Death in Lights

SR Garrae

ISBN: 9798821839404

DEDICATION

To my family.

ALSO BY SR GARRAE

The Casey and Carval series
Death in Focus
Death in Camera
Death in Sight
Death in Frenzy

CONTENTS

ACKNOWLEDGMENTS

Thanks go to Daniela, for all her help, support and encouragement from the very beginning; Joan, for editing and teaching me to speak American English; and the writers' group, for all their help and support.

CHAPTER ONE

"No. I don't care *how* much you think it would be a great team bonding exercise, I'm not coming to any 'cultural experiences'. No."

"But Casey, we could do ballet, or opera, or theatre" – Andy said.

"No." Casey Clement, NYPD detective and a woman who disliked experimental high culture in any form, glared at her colleague.

"Nah," Andy's partner added. Tyler didn't do culture. He did the gym, religiously, and it showed in every sharply-defined muscle of his dark body.

"I could come," O'Leary offered. His grin spread over his moon face.

Andy huffed at the giant of the precinct. "You have to sit at the back of any auditorium so you don't block the lighting and half the audience. I can't see the details from that far away. That's not team bonding, that's…that's…"

"That's my phone," Casey said, cutting through the conversation. "Clement. Okay. There shortly." She swiped off. "We've got a new one. Right up your alley, Andy. Looks like you'll get your team bonding over high culture – this one's experimental theatre – with a corpse."

"Where are we going?"

"Terpsichore Theatre, off West 124th. Let's go."

The team swiftly found the scene of the crime. It wasn't hard: bright yellow *Do-Not-Cross* tape and the bustle and fuss of CSU and the Medical Examiner guided the team in. Dr McDonald's thin, pecking form was already bent over the victim.

"What can you tell us, Dr McDonald?"

He looked up, narrow lips pinched, long, bony fingers encased in blue nitrile. "Little, as yet. It appears that she has been hit above the ear – with what weapon, I cannot yet say – and then strangled."

Casey regarded McDonald with some wonder. He wasn't usually as forthcoming this early in his examination. He was almost pleasant, which

1

made a nice change from his normal acidulated dislike of the entire human race.

"Do you have an estimated time of death?"

"My preliminary conclusion, which may change, is that she was killed within the last fifteen to twenty hours. Rigor mortis is present, but that is not an accurate determinant. The body has reached ambient temperature, but that will also not be conclusive, as the weather is pleasantly warm. I believe her to be an actor," McDonald added.

The team gawped. A conclusion from McDonald before his report?

"How d'you know?" O'Leary asked.

"There are faint traces of stage make-up at her ear, below the site of the blow. I conclude that she had not cleansed it properly." Disapproval tinged his tones.

"Show me?" O'Leary requested.

"You?" McDonald said disbelievingly.

"I know somethin' about theatre make-up," O'Leary clipped. McDonald blinked, but stepped back.

Andy stepped up. "I do too. Let's both have a look."

O'Leary's huge bulk lowered itself to the victim's body, pulling nitrile gloves on to his ham-hands in tandem with Andy's slim, neat form. He drew back locks of black hair – dyed, Casey thought from her place behind O'Leary – from the victim's ear, and examined. Andy touched the corner of her eyelid.

"Yeah," Andy said first. "Heavy make-up, and she didn't get all of it."

"Same," O'Leary added. "Greasepaint's pretty unmistakeable."

All four cops looked at the stage door of the theatre.

"Guess we know where to start," Casey said.

"Where?" panted out their unofficial fifth member, arriving at a run. "What's this one?" His camera was already out and shooting, because Jamie Carval was, first, last and always, a photographer.

Casey looked around, surveying Carval's tall, broad form; brown, messy hair, sparkling blue eyes. "Hey," she said. He was a pleasant view, unlike the corpse, to which she returned her focus. "Actress, we think."

"Actor," Andy corrected. "Actress is old-fashioned. Experimental theatre people don't use it."

Casey stared. "Really? Okay. Anyway, I guess she worked there." She smiled at Carval, dark eyes warming from their cool assessment of the crime scene.

"The Terpsichore?" Carval's brow creased. "Never heard of it."

"Experimental theatre," Andy said from his crouch by the corpse.

"Not my thing," Carval stated.

"You're high culture," Andy pointed out.

2

"No, my shots are high culture," Carval replied with a complete lack of modesty. His arrogance was entirely justified, since he was the most successful reality photographer since Henri Cartier-Bresson. He'd followed up his last blockbuster show, *New York's Ugly Underbelly*, with a show intended to be a small fill-in. *Hands*, however, far from being a fill-in, had been extended from two weeks to four before it had even opened, garnered rave reviews, and was now touring before it moved to a new location in New York and ran for another four weeks. It was phenomenally successful. Carval had declined to tour with it, complaining that he couldn't leave his cops, who were the focus of *Murder on Manhattan*, his next show. No amount of persuasion, promises of perks, or outright bullying by Allan, his manager, had moved him.

He looked at them all with affection: the titanic, multi-muscled bulk of O'Leary; Andy's slim, Chinese-American form; Tyler's hard fitness; and lastly Casey, small, toned but with attractive curves, brunette curls held back in a clip, the heart of their team, darling of his camera and unwilling star of the forthcoming exhibition.

"I'm not high culture," he continued. "I don't do all that ballet and opera that you do. I'd rather go to the ball game."

"Rather see Casey," Tyler said, with typical brevity.

Carval grinned.

"Can we pay some attention to the victim, rather than you kids braiding each other's hair?" Casey snipped.

O'Leary straightened up to his full six-ten. "Let's go see iffen anyone's home." He took two strides over to the stage door, and banged on it. Nothing happened. He banged again, harder. The frame shivered.

O'Leary stepped back to the body, crouching by Andy. "I don't think anyone's here," he grumbled. "That ain't fair. 'S only just before lunchtime."

"You sure?"

The stage door opened. The O'Leary monolith began to stand up, but Casey was already there.

"What?" snapped a gnarled gnome. "Theatre's dark. Next rehearsal tomorrow. Go away. We don't need circus strongmen. Casting's been done for weeks."

"We're not here for a show." Casey showed her shield. "Detective Clement, NYPD."

"What? Cops? Nothing's up here. I didn't call the cops."

"Seein' as there's a corpse outside your door, I think you got that one wrong," O'Leary rumbled across the alley.

The gnome paled to grey, matching his grizzled hair, struggling for breath. "Corpse? No, no. Nothing to do with us. This is a respectable theatre. We don't have corpses. You got it wrong." He bent over, hands on his knees, and drew deep breaths, rattling in his chest.

"Corpsing, maybe," Andy whispered to O'Leary, who tried to stifle a guffaw and almost succeeded. Andy continued his delicate probe for any form of ID.

Casey cast them a *shut-up* glare. "What's your name?"

"Ron. Ron O'Toole."

"Mr O'Toole, I'm sorry to tell you that there is a dead body in the alley."

Ron paled another few shades, gasping. "Dead?" he stammered. "An accident? Why'd you pick on us?"

"We think she may have been an actor."

Ron wobbled on his elderly legs. O'Leary stepped up, and steadied him. "An actor?" Ron forced out, dead white. "No. Can't be." He gulped. "No."

"Easy way to fix it," Tyler said. "Take a look."

Casey looked sympathetically at Ron. "Mr O'Toole, it would be a big help if you could take a look at our victim. Just in case."

"I guess I can be a good citizen," he wobbled.

"Thank you."

Ron was taken the few steps to the body, where Andy was now standing back, a slim wallet in his gloved hands. He didn't say anything about it, and Ron didn't notice, staring, horrified, at the victim.

"That's Isabella!" he gasped, and staggered away, collapsing on to the stage door step. His head fell between his knees, and he took more of the harshly rattling breaths. Casey, watching for small signs, saw only utter shock and upset.

"Isabella?"

"Isabella Farquar."

Andy's eyebrows flicked up and down, tipping the others off that the name didn't match that in the wallet.

"Actors often use stage names," Casey noted. "Was that her real name?"

"I don't know. We all call her Isabella. She's a really nice girl." He sniffed soggily, and blew his nose.

"Could two of us come in, to ask you about Isabella?"

"Uh, sure." Ron struggled to his feet, hands wavering in useless gestures of dismay, eyes damp.

"O'Leary, with me. Tyler, Andy, you get McDonald, CSU, and running her."

"You get all the fun," Andy groused.

"O'Leary knows about drama groups," Casey said. Ron snorted damply behind her, clearly not believing her. "Go on."

"Can I come in?" Carval asked.

Ron looked up, momentarily distracted. "Who's this? He the photographer?" He blew his nose again. "I can't believe it's Isabella. She's so nice." He propped himself on the support of the doorway, still dead white, still snuffling miserably into a Kleenex.

"I'm Jamie Carval, and yeah, I'm the photographer."

"You don't look much like a cop," Ron said, sniffing.

"Cop? I'm not a police photographer. I'm *Carval. New York's Ugly Underbelly. Hands.*"

"Hands? Like that exhibition a coupla months ago?"

"Yes, that one. I took those shots."

"You?" Ron said with unflattering amazement. "Really? You don't look much like you could. You look like an ordinary guy."

Casey suppressed her laughter. O'Leary didn't. Carval's expression was too good to miss.

"But I guess you can come in, and take photos. Nobody'll be here till tomorrow, anyway."

"Thanks," Carval said stiffly. Offence bristled around him.

"I liked that exhibition," Ron quavered, clearly trying to distract himself from the sight of the dead woman. "*Hands*, I mean." He looked at O'Leary. "That was you, wasn't it? Those huge hands pulling up the other one that just left?"

"Sure was," O'Leary said comfortably. "We been pals a long time."

"Come in. I got a kettle, if you want a drink. I sure need one. Poor Isabella."

"Coffee would be great," Casey said. O'Leary nodded.

They followed Ron-the-gnome, still wobbly, into the theatre, through a dingy passage, down to a small room. In contrast to the back-stage passage, it was neat, tidy, and cleanly painted in a fresh, bright cream. Surprisingly, there were three chairs – two folding, one comfortable, worn armchair behind a wooden table. O'Leary squashed himself into one of the folding chairs, Casey took the other.

Carval looked at them, considered his options, and leaned on the doorframe. He knew he couldn't dispossess either of them, and he didn't want to. "Can I take shots in here?" he asked.

"Sure."

"Can I wander? I wanna take shots of the empty theatre."

"Why?"

Carval shrugged. "I never know what I'll see through the lens."

"If you want. Don't do anything dumb."

Carval bridled, but then faded into the background, camera poised. He began with sighting shots of the room, then moved out to the corridor for a perspective shot, contrasting the dark of the passage with the lightness of the room. He'd return to shoot his cops and Ron later, when they'd have forgotten he existed.

5

Ron filled a small kettle and produced tin mugs, instant coffee, and packaged creamer; plus tea for himself. Bringing the cops in, the surprise of meeting Carval, and the domesticity of making drinks were all steadying him, though he was still frighteningly pale and his eyes glistened wetly.

"Black, please," Casey said.

"Light for me," O'Leary followed. "Thanks." He smiled. "Nice little room you have here. Better than a lot I've seen."

"She," Ron said, nodding at Casey, "said you knew about drama." Disbelief was patent.

"Waal, I don't do modern experimental stuff like here," O'Leary replied, "but I do community theatre near home. We tend to do lighter stuff, y'know, Gilbert and Sullivan, musicals, nothin' too difficult. We all got day jobs."

"Musicals?" Ron said, stunned. A little colour returned to his wrinkled face.

"He's a bass," Casey noted, happy to let O'Leary lead and for Ron to get past his upset and relax. They'd extract far more from him that way, and she could watch his reactions. So far, unless he had an Oscar lurking in his room, he'd been genuinely shocked.

"Bass?" O'Leary took mock offence. "I ain't no *bass*. I am a basso profundo." He grinned. "Not much else I could be."

"I guess," Ron said faintly, and slurped back his tea.

"Anyways, you do experimental stuff here, and you're the…?"

"I'm mostly the doorman and late watchman till rehearsals or the show's finished, then I lock up and go home," Ron said, voice less quavery, "but I used to do character parts. Not here, though."

"What're they doin' here?"

"Experimental, like you said. They're rehearsing *A Midsummer Night's Dream.*"

"That's experimental?" Casey asked.

"The way they're doing it, sure."

"How's that?" O'Leary picked up.

"They got an all-male cast except for the Titania role – oh, crap."

"What?"

"Isabella was playing Titania," Ron said. "Oh, *crap*. Carl'll go crazy."

"Huh?"

"We open – we *should* open – in two weeks. Carl didn't like Isabella, but he's gonna be really unhappy about a change this late."

"Why didn't he like her?"

"Wasn't his first choice."

"That's unusual," O'Leary said. "I guess Carl's the director?"

"Yeah. I should tell him." He blew his nose again.

"We'll do that. Please don't say anything to anyone," Casey said.

"Full name?"

"Carl Heyer."

Casey noted it. "How come she wasn't his first choice?"

Ron's blue eyes sparked. He leaned forward confidentially. "You know, it's not cheap to put on a production, but the Finisterres said they'd fund – they liked the concept."

"Sure," O'Leary rumbled.

What concept? Casey thought, but didn't interrupt. Ron was obviously a gossip, which was the best possible start to their investigation. Cynically, he might be a malicious gossip, but it was still a great place to begin.

"Anyway, they're too rich to ignore, and they're financing the whole thing, full cast, no doubling up, so when they said they wanted Isabella for Titania, Carl had to take it."

"Who did he want?"

"He wanted Dacia Kraven, but he had to accept she'd only be the understudy. I mean, he's gonna be delighted she steps up, but it's a huge pain for everyone to adjust this late, no matter how good she is and how well she knows the part. She fit his concept better, he said."

"Mm?"

"I don't *know*," he insinuated, "but I think they were close, you know what I mean?"

"Sure do." O'Leary's light eyes sparkled. "Good pals, like?"

"Yeah. Dacia, she doesn't like being the understudy. Carl doesn't like Isabella, and he was always picking on her. Everybody noticed, but nobody said anything. Carl's got a temper."

"How many in the cast?"

"Twenty-one, plus four understudies who were doing walk on parts too."

"Do you have a list of names?"

"Yeah." Ron reeled off all the names, which Casey wrote down as fast as she could.

"Thanks," she said, when she had finished. "Can you tell us more about Isabella?"

"What d'you wanna know?"

"Anythin' you c'n tell us," O'Leary enticed. "Sounds like you're the man who sees most."

Ron's skinny chest inflated. "Sure do. They all go past here, and most of the time they don't even notice me."

Not only a gossip, but an undervalued, ignored employee. Perfect. They'd be talking to Ron a lot, Casey decided.

"Tell us about Isabella," O'Leary repeated. "We'll wanna know about the others, too, later on after we've met them, but this time we wanna focus on her."

"Okay. Isabella started off really happy about being Titania, but that all went to hell in a hurry when Carl started bitching about every move she made. I reckon he was hoping she'd give up, but she wasn't a quitter and this was her big break. She'd only ever had bit parts before." He stopped, and dabbed his eyes. "She looked soft, but she was as ambitious as anyone, though she was always nice to me. She had the part, and she was going to keep it come hell or high water."

"Mm?" hummed O'Leary.

"Uh…look, I don't know. Isabella had some support, and the funders were on her side, but nobody would challenge Carl. He'd make them pay."

"Apart from Carl, did anyone dislike her, or quarrel with her?"

"Dacia won't be crying that she's gone. Max – he's playing Egeus – might be upset. He was pretty supportive. Carl'll go mad about it first off, but then he'll be delighted he gets Dacia, as soon as he gets over being mad about it being so near to opening. He'll get what he wanted all along."

"I get it. Anythin' else you wanna tell us? We'll be askin' you more later, like I said, but anythin' stand out?"

"Someone's boozing."

Casey jerked. "Why?" she asked sharply.

"Just…a smell, bottles in the Dumpster."

"Who do you think it is?" O'Leary asked, giving Casey a necessary instant to compose herself.

"Dunno. None of them act like they've had a drink."

"Thanks. We'll keep an eye open for anythin' like that."

"You've been a real help," Casey said. "Thanks very much."

"Happy to help," Ron said. "You'll get who did it, won't you? I liked Isabella. She doesn't deserve to be dead." He sniffed again, watery eyes damp.

"We'll do our very best."

"One last thing, could we get a look around the theatre now? Don't wanna disturb them rehearsin' when we're pokin' about."

"Sure. They won't be back till two tomorrow."

O'Leary didn't mention that they'd be doing plenty of disturbing the next day, when they'd want to meet the cast all at once.

"We better catch that photographer so he doesn't sneak in. Don't see Carl being happy if he's taking shots of rehearsal."

"The Finisterres would be," Carval said from the doorway. "They sponsor a *lot* of culture and I bet they've been to my shows. Allan would know."

Ron regarded him sidewise, but said nothing. "Let's tour." He walked the three of them around every inch of the theatre, ending up centre stage.

O'Leary grinned. "To be, or not to be," he began, only for Casey to punch his arm.

"No," she said. "No acting."

"Aww."

"That's great, Mr O'Toole," she said. "We need to seal Isabella's dressing room till I can get CSU out here to search it properly, but we'll be discreet. Do you have a key, and are there any others?"

"Yeah." Ron handed it over. "I don't think there are any spares lying around."

Casey locked the room. "I'll keep the key, so I can pass it to CSU." She smiled at him. "Here's my card, in case you think of anything urgently, but I'm sure we'll need to take advantage of your expertise again."

"Happy to help," he repeated, and escorted them through the backstage labyrinth to the stage door.

As soon as they were out of earshot, Casey called Andy and Tyler. "We got a list of names – though they all sound like stage names – for you to run. I wrote them down, and I'll send you a photo."

"Okay. We're working on Isabella – her real name's running through the system, and Tyler's requesting phones and financials while I do a social media search – real name and stage name."

"What's her real name?" Casey asked.

"Bettina – Betty – Scarfield."

"I can see why she changed it," she said. "Not very theatrical."

"Bet she got a lot of shit in high school," Andy said cynically. "Scarface would be the least of it."

"Yeah. If I send this through now, do you think you can get everything into the system while we're getting back? Rehearsals start at two tomorrow, so I thought we'd join the show at five after."

"Sounds like fun," Andy said. "Gimme a moment?" They could hear him talking to Tyler. "Yeah, that's fine."

"Soon as you can, and we'll brief you when we're back."

"Okay."

Casey snapped a photo of her notes and sent it off. "It's already three-thirty. Let's get back."

"Yeah," said O'Leary, as they all walked to his SUV. "About this boozin' issue. Will you be okay iffen someone's fond of the sauce?"

Casey's shoulders hunched. "Dad's fine," she defended. "He completed his residential rehab, he's got his first thirty-day chip, and he's still dry. He'll have his second one at the end of this month." She didn't say that he'd only had the rehab that his health insurance would fund. He should have taken much longer.

"Waal, that's good," O'Leary agreed, and exchanged glances with Carval, standing almost protectively behind Casey.

Carval looked down at Casey's fragile-seeming form, worried. Her dad had only been out of rehab for a couple of weeks, and in that time Casey had visited him almost every night. While Carval applauded her loyalty to her only family, he wondered what would give when the current case ran hot: her job, her father – or her sleep. He was betting on her sleep. He knew she didn't always – or often – sleep soundly, except when she was curled against him: not that she admitted it, but her eyes told their own tale. Now, with her father at the front of her mind, she sure wasn't sleeping with Carval. The only place he'd seen her in the last two weeks was around the precinct and on this new case.

"Yeah," she said. "It is. He's finally got it."

Maybe he had. Almost three months ago, he'd been in the ER, with the doctor telling him to stop drinking; telling Casey that if he didn't stop, he'd die. Maybe that had been the shock he needed to sober up and stay sober. Maybe. But Carval wouldn't believe that till he saw it. Unfortunately, Casey *needed* to believe it, and he couldn't bear to say otherwise, knowing that she'd deny it all the way.

"Let's get back to the crime," she said, scrambling into the SUV. "Work out our next steps, find out what Andy and Tyler know, then decide how to play it." She gave her enormous partner a smile. "You and Andy get to star with the rehearsal, seeing as you two know about theatre."

"Right now, I wanna know about Isabella," O'Leary said, "so let's start there."

"I want to stay," Carval decided. "The theatre's fascinating, even without anyone in it. I'm going back to talk to Ron some more." He wasn't thinking of the cops or the case, wholly driven by his photographic instincts for a new, exciting set of shots.

"Okay. We won't be doing anything that you'd want to shoot anyway."

CHAPTER TWO

"This is what we got," Casey told Andy and Tyler as she finished her mid-afternoon sandwich, laying out everything Ron O'Toole had told them. "We took a look around the theatre, but I didn't spot anything interesting."

"We set off all the searches, and put in requests for Isabella's phone records and financials," Andy said, "so that's all running. CSU have her cell phone. We're looking for next of kin but I haven't found that yet – a quick look through her public social media showed it was all about theatre and productions and her pals."

"Okay. We want to watch the rehearsal tomorrow."

"Ask?" Tyler queried.

"I think we have to." Casey grimaced. "I'd rather sneak in and watch without them knowing, but I don't think that would go down well with Kent if they complained, and they would."

"Yeah. Don't take chances."

"We hafta keep our noses clean," O'Leary reminded everyone. "No bad PR."

"We'll go in the front – or maybe ask Ron to introduce us."

"Okay."

"That's tomorrow. What about these runs? We have all the stage names, so where shall we start?"

"Social media," Andy said. "Could be a lot there, if we're lucky. Or not," he cynically contradicted himself. "Street cams if there are any, though I'd like a better time window first. Otherwise we'll all go cross-eyed looking at a whole lot of nothing. Five hours is too big of a gap if we can avoid it."

Casey frowned. "I guess we'll see what McDonald comes up with. We've got a lot to cover even without cameras. Do we have her address yet?" she directed at Tyler.

"No." His computer pinged. "Next of kin." Another beep. "Address. Heard you," he grinned.

"Isabella's? Great. We can go tell next of kin and then look around her apartment. We need to get that done by the end of today, even if we run late."

Tyler nodded.

"I'll requisition some uniforms and they can work while we're out," Casey decided. "Maybe we can have Fremont and Larson."

"Adamo," Tyler added.

"Yeah," O'Leary contributed. "He did good last time."

Casey swung off to Sergeant Tully to arrange her staffing. "Can I get Fremont, Larson, and Adamo? I've got about twenty-five people I want to have looked at. Maybe more later."

Tully checked his rosters. "Sure, Detective." He flicked her a sidelong glance. "Got room for another one?"

"If there's one available. Who is it?"

"Henegan."

Casey stared. "Henegan? Why would I want Henegan?"

Tully dropped his voice. "Look, Casey. You know he's trying to get away from Estrolla after that clusterfuck nearly three months back. Estrolla's been picking on him, but he won't mess with you four again if he's got half a brain. It'd be good if you'd take Henegan for this one. If he's crap, lemme know, and I'll deal, but I think he'll be okay. C'mon. Whip him into shape like you did Larson."

Casey made a face. Sure, Henegan had apologised, but...she wasn't anxious to reopen that particular can of worms. She scowled at Tully, who looked her dead in the eye.

"Oh, whatever," she conceded. "But his first screw-up, he's out. No second chances. If I get grief from Estrolla and his pals, you tell Captain Kent you forced Henegan on me."

"Sure thing, Detective. I'll round 'em up and send 'em over."

A few moments later, four uniformed officers arrived at Casey's desk: the big forms of Fremont and Larson, the small, sparky rookie, Adamo – and Henegan, cringing at the back.

O'Leary and Andy blinked at the sight of Henegan, but Casey made a *tell-you-later* gesture and they kept quiet. Tyler joined the mix, casting Henegan a surprised look, followed by a slow assessment. Henegan shivered. "Sergeant sent me," he stammered.

"Huh." Tyler followed up with a hard stare.

Casey took command. Tyler was great at making groups of uniforms work as a team, but it wouldn't work if Henegan was so scared of him he couldn't focus. "Listen up. We got called to a body behind the Terpsichore Theatre this morning. She was an actress, playing Titania in an experimental production of *A Midsummer Night's Dream*, supposed to open in two weeks. We've put the whole cast, the director and the doorman into the databases, but I want you to start on the social media searches for everyone except the victim – Andy already did a quick search, so Tyler'll give you that and you can carry on from there. We also want to look at the Finisterres: the rich guys funding this; and we just got the vic's next of kin. One of you take them and do a full search: runs, social media, the usual. Tyler and I will notify next of kin and search the vic's apartment." She grinned. "The fun part is, most of them'll have two names – real and stage. Twice the work, but I've only got the stage names for the actors so far."

"Is there a boyfriend?" Fremont asked.

"Not that we've found, but we'll ask next of kin. If you think you find one, run him. We'll want to talk to him."

"What about phones or financials?" Larson added.

"Good question." Casey was keen to encourage Larson. After a rocky start, he was turning into a useful officer. "Tyler's already put in the requests on our vic. We'll need some evidence to base a warrant on if we want others – but there'll definitely be some work when we get those."

"What do you want me to do, ma'am?" Adamo queried.

"I'll let you work it out between the four of you. Any disagreements, Fremont makes the call."

"Before you start," Tyler said, "Henegan, a word."

Henegan went white. Casey flicked Tyler a glance, but when he nodded, she didn't interfere. Tyler beckoned Henegan to the break room, and firmly shut the door.

"Guess Casey's giving you a chance."

"Sergeant sent me."

"Wouldn't if she hadn't agreed. We don't work with assholes or anyone we don't trust. One chance. Fuck up, you're out. Mess with Casey or Andy, you'll answer to me and O'Leary. Got it?"

"Yessir," Henegan squeaked. "I wanna make it right."

"Up to you. If Estrolla hassles you, tell me or O'Leary. Not Casey or Andy."

"Yessir."

Henegan fled. Tyler downed a gulp of sports drink and went back out, perfectly satisfied that the shit had been scared right out of Henegan. Unhappily, he had a nagging instinct that there would be trouble from Estrolla and his cronies.

***

"We need to change it around," Casey said to the gathered team. "Tyler, you and me'll take the people who aren't theatre types, so we'll be busy today, and Andy and O'Leary can look after the uniforms and searches.

13

Tomorrow, Andy and O'Leary can stay at the theatre for anything interesting, and we'll supervise the uniforms."

"Yeah?"

"Yeah. I think we'll get more out of the family if they don't think we're associated with the theatre."

"I guess," O'Leary agreed. "Mebbe somethin' unusual'll happen an' we'll get information outta McDonald without needin' a scalpel of our own."

"You can always chase him," Casey suggested. "That'll keep you hopping as you avoid his wrath."

"I'll pass," Andy said wryly. O'Leary humphed.

"Do we have her keys?" Casey asked Tyler.

"Yep. From Andy."

Andy smiled. Casey deduced that Andy had collected them from CSU and passed them to Tyler. "Where'd she live?"

"Walk up in Inwood. Studio."

"How was she paying for that?"

"Wait for her financials, wait for social security number run to finish."

"You mean we don't know yet."

Tyler nodded.

"Next of kin."

"Inwood. Near her apartment."

"Good. Not too much travelling. We've barely got any of today left to waste." She grinned. "We're off. Don't get up to any mischief while we're gone. If we need you to join in, I'll text."

O'Leary flipped her the bird as she went, then turned to his chaotic desk.

***

Twenty minutes later they pulled up at a sandstone-coloured block in Inwood, and took the elevator to the third floor. Casey steeled herself.

"Never gets easier," Tyler said.

"No."

She knocked. "Mrs Scarfield?" she said to the greying woman who opened, showing her badge. "I'm Detective Clement. I'm sorry to tell you" –

The woman crumpled against her doorframe, half-fainting. "Donnie? Not Donnie!"

"Your daughter, Bettina" –

"No!" she howled. "Not Betty? Please not Betty. You're wrong. You have it wrong. I have to call Donnie. He'll tell you you're wrong."

"Mrs Scarfield, please may we come in while you call your husband?"

"Yes, yes," she sobbed. "I have to call Donnie." She stumbled out of the doorway, fumbling blindly for a phone.

14

Casey preceded Tyler into a small, pretty family room: photos of Mrs Scarfield with Donnie and two children on a side table, cream walls with grey-blue furniture and curtains at the window. She winced. "This one's hard."

"All hard."

In the background, Mrs Scarfield was crying down the phone to Donnie, incoherent with grief. As soon as she finished the call, Casey went to her.

"Mrs Scarfield?"

"He'll be home as fast as he can," she wept. "I can't…Betty."

"I'll make you a cup of tea or coffee," Casey said softly. "You should sit down."

"I can't…I'll make it. I have to do something." She was still crying hard, scrubbing her eyes to no purpose, hunched over and somehow twenty years older in two minutes. "What happened? Was there an accident?"

"I'm afraid not. Betty was attacked and killed."

"An attacker? No! Who'd attack her? She didn't have enemies. She didn't have enough money or jewellery to be mugged – who'd do that?" She crumpled again, staggering under the blow. "I don't believe this. How will I tell Maisie?"

"Maisie? Is that your other daughter? I saw the photos in the family room."

"Yes. They were so close. Maisie's only eighteen months older. She'll be heartbroken." Mrs Scarfield jittered from cupboard to hot water to coffee jar to fridge for milk. "They've always been so close," she repeated, through her tears. "How do I tell her?"

"Please, sit down. I'll make coffee since you have everything out. Tell me how you take it?"

"Light."

"I'll put some sugar in."

Mrs Scarfield didn't – couldn't – argue. Casey finished making the coffee and brought it through, with a mug of water for Tyler, who rarely drank coffee.

"Can you tell us about Betty?" she asked gently, loudly enough to be heard over the agonised sobbing. "We know she was a talented actress."

"She was," her mother wept. "She was delighted that she'd been noticed by the Finisterres. They were supporting her. They only pick out a few people and she was one. We were so proud." Her voice cracked. "She put everything into it, worked every hour she could to pay her tuition."

"Dedicated." Casey's sincerity shone.

"Yes. This was her first big break." She broke down again, burying her face in a handful of Kleenex.

"Mrs Scarfield," Tyler asked, "did Betty have a partner?"

"Not right now. She'd had relationships, of course she did, but she broke up with her boyfriend a few weeks back and she was still pretty upset. I think she'd hoped he was the one." She snuffled, and wiped her eyes again. "I'll never see her get married," she wept.

"What was his name?" Casey coaxed.

"David. David Gallagher."

Casey wrote it down, while Tyler took point.

"Did she tell you about anyone annoying her, or who didn't like her?" he followed up.

"No. I mean, there was always jealousy and backbiting, but nothing specific."

"Nothing?"

"She said that the director didn't like her," Mrs Scarfield admitted. "He wanted someone else, but Betty won it. I guess the other woman was put out, but that's acting, isn't it? Surely nobody would hurt Betty just for that?"

"That's what we're trying to find out. Did she have any close friends we could talk to?"

"There's Suzie, Suzie Keller," Mrs Scarfield sniffled. "And Anna Bulitt."

"Thank you."

The door opened, and a mid-height man rushed in. "Eileen," he said, "Eileen," and took her in his arms, crying. "Our poor girl," emerged. "I can't believe it."

Casey gave them some time to lean on each other, before speaking again. "Mr Scarfield, your wife has been really helpful. She's told us about Betty's friends. In case you've heard anything more, do you know if anyone disliked Betty, or was harassing her?"

Donnie Scarfield slumped into the couch, holding his wife against his shoulder, sheet white and aged. "The director was giving her a lot of grief," he said unhappily. "Seemed like it was pretty personal. He said some nasty stuff, but Betty begged me not to interfere. She wanted to handle him herself – to prove she didn't need us to step in. I don't know about anything else. I wish I did. I wish I knew anything to help you." He buried his face in his wife's hair.

"Her ex-boyfriend?"

"No. That little creep dumped her. Thought he was too good to date someone who was trying to make it and waiting tables to support herself. She worked really hard to keep herself afloat. We were so proud of her," he said miserably, as his wife had.

"Where did she work?"

"Mornings, in Carrie's Diner at Broadway and 207th. On days she wasn't rehearsing or in a show, she worked afternoons and evenings in Verdicchio on Amsterdam. She worked so hard…." he said again.

"Thank you. Could you give me Maisie's contact details, Mrs Scarfield?"

"I need to tell her…" she sobbed.

"We'll do that. Give us a little time and then you can speak to her. It'll be easier for you if we break the bad news."

"She works two blocks over. We all stayed close – family matters to us." Both parents were still weeping, shocked. "I don't believe it." She scribbled down the address.

"I'm sorry for your loss," Casey said, taking the paper. "We'll do everything we can to find the perpetrator."

"Thank you."

The detectives let themselves out, and hurried to Maisie's workplace, hoping to get there before either parent could pull themselves together enough to call her. Casey hadn't felt that Betty-Isabella's parents had anything to do with it, but since the Asher Washington case, she'd never discounted family members as potential killers, no matter how upset they seemed to be.

"Thoughts?" she opened.

"Unlikely."

"I agree, but let's meet the sister first. Families can look at things differently, and just because Mom and Dad think the kids are best pals doesn't mean they are."

"Yeah." To Casey's surprise, Tyler carried on. "Like that for my brother and me."

"It was?" Tyler had never mentioned family, let alone a brother, before. His Army service, sure, including his occasional fugues if a truck backfired and sounded like a shot, but not family.

"Yeah."

"Okay." Tyler would only talk if he wanted to. The team never pried: each of them talked if they were ready to. She looked at the front of the block. "We're here."

'Here' was a small door leading upstairs to an office. They rapped on its door, which was opened by a young woman with rainbow hair.

"Detectives Clement and Tyler," Casey said, showing her badge again. "Is Maisie Scarfield here?"

"That's me," the woman said. "Police? Why – are my parents okay?" she panicked. "What happened?"

"Ms Scarfield, I'm sorry to tell you your sister" –

"No!" she screamed. "Betty!"

Heads poked out of doors. "What's wrong? What's happened? Maisie?" A middle-aged woman arrived, cast a filthy glare at the cops, and bundled Maisie into a hug. "What's this?" she demanded.

"Ms Scarfield's sister has been killed," Casey murmured.

"Oh my good God," the woman said. "That's awful." She made a swift decision. "Here, come into this room. I'll get her some hot sweet tea." She

17

steered Maisie and the detectives into a small conference room, and shut the door on the way out. Maisie half-fell into the chair, buried her face in her hands and howled, only diminishing when the other woman returned and pushed a mug of steaming tea at her. "Maisie," she soothed. "Maisie, shhhh. These cops are here to help you. Shhhh." She patted Maisie comfortingly. "I know it's terrible. Take a breath and a drink of tea."

After several minutes, in which the woman gradually managed to calm Maisie to shuddering, gulping tears, she looked up. "I'm Emma," she told them. "I own this business."

"We need to ask Maisie a few questions." Emma's eyebrows rose. "If she wants you to, you can stay," Casey said. "But we need any information Maisie can give us as soon as possible to help us investigate. I'm sure you know time is of the essence in a murder enquiry."

"Murder?" Maisie wept. "No-one would want to murder Betty."

"Your parents said you were close," Casey trailed. Emma cast her a sharp glance, but kept her mouth shut.

"She was my friend. Sure, we squabbled sometimes, but she was my *friend.*"

"I'm sorry," Casey murmured.

"She was just getting her break and she was…she said we'd all be in the front of the mezzanine for the opening night and it's *not fair* that she won't be the star like she should have been. That rat bastard director hated her but she was going to stick it out and show him she had it." Her voice was rising. "He wasn't the only one. Her understudy was stabbing her in the back every chance she got too."

"We'll be looking at both of them," Casey said. "Is there anyone else she mentioned, on or off stage?"

"No…" but Maisie sounded a little doubtful.

"Mmmm?"

"She said that some of the other actors weren't as squeaky clean as the director wanted them all to be. But she didn't tell me any details. Just said that it wasn't fair that he picked on her all the time and never on any of the rest." More tears leaked out.

"Thank you. Your mom said that she'd broken up with her boyfriend a few weeks ago?"

"He broke up with her, you mean. Asshole. We weren't good enough for Mr-aspiring-to-money. He'd have eaten crow when she made it. She was devastated, but in the last few days she'd cheered up again. I thought she might have met someone new, but she didn't say anything if she had."

"I get it," Casey agreed. "Can I have her ex's contact details?" They'd cross-check that it was the same guy her parents knew about.

"Sure. I don't guess it was him, but he's an asshole anyway so grill him like good. David Gallagher. Fancy-ass apartment in Hudson Heights." She looked at Emma through red eyes, and blew her nose. "Please could I get some paper and a pen, and another cup of tea?"

"Sure, honey," Emma said, and went to acquire both.

"I don't want her to hear this," Maisie said, through more tears. "David tried to hit on me, straight after he dumped Betty. I told him to f – um, take a hike, and he said he thought Betty was cheating on him, so I told him he was an asshole and she never would and we had a pretty big argument and he stormed out. I wasn't sorry."

"Anyone else?"

"No. Now what?"

"We investigate, and do our very best to find whoever did this. Here's my card. If you think of anything at all, however small, let us know. Anything can help. We'll be in touch if we need to ask you any more about Betty."

She cried harder as Emma returned with tea, pen and paper. Maisie scrawled down Gallagher's address, and then put her head on her arms.

"Thank you," Casey said quietly. "We'll leave you now."

CHAPTER THREE

"Okay," Casey said, on the sidewalk. "We've got a potentially angry ex-boyfriend, and some strange goings-on back at the theatre. Maisie was pretty hysterical, but you can cover a lot with loud emotions."

Tyler merely nodded.

"Let's go search Isabella's apartment, while I get a couple of officers to canvass those places Isabella worked in. I wanted to get back to the precinct in case the others find anything useful, but that's looking like a lost cause."

"No chance. Way over an hour already. Nearly six."

"I'll give Fremont a call to start on Gallagher, then Larson can take Adamo to talk to the restaurants, while we search."

By the time they'd reached Isabella's block, Casey had briefed Fremont and Larson. They parked, and went up.

"Shit," Tyler said, goggle-eyed, as they entered, sliding on gloves.

"Where do we *start*?" Casey lamented. "This is…how old was she? Because *nobody* older than six should have this many stuffed animals."

"Cushions."

"Pillows. Dolls. It's a temple to kitsch." They exchanged evil glances. "The others should see this," Casey suggested. "We could use some help."

"Yeah."

Casey texted O'Leary to ask him and Andy to join her at the studio apartment, without further commentary. "We'll need them to turn over all this stuff. If she had anything useful, it's probably under a plushie."

"What?" Tyler regarded her with horror. Squishy toys were not his area of expertise.

"One of these," she clarified, pointing at a large stuffed object occupying a small armchair.

"Jesus."

Casey couldn't disagree. She had plump cushions at her apartment – on the couch, where such things belonged. She'd grown out of stuffed animals long ago. "We'd better start. This'll be a long job for a tiny studio. I'll take the bed side of the room, you take the kitchenette side. Whichever of us finishes first gets the bathroom, though you couldn't hide a mouse in there."

They began. Every toy was moved, every stuffed animal, every cushion, revealing only plain white walls. Casey checked under the narrow bed and even its frilly, pale blue coverlet and matching pillows, then, satisfied that the only things there were more toys, moved on to the cheap desk. Tyler opened the cupboards, there being nothing on the draining board or counter of the tiny kitchen area. She was beginning to search it when the noise of O'Leary tromping up the stairs alerted her to the arrival of the others. "They're here," she whispered to Tyler.

Andy opened the door and walked in – one step before he stopped dead, mouth agape. "What" – he began, and was pushed in by O'Leary.

"Don't stand in the – what the *hell?*"

"My eyes, my eyes!" Andy wailed. "This is a crime scene right here. It's a crime against good taste." He wailed again.

"Interesting décor, isn't it?" Casey said cheerfully.

"That's what you call it?" Andy said with utter horror. "I'll have nightmares."

"I ain't never seen anythin' like it," O'Leary mused. "Not even when I've been buyin' presents for all them nieces of mine and Pete's. I'm goin' to have nightmares too, an' they ain't about inheritin' this toy collection." He pulled on his nitrile gloves.

"You mean you wouldn't pay good green dollars for it?"

"Naw. I got my Pete. I don't need no other cuddly thin's."

The other three groaned. "Save it for home," Andy said, also gloving up.

"Didn't Carval tag along?" Casey asked.

"Naw. He's still prowlin' round the theatre."

"Oh," Casey said, flatly. "Let's keep searching here. She must have a laptop. Everyone's got a computer." She ignored her disappointment at Carval's absence. She'd see him later. She hadn't seen much of him lately, what with his show and her dad coming out of rehab. She sent a brief text, simply saying *Abbey later?*

"Phone?"

"That's with CSU," Andy said, "but yeah, she might have used her phone."

"Ugh," Casey said. "Laptops are much easier."

"Not really," Andy said. "I can get as much out of a phone as a laptop."

"Technogeek," Tyler teased.

"I'm *the* technogeek," Andy batted back.

21

"Sure are," Casey confirmed. "There's no-one better." She grinned. "Can you extract that phone from CSU – opened – and work your magic, assuming we don't find a laptop in this shrine to stuffed animals?"

"Definitely." Andy stepped out of the way and made a quick call to CSU. "They'll tell me as soon as they're done with it, but they've got a line."

"They've always got a line," Casey muttered. "Let's finish up."

Finishing up produced nothing useful: no conveniently printed files of bank statements, no helpful anonymous hate mail (in or out), and no signs of a partner, which matched up to what Isabella's parents and sister had said about a breakup, but didn't help in finding if there had been anyone new.

"CSU can screen it for prints or anythin' else tomorrow," O'Leary said, "but that's a washout."

"Yeah. Let's get back to the precinct for a quick round-up, and then, unless we have anything new, start fresh tomorrow. We're way past shift end and Kent won't like it if we stay much later."

***

Back at the precinct, the four officers had hunkered down together to work it out.

"What've you got?" Casey asked Fremont.

"Whole lotta posing for pictures, bigging up their roles – like PR, not like most people use social media."

"Curated," Larson said.

"Huh?" Casey queried.

"He means that it's all faked, staged and carefully selected," Andy clarified, then looked hard at Larson. "You know about it?"

"Some," he said. "Got friends who use it a lot, and they tell me stuff. Don't do it myself."

Fremont chortled. "Don't think you're the type for modelling shots."

"Nup," Larson agreed, unbothered by the friendly insult.

"Okay," Andy said. "If you know a little, Larson, come with me and you can learn a lot more. We always need people who can translate to the techno-challenged like Casey here."

Casey flipped him the bird. "You and Larson can play with the tech toys if you like, but before you start, what did everyone else find?"

Summarised, they'd found a whole lot of nothing. Perfectly posed pictures, and nothing that anyone could take exception to. Isabella's relationship status had changed a month ago to single, and had stayed there.

"What about where she worked?"

"Shock and horror," Larson said cynically, "but they didn't say anythin' useful, ma'am. She'd shown up for her shifts just as usual, and nobody noticed anything changing recently. Everyone seemed to like her, she got

22

good tips. They said she was polite, friendly, didn't think too much of herself."

"That don't sound like anythin'. Anybody at all who didn't like her?" O'Leary asked.

"Not a one."

"Okay, we'll put that on the back-burner for now. We can revisit it if anything points us back to her work," Casey decided. "So right now we got nothing. Do we have financials yet? Or phone records?"

"No," the four officers said.

"Anything on the runs?"

"Uh," Henegan emitted. "Not on the runs, but this guy, Maxwell Stephens. He's been picked up drunk a couple of times."

"How'd you know if he wasn't charged?"

"Uh…me and Grendon picked him up. I recognise him. He made a big fuss about being an actor and since he hadn't been doing anything to annoy anyone and wasn't disorderly, the desk sergeant threw him in the tank and sent him home with a hangover the next morning."

"Good catch," Casey said, without any warmth. Henegan dropped his eyes.

"We got nothing else," Andy said. "Let's give up for tonight, and start again in the morning."

"I guess," Casey said. "Officers, you can quit till tomorrow."

"You sure, ma'am?" Fremont asked.

"Yep. Captain Kent won't authorise overtime if we've got nothing to do, so we'll save it for when we need it."

"Yes'm."

The detectives watched with interest as the four officers went off together, Adamo, smaller than the others, half-skipping to keep up – and Fremont and Larson on each side of Henegan. The arrangement was explained when Officer Estrolla, lurking malignantly at his desk, gave the four departing officers a filthy look and said something, face contorting with anger, to Officer Grendon.

"Abbey time," O'Leary said cheerfully.

"Sounds good."

***

Carval hadn't even thought about going back to the precinct, desperate to download and review his shots. He'd prowled around the theatre, shooting consistently, fascinated by the differences from his usual fare. He raced back to the studio, yelling, "Allan, Allan, come look at this!"

There was no answer, and he remembered that Allan was touring with the *Hands* exhibition, as the only person Carval trusted to get it right. He flicked out his phone.

23

"Allan!" he said, before Allan had even managed *hello*. "Allan, I got another theme. Theatres. Not performances, but rehearsals and backstage and direction and the way the light and shadows fall in the auditorium and on the stage – it's gonna be *great*. You gotta see these as soon as you're back and I haven't even shot any actors yet but I'll get them soon. I think I can make it another big one before I do *Murder on Manhattan Two* and I've still got all those construction sites that aren't done yet and it'll be *great*."

"Jamie…" Allan said feebly, and was run over.

"When you're back you can fix it up. This production where there's been a murder" –

"Some light in the darkness of your non-explanation, at last."

Carval ignored that. "It's funded by the Finisterres, but they don't know I was there yet" –

"Don't talk to them! Leave that to me. If you talk to them they'll whip the copyright out from under you. They're absolute sharks. Do *not* go there until I'm back."

"Okay, okay. But you have to come back soon."

"Jamie, I'll be back early Sunday morning. LA's closing tomorrow. I'll be in New York for two weeks, to get *Murder on Manhattan* open and going, then *you* insisted I go with *Hands* everywhere it went, so I'm off to Pittsburgh." Allan recovered himself. "What about *Murder*? Have you finished that yet?"

"Almost. Is the space booked?"

"Don't insult me. It's been reserved for weeks. You need to finish and get it hung. We open on Thursday for the critics, which I keep telling you. Try listening for a change."

"We're ready. I have enough, any more is extra."

"When did you decide that?" Allan asked cynically.

"Uh, right now. I wanna do a second one with the cops anyway like I said a minute ago and you have to *see* these" –

"You haven't thought it through. I thought so. I want this to go ahead, Jamie, but not on impulse. We'll talk about it when I'm back."

"I'm ready."

"Are your cops?"

"That's… They'll have to be. This'll be huge. I'm not pulling it down or pushing it back for anyone. They wouldn't ask me to, anyway."

"You said it. Try not to get into any trouble before I get back."

"I" –

"Jamie."

"Yes, Mom. I'll be good."

Finally, download complete and satisfaction with his talent at maximum, Carval thought to look at his phone, and found a terse message from Casey, sent a couple of hours earlier. *Abbey later?* He sent back *On my way*, and dashed off.

***

The team settled into its favourite corner in the Abbey pub, with drinks.

"Waal," O'Leary said happily, "this is cosy." He grinned. "How come Henegan's joined the party? He found some spine yet?"

"Sergeant Tully shoved him on to me," Casey groused. "He said Estrolla was giving Henegan grief and we could whip him into shape and keep Estrolla off his back. We've just gotten Larson all smartened up and useful, and we get Henegan."

"The reward for a hard job done well is a harder job," Andy pontificated.

O'Leary frowned furrows into his forehead. "Tully *asked* you to take Henegan?"

"Yeah."

"Waal, ain't that somethin'. 'Specially after all that trouble with Estrolla. Sure, Henegan tried to apologise, but…" He frowned harder. "Sounds to me like someone's been thinkin'. An' it sure wasn't us."

"Kent," Tyler said bleakly.

"Most likely," Andy agreed. "Estrolla's looking for a way to make trouble."

"We've been told to keep our noses so clean they're practically sterile. That's why one of you has to babysit me every time I get my lunch or at shift end," Casey griped.

"You know you love our comp'ny," O'Leary grinned. "You couldn't get nicer 'n' us."

Casey stuck her tongue out at him, then returned to her theme. "Kent's given Estrolla another reason to make trouble."

"Or enough rope to hang himself," Andy pointed out. "He might be hoping that Estrolla blows up so badly even the union can't find a loophole."

"No loss," Tyler said.

"What's no loss?" Carval asked, ambling up with a beer. "Who wants another?" Everyone did. Carval set his drink down beside Casey, and by the time he'd come back with two more beers and two sodas, a chair and a space for him had appeared. "What's no loss?" he repeated.

"Estrolla wouldn't be a loss," Casey summarised. "We got landed with Henegan."

"Kent's plottin'," O'Leary added.

Carval sneaked an arm around Casey, who moved slightly into it and drank her soda. "Plotting?"

"I reckon he's tryin' to tempt Estrolla into somethin' stupid."

"That was *my* theory," Andy complained.

"An' I agree with it." O'Leary sighed, and a small tornado fluttered the beer mats. "That means that we take even more care of Casey here, 'cause the easiest way for Estrolla to do somethin' stupid is to go after her."

"Don't want to lose you," Tyler said, in an unusual display of emotion.

"No. Who'd we have to hide behind?" Andy teased.

"Great," Casey said. "I get to look like the pathetic little girlie everyone has to protect."

"Naw. Ev'ryone heard about the sparrin'." O'Leary looked saintly. "It wasn't me."

"You suggested to Fremont and Larson that they tell the tale, didn't you?" Casey said.

"Why'd you think that?"

"'Cause I know you."

"That ain't no excuse."

"That's not a denial."

"It's a good story."

Casey scowled at her huge partner, which had no effect, and grumbled, which had less. "You and your stories," she humphed, and swallowed her soda.

"Changing the subject," Andy said cheerfully, "before Casey does something mean to O'Leary, why were you so long at the theatre?"

"It was interesting," Carval said, "and I got lots of brilliant shots. You take me to all the best places," he simpered. Everybody laughed. "It'll be the next big exhibition after *Murder on Manhattan One*."

"What?" Casey said sharply.

"*Murder One.* I can't stop. There's got to be a second *Murder on Manhattan*, but the theatres one will be in between. *Behind the Scenes.* I know it's a cliché title but it's *right*."

"No. No, no, no! Isn't one exhibition starring us enough?" Casey's voice rose. "Why do you need to keep going?"

"Because they're great shots!" Carval whipped back. "Haven't we had this argument enough times yet?"

"I thought you were only doing *one* show with us in it. Not a *series*."

"There's too much. Too many things to shoot. I can't possibly get it all into one exhibition."

Casey hunched up, away from his arm.

"Waal, *I* wanna be a star for longer," O'Leary said. "Don't shoot Casey, huh, an' shoot me instead. I'm prettier."

Andy snorted. "You? You're a monster. I'm the good-looking one here."

There was a pause, where Tyler might normally have pitched in. Instead, he was staring at his beer, fingers latched around the bottle.

"Tyler?" Andy said.

"Huh?"

"Are you awake? Carval here's going to do another show about us."

"'Kay." He looked at his beer again.

"You okay?" O'Leary asked, and clapped him on the back.

"Yeah. Thinking."

"D'you want another beer to help that thinkin' along?"

Tyler shrugged. "Guess so."

O'Leary lumbered up to the bar and bought another round. He didn't like the way the evening was going, but he couldn't see what to do about it. Nothing, he'd found, was usually the best plan, at least until he got Casey alone.

"Drink up," he suggested.

Tyler stopped gripping his bottle and looked up. "Got a brother," he said, which bore no relation to the conversation at all. The team, and Carval, waited. "Older. Three years." His fingers locked again. "Mom thought we were best pals. Weren't."

"I get it," O'Leary rumbled. "Families ain't always all roses an' unicorns. My sis is fine. My parents, not so much. Where'd this come from?"

"Dead girl's sister. Said they were friends." He pulled on his beer. "We weren't," he said again. "Went into the Army. Did good." That was an understatement of epic proportions. Tyler was a highly decorated top-class sniper. "Haven't seen him since."

Casey emerged from her hunched sullenness and touched his arm. "It's okay."

Tyler simply shrugged. "Not like Andy. Not like Bigfoot there. Fought, I left. That's all."

It undoubtedly wasn't *all*, but it was likely all he was going to say. The team were about to leave it at that when he took another huge gulp of beer and opened his mouth again.

"Stop letting Marcol fuck up your life, Casey."

"Say *what?*"

"He's sayin', at least he would if he'd use his words more, that you're lettin' Marcol messin' with those photos screw you 'n' Carval up, nearly nine years later. An' he's right." O'Leary might not have started this conversation in front of the team, but since Tyler had opened the door, he'd barrel right through it.

"How did we get there from his family? One minute he tells us he's got a brother and the next he's off on a tangent about Marcol?"

"It don't matter how we got here. You need to listen." O'Leary scowled at her. "We all know you don't like photos, an' it's no wonder. But that ain't Carval's fault. Marcol tried to screw you over at the Academy an' failed, so why're you lettin' him win by drivin' you two apart over more photos?"

Carval sat flabbergasted as O'Leary put a metaphorical boot up Casey's backside.

"Carval c'n shoot as he pleases, an' you c'n react as *you* please, but you're goin' back to old injuries 'cause you're scared."

"I am *not!*" Casey snapped.

"You are, an' that's fine, 'cause I would be too iffen I was goin' to be front an' centre with a shithead like Estrolla gunnin' for me an' Marcol makin' mischief in the background. But you're lettin' bein' scared stop you thinkin', an' that's where you're bein' dumb."

"I don't have to listen to this" –

"Do," Tyler contradicted, echoed by Andy. Carval's arm slid further around behind her, which would stop her leaving if she tried to – or get broken in the scuffle. He untucked it.

"You don't hafta, but likely you'll regret it iffen you don't."

Casey glared. The O'Leary juggernaut, amply flanked by Tyler and Andy, rolled right on, flattening everything in its path.

"Iffen you were thinkin', you'd be thinkin' it's time to stop lettin' Marcol dictate your reactions" –

"*Enough!*" Casey ordered. "Stop. Talking."

"Naw" –

"*Stop.*" Even O'Leary didn't disobey that tone from Casey. "I need to think. *Shut up.*" She shoved her chair backwards, and leaned her elbows on her knees, head down. The men exchanged silent glances over her bent head, but didn't talk. After a moment, she surged up. Tyler, braver than the others, caught her wrist. "I'm going to the *restroom*," she bit. "Let go." Tyler did. He wasn't *that* brave. Women's restrooms were a mystery that Detective Jayvon Tyler did not need to solve.

Casey slammed into the restroom, utterly infuriated. That overgrown *oaf* didn't know what he was talking about. She wasn't *scared*, she simply loathed photos. It was perfectly reasonable not to want a second show featuring her and her team.

Haven't we had this argument enough times yet? Enough times to make her views perfectly clear.

Enough times to make Carval's views equally clear.

Well, *fuck*. Her overgrown, oversized partner might have a point. *Fuck.* She hated it when O'Leary was right about relationship matters. She stood in the restroom and cursed liberally until she felt better, which took several repetitions.

She stalked back to the table. "I don't want to talk about it any more," she stated.

"'Kay," O'Leary said, grinning evilly. "So long as you think about it later."

"Shut up." She knew that O'Leary knew that she knew that he was right. Ugh. She downed her soda in a conversation closing-down manner, ignoring O'Leary's smirking face. Carval's arm sneaked around her again, and she didn't pull away.

When the evening wound up, she smiled up at him. "Wanna come back?"

"Sure."

CHAPTER FOUR

Carval looked around Casey's cosy apartment, warm-toned and welcoming, and noticed small signs of unusual neglect. Dishes still in the sink, a half-finished cup of coffee (and if that wasn't worrying, nothing was), an unmade bed visible through the bedroom door. Nothing significant – nothing that he didn't do at his own apartment – but Casey was tidy in all aspects of her life: home and work. Her pristine desk was a standing joke with the team. Casey didn't tolerate mess, or messy thinking.

She followed his gaze, and shrugged. "Dad needed me."

"Have you seen my apartment recently?" he replied. "I don't have any excuse and it's messier than this."

She shrugged again. "I'll fix it later. It's not important." She began to make coffee. "Go sit down."

Carval did. He'd known she was spending a lot of time with her father, following his release from another round of residential rehab, but the relative untidiness of her apartment suggested that she'd been spending far more time there than he'd realised. It certainly explained why she hadn't been spending time with him. There were only twenty-four hours in a day.

However, he was here, and so was she, and that meant –

"We need to talk," she said, and his heart stopped.

"We do?" he said, commendably calmly.

"About what O'Leary said." She put the coffee on the table, and sat down, facing him. Her brow creased. "Did you think...oh. No. I didn't mean that, and if I did I wouldn't start with *we need to talk*. I'd point my Glock at you and tell you we were done."

Carval managed a twisted smile. "I guess that would be pretty clear."

Casey produced an equally wry face. "Yeah. But that's not what I want to talk about." She tugged his arm around her. "That's better," she said.

30

"I…look, I know I haven't seen you much since Dad got home, outside the precinct. But there's nobody else to make sure he's okay."

"I get it. Sure, I'd like to see you more, but…family, yeah?"

"Mm," Casey said. "Yeah, but…anyway. That wasn't what I wanted to say. Uh…are you *really* planning a second show about us?"

"Yep. I wouldn't joke about that."

"Why?"

"Why a second show? Because there's much more about all of you and the crimes and CSU and McDonald and even Renfrew. I can't get it all into one show." He took a breath. "Why no jokes? Because I won't lie to you. I told you all up front. Photography is my life. I don't mess around with it and I don't let *anyone* tell me what to do and how to do it. You know that. Nobody decides what I shoot and what I show but me."

"Not even Allan?"

"Not even Allan." Carval grinned, suddenly boyish. "Though I listen to him, even if he thinks I don't."

Casey raised an eyebrow.

"I do. Don't tell him that, though. He'll fuss and nag more."

"He only does it 'cause you need to be fussed and nagged at."

Carval pouted at her. "I don't." He grinned again. "I just let him think I do. It makes him happy." He blinked. "What did you want to talk about? The second show? The first one – we're about ready to go with that."

"Uh…sort of. Not the show. Photos. Marcol. What O'Leary said."

Carval boggled at her. Casey didn't talk about things like that unless she absolutely had to, which had normally coincided with moments of high emotion – absolute fury or absolute misery. "You do? Uh, I mean, sure."

For someone who wanted to talk, Casey wasn't making any noise. Carval cuddled her closer, and with remarkable good sense, kept his mouth shut while he waited, tracing little patterns on her arm and sipping his coffee.

"I don't like photos. Now. I liked them fine before the Academy. Somewhere there's a photo of me with Mom and Dad, graduating from Stanford. I put it away. I only kept that one" – she pointed at it – "with Mom and Dad at my Academy graduation. Marcol…you know the story. Stole one of your shots and tried to use it to make me look like a cheap slut, doing it on my back." She took a breath, dragging herself back to calm. "Till you showed up, it didn't matter. No-one would be taking photos of me." Another breath. "Except you did. Everything's centred on that one shot of me, and even though you're shooting the team, it started with that." She paused. "Then you poked the bear."

"Yeah." He had. Furious that *his shot* had been stolen and used to shame Casey, he'd gone after Marcol. *Playing the hero*, Casey had said, and it certainly hadn't been a compliment.

"We're trying to deal with Marcol's malice, and he's working through all his pals to fuck the team up. Your photos are collateral damage."

Carval squawked.

"Not to you, sure," she said, "but to Marcol, it is." Her face changed, hardened. "I am *not having it*," she announced in tones of doom. "I am *not having* fucking *Marcol* dictating my life." She stood up and started to pace, heels clacking on her wooden floor. "I *hate* it when O'Leary's right."

Carval's pulse kicked up to about two hundred beats per minute. He told himself firmly that hyperventilating wasn't cool, but his heart was still hammering.

"You shoot as much as you want. This isn't about you. It's about me. I won't let that rat bastard mess me around again. You do what you need to do and I'll deal with it. You didn't try and interfere in my job, even when I got hurt, so I won't interfere with yours." She sat down again. "But you'd better make these the best damn shows *ever*, 'cause if I'm going down I'm going down fighting."

"Blaze of glory," Carval teased, though, from Casey's tone, mutually assured destruction wasn't out of the question.

"Yeah." She smiled nastily. "Let's *do* this. I've had enough of Marcol. I ignored him for years till this blew up, and I'm not letting him back into my head to screw me over again."

"Meaning?" Carval asked.

"Meaning I won't let him split us up because of *photographs*. I don't like them. But it's not up to him. It's up to us and he isn't getting in the way." She turned within his arm, eyes blazing, hauled his head down and kissed him challengingly.

Carval never backed down from a challenge. Casey had the initial advantage, but he had size on his side. He let her kiss him as violently as she pleased – but when she lifted off, she was in his lap.

"That's cheating!" she said indignantly.

"Yep." Unrepentantly, he kissed the tip of her nose. "So's that. And this." He stood up with her in his arms, ignored her commentary on oversized cavemen, and carried her to her bedroom, where shortly she proved how much she'd missed his company.

***

When Casey's nuclear-attack-warning alarm screeched, Carval jerked into shocked life, and only then discovered that he was still at Casey's with the woman herself curled up against him. He liked that. Casey asleep was a cosy, cuddlable bundle; soft and warm. As soon as she cranked her eyelids open, though, she'd be straight back to her daytime alpha personality. He liked that too, and his camera liked it even more.

The thought took him back to his other priority, *Murder on Manhattan*, abbreviated to *Murder One*, which made him smile.

"Wha's funny?" Casey grumbled, trying to pull the pillow over her head while hitting the snooze button.

"Nothing," Carval said, not being dumb. Telling Casey that she was small, cute and adorable, while she was scrubbing her eyes to wake up, was roughly equivalent to patting a hungry tiger on the head and then wondering why you were dead. "Good dreams."

"Ugh," Casey said, as the snooze expired and the alarm screeched again. She rolled out of bed, clad only in a sloppy sleep tee. "What time's it?"

"Whenever you set the alarm for, so, by definition, far too early."

"Ugh." Casey didn't get much beyond *ugh* until after her first espresso had hit her stomach. She activated her single functioning neuron to the setting of *make-coffee-drink-coffee*, threw espresso down her throat, and finally achieved intelligence. "Work."

"Yes." Carval managed a sleepy smile. "I'm going home. Allan's back tomorrow and we need to plan how to hang *Murder One*."

Casey grimaced. "Can we see it first, like we did with *Hands*?"

"If you want. It won't be ready till Wednesday afternoon anyway. It's much bigger, and we need a lot more time to get it right." He eased out of bed and watched caffeinated Casey watching him. He couldn't resist a small flex, spoilt by a large yawn.

She grinned and wolf-whistled, then whipped into the bathroom. Less than twenty minutes later she was showered, dressed, and wearing her usual minimal make-up: mascara and lip-gloss. "Bring the keys with you," she said. "See you later."

"Sure," Carval yawned, his momentary wakefulness dissipating as the door closed. He'd just go back to bed for a minute or two. He breathed in the light scent of Casey's shower gel, and was asleep again in seconds.

***

"Clement, my office," Captain Kent said as he walked through the door.

She'd been happily making a lovely logical list of everything they wanted or had to do as a start to her shift. "Sir." Oh, God, what had she done? She searched her conscience as she nervously followed him to his lair, and found not a single misdemeanour. What was he doing in on a Saturday? Captains should stay out of the way at all times, and especially when Casey was on weekend shifts.

"Close the door." She obeyed, knees trembling. "I requested Sergeant Tully to assign Officer Henegan to you the next time you asked for officers."

"Sir?"

"I want him detached from Estrolla. Your team has improved Larson, you can try to improve Henegan. If he wants to make amends for his behaviour toward you" – *What?* When had Kent noticed that? – "this is his chance."

"Yes, sir."

"If he fails, I won't blame you." Kent regarded her sourly. "But if he does, you are to tell me or Sergeant Tully right away. And, Clement, if there is any problem with Officer Estrolla or his cronies, you are to report immediately. That's an order."

"Yes, sir."

"Dismissed."

Casey fled Kent's intimidating presence.

Behind her, Kent considered his limited options. He could have transferred the whole damn mess of Estrolla and his henchmen to another precinct, which had been a tempting idea. However, he didn't like shifting problems rather than dealing with them, so he'd taken another route. Detach the officers who might, if they acquired some guts and a spine, be worth keeping, such as Henegan, who'd at least tried to apologise and make amends, then deal with the hard core of bad apples when they finally overstepped so far that God Himself wouldn't be able to save their sorry asses.

As long as Clement and her team could keep their tempers, that would be fine. Kent wouldn't tolerate dissent or conduct unbecoming from anyone.

He turned to the urgent reports from 1PP which had brought him in, hoping to have a quiet two hours to clear them. He sure hadn't had that the day before.

***

Casey parked Kent's commentary until she needed to think about it, which was definitely not now. Right now, she needed to get CSU into the theatre and Isabella's apartment. She dialled.

"Hey, Evan."

"Not you again, Casey. Why am I always on shift when you have a case?"

"That's not nice."

"I'm still waiting for my champagne for all the miracles I do for you."

"You'll get your reward," she laughed. "In fact, I have a reward for you."

"I know I won't like this," Evan muttered.

"Two nice, easy, clean searches. One studio apartment, and one dressing room at the Terpsichore Theatre. See, no problems."

"Casey, why me?"

34

"Because I have your number and I know where you live," she teased.

"This is harassment."

"You like me really."

"I like your interesting cases."

"That'll do. I even have a contact for you at the theatre, and the keys to the apartment and dressing room."

"You wanna be there?"

"Not at the apartment. We looked at that yesterday, but yes at the theatre if I can. O'Leary and me."

"Isn't it always?"

"Yep. Thanks, Evan," Casey said. "Call me when you're on your way to the theatre, and let me know what you find in the apartment."

Evan spluttered. "I always do. If I don't, you come asking."

"Tenacious, that's me."

"Like a pit bull."

Evan cut the call as O'Leary lumbered in.

"Mornin'."

"Hey. CSU are briefed. We'll go see the dressing room with them. I'm leaving the apartment to them – I don't need to see that again. I might suffocate in stuffed animals."

O'Leary chortled happily. "We could send Andy back. An' Tyler. He needs a softer side."

"That's what Allie's for," Casey pointed out. "He even brought her to your birthday party."

"Yeah," O'Leary grinned. "An' weren't they adorable? Cuter 'n' kittens."

Casey grinned right back at him. O'Leary's party had been great, and the absolute best fun had been teasing Tyler about Allie, music major and sometime model, afterwards.

"She's far too pretty for him," O'Leary carried on. "She's nearly as pretty as me."

Casey choked on the last of her coffee. "Are you trying to kill me?"

"Naw. Who'd partner me iffen I did?"

"Some poor fool…hey, maybe you could have Feggetter. He's good."

"Mebbe."

Casey refocused. "Kent hauled me in first thing to tell me he'd assigned Henegan to us. This is his chance to make good."

"Told you so," O'Leary said smugly. "Guess we'd better try 'n' straighten him out?"

"Guess so."

"C'mon then. I need to get a coffee, an' you always need to get another coffee. Let's go make them an' think about how to turn Henegan into a fine upstanding officer of the law."

"Brain transplant," Casey said bitterly. "Followed by the insertion of a backbone, possibly through his gutless ass."

"Ain't that illegal?"

She laughed. "Coffee, Dr Frankenstein."

"That's mean."

"Mean's my middle name."

A double espresso for Casey and a bucket of white Americano for O'Leary later, the necessary conditions for coherent thought had been achieved.

"I got an idea," O'Leary said.

"Mm?"

"Take him along to the CSU search at the theatre with us."

"I'm really glad you said *us* there, because if you think I'm going anywhere alone with Henegan, I'd have you checked out by a shrink."

O'Leary smiled. "An' if you were suggestin' it, I'd get Renfrew back here to check you out."

Casey made a superstitious gesture of aversion. "Anything but that. At least this case isn't likely to involve the FBI."

"Anyways, how about we take him?"

"Seems a little unfair on the other three."

"Aw, c'mon. They all got to go places with us before. They're not goin' to be all jealous-like. An' if they are, waal, we c'n manage them with some straight talkin' and that glare of yourn."

"I guess." She peeked up at him. "Do you think Henegan wants to make amends, like Kent said?"

"I dunno. I'm not bettin' either way. I don't think he's got the smarts to plan it this way, but we both know that someone else" – the name *Marcol* hung in the air – "does." He frowned. "I don't think so, though. I think he's tryin', but the man's as weak as the coffee from the vendin' machine."

"Mm. I wish I thought he was sorry."

"You're just nat'rally suspicious."

"Yeah."

"C'mon. Let's go give Henegan the good news about his field trip."

They found Henegan sitting within a protective ring of Fremont, Larson, and Adamo, all of them working on other matters until some information arrived on Isabella or any of the persons of interest so far identified.

"Henegan," Casey said. His head jerked up, worry, tending to terror, on his face. "O'Leary and I are going to join CSU to search Isabella's dressing room. You're coming too." His terror didn't abate. "It'll be good experience."

"Yes'm," he squeaked. His hand started to salute, and stopped at Casey's look.

"We'll let you know when we go. I'm waiting for CSU to confirm."

"Yes'm," he said again.

"Fremont." Casey turned her attention away from Henegan's quivers. "Anything new?"

"No'm. Detective Tyler and Detective Chee haven't gotten the phone records or financials through yet, but they'll pass them on when they get them and tell us what they're looking for."

"Okay." Casey looked up at O'Leary, then back at the officers. "Did one of you run David Gallagher?"

"Yes'm," Adamo replied. "I have his address and workplace here. Matches what Ms Scarfield told you."

"Anything interesting?"

"No record, but his social media's all like he's some rich big shot, except he isn't."

"Do you think he wants to be?"

"Yeah, but it's all bullshit." Adamo clapped a hand over his mouth and turned red. "Uh, sorry, ma'am."

"I've heard it all, and much worse," Casey pointed out. "If you'd say it in front of Tyler, you can say it in front of me." She assessed his squirm. "Don't tell me your mama wouldn't like it. She's not here. I am. You treat me the same as you treat the men."

Adamo nodded, wincing at the rebuke. Casey swung off to see if she had autopsy results yet.

"You slapped him down pretty hard," O'Leary said.

"Yep. If he starts thinking he has to do it differently because I'm a woman, then he'll start trying to do it in bad situations and it'll all go wrong in a hurry. He needs to learn that a cop is a cop is a cop: male, female, or any identifier in between. You treat them all the same. Save the differences for when you need it – like when we need a giant, we call you," she grinned, "and when we need a shooter, we call Tyler."

"An' when we wanna know about culture an' computers, that's Andy."

"Yeah." She refocused. "I spent some time this morning making a list, before Kent hauled me in." She scowled at the sheets of paper, which most unreasonably failed to cower and resolve themselves into answers. "We have a lot to do."

"We always do," O'Leary pointed out. "What've you got there that we c'n start with?"

"We're going back to the theatre this afternoon, so check off that one. Tyler and Andy should go find Gallagher and talk to him this morning."

"What about the rest of the cast, seein' as Maisie thought there were others doin' bad things?"

"Yeah. We ought to talk to the boozer – Maxwell Stephens." Casey's face twisted. The last thing she wanted was to deal with an alcoholic.

O'Leary didn't comment. Offering to do it for her, or suggesting that the others should do it, wouldn't go down well. Casey faced down her difficulties. "We'll do that after we've searched Isabella's dressing room and seen the rehearsal. Who's got Stephens' address?" she called to the officers.

"Me, ma'am," Fremont offered. "I'll send it to you now. We're making a list of all of them, but we're not quite done yet. I'll send you that later."

"Okay." Casey looked around. Andy had slipped quietly in while she was talking. "Andy, do you have Isabella's phone yet?"

"No. CSU aren't done. I told you that earlier."

"You and Tyler talk to Gallagher, then, and O'Leary and I'll take Henegan to search the dressing room. We'll send him back with anything interesting. Depending how long the search takes, we'll come back here for lunch and then go back for rehearsal at two, or simply stay there for the rehearsal. I'll let you know which."

"Till I get financials, there's not much to do here." Andy wandered over to the officers. "You got Gallagher's address?"

"Sure, Detective." Adamo handed it over.

"Thanks." Andy came back to the other two as Tyler arrived. "We're taking the boyfriend," he said to his partner. "No phone, no financials yet. Let's go make you happy with a nice interrogation of a non-theatre person."

Casey's phone rang. "Evan? Okay, see you at the theatre."

The detectives departed together, Henegan trailing them. Outside, they split up: Casey and O'Leary, with the officer, to O'Leary's massive SUV. Casey claimed shotgun without a word, texting Carval as soon as her seatbelt was on; Henegan relegated to the back seat, where he sat in silence, exuding nervousness. O'Leary thumped in and drove off with his normal cheerful demeanour.

CHAPTER FIVE

Casey rapped on the stage door, flanked by the two men.

"Who's there – oh, it's you again," Ron said. "With another one." He scrutinised Henegan. "Why's he got a uniform on and you two don't? Not that you'd get a uniform to fit you," he said to O'Leary.

"We're still investigating Isabella's murder," Casey rebuked.

"Yeah. But if I don't laugh, I'll start crying, and if I do that I won't stop," Ron bit back. "She was nice to me. Came and chatted and drank my tea without complaining. Don't you go thinking I don't care. I do."

"I'm sorry," Casey said, awkwardly. Ron made a *don't-mention-it* gesture. She smiled at him, then grinned. "Detective O'Leary does have a uniform, though. We made it out of a navy circus tent."

Ron laughed, though it had a forced edge. "What's it today? Thumbscrews, the rack? Yorick's skull?"

"None of the above," Casey replied. "CSU is coming to search Isabella's dressing room, and Officer Henegan here will help."

"That would be them, then?" Ron said, looking past Casey's shoulder.

"Yeah. Hey, Evan. You came yourself?"

"It's my turn for a trip out." Evan's pasty-pale face indicated that trips out weren't a major part of his job description. "I thought I'd march you down to the liquor store once we were done, for that champagne you keep promising me."

O'Leary chortled, but remembering that they weren't in the precinct, didn't make jokes. "C'mon. Mr O'Toole here is the doorman and caretaker, and a character actor. He'll show us to the right room."

Ron led the way. Casey walked with Evan, who didn't appreciate the compliment, and O'Leary and Henegan brought up the rear. Henegan seemed remarkably nervous, Casey thought. Surely he'd been allowed to do searches previously?

"Uh, Detective?" Henegan whispered to O'Leary. "Uh, can I...can we...uh, I need to talk to you."

"Me?" O'Leary tried to murmur, and failed.

"Yeah."

"Now?"

"*Yes*. Before the search."

"'Kay." He reached out and tapped Casey's dark head. "Need a minute," he said.

"Should have gone before you left," Ron snipped. "There on the right."

O'Leary almost dragged Henegan into the men's restroom. "What the hell is this about?" he said menacingly. His hayseed persona had dropped. Henegan shook in his shoes. "We got a job to do and you're not doin' it."

"I don't know what to do!" Henegan wailed. "Sure, I've been out on patrol with Estrolla but I've never been on a proper search and" –

"Never? You haven't gone searchin' with Estrolla or Grendon?"

"No. They did it all." He cringed.

"'Kay. An' what else? I c'n see there's more."

"Uh..."

"You need to grow a spine. What is it?"

"Uh, nothing more. I dunno what to do and everyone knows that you four eat idiots for breakfast and I don't wanna be an idiot."

O'Leary thought: *more of an idiot*, and, not being an idiot himself, wondered if Estrolla or Grendon had been hassling Henegan. If they had, he wouldn't get it out of Henegan.

"You watch an' learn. Don't touch anythin' 'less we tell you to, but ask if you wanna know somethin'."

"Yessir."

"An' you don't *sir* me. You c'n call Casey *ma'am*, like the other officers do, but leave the *sir* for the sergeants an' the captain."

"But I thought..."

"Why?" O'Leary inquired.

"Other detectives want it," Henegan muttered.

O'Leary parked the problem, to be discussed with the team sometime. "Not us. We don't need it. An' Casey don't much like *ma'am*, but she's in charge so you use it." He grinned. "C'mon. Iffen we don't go search there'll be trouble an' fuss, an' that ain't no fun."

Under O'Leary's gigantic reassurance, Henegan straightened up and trotted along beside him – necessary to match the big man's seven-league strides. Shortly, they entered the now-unsealed dressing room. Evan was already carefully photographing, stubby fingers in blue nitrile gloves turning over items. Casey, also gloved, was examining the top of the vanity unit.

"That's not much like her apartment," O'Leary said. "It's all tidy an' there ain't no stuffed animals."

"I guess she kept those for her private life."

"Stuffed animals?" Henegan said.

"Her apartment had all these cute li'l fluffy toys."

Henegan shuddered, which endeared him to Casey more than almost anything else could have done. "Oh," he said, with a distinct flavour of *ugh*.

"Out of the way," Evan instructed all three of them. "Officer, put on some gloves before you touch anything." He handed a pair to Henegan.

"'Kay," O'Leary said to Henegan. "Evan here's taken his photos, an' he's goin' to dust for prints an' spray for blood. He'll do a UV light scan for other bodily fluids."

"Like, um, sex fluids?"

"Or saliva, urine, sweat…" Casey suggested.

"Bodily fluids," Evan said firmly. "I'll determine the type at the lab." He looked at the three of them. "Go get coffee or something. You're in my way." He scraped up a sample and dropped it into a tube.

The detectives and Henegan did as they were told, and when they returned, Evan was finishing up. He smiled at Casey. "All yours," he said. "I'll take everything back to the lab."

"When will I get results?"

"When I get to them. There's a line, Casey. You know there's always a line."

Casey grumbled, but she couldn't jump the line. That was, Evan wouldn't let her jump the line.

"Okay," she said. "O'Leary, Henegan, time to search."

"What do I do?" Henegan asked.

Casey opened her mouth on a scathing blast of criticism, but was overridden by O'Leary. "We received information that Isabella knew that others were behavin' badly. Anythin' that might give us a clue about that. Letters, anythin' financial, photos – iffen you see anythin' that isn't stage make-up an' costumes, sing out so we c'n look. If you find a computer or phone, though that ain't likely, tell us right away."

"Okay."

Casey took the drawers of the vanity. She might have to work with Henegan, but she didn't have to like it. O'Leary could deal with him. Henegan was an unknown and potentially hostile quantity, as far as she was concerned, and since he'd had no backbone nearly three months previously, she couldn't trust him not to flip-flop back to Estrolla and Marcol's background malice.

"Mr O'Toole?" Casey called down the corridor. Ron arrived.

"Yeah?"

"Is this supposed to be locked?" She prodded at a drawer of the vanity.

"I guess," he said doubtfully. "I don't have keys, though."

41

Casey tugged out her phone, and called Andy. "It's me. I don't remember any keys at Isabella's apartment, but there's a locked drawer in her dressing room. Were there keys on her body or did CSU pick any up at the scene?"

"There weren't any keys in her apartment, but I gave the keyring to CSU on the way – we'll be at Gallagher's office shortly so make this quick."

"Was there a drawer key or similar on the ring?"

"There were several keys. Only one looked like it might fit her door."

"I'll call CSU."

While she waited for CSU to answer, Casey's mind whirred. Several small keys indicated several lockable things – maybe a safe, maybe drawers. But there was only one locked drawer here, so where were the others? Her fingers tapped impatiently on the vanity. "Hey, it's Casey Clement," she said briskly. "The Isabella Farquar/Betty Scarfield case. Do you have the keyring there?"

"Hi, Casey, how are you?" the tech said sarcastically. "Yes, I do."

"Can you see what other keys are on it? I have a locked drawer here and if you have the keyring I'll need to come pick it up."

"Send someone," O'Leary's bass muttered from the other side of the room.

"Or send someone. How long'll you be there?"

"Yes, there are other keys on it. We'll be about another hour. There's a couple of different looking hairs in the drain of the shower, so we're searching there."

"I'll send an officer. Thanks."

"No problem."

Casey cut that call and immediately dialled again. "Fremont? I need a keyring picked up from Isabella's apartment. You got time?"

"Sure, ma'am."

"Leave CSU the door key, so they can lock up, and bring all the rest to me at the Terpsichore."

"Yes'm. On it."

"That's in progress." Casey looked round. Henegan had slumped slightly. "You got a problem, Henegan?" she snapped.

"No'm. I could've gone."

"No. You're learning how to search properly." Not to mention that she wasn't letting him out of her or O'Leary's sight until she was damn sure he wouldn't screw up – accidentally or deliberately. "Carry on with the wardrobe."

Henegan turned back to the job he was supposed to be doing. O'Leary watched him from the corner of his eye. "You need to check for pockets, an' iffen you find 'em, go through 'em. People's pockets oftentimes have interestin' contents." He grinned. "Start again."

Casey efficiently searched down the sides of the cushioned chairs. "You should always lift cushions and poke down the edges of furniture," she said. "It's a total cliché but you can sometimes find things."

"Uh, here's something," Henegan said diffidently. "There's a shelf in this wardrobe that was mostly hidden by the clothes."

O'Leary shunted Henegan aside, and carefully examined the shelf. "Papers," he said, "and a box. Locked." He shook it delicately. "It rattles. When Fremont gets here, I reckon we'll find that one of them keys on the ring unlocks this."

"Most likely," Casey said absently. "When we've opened it, I want to have another chat with Ron. I keep coming back to that comment about others doing dirty deeds."

"Are you thinkin' what I'm thinkin', or are we bein' cynical?"

"I think we're thinking the same."

"Yeah. Thought so."

Henegan looked bewildered. Neither detective felt like explaining, since a certain degree of deduction would have shown him the answer.

"When we get the keys, we'll see what's there," Casey said. "You found it, so you can open it." Henegan looked like Christmas had come early. O'Leary cast Casey a *what* glance, which received back a small headshake. "Until then, keep looking through that wardrobe."

"Yes'm."

Around half an hour later Fremont showed up, escorted by Ron, and produced a handful of keys on a novelty fluffy panda keyring. Casey regarded it with horror.

"Wow," said O'Leary. "Pandas?"

"Do you need anything else, ma'am?" Fremont asked.

"Not yet, thanks. Have we got phone records or financials yet?"

"No'm."

Casey muttered horribly. "They should be faster. See you back at the precinct." Fremont left. "Henegan, here are the keys. Bring that box on to the vanity, and open it."

Henegan tried two or three keys before finding the correct one. All three cops peered into the box, but it was Casey who lifted the contents out.

"Well, well," she hummed happily. "Look what we have here. I think this is a diary."

"We like diaries," O'Leary agreed.

"Is there another key on that ring?" she asked Henegan. "This diary's locked."

"Yes'm," he quivered, and passed the ring across.

Casey selected a small key, and wiggled it in the pink padlock on the pink, butterfly-decorated book. "I can't imagine anyone expecting this to have anything more interesting than *Betty hearts David*," she snipped, "plus her heartbreak when he ditched her."

"You ain't sympathetic?"

"Nope. It's not my job to be sympathetic, it's my job to catch whoever did it." She looked down at the book, and opened it. "What the hell?"

"What?" said the other two.

"This isn't a diary," Casey said, and stopped, frantically flipping pages. "Andy needs to look at this. This is an account book – but I don't know whether she was balancing her check book and grocery bills or something else."

"How come?"

"Abbreviations," Casey said disgustedly. "Look at this so-called handwriting. That's not handwriting, it's chicken scratches."

"Like you do calligraphy?" O'Leary teased. Casey's own handwriting was notoriously dreadful. Andy threatened her with calligraphy classes every few weeks, and had displayed his own beautifully constructed brushwork at every opportunity, until Casey had threatened him with being drowned in the ink and then pointed out that his actual handwriting was almost as bad as hers.

"Yeah." Casey flicked a glance at Henegan, and O'Leary dropped the teasing. No point in providing ammunition. "Anyway, it's potentially useful. Anything else in pockets or that closet, Henegan?"

"No'm."

"We'll take this back." She dropped it into an evidence bag. "What about the papers?"

"Complicated," O'Leary said. "I'll bag 'em and look properly when we get back."

"Then let's open up this drawer." Casey took the keyring from Henegan and started trying likely-sized keys in the lock. The third one turned over. "More papers. Another bag, please?" O'Leary handed one over, and Casey squeezed the bundle of papers into it. "Okay." She felt around in the drawer, opened all the others to make sure there was nothing lurking, then removed each drawer from the vanity. "In case something's dropped down behind – or been hidden there," she explained, crouching down to examine it with the aid of the flashlight on her phone. "Nothing," she said.

Another hour later, they hadn't found anything else interesting, and left for the precinct to drop off the papers and account book. She texted Andy to ask him and Tyler to come back to the bullpen to share notes, before returning to the theatre for the rehearsal.

***

44

"David Gallagher, please," Andy said to the security guard at the mundane office building. Gallagher hadn't been at the address they'd had for him, so despite it being Saturday, they had tried his workplace.

"Sure," he said boredly, barely looking at them. "I'll call him down." He tapped a number and lifted the receiver. "Dave? Got visitors for you. Come down." He turned to Andy. "There's a room here, with a vending machine if you want a drink." He pointed. "Dave'll be here in a minute. I'll tell him where you are."

"Thanks."

Andy and Tyler settled themselves in the sparsely furnished room, already planning to grill Gallagher on the difference between his social media persona and his employment.

A tall man walked in. "I'm David Gallagher," he announced. The cops examined him. Broad but not overly fit; a suit which hoped to be stylish but had come off the rack, a tie that screamed *trying too hard to be cool*, decorated with pink elephants. His attempt to look like a rich young professional was ruined by the pen in his shirt pocket, which was slowly staining the seam with blue ink. Neither cop felt like pointing out the leakage.

"Detectives Chee and Tyler," Andy stated.

Gallagher regarded them with dislike. "What d'you want? I'm busy."

"Betty Scarfield."

"What about her? She's just another actress wannabe."

"She's your girlfriend."

"Nope. We broke up almost a month ago. She was holding me back."

"How so?" Andy asked.

Gallagher checked that the door to the room was firmly shut. "I got the chance of a promotion, a big jump up. It's in Chicago. Betty didn't want me to take it – said she wasn't moving outta New York when her career was starting to move. I mean, what career? She's barely doing off-off-off Broadway and it's all that experimental crap that no-one wants to go see anyway."

Tyler caught Andy's expression, and tapped his foot on Andy's highly shined shoe, warning him not to comment on cultural matters. They'd be here for hours and learn nothing if Andy started on culture.

"I told her my career would keep a roof over my head," Gallagher continued, "and if she wanted to stay stuck in her teen-dream with those dumb stuffed animals, living on ramen, it was her problem not mine. She could come with me or not, but I wasn't going to turn this down for her."

After he finished, the cops let the silence continue.

He finally sat down, expression changing. "She could have worked in Chicago. It wouldn't have made a difference, I didn't think. There's a lot of opportunities there. I tried to tell her that." He stared at the surface of the table, hands tightening on each other. "She'd have been a bigger fish there."

He looked straight at Andy. "She has talent. But she won't – it was New York or nothing." His face twisted, then crumpled. "I would've married her. I would have...but she wouldn't come with me."

"I thought you said she was holding you back?"

"Because she wouldn't come with me. This is huge. I'll go from being a cost accountant to being a full financial controller, in a much bigger company with more opportunity. I got my CPA three years ago and now I have real experience. But she doesn't want to come, so we broke up. She got totally mad about it but it was her fault really. If she won't give up her dream, why should I give up mine? She won't compromise. Going for some role in Shakespeare so far off-Broadway she was practically in Pittsburgh was more important."

Gallagher stopped. "Hang on a minute. Why are you here? Has Betty been arrested?"

"Why would you think that?"

"Because she hated the girl she was up against for the role. Uh...Dacia something. Betty said she was always saying how much better she'd be. Did they get into a fight or something? Betty wouldn't have started anything, but...she might've finished it."

"No. I'm sorry to tell you, Mr Gallagher, but Betty is dead."

He gaped, dumbstruck, colour draining from his skin. Then, "What? Dead? *Why?*" he gasped, gulping air. "What *happened?*"

"You tell us," Tyler said bleakly, though they'd both noted that Gallagher had consistently talked about Betty as if she were alive.

Gallagher paused, horrified, then jerked straight up in his chair, white lipped and furious, shock and upset burned away. "*What?* I'm a *suspect?* That's total crap. I broke up with her. She didn't ditch me. I haven't seen her since we split."

"You hit on her sister."

"*Maisie?* You're kidding me. I wouldn't hit on Maisie if you paid me."

"She says you did."

"That conniving little *bitch!*" Gallagher exploded. "She cooked that up because she was mad I ditched Betty. That pair stuck together like glue. Maisie thought and acted just like Betty – sure, Maisie wasn't an actress but she bought into all Betty's dramas like it was her." Fury sparked from his eyes. "Maisie'd do anything for the drama. I bet she told you she didn't want anyone else to hear it."

Tyler made a note. Casey had said something about that when they debriefed.

"Anyway, I never did it. I haven't seen her and we're close to year end here. I've been piling on the hours. I bet if you ask her when it was she won't be able to tell you, 'cause she knows it never happened and I can prove it."

"How?"

"Swipe cards," Gallagher stated. "We have to swipe in and out of the accounts office and somewhere someone records it. I'll get you the office manager and she can pull the records so you can see I was here till nearly ten for most of the last month."

"Where were you between six p.m. Thursday and noon yesterday?"

"Six till elevenish, at work, like today. Year end, like I said. After that? Asleep in my bed." He thought for a moment. "Alarm goes off at quarter of six, out at quarter after – shower, shave, then I get coffee on the way here."

"Where do you live?" Andy asked, to make sure they'd gone to the correct address. The databases could be out of date.

"Hudson Heights. Bennett Avenue." That was the address they had. He pulled out a notebook and scrawled the full address on it, ripped the sheet out and shoved it at them. "I get the subway from 191st to 110th. You can check my travel. I got my coffee at Peaky Barista on Broadway. You can check. I always go there, every day. I probably swiped in here at quarter after seven, maybe closer to half past? I was here all the time." He flicked his focus from Andy to Tyler and back again, frantic. "You can check everything!"

"We will," Tyler said.

"I didn't kill her and Maisie's *lying!*" he flung back. His head dropped, and the silence rolled out for a moment or two. Andy broke it.

"Did you know that Betty had won the role in the Shakespeare play?"

"No – she did?" He slumped, defeated and miserable. "She'd never have come with me, then. Not if she had a role." His shoulders hunched.

"Do you know anything about the Finisterres?" Tyler asked.

"Oh, them. Betty called them her fairy godparents, because they were helping her. She thought it meant she'd be a star. Did they help her get that role?"

"We think so."

"Maybe she was right, then. She said they could make or break anyone." His mouth pinched. "Maybe she would have made it, with them behind her."

"Was there anyone who disliked her, or that she'd argued with?"

"I guess the girl she beat out for the role wasn't happy, but I don't know about anyone else. She hadn't gotten the role when we split." He looked up, and to their surprise, the cops noticed that his eyes were damp. "I should've believed in her. Even if we'd broken up, I could still have believed she'd make it, but I didn't."

"Apart from Maisie, who would know if Betty had any enemies, or recent arguments?"

Gallagher thought. "Her girlfriends, most likely. Suzie and Anna. She saw them a lot."

"Last names?" Tyler queried.

"Uh, Kellman – no, Keller, and Bulitt."

"Thank you. Is there anything else you can tell us or that you can remember?"

"No." He shuddered. "I'm sorry. I wish…" He couldn't finish.

"Here's my card," Andy said. "If you think of anything, call us. We might want to talk to you again."

"Whatever. You get the guy, yeah?" But his voice cracked as he tried to gather himself.

"That's our job. Thank you, Mr Gallagher."

CHAPTER SIX

"Unexpected," Tyler said, on the way back to the precinct.

"Yeah. Interesting – especially if we can prove that Maisie lied. Something's squirrely here. Sounds like we don't even have half the story yet."

"Why'd she try to finger Gallagher?"

"That is the question. Maybe she wanted to find out whether 'tis nobler in the mind to suffer" –

"What the hell?"

"Or maybe she wanted him to suffer the slings and arrows of outrageous fortune?"

"That culture?"

Andy sighed. "Don't you recognise *Hamlet* when you hear it? That's from the most famous soliloquy in the whole English-speaking world, you Philistine."

"From the Bronx. Not Philly."

Andy squawked indignantly, and then looked at Tyler's gleaming grin. "You're playing with me."

"Took you long enough. Course I know it. *To be or not to be*," he began. "Learned it in high school." He laughed. "Gotcha."

Andy grumbled. Tyler grinned some more. He was still grinning when they reached the bullpen, where Casey and O'Leary had arrived only a moment ahead of them.

"Thanks for your help," Casey said to Henegan. "Go join Fremont and see if there's something you can do there. We'll call on you when there's more."

"Yes'm," he stuttered, and left the group, heading for the break room.

"Still searchin' for his spine," O'Leary commented.

"We're stuck with him till he either shapes up or screws up," Casey replied. "We can try to knock him into shape. Kudos for us, and we don't have to be pals with him."

"Not allowed to teach sparring," Tyler noted.

"Shame Kent stopped us. I enjoyed giving our last lesson." Casey smiled sharply. Officers Estrolla, Grendon and a few pals had learned that size mattered. Specifically, O'Leary's size. They'd also learned that speed and sneakiness beat unfit size. It had been thoroughly satisfactory, but as part of Captain Kent's orders to keep their noses clean until after *Murder on Manhattan* had opened, the team had been ordered not to hold any more sparring sessions with officers who didn't like them.

"What's made you so happy?" O'Leary enquired, noticing Tyler's wide grin.

"Andy," Tyler said, with an even wider grin. "Culture."

"Turns out Tyler knows some Shakespeare," Andy muttered. "Next we'll find he can dance."

"Don't dance."

"You danced with Allie at my party," O'Leary said smugly. "There you were, cheek to cheek. Awwww."

Tyler's dark skin tinged with red. "Still don't do that ballet shit Andy watches."

Casey took pity on Tyler, unusually. "What did Gallagher say?" she diverted, while storing up the possibility of teasing Tyler later.

"Maisie lied."

"What?"

"He said," Andy picked up, "that he wouldn't have hit on Maisie if you paid him, and that she was a total drama queen who'd support her sister no matter what."

"Convincing," Tyler said. "Easy to check."

"We'll have to. Looks like we need another interview with Maisie."

"Why'd she lie, though?" O'Leary asked.

"That's what we wondered. Maybe Betty-Isabella wasn't as nice as her parents made out?"

"It's goin' to be interestin' talkin' to all them actors, ain't it? An' we got all them papers, too."

"Papers?" Andy said, electrified. "What kind of papers?"

"Looked like an account book. Lotsa numbers an' weird abbreviations." O'Leary waggled the evidence bag.

"Give it here," Andy demanded, grabbed it from O'Leary's giant paw and started to flick through the pages. Four flicks in, he stumbled to his desk without taking his eyes from the book, and plumped down. Shortly, he grabbed paper and a pen, and started making notes, muttering all the while.

"Leave him," Tyler said. "Pull him out for the theatre."

"What are you seeing?" Casey said to Andy, barely two minutes later. "Give me a chance."

While Casey and Andy argued, out of the corner of his eye, O'Leary noticed Estrolla heading for the break room, shadowed by Grendon. He hummed thoughtfully, and then tapped Tyler. "Wanna drink?" he murmured. "'Cause I think somethin's goin' down in the break room an' I wanna know what."

Tyler nodded, and they slipped away, not concealing their approach to the break room, but certainly not announcing it. Henegan was, shakily, drinking a coffee, Estrolla and Grendon eyed up the fridge.

"You were out with Clement's team," Estrolla noted.

"Sergeant assigned me," Henegan defended.

"Guess you couldn't argue."

"No."

"Huh." Estrolla smiled toothily, and left.

Tyler and O'Leary strode in as he did. "Coffee?" O'Leary asked. Henegan startled, and spilled his coffee. He began to make more.

"Sports drink."

"Your funeral, but I don't get how you ain't bright blue like a Smurf from drinkin' that stuff."

Tyler scowled. Henegan completed his coffee-making, and tried to scuttle out, forestalled by Tyler's arm. "One chance," Tyler said. Henegan paled, and fled.

"What was that?"

"Told him he got one chance. Reminding him."

O'Leary smiled slowly. "Nice," he said meaningfully. "Iffen we could find him a backbone, that'd be good."

"Yeah."

O'Leary, despite his hayseed drawl and carefully cultivated dumb demeanour, was an intelligent man, currently applying his intelligence to Henegan's behaviour in the break room. Sure, he'd been nervous, but that seemed to be his natural state of being. What he had *also* been, O'Leary noted, was shaky. Hmm. Estrolla was a nasty piece of work.

He parked it for further thought later, and reminded himself that one of them should be with Casey every time she left the building. Keeping eyes on the situation wouldn't be a bad plan.

"Not alone," Tyler said, following O'Leary's thought and gaze at Estrolla. "You or me with her."

"Yep."

They ambled back to Casey and Andy, perfectly in harmony.

***

After lunch, the four cops returned to the theatre, where Ron let them in and escorted them to the stalls. They were followed by Carval, who'd shown up at the precinct demanding to know when they'd go to the rehearsal.

"Mr Heyer," Ron said apologetically.

"No," a man snapped, without even looking. "Out."

"Mr Heyer…"

"One more interruption and I'll have you fired."

"Carl Heyer?" Casey said coldly, "NYPD."

Heyer turned around. "You're disturbing my rehearsal."

"Murder disturbs a lot of things." Casey looked him up and down with disbelieving contempt.

"Murder? The only murder I know about is the way Isabella murdered Titania on this very stage!" He stamped his foot. "She's late for rehearsal. I don't care how much is riding on it, if she's not here in one minute, she's *out!*"

"She won't be here." Casey's tone was glacial.

"Why the *fuck* not? Don't tell me you arrested her? What'd she do? Crime of impersonating an actor?"

"Mr Heyer, Isabella Farquar was found dead outside the stage door yesterday."

Heyer abruptly stopped his dramatics. "What?" he choked. "What happened?" He supported himself on the side pillar of the stage, shaking. "She's dead? You're sure it's Isabella?" Heyer paused, still pale and shuddering. "That's terrible. But the show *has* to go on, even in the face of such tragedy. We open in two weeks, and her accident and demise must take second place. Dacia! Get out here! You're on. Titania."

Casey assessed Heyer as genuinely shocked, but so self-absorbed that he was incapable of counterfeiting upset.

The rest of the cast babbled frantically, then displayed enough histrionic distress to make all their apparent upset seem completely insincere.

"Silence!" Casey yelled from the front of the stalls.

A twenty-something woman appeared from the wings.

"*Stop.*" Casey's word halted her. "Mr Heyer. This is a *murder* investigation. Your play is secondary. Co-operate and you might be able to start today's rehearsal. Don't, and I'll take you down to the precinct and ask my questions there. Then I'll take the cast one at a time, sequentially." Heyer began to protest. "Or, you can let me deal with this, and further questions will be asked at a more convenient time."

It finally dawned on Heyer that Casey was entirely serious. He waved dismissively at Ron. "House lights," he said, and the auditorium lit up. Heyer stayed on the stage, above the cops, in a clear attempt at a power play.

"Come down here," Casey said.

"I c'n give you a hand, iffen there's no steps," O'Leary offered, and stood at the edge of the stage. Suddenly, Heyer didn't look sure of himself.

"Anything to assist," he said snidely, but came down the steps on the left-hand side.

The team sized him up. He was dressed in a dark green velvet jacket, floppy bow tie, Prohibition-era pants and spats. His dark hair, slightly too long, was greased back, and he sported a goatee. There was an odd aroma about him, which Casey couldn't identify.

"Andy, Tyler, O'Leary, can you start getting everyone else's full name – and legal name, not just stage name – and details, usual basic questions?" The men nodded, and moved on to the stage.

"Full name?" she rapped at Heyer.

He blinked. It didn't seem like anyone had taken that tone to him since he was out of diapers. "I beg your pardon?"

"Full name," Casey repeated.

"Carl Tarran Heyer."

"Is that your birth name or is it a stage name?"

"Birth," he said sulkily.

"Occupation."

"Theatre director."

"Mr Heyer. Earlier yesterday the body of Isabella Farquar, also known as Bettina Scarfield, was found close to the stage door of this theatre. I understand that she had been cast in your production as Titania."

Casey didn't say how she knew that, and Heyer didn't have the brains to notice. His brows had drawn into a scowl, and whatever, extremely limited, upset he'd felt at Isabella's death had gone. Casey wasn't impressed.

"I never wanted her," he snapped. "Dacia's got more talent in her little finger than Isabella had in her whole body, but Isabella was forced on me by the Finisterres and I needed their funding. My artistic vision demands that the cast be exactly as I envisage it and Isabella was totally wrong. It would have been a laughingstock. She was hopelessly inadequate."

"Your vision?"

Heyer's voice rose. "My concept is a completely new take on *A Midsummer Night's Dream*, focused on how the Oberon-Titania dynamic represents the patriarchal hierarchy of sexual dominance and women's subjugation in a male-dominated society and zeitgeist, with all other relationships being male-male to show that outmoded definitions of the characters' sexuality have no place in the theatre, and also to refer back to the original intentions of the Bard where all actors" –

"Were male," Casey said, already tired of this pretentious piece of bogus artistic integrity. Heyer stopped, thwarted. "Basic tenet of Shakespeare's time."

"Yes. Every part except Titania is male. Titania must be obviously female in form. My vision demands that she is tiny, with long dark tresses, barely bound up, clearly physically weaker and smaller than everyone else. Isabella was too tall, her hair was too short, and she had too little" – his hands made a gesture around his chest. "You're much more the right type," he added. Casey wasn't flattered. "It is *essential* that she is well-endowed, to emphasise the animalism of female sexuality in contrast to the purity of male bonding and friendship, exemplified by men's physical stature and beauty. You" –

Casey interrupted him. "Why did you cast her?"

"I said," he snapped, "I didn't. She was forced on me as a condition of the Finisterres' funding. I can't afford to cross them. Nobody can. They had ruined the whole impact of the production with the crudity of filthy lucre."

"I see. Did anybody have a problem with Isabella?"

"Only that she couldn't act and was completely wrong for the part. Otherwise, no. We are a close-knit group, united by my vision."

If Casey heard the words *my vision* one more time, she'd vomit, preferably all over Heyer's pretentiously polished spats.

"Was anyone else forced on you as a condition of the funding?"

"No, thank God. Now that Isabella is so tragically gone, I can realise my *Dream* as it should be."

"That's all. I'll want to talk to you again. Two of my team will remain to watch the rehearsal."

"What?"

"Procedure," Casey snapped.

It wasn't. But she couldn't flat out ask *who's boozing, who's in bed with whom?* without giving Ron away, which she didn't want to do. Ron, treated nicely, would be their unwitting eyes and ears. If Andy and O'Leary remained, they could pick up all sorts of clues from the way the actors interacted with each other and with Heyer, and meanwhile she and Tyler could remove themselves from the drama to work with the flow of other leads and information, using all the normal, factual, and definitely *not* over-dramatic steps of an investigation.

"Who's *that*?" Heyer cried, more disturbed by Carval than by the news of Isabella's death. "What's he doing?" Carval's camera flashed again. "You! Get down here!"

Carval strolled up, still shooting, and smiled. "I'm Carval. Who're you?"

Heyer had been winding up to a diatribe, but on hearing the name, he stopped. "Carval? *Jamie* Carval? The photographer?"

"That's me."

"Oh." Heyer deflated instantly. That, it seemed, was that. Or not quite. "Is this for an exhibition? Would we be credited as subjects? We could use some good PR."

"I don't know yet," Carval said. Heyer slumped. Carval moved off, still shooting, before any further conversation distracted him.

"If he – *Jamie Carval* – wants to watch and shoot, he can," Heyer said, an obsequious note creeping into his voice.

"Up to him," Casey clipped. "We'll finish with the others, and then you can continue. Everyone is to leave their contact details, because we *will* have more questions later."

"If you have to."

"This is a murder."

"Everyone will co-operate," Heyer opined.

Casey wasn't sure. Heyer's self-absorbed reaction didn't give her any confidence that she could expect co-operation. She was already formulating a list of follow-up questions, but she needed the team's first pass before she blundered in on the wrong foot. Better to take longer now, and get it right.

She dismissed Heyer, and joined the rest on the stage. "Has anyone talked to Dacia?" she asked.

"Naw," O'Leary replied. The other two shook their heads.

"I'll start with her. How're we doing?"

"Done a couple each," O'Leary summarised, "got a couple more each to go. Chat after we're done."

"Okay." Casey looked around, spotted her prey, and swung over. "Dacia?"

"Yes?" she wavered. She was indeed tiny, far shorter than Casey, who was barely middle-height. Straight, pure black hair (Casey suspected dye, just as Isabella had had dyed hair) fell past her bottom half-way to her knees. As indicated, she was a perfect, hourglass shape; tiny waist to match her tiny height, curvy hips and generous chest, which, astonishingly, didn't look artificially enhanced. "What's happened? You said *murder*, but who'd want to murder anyone?" Her eyes were wide.

"Isabella Farquar is dead."

Dacia gasped, but for an instant ambition flickered in her face, before she produced tears and shock. "That's terrible," she said in a shaky, little-girl voice which impressed Casey not one iota. "I can't imagine who'd do that." Her fingers knotted together, then unknotted, quivering.

"Yes, it's terrible," Casey said, making a snap decision to shock her, "and you're the one who's benefited most."

"What?" Dacia paled.

"Carl wanted you in the part, and you were jealous that you hadn't gotten it – and now you have."

Dacia's dismay disappeared. "I'm a far better actor than she is – was! I deserved this part and I'm not sorry I have it, but I'm sorry she's dead. I didn't kill her. How would I manage that without shooting her? I'm six inches shorter and thirty pounds lighter than she was, and you can check that I don't own a gun."

"We will." Casey regarded her. "We'll be checking up on you. Anything you want to tell me before I find it?"

Dacia scowled, which wasn't an act. "I was furious about only being the understudy, and I wasn't shy about saying so."

"Full name – stage name and real name, please – and contact details. We'll talk to you again later."

Dacia gave her details. Casey looked around, saw that everyone was finishing up, and left the stage. The rest of the team joined her in the stalls.

"Done," Tyler said with customary brevity.

"We'll check the contact details against what we already have – make sure they're telling the truth. When we've run them, we'll start on individual interviews and alibis. I'm not doing that where everyone can hear."

Tyler nodded.

"I got Max – Maxwell Stephens. Egeus," O'Leary said quietly. "I agree with Henegan, he's the boozer. He's really upset."

Casey winced. "Okay."

In a few moments, they'd shared all the information.

"Ev'ryone seemed pretty shook up and upset that she was dead," O'Leary noted, "but they're all actors, so that don't mean nothin'."

"We need to start running everything," Casey summarised. "Andy, O'Leary, you two stay and watch the rehearsal. Heyer's agreed. You know what you're looking at. I've had a bellyful of Heyer's *vision* – something about the chauvinist zeitgeist" – both men snorted – "but you're more likely to notice if anyone looks too friendly or a lot unfriendly – or anyone else had a drink, smoke or snort. O'Leary, keep a close eye on Egeus."

"Sure."

She thought briefly. "Can you record the rehearsal on your phones?"

"Maybe," Andy said. "We'll try."

"That way we can have a better look back at the precinct, to see if it ties up with our first thoughts."

Carval ghosted up behind her. "I'm staying. I wanna shoot the theatre while they're rehearsing and it's got lights and people. It's fascinating."

"Up to you. Heyer'll let you do anything you please. If you hear anything outside your camera clicking, let us know." Her smile belied her snippy words. "See you later," she said generally.

"Later," Tyler added.

Carval ghosted off again. Andy and O'Leary took seats a little way apart at the front of the mezzanine.

"Is this team bondin'?" O'Leary asked.

"Guess so," Andy said. "It wasn't quite what I meant."

"Naw."

"Why'd Casey leave us here?"

"You watch it, I do community theatre. Guess she thinks we know enough."

"Or she doesn't want to suffer through it," Andy said acidly. "Who is this pompous ass Heyer, anyway? I've never heard of him."

"Dunno. Wish I had some popcorn, though."

They settled back in their seats, and started their phone videos.

Less than five minutes in, Andy's teeth were clenched so hard that the video picked up their grinding. O'Leary's jaw had dropped open.

"Stop!" Heyer shrieked. "Lysander, you're supposed to be in love with Hermia! Put some emotion into it. You're not in a drag club."

"What's this crap?" O'Leary asked. "We do better in my group and we ain't professionals."

"Heyer doesn't have a clue," Andy said. "He might have a vision but it sure isn't translating into the performance."

"Casey's lucky to be out of it," O'Leary said.

They turned back to the stage, wincing.

"Act Two, Scene Two," Heyer enunciated. "I need to feel the menace here. They *hate* each other, but there's unstoppable sexual attraction. Show it! You aren't two schoolyard babies. Oberon, *intimidate*. Titania, feel the *fear*. He can kill you with a touch, but you're still fighting against him and against your own desires. Oberon, hatred and *desire*! Go to!"

"Ill met by moonlight, proud Titania."

The instant Dacia stepped out and spoke, everything changed. "What, jealous Oberon!" she began, and the stage electrified. Heyer's vision manifested around her: a tiny, apparently feeble woman, surrounded by testosterone.

"Wow," O'Leary whispered.

"Dear God," Andy countered. "She's *really* got it. Look at them respond."

They did. Suddenly, the production took shape.

CHAPTER SEVEN

"Cross-check," Tyler said, referring to the cast's real names, as he and Casey strolled into the bullpen.

"Yep. Then we can set the databases going again, and maybe Larson and Fremont would like to do a little social media investigation before Andy gets back." She grinned. "Wonder how they're enjoying the show."

Tyler smirked. "Mean."

"My middle name. If I'd known you wanted to see it" –

"No way."

Casey's eyes glinted. "You sure? Some culture would balance out all that gym work."

"Nope." Tyler scowled.

"Let's go make our four uniforms busy, happy people. We have all those real names, and we need to add the two friends to the next of kin and the Finisterres."

"Sounds good."

They descended upon their four victims. "We gave you stage names," Casey said, smiling happily. "Here are the real names. Reference them to the stage names and see if you can dig anything more out of them than we did."

"Add two more – her friends. Anna Bulitt and Suzie Keller."

Fremont grinned. "Yes'm," he said. "Henegan, you take the friends, and the three of us'll divide up the real names."

"Okay," Henegan agreed. He didn't exactly look happy, but when he caught Fremont and Larson's twin hard stares, he put his head down to begin.

"I think there's some attitude adjusting going on," Casey said dryly as she and Tyler wandered back to their desks.

Tyler nodded. "Larson's improved. Did good there."

"If I'd known we'd get Henegan, I wouldn't have bothered."

Tyler lifted eyebrows at her.

"Oh, okay. If we can't fix him, no-one can."

Another nod.

"Now what?"

"Autopsy?"

"Good point. Maybe McDonald's sent something, but no way will we have tox. He tells me every time that it takes more than twenty-four hours."

She tapped hopefully, and made a face. "Not yet. D'you think Andy'll explode if we look through those papers and account book?"

"Papers. Leave the book."

"He's put Post-Its in it." Casey poked at one of them.

"Your funeral."

"Let's take one bag of papers each, and see if we can make sense of them."

***

Some two hours later, Casey's eyes were crossing and the papers were obdurately refusing to tell her anything useful. Fortunately, before her head exploded or she planned a Monday strangulation of an innocent bank clerk in order to extract Isabella's financials, Andy and O'Leary returned.

"You made me sit through the worst production I've ever seen!" Andy accused.

"Naw, that's not fair," O'Leary said. "The first ten minutes were dire, but then that mini-Dacia woman came on, and wow!"

"Wow?" Casey repeated.

"She *shone*," Andy elaborated. "It was electric. Suddenly I could see that pretentious ass's vision and it *worked*."

"You have got to be kidding me," Casey said. "All that crap he spouted about his vision and it's *good*?"

Andy nodded.

Casey boggled, then recovered herself. "Motives. Dacia wanted to be the star, and it sounds like she's up there. Heyer wanted his vision, and it sounds like *he* was right about casting Dacia. Removing Isabella from the show suited both of them. Neither of them were sad about her death."

"Now we got two strong motives," O'Leary rumbled.

"In it together?" Tyler queried.

"They might be. Does that make two and a half motives or just one?" Casey wondered.

"Dunno. I don't remember my math."

"Says the man who aced high school math," she tossed back at O'Leary. "Or were you fibbing about that?"

O'Leary blushed. "Naw, but that was a long time ago."

59

"Two motives," Tyler reminded them.

"We haven't even started to get any useful information on the usual suspects – cast, boyfriend, friends, family, money providers, never mind anything in her financials," Casey gloomed. "Her sister implied the boyfriend thought Isabella was cheating, and said he hit on her, but he says Maisie's lying, so there's another couple of motives. Then Maisie said there were dubious goings-on in the theatre cast, so there's even more."

"Lots of motives. Just what we like."

"Do we?" Casey said even more gloomily. "Where's Carval?"

"He's still shootin' at the theatre. Got a bee in his bonnet about it."

"Oh." She stretched. "Coffee."

Back from the break room, Casey had left Andy to continue his investigation of the account book, and contemplated her list of actors. "Have you got the cross-referenced list of names – real to stage?" she asked Tyler.

He nodded. "Here." It landed on her desk.

Casey read down it, then surged over to Andy. "These names – look at the initials. They match with some of the entries in that book."

Andy scanned the list. "Yeah – but how did she know the real names?"

"Why?" Casey added. "Is it normal to need to know the real names? Surely she'd have called them by their stage names."

"You'd think," Andy said. "Weird to find out real names. I wanna check this to her bank records."

"You're thinking she was putting the squeeze on," Casey suggested.

"Yeah."

"Hm. I wonder how much Maisie knew about that – and whether she was gearing up to try the same thing, starting with Gallagher."

"That's a stretch," Andy scoffed.

"Yeah…but…anyway, I'm not ruling it out. It's too early to rule anything out." She smiled. "Everyone's a suspect except us four."

"What am I suspected of?" Carval said from over her shoulder, appearing as if by magic.

"Inflicting torture on innocent NYPD detectives," Casey flipped back.

"Yeah. About that – you mean the exhibition, don't you? Allan's back tomorrow so we'll start hanging stuff immediately."

"Already?"

"Yep. I told you we need till Wednesday to get it right, and – oh God."

"What?"

Carval coloured. "Uh…Captain Kent allowed me to shoot here, but he had a price."

"Yes?" Casey said suspiciously.

"I had to promise that I'd give his wife a personal tour before opening. Oh God. I'd better go see him. Why's he in on a Saturday anyway?"

"To keep us on our toes. Good luck," Casey said mordantly. Kent wasn't a notable culture fan, but his wife was. She sniggered evilly. Carval wouldn't get much change out of Kent. Especially not if he mentioned *Murder on Manhattan Two*.

Carval made his way to Kent's austere office, and knocked. Barging in would be unwise. Kent ran a tight ship, and he didn't tolerate disobedience, insolence, or any form of unethical conduct. By the book was his middle name. On the other hand, he generally let his misfit team get on with their investigations without interfering, beyond requiring occasional progress reports.

"Come," Kent's stentorian tones commanded. Carval sidled in. "What do you want?" Kent could have been less welcoming, but only by firing his gun point-blank at Carval.

"My exhibition is almost ready," Carval said. "You agreed with Allan that your wife would have a private tour before we open. We expect to open Thursday for the critic's previews, before we let the public in on Friday. It'll run for four months, minimum," he added smugly.

"You could take my wife – and me" – Carval yelped – "around on Wednesday evening," Kent decided. "Fine. I'll tell her."

"Okay." Carval started for the door.

"Does this mean you're done with my precinct?"

Carval stopped dead, and slowly turned around. He'd hoped that Kent wouldn't ask that. "No."

"What?" Kent's irritation cracked through the air, his square face reddening. "What do you mean, no?"

"I mean I'm not done. There's enough for a second exhibition at an absolute minimum, and I'm going to shoot it." As ever, any attempt at hindering Carval's photography went down badly. "There's too much here to miss. There will be another exhibition."

"If I say no?"

"Someone else will say yes. Or 1PP will see how successful it's been and tell you to let me back." Carval scowled back at Kent. "Or you could accept it. I don't get in the way of your precinct and Casey and her team are happy to let me tag along. I don't get in their way either."

"Clement's *happy* with this?" Kent jabbed. "I don't believe you."

"Yes. I don't get in the way of her job and she doesn't get in the way of mine."

Kent self-ejected from his chair and stormed to his office door. "Clement!" he bellowed. "My office, now!"

Casey hurried in and stood at parade attention. "Sir?"

"Carval informs me that you are happy" – Kent's inflection on the word spoke volumes – "that he intends to shoot a second exhibition in this precinct. Would you care to confirm that?"

"Sir, I'm not exactly *happy*. But he doesn't interfere with my job and I won't stop him doing his. Unless you specifically order me to, sir."

"Do you want me to?"

"No. I can fight my own battles with Carval. If I wanted him to stop, sir, I wouldn't hide behind you." Behind her, Carval boggled slightly. Sure, she'd *said* she wouldn't get in his way…but up until right this minute he hadn't fully believed her.

"Dismissed, Clement," Kent growled. "You, stay."

Casey scarpered. Carval stayed put, holding Kent's annoyed gaze.

"Don't get in my team's way," Kent snapped. "Dismissed."

Carval fled, before Kent could change his mind. He decided that a soothing coffee would improve the afternoon, and diverted himself to the break room, where he found two relatively clean mugs and began to brew. As he waited, through some quirk of the precinct acoustics, he could hear an unpleasant voice berating some unlucky person.

"Tully might've assigned you, but that doesn't mean you go kissing ass." An indistinct mumble replied. "You keep me informed." Another, unhappier, mumble. "I'm senior. You *take* orders. Capisce?" Miserable agreement followed.

Carval wandered out, pondering, but he didn't waste much time on it once he found his way to Casey's desk, on which he placed her espresso. He hadn't recognised either the voice or the mumble, which wasn't surprising since his entire existence was centred around sight and pictures, not hearing and sounds. He'd probably recognise the team's voices, and Allan's, but that was about it. He didn't care about that, only about his exhibition. On balance, he thought the discussion with Kent could have gone a lot worse, but he hoped that Mrs Kent was a little less abrasive than her stern husband.

"Thanks," Casey said automatically, staring at her board as she downed the liquid. "Have we got financials or phone records yet?"

"No."

"Why not?" she complained rhetorically. "What are they doing?"

"Annoyin' you," O'Leary grinned. "Just like always."

Casey grinned back ruefully. "Yeah. But why can't I have it right away?"

"Because that's life," Andy said bluntly. "We can't always get what we want."

"We don't even get what we need," O'Leary added, and hummed. Andy fixed him with a horrible glare, which achieved nothing. O'Leary happily hummed on, tunefully.

"I don't want to interview again without knowing what that book and those papers mean," Casey grumbled. "I wanna hit them where it hurts."

"Phone company," Tyler suggested, meaning that he'd try to get information from them.

Carval wandered around, idly shooting the precinct, not selecting shots. No-one noticed him: just another part of the misfit team.

That would change, in a few days. The *Hands* exhibition hadn't registered with the precinct. *Murder on Manhattan* certainly would. He wandered back towards his cops, barely registering a hostile glance from Officer Estrolla and his pal, Grendon.

"We won't get anything tonight?" Casey carped as he returned. "Why not?"

"Because the phone company haven't pulled the records," Andy said, sufficiently patiently for it not to be the first repetition. "It's ten minutes till shift end, and we're not getting anything tonight. Banks don't work on a Saturday or Sunday. Let's all go home and start fresh in the morning."

"If we must," Casey muttered.

"Let's go to the Abbey," O'Leary suggested. "Casey here could use a beer to soften her disappointment."

"Can't," she said. "I have to go see my dad."

O'Leary regarded her worriedly. "You been there pretty much every night, 'cept yesterday, since he came outta rehab," he murmured.

"He needs me."

"I get it," the big man said softly, "but sometime he has to do it himself. You can't hold him on the wagon forever."

"I'm not," Casey said defensively. "I'm supporting him, that's all. Family's supposed to do that."

"Mm," O'Leary hummed sceptically. "An' when are you sleepin'? 'Cause you don't look like you've slept good for weeks."

"I'm *fine*," Casey snapped. Truthfully, the only nights she'd slept soundly since her father started rehab had been the nights she'd spent with Carval. O'Leary didn't need to know that, but from his expression, he had guessed. O'Leary was far too sharp, and knew her far too well, to be deceived or put off.

As if he'd heard her thought, O'Leary flicked an inquiring glance at Carval.

"Oh, no," Carval said. "I'm not getting involved. You want answers, you get them from Casey."

O'Leary grinned. "But she ain't answerin' me."

"Not my problem," Carval pointed out. "Being shot would be my problem, and that's what answering for Casey would get me. I don't want to be shot."

"Man's got sense," Tyler approved. "Casey hasn't."

"What?" Casey squawked.

"Bigfoot's right. Can't hold him dry forever."

"I have to try," she hissed. "He has to stay dry or he'll *die*." She stopped. "He has to stay dry till after this damn exhibition, too."

"*What?*" exclaimed four men at once.

"Get real," she snapped. "We were told to stay squeaky clean. *Everyone's* going to be watching us, and you know as well as I do that everybody'll hate us even more as soon as it opens. If Dad gets picked up and charged, some sonofabitch'll leak it to discredit me, just to add to the PR circus. Then they'll start looking for the rest of our histories. We've enough problems with Estrolla and his gang already. Kent's hovering like an attack hornet" – O'Leary muffled a snort of laughter – "and God knows who at 1PP's looking for an excuse to go after us 'cause they're best pals with Marcol. We're under the microscope and I have to keep Dad out of it so he doesn't make it worse."

"Does your dad even know about the exhibition?" Carval suddenly asked.

Casey coloured uncomfortably. "No."

"No?" the other three chorused.

"What the hell?" O'Leary added. "Casey, what'cha doin'? You gotta tell him before it opens. C'n you imagine what he'll do when he reads the papers?"

"He isn't interested in that sort of thing," she defended.

"He won't be able to miss it." Andy pointed out. "It's not that it's culture, it's that it's the NYPD. It won't be on the front pages, sure, but it won't be hidden in the critics' reviews."

Casey crumpled. "It won't? Crap. I was hoping..." She trailed off. She'd hoped she could keep it from her father. She couldn't stand it if he was enthusiastic. She'd be devastated if he simply didn't care.

"Tell him," Tyler instructed.

"I guess," she said miserably. "That won't improve this evening."

O'Leary patted her shoulder. "It won't get any better for waitin'," he consoled. "Just do it, an' then it's done."

Casey stood up, and set her shoulders squarely, straightening. "Yeah. See you all tomorrow." Her tone dismissed them all, and she walked to the stairwell alone.

"Wait," O'Leary said. She stopped, and he caught up to her. "Not on your own. Remember?"

She grimaced at him, but O'Leary was pleasantly implacable as he escorted her to her car. "We can't have you gettin' into trouble, c'n we? I'll be the best-lookin' cop in the PR photos. I don't want you spoilin' it with bruises. You'd ruin my reputation."

Casey managed a laugh. O'Leary wasn't a handsome man, though his many muscles were truly impressive. "I'll take care."

"You do that. Seeya."

She waved, and drove off.

O'Leary ambled back upstairs to the bullpen, where the other three were waiting for him. Tyler nodded once, sharply. "Estrolla was looking."

"Thought so," O'Leary replied. "Too bad. Abbey?"

Tyler nodded again.

"Sure," Carval said.

"If we have to," Andy complained. "What's wrong with a tea bar?"

"No beer."

"Beer is overrated."

O'Leary gasped in horror, and made for the door before Andy could blaspheme any more.

***

Casey pulled up at her father's Brooklyn apartment, picked up the bag full of the evening's dinner, and forcibly calmed her face and body before entering. She knocked, but only as a warning that she was there, opening the door with her key, observing every small hint and clue to her father's state.

Sober.

She hid her relief, and smiled. "Hey, Dad. I brought dinner. Pulled pork, salad, and a peach pie."

"Sounds lovely, Catkin. There's sodas in the fridge." He smiled vaguely. "It's great that you come round as often. Seeing you helps."

Guilt sliced at her. She hadn't wanted to come. She'd wanted to go to the Abbey with the team, and then go home with Carval, or he with her. Instead, she was here, picking at an indifferent ready-made meal and trying to make banal conversation, before opening the real issue.

"That's good."

"I don't know what I'd do without you."

Drink yourself to death, that's what you'd do. That's why I'm here. That's why I'm barely leaving you alone. I can't let you die.

"What did you do today?" Casey asked, desperate to pretend that they were a normal family, having a normal dinner together: that they hadn't been shredded by her mother's death in a road accident that might have been caused by her brain cancer; that they weren't broken by her father's swift drowning of his grief in rye whiskey.

"I went to the store, and to the meeting. Then I took a walk through the park, and came home. It's been a lovely day, so I thought I'd enjoy the sunshine." He smiled. "There was this cute spaniel in the park, like my dog when I was young. Maybe I should get another one?"

"I don't think a dog would be happy in an apartment," Casey said, despite knowing that many city-dwellers managed fine. She meant *you'd forget to take care of it if you fell off the wagon*, but chided herself for her lack of

65

confidence in him. He'd been dry for weeks. "Maybe a hamster?" she said, consciously mischievous to hide her mistrust.

Her father made a face. "Too much like a mouse. What if it escaped? I'd never find it." For a moment, his gamin smile was exactly as he'd used to be. "It might nibble my toes."

Casey giggled, and suddenly they were family again. Even the indifferent food tasted better, for an instant, but then she raised her eyes to meet her dad's gaze, and saw the yellowing sclera, the few broken veins in cheeks and nose, the tiny hints of blurring vision; heard the lack of clarity in his voice.

Nothing was the way it had been. Nothing. But if she tried hard enough, supported him enough, was simply *there* with him enough…maybe it could be. Maybe. Her momentary happiness dissipated, replaced by hard resolve. She couldn't, wouldn't, let him drown.

"Fine, no hamsters," she said lightly. "Maybe a goldfish." Her father made a noise of disagreement, and the conversation moved on, until Casey sat at the dinner table, finishing her peach pie, wondering how to open the latest problem. The sweet pie turned acid in her throat.

"Dad?"

"Mm?"

"Dad, there's something I need to tell you."

"Is something wrong?" he worried. "Catkin, you're not sick" –

"No. Nothing like that." Thank God. That would really be the last straw. "Uh, Dad, have you ever heard of the photographer Jamie Carval?"

His forehead wrinkled. "Carval? Uh…no. Not that I can remember."

His memory had holes in it, thanks to his drinking. His failure to remember meant nothing.

"*New York's Ugly Underbelly* – the photo exhibition almost two years ago?"

His eyes cleared. "Yeah…I think I heard about it. Not my thing. I'm sure I didn't go see it." Hazy reminiscence crossed his face. "Your mom would have gone, and dragged me along."

Casey winced, but her father didn't notice. "That exhibition was Jamie Carval's." She stopped. "Um, he's got a new exhibition opening on Thursday."

"Yes?" her father said, confusedly. "Do you want to go? It isn't my thing. If you want to go to the ball game, I'll come. We haven't been to a ball game in years."

"No…It's about us. Me and my team, I mean."

Her dad stared at her, completely befuddled. "Say what?"

"He's been photographing us. We're" – she cringed – "the focus of it."

"You are?" He smiled, still confused, but delighted. "That's great."

She couldn't bear to spoil his happiness by telling him that she hated it; that she didn't want to be the star of any show.

"I'd better come see it," he decided, and her heart crashed through the floor.

"I thought it wasn't your thing," she tried.

"I can't miss seeing my daughter in a big show."

Why not? Casey thought bitterly. It wasn't like she was a child in the school play, wanting her parents to watch. She wished she'd never mentioned it. She certainly wouldn't tell him that she and Carval were in a relationship: that was still too fragile to touch.

She made it through the remains of the evening, pleaded a headache to escape early, telling him she'd see him Monday, and went home, guiltily conscious that she didn't want him to go to the exhibition, especially not with her.

On the other hand, she mused bleakly, if he came to the show with her, then it wouldn't be the public viewings, it would only be the team. Less chance of difficulties – and more chance to get him out of it without a fuss. But, on yet another hand, he'd meet Carval, and she'd done everything she could to make sure that they didn't meet. She couldn't stand the pity she'd see in Carval's eyes; she couldn't stand the contrast between Carval's blazing presence and her father's half-dissolved vagueness.

She made herself a coffee, and tried to calm down, but worries ran around her head like hamsters on a wheel: what if he came, what if he was drunk (*but he's dry*, she told herself), what if the media found him, what if Marcol or his cronies leaked his history? So many bad outcomes, and she couldn't think of a single good one. The best she could hope for would be that he was embarrassingly parentally proud, and that nobody noticed him. The cold space in her stomach grew, not solaced by her hot coffee.

Eventually, she went to bed. After fitful sleep, she woke unrefreshed, with no solutions.

CHAPTER EIGHT

"Mornin'," O'Leary said cheerfully. Casey grunted. "Coffee?" Another grunt. "Guess that's a yes." She managed a nod. "C'mon." He hauled her up, and pushed her gently towards the break room and their machine. O'Leary brewed his own barrel of coffee, made Casey's and handed it over, and wandered out to join Tyler and Andy. "We got anythin' new yet?"

"Nope, but it's barely eight. If we haven't seen anything in an hour, we'll chase. I was thinking about Maisie." Casey frowned.

"Mm?" the world's biggest bumblebee buzzed. "What'cha thinkin'?"

"I wondered if she knew what her sister might have been doing? And whether it might have happened before?"

"That's a stretch. You sure you ain't doin' yoga on the side? You're stretchin' like you are."

"I don't do anything that would twist me into a pretzel," Casey pointed out. "I don't bend like that. Running and some sparring's enough for me, with all the drills we do. I leave yoga to Andy. He can tie himself into knots."

"Let's get some work done," O'Leary said, before Andy retaliated and it all went downhill fast. "Surely we'll get somethin' soon?"

As Tyler and Andy moved away, O'Leary looked down at Casey. "Now that you've finished tryin' to divert me, what's up? All that about Maisie bein' in on it an' then seizin' on yoga was so's I couldn't spot it."

"I hate you," Casey grumbled. "I don't wanna talk about it."

"Waal, you c'n buy me lunch, an' tell me all about it then." He ignored Casey's disagreeable noise, and clumped back to his own chaotic desk, just as there was a happy yelp from Casey. "We got somethin'?"

"Phone records. Tyler, you're the best." She flicked them on to Tyler, whose sniper's eyesight, she thought, gave him extra-good pattern recognition.

"Phone contacts from CSU?" Tyler said to Andy.

"Nope."

Tyler called them. "Coming."

"You got that video from yesterday?" Casey asked O'Leary.

"Yup."

"Andy, you tie it together with yours and then you and Tyler can review the interactions and come up with our interrogation list."

"I'll harass Isabella's bank first thing tomorrow," Andy said, "so now I'll stitch those videos together. What'll you do?" he asked Casey and O'Leary.

"Polish my nails," O'Leary teased, "then Casey's."

"Search the backgrounds of all the actors," Casey corrected. "No nail polishing here."

"You're no fun," O'Leary complained, but ambled over. "Give me half of them."

Casey handed over a copy of her list with a line around halfway down. "Top or bottom?"

"Top."

"Okay."

"Is Carval coming in? I want his shots when I'm done," Andy said.

"Don't know. He and Allan were starting to hang the exhibition."

"I'll call him."

The team set to. Tyler enlisted Fremont for his phone matching; Andy acquired Larson, to show him some of the skills of the precinct's top technogeek. Casey and O'Leary started analysing the limited information from the databases and social media. As Henegan had said, Maxwell Stephens had been picked up drunk a couple of times, but not charged. That was it, it seemed.

"Waal, that was a whole lotta nothin'," O'Leary humphed. "I always thought actors got up to mischief, but this lot are borin' as all get out."

"What was in that book of Isabella's? There must be something dodgy." Casey thought. "There could easily be. If you annoy the director, or someone more famous than you, what's your chance of getting another role?"

"Slim to none," O'Leary agreed.

"Plenty could be going on that never gets reported or mentioned."

"Sure could."

"Why do I suddenly see hours of interviewing in our future?" Casey asked the air.

"Aw, c'mon. We like interviewing. It's fun. I get to look like the bad cop an' you get to be it."

Casey grinned. "Before we get to that, let's have a look at the Finisterres, and at Isabella's family."

"Sure. An' when we've done that, it'll be lunchtime, an' you owe me lunch."

"Elephant," Casey said. "You never forget anything."

"Not when it's you buyin'. Who're these Finisterres?"

"They're the money guys." Casey scanned the search data. "Wow. Lots of money. They fund at least three experimental productions every year."

"Where'd it all come from?"

"Good question." She scrolled further down. "It doesn't say here, just that they fund a lot."

"Mm," O'Leary hummed. "Wonder why they backed Isabella if Dacia was much more talented?"

"Now who's stretching? That's even further than I went."

"I got longer arms than you," O'Leary pointed out.

"And an over-active imagination."

"Yeah, most likely. But like you said earlier, I'm not rulin' anythin' out. Let's set Henegan or Adamo on a deeper dive."

"If you want. I'd rather have Adamo, but I don't want to annoy Tully. Pick whoever you want."

"Henegan," O'Leary decided. "'Cause I want him under my eye."

Casey's grimace altered to questioning. "Really?"

"Yeah. I think Estrolla's out to make trouble an' if I c'n head it off, that'll be better than anythin' else."

"I don't agree. I think Kent slapped him down and he'll sulk and throw dirty looks around. But if it makes you happy," she added quickly, "you can keep walking me to my car at the end of shift."

"It makes me happy," he said, smiling seraphically. "Anyways, I'll go brief him, an' you c'n keep lookin' for somethin' interestin'." O'Leary wandered off, and Casey went back to her data.

***

"I spoke to Kent about showing his wife around," Carval said to Allan as they surveyed the exhibition space. "He's coming too."

"Both of them? I didn't get the impression Kent was interested."

"He's not. I guess he's doing it for his wife. He'll glower at the walls."

"If you don't get on with this, he'll be staring at empty walls."

"Don't fuss. I'm thinking. I need to place the centrepiece of Casey first, and then everything'll flow from that."

"You haven't thought about that already?" Allan snipped.

"Of course I did, but I wasn't standing in the space. Stop fussing and distracting me." Carval revolved a few times, slowly, assessing the light, the entrance, the rooms… "Here," he finally decided. "Right here."

Allan made a note. "If you've settled on that, can we get on with the rest of it?"

"I need to hang it. It has to be in place before I decide on the rest, because I need to see the lighting and the way it falls for best effect. This'll knock them flat on their critical asses and it has to be *right*. This shot will set the tone of the whole exhibition."

"Yes, Jamie," Allan said patiently, resisting the urge to roll his eyes. "You do this every time. I know. You don't need to tell me. Go get a coffee while I talk to the curator."

Carval hurried off to get a coffee, before Allan found something less pleasant for him to do. A few moments later, in the gallery's café, his phone rang.

"Carval," he said, then, "Hey, Andy."

"Hey. I've been combining our videos, and I want to see your shots of the theatre while we were interviewing – evidence," he added, which stopped Carval's protest in its tracks. He wouldn't normally allow anyone near his raw shots, but *evidence* made it a different matter.

"When? Allan's talking to the gallery staff about hanging, but we have a lot more to do today."

"Can you come over at lunchtime?"

"I guess," Carval said, "but I can't stay long. Can I download and scoot? I can always come back at the end of the day when we're done here."

"Sure," Andy said equably. "Let me know when you'll show up."

"Yeah. Gotta go. Allan's looking for me."

Carval tipped his coffee back in one long slug, and bounced up to return to the arrangement of shots, options boiling up in his brain.

"What is – oh, *wow!*" He stopped cold in front of the centrepiece. "They'll *die* when they see this. I'll be *stratospheric*." He stepped back. "Put the lighting on it," he ordered, utterly forgetting courtesy in his passion to get it right.

Allan, excusing the rudeness as he recognised Carval's complete absorption, signalled to the tech to be ready to realign the lighting – several times, going on past experience – and switched on.

"No. It needs to be up a little – down a little – stop! Right there. Don't let *anyone* move that light."

"We won't," Allan placated. "We'll check it again – all three of us – five minutes before opening."

"We sure will," Carval decreed. He stared at his centrepiece with enormous satisfaction. It was *perfect*. "Okay," he said. "Let's get the next section fixed up."

Three hours of intense work later, his phone rang. "What?" he snapped, having been removed from his stunning arrangements.

"It's Andy."

Carval returned to the real world. "Yes?"

"Are you showing up or not?"

"But – oh, *crap*. I lost track of time." He looked frantically around. "Allan? Allan! I have to go to the precinct for an hour. Don't let anyone move *anything* till I get back. Go get lunch or something."

Allan tutted. "Be quick. We're making great progress and I don't want to lose momentum."

"Tell Allan I'll send you back asap," Andy said.

"There shortly." Carval looked around for his camera, and discovered it, in its satchel, in the corner where he'd left it. "Andy says he'll send me back shortly," he said, "just like I'm a school kid."

"There are some similarities," Allan pointed out. "Starting with your ability to get distracted by almost anything."

"If I hadn't been distracted by Casey's team, we wouldn't have an exhibition at all," Carval snipped. "The faster I go, the faster I'll be back."

"Go. Don't get distracted by construction sites, theatres, Casey, the other cops…"

"Stop it, Mom!"

Carval fled before Allan could berate him further.

***

"C'mon, Casey."

"Uh?" Casey dragged her head out of the endless search data to gaze vaguely at O'Leary. "What?"

"You owe me lunch. C'mon. The food truck has mac 'n' cheese, an' it's sunny, so let's go get it an' sit in Sakura Park. You could do with some sunshine. You're as pale as a ghost."

"Like you're Mr Suntan."

O'Leary merely smiled. "I'm hungry. Let's go."

Casey stood up, ignored the scowls from Officers Estrolla and Grendon with consummate ease, and left, half-running to keep up with O'Leary. "Slow down. Running's bad for my digestion."

"Only if you do it after you've eaten. You go runnin' for fun."

That was true. Casey found that running cleared her head – or if it didn't, it tired her out so that she had a chance of sleeping. However, she didn't need to have O'Leary commenting on her complexion or exercise regime. "I like running, just not in dress pants and shoes."

"Fair enough."

They bought their lunches, and found a comfortable bench in the sunshine.

"What's up?"

"Nothing. I'm fine."

"That means you ain't fine at all. What did your dad do?"

Casey heard *this time*.

"Nothing." She took her coffee from O'Leary's massive paw. "He's doing fine."

"An'?"

Casey gave up. O'Leary would keep asking – albeit out of anyone else's hearing – until she answered. "He wants to come see the exhibition."

O'Leary's massive jaw dented the grass on its way to the magma layer. "You gotta be kiddin' me. What's he want to do that for?"

"He wants to see me in the show," she spat. "Just like when I was in grade school and an angel at the back of the Nativity." She winced. "At least then he did it because he cared." She stopped short. "I…I didn't mean that."

"Naw?"

"No. He *does* care."

"Iffen you say so." But O'Leary's scepticism was patent.

"He *does*," she insisted. "But that's not the point."

"What's the point, then? You dragged me all the way out here, an' while it's nice to see the sunshine, I don't guess that's it."

"You dragged me, you big lunk. You're the one who wanted to know what was up, and I told you."

"Yeah, an' you said your dad carin' isn't the point about this here exhibition. What is the point?" he repeated.

"I can't let him go around it on a public showing," she admitted. "So…uh…"

"You thought he could come around with all of us. Waal, that ain't such a bad plan."

"He doesn't know about Carval."

"Huh? You mean he doesn't know that it's Carval takin' photos, or he doesn't know that you an' Carval are seein' each other?"

"He doesn't know we're" – she searched for an appropriately neutral word – "involved."

"Sweethearts," O'Leary teased, and dropped the smile when he saw her face. "Oh. That's complicated, sure, but 't ain't like you're kissin' in public. You don't even hold his hand, most times."

"I don't want them to meet."

O'Leary's elephantine jaw dropped again. "You what? Surely you ain't ashamed of your boy?" Her mouth opened on a furious denial. "Naw, an' I know that. But whether you say it or not, an' mostly it's not, you're ashamed of your dad. I get it, an' you know I know about parents you don't wanna admit to."

He did. O'Leary's parents had as good as disowned him the day he'd told them he was gay, more than ten years ago. As far as Casey knew, he'd barely seen them since. They hadn't even come to his wedding to Pete. *Unreconstructed*, O'Leary had said once, putting off his down-home pretence.

73

Homophobic, red-necked assholes, Casey had thought, and been delighted she'd never had to meet them.

"I'm not!" Casey denied, and both of them heard the doubt. "But…" She turned away from him to look towards the General Grant memorial, hidden by the leafy trees.

"Mm?"

"It'll be a disaster. Carval sky high on the exhibition and total success, and Dad…not even interested. He never was. Mom was. She liked exhibitions and museums and art. Dad…"

"But he wanted to go to that new African-American museum down in DC," O'Leary said.

Casey winced. He'd drunkenly gone to the airport, to try to go, and been arrested for it. "Only to look at the architecture. He wasn't interested in the contents, even when he talked about it sober. *I* wanted to see the exhibits. He'd probably have gone for coffee, or examined the structure." She exhaled. "Anyway. Everyone'll know he's not interested."

"That ain't all," her enormous partner said. "You're worried he'll embarrass you, an' you don't want him lookin' like a bum in front of us an' your boy."

"He won't. He's *dry.*"

"Sure he is, now." The words *but for how long* hung between them. "But that ain't what I mean. Your dad hasn't any passion, an' all of us do, an' you an' Carval most of all. Everyone's goin' to see that your dad's basically given up."

"Yeah," she sighed. "Even sober, he doesn't care about anything much any more. He only ever wanted Mom, and she's gone."

O'Leary regarded her bent head, and patted her gently on the back. He'd heard this a few times in the last year, and he was beginning to believe it. Casey had told him how her dad had said she shouldn't be a cop, and then that he'd asked her to betray all her ethics and morals, and fix it so that his arrest would go away. "Iffen he don't care about you, why's he comin'?"

"I'm the last link to Mom," she said miserably. "Mom would've cared."

O'Leary carefully didn't mention that not five minutes ago Casey had vehemently insisted that her dad did care about her. Pointing out inconsistencies was for the interrogation room, not his pal.

"Waal," he said, "you can't stop him comin', 'cause then he'll know there's somethin' up. But if he comes the same night we do, then we c'n all make sure there's no trouble."

"I guess."

"C'mon, then. Let's get back, an' get more coffee from your li'l place on the way. Mebbe somethin's come in while we've been havin' our lunch."

***

74

Something had indeed come in while Casey and O'Leary had been having their lunch. When they returned, Carval was leaning over Andy's desk, fingers tapping impatiently.

"I'm downloading as fast as it'll go," Andy said. "You plugged it in, you know that. Go make coffee, or something."

"I need to get back."

"We *know*," Andy said, in a tone that indicated that he and Tyler had known that several repetitions previously. "It's almost done."

Carval looked up, and spotted Casey. "Hey," he said. "I nearly missed you. I have to get back to the gallery before Allan puts out a BOLO on me."

"We'll help," Andy said.

Carval ignored him. "I'll be back around shift end – five?"

"Yeah." Casey smiled at him. "See you then."

"It's done," Andy said, and disconnected. "Off you go. Should I call Allan to tell him you're on your way?"

"Not you too," Carval complained. "Allan fusses enough for ten and I don't need a nanny." All four cops regarded him. "I don't!"

"An' if you see somethin' interestin' through that lens of yours?" O'Leary asked pointedly.

Carval coloured. "Uh…Nope. Not today. I have to hang the exhibition and nobody else can get it right."

"When do we get to see it?" Andy asked.

"If you don't want to be in with the public, the only chance is Wednesday. I gotta go," he said, frantically looking at his watch. "See you later." He dashed out in a flurry of chaotically harassed energy and a ringing phone, which the team rapidly and correctly deduced to be Allan.

75

CHAPTER NINE

"Do we have anything new?" Casey asked.

Tyler grinned. "Phone records."

"I knew that," Casey grumbled.

"I stitched the videos together," Andy added, "just this minute, and Tyler'll cross-check with Carval's photos – he's better at seeing the links."

"We'll go interview the Finisterres," Casey decided.

"Not me?" Andy complained. "You don't know anything about theatre."

"That's the point. O'Leary does, but I'll be fresh eyes."

***

Casey and O'Leary found the Finisterres' home in a modern block that gave the impression of containing corporate robots all in the sole business of making money, right up until the doorman allowed them through and they were ushered into the Finisterres' abode.

"Wow," O'Leary said. "That's...not like the outside."

Casey simply stared, wordless. She liked purple. In small quantities, occasionally. A deep violet accent wall, with midnight blue, gold-flecked, gauzy curtains sweeping from ceiling to floor on each side, held back with thick golden cords...hadn't figured in her interior décor choices. "It's like a stage," she said.

"Oh, how *smart* of you," a voice fluted. The cops whipped around. "It *is* intended to convey the impression of a stage, but I didn't expect you to recognise it as quickly." The piping voice belonged to a small woman, dressed in a deep purple robe and purple mules; sporting dangling amethyst earrings and a slight shade of purple in her hair.

"Mrs Finisterre? Detectives Clement and O'Leary."

"I am Claudia Finisterre. Delighted to meet you. Detectives? How interesting. Do come through." Claudia evidently didn't find it curious that two detectives had come to her door. "Now, where is Henry? Henry darling, we have visitors."

"Coming, my love." Another fluting voice, tenor to Claudia's soprano.

"Henry, they're *detectives*."

"How fascinating. I don't think we've ever met genuine detectives." Henry appeared, clad in a velvet smoking-jacket in a similar shade of violet to his wife's robe, midnight blue dress pants and gleaming black shoes. Casey had to exercise supreme control not to gawp at his attire, which was straight out of Oscar Wilde. "Do sit down, Detectives. May I offer you tea?"

Casey, astonished by the Finisterres' lack of panic, considered asking for coffee, and then decided against it. "Yes, thank you," she said. O'Leary followed her lead. She noted with some interest that neither Finisterre had blinked an eyelid at O'Leary's size or the mismatch of their pairing. Behind a bland expression, she assessed them, and concluded that the fluting, fluttery behaviour concealed considerable intelligence and assurance.

"Excellent. Earl Grey, Oolong, or Lapsang Souchong?"

The choice was way beyond Casey's knowledge of tea, which was confined to knowing that some uncivilised people, and the British, drank it instead of coffee. "Earl Grey, please."

"Me too, please," O'Leary added.

Claudia rang a small bell, and a neat young woman appeared. "Tea, Madeleine, if you please. Earl Grey for our guests." Madeleine disappeared again.

"Detectives, what brings you to our door? Has there been some trouble in our building?"

"We'd like to talk to you about Isabella Farquar," Casey said, and watched them closely.

"Isabella?" Claudia dabbed at her eyes. "Such a tragedy. Carl informed us that she had died suddenly and that Dacia Kraven would have to take over."

That explained why they weren't nervous, Casey thought bitterly, though Carl clearly hadn't provided any details.

"A huge loss to the acting community," Henry added. "But that doesn't need police enquiries, surely?"

Claudia blinked rapidly. "We believed that she would be outstandingly successful. This is a tragedy," she repeated. "Are you here *investigating?*" she asked suddenly. Her voice shook. "Why?" She clutched her husband's hand, their fingers white. They couldn't take their eyes from Casey.

"Isabella was murdered," Casey said bluntly.

Both Finisterres recoiled. "*Murdered?* Who would *murder* Isabella?"

"That's what I'm trying to find out," she said. "Before I ask you about Isabella, I'd like to know more about your role in the theatre world first, to put her talent and actions in their proper context." She projected calm interest. "I understand you fund between two and four experimental productions every year?"

Claudia calmed her breathing, her fingers still twisting in Henry's. "We do. Of course, we don't only fund theatre. We also support independent film-makers, musicians – we watch all the student recitals at Juilliard, the Steinhardt, and the Manhattan School of Music, and outside New York, too – and all forms of culture."

"I see," Casey said, thinking that she might have a chat with Tyler's girlfriend Allie, who was majoring in music at the Steinhardt, and see what she knew. "How do you fund your choices?"

Claudia and Henry exchanged an embarrassed look. "You see," Claudia began, and consciously straightened up, "we are both deeply interested in helping young people to achieve their artistic dreams, and we're happy to use our resources to do that." She caught Casey's look. "My parents were extremely well-off, as were Henry's. We inherited, and invested profitably."

"What did they do?" O'Leary asked, which was clearly the wrong question. Or the right one, from the way the Finisterres were squirming.

"We don't discuss money," Claudia said.

"I'm afraid you'll have to tell me," Casey said, "or I'll need to investigate the source of funds." She decided to soften the blow. "It's possible that someone was trying to find dirt on everyone involved in the Midsummer Night's Dream production."

"How dare someone try to besmirch our reputation!" Claudia declaimed. "We have nothing of that nature to hide. However, we do not want our funding sources known. We've spent *years* practising philanthropy and" –

"Darling," Henry said, much more quietly, "I'm sure these detectives are not here to betray our secrets to the tabloids. Isabella was murdered, and she deserves our help."

Claudia shut up.

"It wasn't an inheritance. Ten years after we were married, we won the lottery – the Powerball jackpot. Thirty-eight million dollars." O'Leary whistled. Casey gasped. "It was lifechanging."

"I bet."

"When we realised we'd won, before we collected, we set it up so that we'd be anonymous. We had a good attorney and investment advisor, and for a while we let the funds accumulate. Then" –

"Then we realised that the money was growing faster than we would ever be able to spend," Claudia said. A different type of pain swept over her face. "We didn't" – Casey heard *couldn't* – "have a family."

"We had met at a community theatre group, and although neither of us was good enough to progress, too many of the cast were talented but couldn't afford to take it further. When we came into money, we decided to use it to help."

"Then the money kept growing, and we branched out a little into musicians, and then theatre productions, so we could help even more." She dropped her eyes.

"Why'd you keep it secret?" O'Leary asked bluntly.

"Because other patrons of the arts can be a touch..."

"Snobbish," Henry stated. "And of course there are always people who are less, mm, ethical."

"To be taken seriously, we had to appear to come from a good background. We allowed everyone to think that we came from old money, and had inherited."

"I see," Casey said. "Would that still matter?"

"The tabloids will turn on anyone," Henry said bleakly, "especially anyone they think has succeeded under false pretences."

Casey studiedly didn't react, but the bitter words hit home. That could be her, in a week or so.

"You'd chosen Isabella," O'Leary said, taking over. His usual homespun accent was missing. "Why her?"

"She had talent. She could never have taken roles as a powerful woman – she would never have succeeded as Lady Macbeth, but she could have been a great Desdemona," Claudia explained. "She deserved a chance."

"Why Carl Heyer's production of the *Dream*?" O'Leary asked. Casey stayed quiet.

"It came up. We wanted Isabella to get her chance, and this was it."

"What about Dacia Kraven? She was Heyer's preference."

Silence fell. The Finisterres looked at each other, at the floor, at their shoes. The detectives waited them out.

"Yes, she would have been better in the role. But she wasn't our protégée, and Isabella was. I wanted Isabella to have the chance. I insisted." From Henry's expression, Casey knew that he hadn't totally agreed with Claudia. "Dacia would always have succeeded. She has an amazing talent and the drive. Hard-faced..." She stopped hurriedly, but Casey would have bet on the next word being *bitch*. The fluting act had dropped away.

"Darling..." Henry tried to cover the momentary flash of dislike for Dacia.

"It's all right." She turned to Casey. "Dacia would do anything, *anything*, to succeed. I've seen her upstaging, failing to pass on messages, all that sort of thing. She's viciously ambitious – of course one needs to be ambitious, but she is plain nasty. I would never have supported her. I don't believe in ill-gotten success, and that's the route she takes whenever her talent isn't enough. I had the chance to throw a wrench in her plans and I took it."

"I see," O'Leary said, without a single hint of condemnation. "Don't reward bad behaviour."

"Exactly."

"I wasn't as sure," Henry admitted. "She isn't a nice person, but she would have been a better fit for Carl's *Dream* than Isabella. Still, I wasn't so bothered that I would have argued with Claudia about it, and I don't want to reward bad behaviour either. We don't have to agree about everything to be happy, do we?" He caught her gaze, and smiled lovingly.

"You said Dacia would have done anything to succeed," O'Leary noted. "How far would she have gone?"

The Finisterres stared at him. "Are you implying that *Dacia* might have done this?" Henry said disbelievingly. "That's not possible."

"Not even Dacia would go that far. It's not a starring role in Hollywood's latest blockbuster, and even if this was a chance for the lead – only – female to be noticed by an agent, it really isn't likely. Carl...I don't want to be mean, but he's not first rank as a director. This is as far as he'll get, unless something astonishing happens. We agreed to fund, but the concept is..." Claudia cast around for the right word. "...unusual. Of course we told him that we found it interesting, but..." She trailed off.

"I watched the rehearsal," O'Leary said, "with Dacia. I've done some actin'. It looked to me as if, once Dacia opened up, there was something there. I have some video here on my phone."

Casey continued to let her partner lead. Though she was desperate to speed matters up, O'Leary was taking a better tack. The Finisterres crowded around him as he started it off.

"Oh, *my!*" Henry exclaimed.

"I had never thought it could work," Claudia added. "That's astonishing." She turned to her husband. "My love, I think that we might actually have something here. We must go and observe. If Carl can pull this together, I will quite forgive his pomposity and pretentiousness."

"Until the next time," Henry said. "He can be terribly irritating. I would have understood perfectly if somebody had attacked him, but Isabella was perfectly pleasant."

"Was she?" Casey asked, without inflection.

"Oh, yes. She never said anything to upset anyone."

"She was careful about that," Claudia noted.

"As if it didn't come naturally?" Casey asked.

"As if she couldn't be bothered."

"I'm sorry?"

"It was as if…you know how there are people who always turn the other cheek, no matter what you do or say, and it's because nothing you can do gets through their niceness?"

Casey and O'Leary rarely met the sort of people who turned the other cheek. Mostly, they met the sort of people who'd put a bullet through one cheek, never mind the other.

"I guess," O'Leary said.

"Isabella behaved like that, sometimes."

"Did you feel it was insincere?"

The Finisterres considered that. "No," Henry said doubtfully. "But it can be difficult to tell with actors. They wouldn't be successful if they couldn't counterfeit emotions realistically. I couldn't say." His lips turned down, sadness sliding through his eyes.

"Going back to Dacia," Casey said gently, "could she have been that desperate? You've seen some of the video, and how good she is."

Claudia gazed at her husband. "I would never have thought so," she said. "But *vaulting ambition, which o'er leaps itself?* Ambition can drive you to deeds you would never have contemplated. Macbeth killed a king…Dacia might have killed a rival."

"We don't know," Henry summarised.

"You funded this production – how did you decide on that?"

The Finisterres exchanged cynical glances. "We could persuade" – Casey and O'Leary heard *coerce* – "Carl to cast Isabella. Nobody else would have funded him and, as we said, we didn't think that his concept had real artistic merit – though we'll have to rethink that, based on your video."

"I see. Carl Heyer isn't a top-rated experimental director, you said…?"

"No."

Casey made a *tell-me-more* gesture, and O'Leary exuded interest.

"Carl has been around for some time," Henry explained. "He had been moderately successful – for experimental theatre" –

"Meaning?"

"Around one-third of the productions he directed covered their costs. None of them provided significant returns."

"Thank you."

"He was unpopular with the actors, too. Highly demanding, which is not unusual, but in such a way as to demean their talent. He has a nasty temper, and he doesn't try to restrain it. He believes, and behaves as if, he were Francis Ford Coppola, when he is simply a hack."

"Would actors refuse to work with him?"

The Finisterres gaped. "Oh, no. Nobody can afford to turn down roles when they're offered. All but the most famous actors have to take anything they can get."

Casey remembered saying that people wouldn't win new roles if they made trouble, and noted the confirmation.

"Carl did the casting?"

"Except for Isabella, yes. We were informed but not involved, though we are familiar with some of the actors."

"How did he choose his cast?"

"At least as much on looks as ability," Claudia snipped. "His *vision*" –the cynical inflection implied a whole drama in itself – "demanded that the majority of the characters were played by handsome, athletic young men."

"He demanded physical beauty," Henry added, "claiming that it was as Shakespeare would have had it. It was entirely coincidental that Carl enjoys attractive men." Another whole play arrived from his sarcasm.

"The exceptions were Theseus, Philostrate and Egeus, as older, but still handsome, men, and the rude mechanicals." O'Leary nodded knowledgeably. "And Dacia as Titania, of course."

"We insisted on Isabella. He was extremely unhappy, but if he wanted to put on the production, he couldn't refuse."

"He couldn't have funded it elsewhere, or himself?"

"Carl? My dears, he wouldn't invest two cents. He plays the starving artist, though I don't know why, since he makes it clear that he comes from a wealthy background."

"Did any of the rest of the cast have a problem with Isabella?" O'Leary put in.

"We can only comment on those we know best," Claudia replied. "Julius, Maxwell and Vincent – oh, and Cordell." Casey recognised the names as Theseus, Egeus, Bottom and (she discreetly consulted her list) Philostrate. "I wasn't aware of anyone except Carl and Dacia having a problem with Isabella."

"We have to ask this," Casey apologised. "Are you aware of anything" – she picked the least offensive word she could think of – "untoward around Carl or anyone associated with the production?"

Both Finisterres winced.

"We…well, *rumour is a pipe blown by surmises, jealousies, conjectures,* but…some rumours are more persistent than others."

Casey waited.

"There are whispers that Carl's temper isn't confined to words, but that he can get physical – throwing things, though not punches," Claudia admitted, "and everyone knows that Max – Maxwell – is a little too fond of the bottle. Julius is gay, but nobody these days worries about that, surely?"

O'Leary shook his enormous head. "Don't see it, myself," he said. "Weren't you suggestin' that Carl is too?"

"Carl…is indiscriminate. Men, women, whatever, and he is pushy. Vincent…" She stopped. "There were rumours that he used to be a boxer, but why would anyone care? It made his face perfect for character parts. I haven't heard of anything that would be noteworthy."

"Cordell?" Casey said, when Claudia had finished talking.

"Cordell," Henry said heavily. "Yes. *Rumour doth double*, but there have been a lot of rumours around Cordell."

"If they're not true, we'll discount them." *After a thorough investigation*, she thought.

"Oh, in that case..." Claudia's voice dropped. "Bad attitudes." Her mouth twisted. "Sexism, racism, anything that wasn't straight white male. Harassment. A lot of actors hesitated when they knew he was part of the cast."

"But you said they couldn't afford to turn down parts."

"No." Henry didn't say anything more.

Casey and O'Leary parked Cordell's potential bad behaviour for later. "Is there anything else about anyone else?"

"Not that we know of, but the rest of the cast are young."

"Thank you. One more thing, could you tell us where you were on Thursday night and Friday morning, please?"

"Are you asking us for an *alibi*?"

"Yes," Casey said bluntly.

"My goodness! I have never been asked for an alibi before."

"Have you ever been involved in a criminal investigation before?" Casey queried.

Claudia stopped her Lady Bracknell imitation and regarded Casey with some respect. "No. You have to ask, of course." Her brow wrinkled. "May I get my diary?"

"Sure." Casey turned to Henry. "Do you need to get yours?"

"No. I would have been with Claudia." He smiled, a touch embarrassed. "She's much better at organising than I am, so she keeps our diary. If I don't tell her about something, and it doesn't go in the diary, then we get into a real muddle, and she's disappointed with me. I try not to do that," he finished, with an elfin smile.

"He rarely forgets to tell me," Claudia said, and dropped a fond peck on Henry's silvering head. "Let me see: Thursday." She rustled through pages. "I have nothing for Thursday night, or Friday morning." Suddenly she looked older, and a little frightened. "Does that mean we have no alibi? We could be *suspected?*"

"There are lots of ways to rule people out," Casey said, which wasn't an answer, but reassured the Finisterres. "We often rule people out through street camera footage."

Claudia and Henry sighed in joint relief. "Of course we would have been here, but on our own. We frequently have guests for a small soirée to

83

discuss cultural matters, but not on those days. Our last one was – good gracious, Henry, we haven't held a supper for over a month."

"Really? How remiss of us. Of course, the last one was after we visited the *Hands* exhibition, and we had decided that we would wait until after opening night of the *Dream*." He turned to Casey, brow furrowed. "Will your investigations prevent the *Dream* opening as planned?"

"That depends on what we find," Casey said.

"Oh. Oh, dear. Perhaps we should have a back-up plan? What else might we wish to discuss?"

Casey didn't suggest that they should visit *Murder on Manhattan*, and on catching her expression, O'Leary didn't either.

"Thank you for your time," she said, and they left.

CHAPTER TEN

"Waal, that was interestin'," O'Leary said, yokel drawl back in place.

"Yeah. It's always interesting when you talk like a normal person, not a haystack."

O'Leary grinned. "Iffen I sounded like a haystack, they'd never have believed in us. Still an' all, sounds like there was a lot goin' on under the surface."

"It sure does. The Finisterres were interesting. Trying hard to be artistic types, but when it came down to it they dropped the fluttering and were pretty sharp. They got over their initial shock pretty fast."

"Yeah." O'Leary opened his SUV, and heaved himself in. Casey clambered up to the passenger seat. "Lucky they didn't want to talk about photos, huh?"

"Too right. If they'd known we were most of the hands in *Hands*, we'd never have gotten out. We'd have been exhibited at their next soirée."

"I'd enjoy that," O'Leary said happily. "I ain't never been a cultural icon before. I could've talked to all them cultural people."

"I'd rather not," Casey said flatly. "I'm not going near the gallery once the exhibition opens." She clicked her seatbelt in place. "Let's get back to the bullpen and figure the Finisterres' gossip into the background runs. None of this came up, except Maxwell's boozing."

"Naw. We thought it wouldn't." He started the engine.

***

"Come see this video, Andy said to Tyler, "along with Carval's shots. I want your opinion."

"'Kay." Tyler marched over, wearing a distinctly unimpressed expression. "Go."

Tyler had as much interest in theatre as he did in polishing his nails crimson and wearing lipstick. However, Tyler's ability to spot small visual cues and clues was unmatched, and Andy's eyes were already bleeding from watching it.

"People *pay* to see this shit?" Tyler carped. "Why not a sports video?"

"'Cause we didn't get a sports murder. Culture's good for you." Andy smiled angelically. "Anyway, I thought you'd be getting into culture."

Tyler raised eyebrows, with a side order of scowling. Andy's smile brightened. A minute or two passed. "Stop. Back. Stop." He peered at the screen. "Look."

"Someone – Philostrate, that's Cordell Andrews – doesn't like Bottom, or Egeus, do they? Who're Bottom and Egeus?" – Andy consulted the cast list – "Vincent Younger and Maxwell Stephens – Maxwell's our drunk."

"Yeah." Tyler paused. "'Bout that."

"Mm?"

"Casey okay with drunks?"

Andy stared. "I hadn't thought of that. I don't see why not – as long as they're not her dad. She never lets anything personal interfere with the job."

"'Kay – for now."

"You think there's an issue?"

"She's coddling him. Can't last. Show's soon."

Andy shrugged. "She'll do what she thinks is right. She always does."

"Should cut him loose," Tyler said, unusually judgemental.

"She won't thank you for saying so. Leave it. We'll be there if she needs us."

"When," Tyler said cynically.

"Whatever. Can we go back to the video?"

Tyler nodded.

Two hours of footage later, they had plenty to think about.

"It doesn't look like any of them liked any of them, does it?"

"Nearly. Coupla pals. Vincent and Maxwell."

"Some of those younger ones – the fairies" –

"Not PC."

"No, that's the role. They're part of the Fairy Court. Oberon and Titania – that's Dacia – are King and Queen of the fairies, and those four are servants."

"'Kay."

"They look pretty friendly, though they're avoiding Cordell. It's the older ones who have problems."

"Problems?" O'Leary rumbled over their desks. "We got news about problems too."

"Time to compare notes," Casey decreed.

Shortly, Casey's murder board became busy with photos and commentary.

"All the older ones hated each other and Heyer? Is that what we're saying? We know that Maxwell's a drunk" – Casey forced herself not to wince – "and the Finisterres said that Cordell's a really unpleasant type – a lot of rumours about harassment."

"Yes," Andy said. "But if Cordell was such a pain, and hated Maxwell and Vincent, then why kill Isabella?"

"Same for Carl," O'Leary rumbled. "Not a nice guy."

"Claudia Finisterre said that she thought Isabella was one of those nicey-nice types, but I don't see how that fits with blackmail."

"I don't see how it fits with her lifestyle," O'Leary added. "That li'l apartment didn't say *money* to me."

"No," Tyler agreed.

"Let's go back a step," Casey suggested. "Why did we think Isabella might be blackmailing?"

"The journal, with real and stage names," Andy said. "As soon as I get financials, next on my list is using them to see if she had unexplained income."

"Sounds good." She grinned. "Before that, Tyler, we have something specially for you." Tyler's face showed severe suspicion. "The Finisterres don't only fund theatre, they fund music. They attend recitals at all of the major music schools in Manhattan. I want to talk to Allie about whether she's noticed them." Andy snorted. Tyler stared.

"You still in touch with her?" O'Leary inquired mischievously. "'Cause if not, I think Andy needs a nice, cultured friend."

"Yeah," Tyler said, looking as if he'd been hit with a boulder. "Get her here tomorrow."

"Why not today?"

"It's already after five," the stern tones of Captain Kent interjected. "Is there anything you have which justifies overtime?"

The team regarded each other unhappily.

"No, sir," Casey eventually said.

"Then you will leave at the end of shift."

"Yes, sir."

"Where is Carval?"

"He's not here, sir. He said he'd be back around five."

"When he arrives, send him to my office." Kent scowled at his watch, which indicated ten past five. "At once."

"Yes, sir."

Kent stalked off, glaring indiscriminately around the bullpen, which had become extremely and obviously busy.

"Allie tomorrow, then," Casey grumped. "Couldn't Kent have taken today off?"

"He'll be off tomorrow. Guess he's puttin' together reports for 1PP. You know he's in some weekends."

Some fifteen minutes later, only just before shift end, Carval ambled in, grinning widely enough to light up the street.

"Cheerful, ain't'cha?" O'Leary said.

"Yep. It'll be *amazing*. We've only hung part of it and it'll knock everybody *dead*."

"I'm glad you're happy," Casey said, "because Kent wants to see you, stat."

"Why?" Carval said suspiciously.

"He didn't say. You better get in there."

His upbeat mood dented, Carval hurried across to Kent's office and knocked.

"Come in."

"You want to see me."

"Yes. I've spoken to my wife. She'll" – Kent's choleric expression twisted – "be delighted to visit your exhibition next Wednesday. I will also attend."

"Six?"

"Yes."

"Fine." Carval turned to leave.

"There's another thing."

"Yes?"

"Will Clement's team visit the exhibition before it opens?"

"Yes," Carval said cautiously, scenting danger.

"I want them to attend on Wednesday with me. I want to see their reactions before we even think about putting them in front of the media hyenas."

Carval's jaw dropped. "You what? But" –

"Clement's team will visit at the same time I do, and not before. I want to see how they react before we – the NYPD – decide about media appearances." Kent frowned. "Dismissed."

Carval's feet took Carval's fried brain out of Kent's office. That was…a horrible thought, on many levels. Firstly, to Carval's credit, he'd wanted to ensure that the team was – not *happy*, but content with the show. Less creditably, he'd wanted to show Casey how much his camera loved her. Completely discreditably, he'd wanted to be close to Casey, and he couldn't do that if he had to answer all Mrs Kent's questions. He couldn't be near Casey at all, because even if *he* managed it, *she'd* be as far away from either Kent as she could manage. She'd scuttle off like a panicked rabbit if either came within ten yards of her. He'd better warn Allan. He'd *intended* the team to see the full exhibition *after* he'd gotten rid of the Kents – sure, it would have been late, but they wouldn't have minded if it kept them away from their captain.

"What's wrong?" Casey asked.

"I need a drink," Carval said. "We – all of you – we need to talk."

"Go get them in," O'Leary said, "an' we'll be there in a few minutes. Iffen you feel like startin' on yours, go ahead. You've gone green, an' grass don't talk so good."

Carval went.

"You could have let him explain," Casey said irritably.

"Not here," O'Leary countered. "Look at all them waggling ears." A number of speculative glances were being directed at the team, along with some nastily hopeful looks.

"We'll tidy up and go," Casey said. Remarkably quickly, they cleared their desks and left.

***

Carval reached the Abbey and ordered for everyone, barely steering away from a shot of whiskey for himself. He could see the outline of the next few minutes, and it was ugly. It didn't stop him flicking up his camera and shooting the team as they walked in, one unit, with Casey in the lead. As ever, he contrasted it with the hostility of the first time he'd taken that shot, and as ever, was relieved that they had accepted him.

"What's this about?" Casey demanded, before she'd even sat down.

"You know Kent demanded that his wife get a private tour before we open?"

"Naw."

"What?"

"The *fuck*?"

Casey sighed. "Yeah, you said. What's that got to do with us?"

"He's insisting you've all to be there at the same time, and absolutely not before."

She downed her entire bottle of beer in one slug, white to the lips. "He can't – I can't."

"What's wrong?" Carval slipped an arm around the back of her chair.

"I didn't get a chance to tell you," she said miserably. "Dad wants to see the show with me."

"Fuck." Carval's beer also disappeared in one long draught.

"It would've been okay with the team. Kent... How do I do this?"

Silence surrounded the group. Everyone knew that Casey's dad was a problem. Everyone but Casey knew that she couldn't hold him together for ever, unless he wanted to change. So far, he hadn't been dry for long. Andy whisked up to the bar and whisked back with another round of much-needed drinks.

"With us," Tyler said, unusually loquacious. "Let us help. Keep your dad away from Kent. All of us."

"You can?"

"Sure we can," O'Leary rumbled. "Your pa's a li'l thing, like you. He won't be no trouble to us. Carval here'll look after Kent an' Missus Kent, an' we'll take care of your pa."

"Yeah," Andy chimed in. "We got this. No problem."

Casey looked sceptically at him, ruined by her soggy sniff. "He is a problem. But...uh... Thanks." She stared at the table top and her beer. Under the table, Carval put a comforting hand on her knee. "I wish he wasn't coming," she whispered. "But I can't stop it. He'd never understand." He'd feel rejected, and fall straight back into the bottle from which she was fighting to keep him. He couldn't fight for himself, if he didn't have her support.

She didn't think *if he didn't have her to cling to.*

"He's dry," she went on, talking only to herself. "I have to keep him dry."

Four pairs of eyes met above her bowed head, sharing disagreement that they wouldn't voice.

"We c'n manage for an evenin'," O'Leary repeated. "It don't make no nevermind to us. Anyways, mebbe we'll get some cute tales of baby Casey."

"There are no tales," she snipped, and closed her lips on *if he even remembered them through the booze.* She couldn't think like that.

"Waal, that's as mebbe. Won't stop us tryin'."

"If you do, I'll call Pete."

"He won't tell you anythin', 'cause there's nothin' to tell." O'Leary's moon face grinned at her. "That Allie-girl of Tyler's, that might be different. I bet there's some good tales there."

"No," Tyler stated.

"Aw, c'mon."

"No."

"Waal, that leaves Andy. Who's goin' to tell us tales about Andy?"

"Nobody."

"None of you are any fun at all," O'Leary complained.

"Nope," they chorused. The big man humphed.

Casey drained her beer. "Time for me to go home," she said, and attempted a smile.

Carval flashed her a glance, and received only a small shake of her head. She was gone before they'd finished saying goodnight.

"She didn't wait to find out why Kent said it."

"Why did he?"

"Because he wants to see how you all react before he decides how to handle the media."

"Shit," Tyler summed up.

"If we make a fuss, d'you think we'll get let off the media hype?"

"I don't know," Carval said heavily. "If I'd known her dad was coming..."

"You'd have done what?" Andy said. "You wouldn't have told Kent that, would you?"

"No. I don't talk about you guys to anyone, and especially not to Kent. Not even to Allan."

"That's true," Andy said to the other two. "Allan didn't know anything about us, remember?"

"Yeah," O'Leary agreed. Tyler nodded.

"When – oh. It must have been last night." Carval deduced. "She said she hadn't had a chance to tell me, and yesterday we told her to tell him before he found out from the press."

"She told me at lunchtime," O'Leary said smugly, "but only 'cause she looked like hell this mornin' an' I pushed."

"That doesn't solve the problem," Andy said.

"No problem. We deal with Casey's dad. Carval takes Kent." Tyler sounded as if it was that simple, and maybe, to him, it was.

"I guess," O'Leary said doubtfully. "Anyways, I'm out. Seeya tomorrow."

"Me too," Carval said, and the party broke up.

"Need a ride?" O'Leary asked Carval.

"No, but you want to talk."

"The boy ain't dumb," the mountain said to the air. "Yeah. Were you plannin' on goin' by Casey's apartment?"

"I was."

"C'n I tag along?"

"Why?"

"Because the three of us need to talk. Tyler has the right of it, but 't ain't as simple as he wants it to be."

"Nothing ever is," Carval gloomed as they pulled out.

"Nup. 'Specially not with Casey an' her pa." O'Leary's brow creased into crevasses. "What's she told you 'bout him?"

"He drinks. He's done a couple of rounds of residential rehab. He's been picked up drunk plenty, and had two arrests – so far."

"Yeah. She told you *why* he drinks?"

"No. Well, half a sentence about her mom having a tumour."

"'Kay. Didn't think so. It's time you knew the whole story."

"Only if she wants to tell me. I'm not pushing for something she doesn't want to give." He smiled wryly. "It might be fatal, and I like living with all my limbs attached."

"Waal, they say it helps."

Carval grinned as they pulled up outside Casey's apartment block. "I can always hide behind you."

O'Leary grinned right back. "Naw. I'll hide behind you."

Carval sardonically gestured him to take the lead at Casey's door. "No way."

"Oh." Casey opened it, only her head visible. "What are you doing here?"

"Visitin' you," O'Leary said. "I hear you got good coffee."

Casey scowled. "I was hoping for a nice, quiet, *solitary* evening."

"Aw, that's not nice. I even brought your boyfriend."

"Carval?"

Carval squeezed past O'Leary. "I was going to drop by anyway, and O'Leary said he'd tag along."

"I guess you can come in," she said ungraciously.

"An' have coffee?" O'Leary hoped.

"Okay," she grudged. "But I don't have any cookies. If I did, I wouldn't share them with you."

"Mean. You're always mean to me." He stepped inside.

Carval followed him, and abruptly realised that Casey was wrapped in a soft, dark green, oversized robe which looked as if it would go around her another few times without a problem. He hadn't seen it before.

"I didn't expect visitors," she said defensively, and pulled the cord around her waist tighter.

"Naw, I didn't think so. 'S why I'm here. Dunno why Carval's here, gettin' glared at, but I guess even spitfires like you c'n find love."

Casey's glare tried to burn a hole through O'Leary's head, but sadly failed. The heat of her blush might have worked better. Carval, prudently, stayed silent.

"C'mon. I could use a coffee." O'Leary regarded her plaintively. "Otherwise I'll fall asleep on your couch."

"I thought we agreed you're too big to fall asleep anywhere in my apartment? If you're that tired, go home." But she began to make coffee with the Gaggia in the little kitchen. "Why are you here?"

"Waal," O'Leary began, and then hesitated, sitting down on the couch. Carval took a chair.

"Oh." Casey said flatly. "You wanna talk about Dad."

"Stop investigatin' an' deducin' at me. 'S not fair."

"I'll stop as soon as you stop playing at being Dear Abby."

"C'n I get that coffee before you start gettin' mad at me?"

Casey put the coffee down with a decided clunk. "There. Say what you want to and then maybe I can have some peace?"

"Okay," O'Leary said heavily, and cupped his large mug. "Waal, we all know your pa's clingin' on to the wagon, an' you're makin' sure he does. But how's he goin' to react to all those pictures of you? 'Cause some of 'em ain't exactly how he thinks his li'l girl is."

Casey, who'd opened her mouth in protest at O'Leary's first comment, shut it abruptly.

"You don't like rememberin', but didn't he say you should'a been a lawyer, after he got himself arrested at JFK?" She nodded, face twisting at the memory. "An' Carval took photos of you all purple an' yellow." Carval nodded. "An' there's a whole bunch of shots of you interviewin', an' since you're scary for all you're small, that's goin' to come through. I don't need to see them to know that." He shrugged his huge shoulders, nearly knocking into Casey. "What's he goin' to do when he's made to see who you really are, when you're not pretendin' so's he stays on the wagon? You can't keep pretendin' once he sees this show."

During O'Leary's commentary, Casey had paled to almost transparent. Her lips were moving, but fortunately no sound emerged, since it didn't look like language suitable for church.

Finally, she made her vocal cords work. "First you tell me to tell him about the show, so he doesn't find out from the media. That made him want to come see it. Then Kent gets in the mix and I have to parade my dad in front of him, and even if you'll keep him out of Kent's way, that doesn't mean Kent will stay out of Dad's way. Kent knows about Dad's…issues, and likely he'll take the chance to find out if Dad'll stand up to the PR circus and the vultures that run it. That'll be fun." Her eyes blazed. "And *now* you tell me seeing the exhibition'll show Dad once and for all that I'm not who he thinks I am and I'm not who he wants me to be."

"Your pa doesn't need to be in Kent's way," O'Leary said. "He c'n come later. Kent isn't cultural, so likely he'll want to go pretty soon after he's walked around."

"Maximum of an hour, if you're not interested," Carval added. "His wife is, so give it two hours and tell your dad to show up around eight."

She took a breath. "That might fix Kent, but it's not about Kent. He's a sideshow. What it *still* all adds up to is that as soon as Dad sees the exhibition and realises I'm never, *ever* going to be the good little lawyer he wanted, he'll go straight back to the bottle. The same bottle I've been trying to keep him out of because I thought that this time he might have listened at rehab and tried to stay dry." Her eyes glistened, lips bloodless, voice icy. "But he won't. That's what you're saying. He'll find out the truth and he'll dive straight back into the bottle that'll kill him. Maybe it won't, next time.

Maybe the time after, or after that. But it'll kill him soon. If he's arrested again, the press'll get hold of it."

She turned to O'Leary. "You heard them – the Finisterres. Telling us that the press loved to tear down anyone they thought had hidden the truth. I haven't *hidden* anything, but they'll tear Dad apart and then they'll start on me."

O'Leary opened his maw, but Casey barrelled over whatever he might have said. "*We* won't tell, and Kent sure won't, but Birkett? He'll be leaking to the press as fast as he can turn the faucet on. Marcol won't even need to tell him to do it. Estrolla'd love to have something real to hit me with. He's still sore, and even if he's not dumb enough to try meeting me in a dark alley, I can't go out of the precinct alone."

She gulped convulsively. "How do we fix this one?" she asked, misery under her harsh tones. "How?"

CHAPTER ELEVEN

"We can't," O'Leary said. "We never could fix your pa. Only your pa can fix himself, an' mebbe he will, this time." His glance at Carval said that he didn't believe it. Carval's return look said *me neither*.

"I can't let him die," Casey said.

"You keep sayin' that, but short of lockin' him in his apartment, how're you goin' to stop him? You can't be with him twenty-four/seven."

Casey walked to the window, staring out into the twilight and the approaching night. "Maybe not. But I can be there as much as he needs me."

Carval joined her. "You can. But how much good will it do? He's got to want to do it, and sometime you'll have to watch him try, or not try."

"He *is* trying."

"How do you know? You're there nearly every minute you're not at work, so he can't sneak anything past you. He won't get blackout drunk in front of you, will he?"

Casey stared at the gloom outside. "No," she dragged.

O'Leary watched, staying silent.

"You'll only know if he's staying dry if you give him a chance" –

"Have you already forgotten what I said yesterday? He needs to stay dry until *your* damn exhibition has opened so that *we* can't be ripped apart because of him!"

"Don't make this a *them* and *us* situation," Carval flung back. "And don't blame me for *your* choices."

"My *choices*? What choices? Keep him dry or let him die? That's not a choice. That's" –

"Not up to you," O'Leary said over her. "That's your pa's choice. Stay dry, or not, an' take the consequences."

"You too?"

"I said it first," he pointed out. "Carval hasn't said anything that I haven't said to you way before he ever showed up, talkin' about exhibitions an' takin' shots. He didn't cause it an' he sure can't control it – an' neither c'n you." He smiled ruefully. "Didn't cause, can't cure, can't control. That's what they say, don't they?" He waited, but received no answer. "Anyways, this was never Carval's fault. Your pa's been slidin' ever since your mom passed."

"Yeah."

"Mebbe tell him about it, so's he knows where your pa is at – an' doesn't say anythin' dumb next week."

Carval snapped his mouth shut before *I wouldn't* escaped. "Only if you want to," he said instead. "It's fine if you don't. I don't have any right to know and I won't push you to tell me things you want to keep private." Behind Casey's back, O'Leary nodded approvingly.

Casey looked miserably between them. "The others know," she sighed. "You might as well." She stopped there, returning to the couch and taking a sip of her espresso, eyes on the floor, hunched unhappily into the oversized robe. Hiding, both men thought, from her memories.

Eventually, she raised her gaze to meet Carval's blue eyes, though he didn't think she saw him. "Eight years ago, Mom died – a traffic accident. She was on her own. It was dark, and sleeting. Early December weather. She skidded, they said, and ran straight into a concrete abutment. Died instantly." She swallowed, and continued in the same dead tone. "They did an autopsy. We didn't know about the brain cancer until then. Glioblastoma, they called it." The lack of hitch in the pronunciation indicated that Casey had heard, or used, the word frequently. "An aggressive form, which they couldn't have cured. She'd have gotten worse and worse and in pain... It explained so much. She'd been forgetful, sometimes shaky. We all said that it was just her, and we *laughed* about it together." Tears pooled, but didn't fall. "I wonder if she knew. If it wasn't an accident, but..." The two men heard the word, heavy and loud in the silent apartment.

Casey sipped her coffee. "Dad was – we both were – devastated. We could barely organise the funeral, but we supported each other and got through it." She swallowed again. "That's what I thought. I was in uniform then, with O'Leary." As if he weren't in the room. "He got me through. There..." She turned to him. "You were there all the way. Came to the morgue to pick me up after we had to ID her. Took me home, and Dad." Another swallow, then another sip. "You were at the funeral. I don't remember how I got home but you must have taken me."

O'Leary gave a wordless rumble, and briefly hugged her. "Pals," he emitted, which Carval thought barely *started* to cover what they were. Casey's actions to cover for O'Leary and Pete made perfect sense.

96

She looked back towards, but through, Carval. "After Christmas, everything seemed to be okay – as okay as it ever could be. We grieved together, but we went to work – Dad was an architect, and I was still in uniform, working shifts. O'Leary and I were a permanent partnership by then. Easier for the captain. If I had a wobble because of Mom, he was there, covering. I thought it was getting better, slowly, like grief does: some days bad, some a little better. I missed her so much." Liquid puddled, and a drop escaped. She wiped it away. "So did Dad."

She stopped, stood, trudged to the window and stared out at the darkening evening again. "I didn't notice for a while. Maybe if I hadn't been burying myself in overtime so I didn't have time to think about Mom, I'd have seen it sooner. Maybe not. Mom and Dad used to have a nightcap together, not every night, but often. Whatever. I didn't notice that he was having one every night, then I didn't notice that it was larger, and then I didn't notice that it was two. Or three. He was still going out to work, and coming home."

Carval's face asked the question.

"I was renting a cheap apartment. I didn't live with them after Stanford. When the estate was settled, Mom had left me a good chunk, and I used it as a deposit to buy this apartment. I invited Dad around to see it, before I started changing it – I thought he'd have some good ideas." She didn't turn from the window, so that they couldn't see her face, but both men knew that she was on the verge of tears. "If he'd been sober," she said in frozen tones, "he might've. But he wasn't." Her breath came jaggedly. "The next day, he apologised, and apologised, and promised not to do it again. For a while, it seemed like it was working. Months. I thought he'd gotten a handle on it."

Her shoulders slumped. "Then it happened again. Same thing. Same result. Months dry. And again. And again. He lost his job. He downsized. Then they started getting closer together, then he started getting picked up and flung in the tank, and now he's getting arrested and charged. All because Mom died and he can't bear to be without her."

Carval could see her haunted, agonised expression reflected in the window. He couldn't stand it any longer: went to stand behind her and loosely wrap her in. Suddenly she turned into him, burying her face in his sweater. He tucked her close, and didn't say a word, stroking gently over her back. O'Leary stayed so silent that he might not have been there at all.

"They wanted me to be a lawyer," she choked into the wool. "I've disappointed them both. Dad *said so*. He *said* I should've been a lawyer. Maybe if I had been then he wouldn't..."

"Disease doesn't care about profession," Carval said softly, looking around the room. His eye fell on the single photo on the occasional table by the window: Casey's Academy graduation, with both parents smiling widely, clearly and sincerely delighted with their daughter. "From that photo, I don't think they were disappointed at all."

"Then," she muttered bitterly. "Dad *said* I should've been a lawyer," she repeated harshly.

"Your dad's a drunk, and anything he says when he's drunk is nonsense," Carval bit out, and stopped Casey pulling away.

"He's dry!"

"Because you're there every fucking *minute* you're not at work, making sure he is, and you'll keep doing that till the show opens." He set her a few inches away, and kept his hands on her shoulders. "But what then? How long can you keep doing this? You have to sleep sometime. You have to take a break. Otherwise you'll get sick, and then what? You can't look after him if you're sick, and he sure as hell won't be able to look after you." He stopped, abruptly aware that he was almost shouting. "You have to think this through, Casey. Don't keep going till you break," he said more softly. "You can't keep him warm by setting yourself on fire."

He looked down at her white face and pinched lips, and pulled her right back in against him. "Just think, okay?"

Over Casey's dark head, Carval's gaze met O'Leary's. The big man shrugged. *Up to you*, it said. Carval cossetted, and stayed quiet. O'Leary frowned briefly, then took the coffee mugs to the kitchen, waved his fingers at Carval, and departed without any noise. Helpfully, that left the couch empty for Carval to sit himself and his coddled Casey down. As he did, he noticed the damp patch on his sweater. He petted, and didn't say anything.

After some considerable time, Casey detached herself from Carval's enclosing embrace, and scrubbed at her eyes, yawning widely. "What will I do?" she asked miserably. "There aren't any good options any more. I have to hope that he stays dry when I'm not looking. I've tried so hard and I'm so tired..."

"Curl in, and go to sleep," Carval soothed. "Don't worry about it tonight."

"I'm going to bed," she said pettishly. "It's comfy."

"Yep." Carval didn't point out that if she was, *he* was, so that he could keep her safely with him and help her sleep.

Casey stood up, wobbled, and stumbled off, eyes half closed already, to fall into bed, barely remembering to shed her robe, which puddled on the floor. She curled into a small, tight ball, buried under the comforter. Carval took the three strides to the bed, pecked a kiss on the top of her head, the only available area, and murmured, "I'll be there shortly." He didn't think she heard, but he had no intention of leaving her alone tonight.

He slipped out of the bedroom, doused its light, pulled the door mostly shut, and went to make himself another coffee and see if there was anything to eat. He found enough bread and ham to scrabble together a sandwich, and munched it while thinking about Casey's story. Her spare, cold words had covered years of disappointment and heartache – nearly eight years, he thought suddenly. That was a lot of pain to bear.

He agreed with O'Leary that Casey's father would have a horrible shock when he saw the truth about his daughter and, to a lesser extent, her team. Casey had said it: *you've sucked out our souls and you'll pin them to the gallery walls.* Most parents would be proud if their child were the focus of a major exhibition. Carval wasn't at all sure that Casey's father would be.

He wasn't sure that Casey would be, either, and he wouldn't be done before Wednesday. There would be no chance to show it to her beforehand – even if Kent hadn't forbidden it. That wouldn't have mattered to Carval: he had no loyalty to Kent and he would happily have ignored him – however, Casey knew about the order and she wouldn't disobey. There were no good answers here. There might not be any good outcomes, either.

He washed up his plate and the mugs, and, in an unusual moment of understanding, looked around to see if he should do a little tidying up. He'd never have bothered in his own apartment: his cleaning service took care of that, but Casey, as far as he knew, did her own cleaning. It looked like she'd done it: everything was as clean and tidy as usual, now that he'd washed up. He found a towel, dried the dishes, and put them away, perfectly familiar with their proper place. That done, he took the trash out. It was such a small thing, but he knew it would be more appreciated than buying her flowers.

Back in the apartment, he looked around, decided that it was tidy enough that he couldn't make a difference, checked his watch, found that it was barely eight-thirty, and called Allan.

"Yes, Jamie? Do you know what time it is? I finished work nearly three hours ago."

"Yes, but you need to know this."

"Oh, God. What now?"

"Don't be like that. It's not exactly a problem."

"That's not reassuring."

"I was being good!" Carval said indignantly, remembered that Casey was sleeping, and dropped his voice. "I went to fix up when Kent and his wife would have that tour you forced on me."

"And?" Allan said suspiciously.

"That was fine. He said six on Wednesday."

"What's the problem?"

"Two problems."

Allan emitted an unhappy squeak-wail.

"One: Kent insists that the team be there at the same time, so he can see how they react and decide about their exposure to the PR machine based on that."

"Okay," Allan said, "that's not dumb. That's not a problem, is it?"

"Um…"

"Jamie," Allan said firmly.

"Casey told her dad about the exhibition – she hadn't said anything, so we told her she had to so he wasn't surprised by the PR and, er" – he hadn't said this to Casey – "doesn't turn up drunk to the public show."

"Still not dumb."

"He wants to see it. With Casey."

"Oh. Why is this a problem?"

"Because he's been telling Casey she should've been a lawyer, when he's drunk. When he sees this show, he'll find out that his daughter isn't anything like he thinks she should be."

"Ye-es?" Allan elongated the word.

"We can't let him into the public show, because it would be a disaster, and anyway Casey won't go within a mile of the public show. He has to come when the team does, though he'll come later, and Kent might still be there, and though the team'll take care of him, it'll be horrible. What do we do?"

There was a silence on Allan's end of the phone. Then, "Let me think about it. It's a big exhibition, and there are several different rooms. I'll see what we can do to keep them apart, but if one of them makes a point of meeting the other, I don't know what we'll do. I guess O'Leary can carry her dad out, if we have to, but that's pretty sub-optimal."

"You don't say," Carval said acidly. "It'll be bad enough for Casey seeing the shots. Add her dad in, and this has all the makings of a complete disaster."

"I don't want your Casey to be hurt either, Jamie," Allan chided. "I like her, and she's good for you. I'll do everything I can to find a way to make this go with as few hitches as we can manage."

"Thanks," Carval said, heartfelt.

"Goodnight. I'll see you first thing tomorrow at the gallery and we'll carry on. We have plenty still to do."

"I know. But it'll be *great*. Best ever. They'll *die* to see it."

"Let's see. Don't get ahead of yourself."

"It'll be *amazing*," Carval repeated. "You know it will."

"Night. See you tomorrow." Allan rang off.

Carval, more relieved than he'd have admitted that Allan was supportive, poked his head into the bedroom, found that Casey hadn't moved an inch, and went back out, wondering what to do until he was tired enough to sleep. He'd never been here without Casey being with him or one of them needing to get out and start the day, and the chance to look around would give him a window into parts of her life about which he hadn't previously known or inquired.

First off, he looked at her little stone bird, at which he'd never looked carefully before. It was the only piece of bric-a-brac that she had, he realised. He picked it up, examining the delicate carving of the orange beak, the grooves on the amethyst of its folded wings and tail. That done, he put it back and moved on.

No ornaments, only the bird; no photos – no surprise – except of her Academy graduation. He lifted it, noting the likenesses to both her parents: her mother's dark curls and shapely figure, her father's facial shape and deep brown eyes. Technically, it wasn't a great shot: exactly what he'd expect from a commercial photographer surviving on easy, frequent shoots with a guaranteed market of doting relatives and proud parents. However, even this unskilled (from Carval's elevated perspective) hack snapper had caught Casey's brilliantly photogenic face: the happiness and pride of her parents and the love enclosing the three of them. He wished, for a moment, that he could have been there; that he could have taken the shots and shown, as only he could, their family bonds.

All broken by her mother's death and her father's fall. Before that, he knew, she'd been driven by her own ambition and pride – and then to prove to that sonofabitch Marcol that she was the absolute best. After her mother's death, she'd channelled everything into her work. She'd said it: *If I hadn't been burying myself in overtime so that I didn't have time to think about Mom.* Everything directed to success, but no happiness. That first shot he'd taken…was of fierce, focused drive in every cell. Since then, he'd captured different aspects of her ability, but nowhere at work had she ever exhibited the slightest softness. Even with him, he'd never seen on her face the full-hearted joy of the graduation photo. He put it down again, and turned away to her bookshelves.

Carval rarely read fiction, preferring photographic technical literature, but he was interested in what Casey read. A wide variety, he found: everything from classics to paranormal romance. The latter amused him: he wouldn't have thought that his fierce Casey would be frivolous. He selected a thriller, and began to read.

A couple of hours and another coffee later, he was tired enough to sleep without disturbing Casey with restlessness and fidgeting. He put himself to bed, and slid a comforting hand on to her waist. She curled towards him as he drifted into dreams.

CHAPTER TWELVE

Casey woke to her alarm and the large, gently whiffling presence of Carval, whom she hadn't noticed joining her. She'd have liked to pull the covers back over her head and stay buried until around September, when the exhibition might have left New York, but she couldn't be that lucky. There was a murder to solve, and she'd better get on with it. She lurched out of bed and into probably-protozoan life, which would only develop intelligence after her first two espressos.

An hour later, she'd acquired intelligence, and sat at her desk in the bullpen with yet another coffee, remembering that Tyler would be bringing Allie in that morning so that they could find out what she knew about the Finisterres. She grinned mischievously for an instant. Teasing Tyler would be fun, and Allie's effect on the bullpen was always amusing, even if the floor would need to be mopped to remove the drool.

She turned to her murder board. The key thing, she decided, was Isabella's financials. If she hadn't been blackmailing, what on earth was that book all about, and what did the papers mean? They'd been a mess of press clippings and cryptic notes, but they hadn't borne any obvious relation to the account book.

She sighed. Maybe Andy would spot something. He was already in, chasing the bank clerk and, from his happy smile, getting somewhere. Meanwhile, she would think about interviewing the cast. The team would take the older members, but the officers could take the ones where there hadn't been any evidence of dislike. She'd give them a list of questions, and pair them. She scowled at the thought. She'd have preferred to keep Fremont and the now-useful, even good, Larson together, but Adamo was far too new to be left unsupervised. He would need to be paired with an experienced officer, and she didn't trust Henegan as far as she could see him. Her scowl strengthened. Still, Larson had made some impression on

Henegan, which meant Fremont with Adamo, and Larson with Henegan, she supposed. Ugh.

"What's with the scowl?" O'Leary asked, passing by with his bucket of coffee, and carefully also passing by any discussion of the previous evening, unless Casey opened the conversation. He didn't think that was likely.

"Interviewing the actors. I thought we could leave the easier ones to the officers, and we'll take the ones where it looked like they all hated each other. We can pair up Fremont and Adamo, and Larson and Henegan. Adamo's still a rookie."

"An' you ain't sure of Henegan. An' it'll be you an' me, an' Andy an' Tyler, as usual?"

"Yep. One theatre type," she said, "and one regular person to keep it real."

He frowned briefly. "You didn't think of puttin' one officer with one of us?"

"No. Do you think we should?"

"Mebbe. We c'n teach 'em faster that way. Think about it." He grinned. "Think how scared they'll be when they see you terrorisin'."

Casey raised her eyebrows. "I thought we wanted to keep three of them? I'll think about it, and we can discuss it later. First, though, we've got Allie coming in for a chat to tell us about the Finisterres."

O'Leary chortled happily. "Funny how Tyler didn't deny bein' able to ask her in on short notice."

Casey managed a faint smile. "Isn't it? I guess they're together."

O'Leary shook his head wonderingly. "I guess them dancin' cheek to cheek should've told a good detective that, but Allie got no taste at all. Here's me, all handsome" – Casey choked and had to be patted on the back – "an' cultured, an' there's Andy, who's got culture comin' out of his ears, an' even if he's an inch shorter than her, he's quite pretty when he tries – an' who does she like? Tyler. I mean, what's he got that we don't?"

"Bravery," Casey pointed out. "He's a hero. You wouldn't be interested in Allie anyway."

"Waal, you might be right there." He grinned massively. "Here's Tyler."

"When's Allie getting here?" Casey asked blandly.

Tyler consulted his watch. "Thirty," he said.

"You didn't bring her with you?"

Tyler gave back a completely bored face. "Thirty."

"I'll talk to her," Casey said. "Otherwise, when Andy gets here, let's work out what we do first today." Her email pinged as Andy arrived. "Autopsy!" she cheered. "What've we got here?"

She scrolled down, skimming the summary. "That's weird."

"What?" everyone asked.

"We knew she'd been bashed on the head and strangled, but this says that tox shows that she'd been drugged. Roofied. Stomach contents showed a little alcohol and some chicken. McDonald theorises that the drug was administered at the time of the meal or drink."

"Not roofies again," Andy said.

"Don't tell Allie," Tyler ordered.

"I wasn't going to."

Allie-the-sometime-model had helped with a sting operation where some nasty pieces of work had been drugging, raping and murdering models; filming it all and selling the films on the dark web. She'd been roofied in the process, though the team – particularly Tyler – had kept her safe. Though Tyler was resolutely silent on the subject, after the cheek-to-cheek dancing at O'Leary's birthday party, it was pretty clear that they were dating.

"Why dope her?"

"To kill her quietly," Andy proposed.

"Yeah."

"Why bother bashing her on the head if she was doped?" Casey's brow creased for an instant. "That changes things. We need to know whether there was a rehearsal on Thursday afternoon, and start from there. If there was, then when did she leave, where did she go, who with?" She stared into the distance. "Andy – no, O'Leary, you talk to Ron, find out about rehearsal. Andy, once we know, you get started on street cams around the area" –

"There aren't any."

"What?" Casey stared.

"When I was checking yesterday, that area's almost completely empty."

"Waal, shit." O'Leary summed it up perfectly.

"Hell. That means we have to hope for witnesses."

"Gas station and sandwich bar," Tyler said.

"Maybe they have cameras?"

"Might."

"I guess we'll have to go with that. Maybe the gas station attendant'll have seen something?"

"Mebbe I'll have a longer chat with Ron," O'Leary said. "He knew about most thin's."

"Good idea. Could Maisie know who she'd have a drink or a meal with? If they were that close you'd think she would. Or anything on her phone? Andy, did you get the phone yet? New boyfriend? Why wouldn't Maisie tell us?"

"Yes, I picked it up from CSU on the way in, but I've got that account book too," Andy pointed out, "and I've started there and on the financials. Can one of you take the phone? Tyler?"

"Sure. Goes with the records." Tyler took the unlocked phone from Andy, and marched off to his desk to start investigating the calls and messages. Casey considered her new complication, and scowled ferociously at her desk. Doped? That was nasty.

A disturbance penetrated her thinking. She looked up, to find the door from the stairway opening and –

Oh. Yes. She might need to stand on her chair to avoid drowning, as the bullpen's collective tongues drooled across the linoleum. Allie, five-foot-ten of stunning Latina gorgeousness, had arrived. Tyler stood up.

"Hello," Officer Estrolla oozed, approaching Allie. "Can I help you?"

"No, thanks," Allie said. "I'm seeing Detective Clement."

Estrolla stood in front of her. "She's really busy today. I can take your statement." He smirked. "I'm much better company."

"No, thank you," Allie repeated.

"Out of the way, Estrolla," Tyler ordered. Estrolla scowled. "Move!" Estrolla did.

"Sorry," Tyler said.

"Hi!" Allie bounced, all her enthusiasm restored as soon as Estrolla was removed. "Is Casey here?"

"I am," Casey said, smiling. Allie's little-girl voice and profuse use of exclamation points weren't her favourite style, but Allie herself had won a lifetime's credit for her behaviour and bravery on the murdered models case, which, with her undoubted intelligence, gave her a pass on the voice.

"Hi! I didn't expect to be back here! Is it another operation? The last one paid so much of my tuition I'd love to do it again!"

"Not this time." Allie's face fell, with which Casey could sympathise. Tuition costs at the Steinhardt were no joke. "But we do need your help again."

"Sure! What is it?" She noticed O'Leary, and gave him a smile that knocked half the bullpen unconscious. "Hi!"

"Hey," O'Leary rumbled. "Lookin' good there. Why'd you waste it on Tyler?"

Allie smiled more widely, and the rest of the bullpen hit the floor, prostrating themselves in admiration. "I like him!" she said. O'Leary grinned.

"Someone has to," Casey said. "Allie, we have a case with a dead actress, and there's a couple involved called the Finisterres."

"You've met them? They're amazing! I mean, they have zillions! They come to all the recitals and take notes and they pick the ones they like best!" She blushed crimson.

"Have they approached you?" Casey asked.

105

"Uh, yes," Allie stammered. "But I didn't say to anyone, not even Tyler, because until they actually get you something it's pretty presumptuous and it could all go wrong!"

"Congratulations," Casey said, echoed by the other three. Not accidentally, they were screening Allie from Estrolla, who was leering from his desk.

"Amazing," Andy complimented.

Tyler smiled like he'd won the lottery, and patted her shoulder proudly, which said more to the other three than all the words in *War and Peace*. "Should've told me," he said. "Wouldn't tell."

"I don't wanna jinx it! I haven't even told my mom!"

"You've met them?" Casey said. "What did you think of them?"

Allie considered. Despite the cloud of exclamation points spattering her sentences, she was pretty sharp when it mattered. "They behave, like, all fluttery and fluffy," she said. "Lots of pitch and tone changes so they sound totally artificial and dumb, and totally stagey, but they're much tougher than they show." The exclamation points dropped away.

"Why?"

"Just...when they're watching they're a lot more focused than it looks when they're chatting. Their eyes don't match their voices and gestures – they're really assessing us. I guess it's not surprising, if they're thinking about financial support?"

Casey grinned. "That's pretty much what I thought."

"About what?" Carval interjected, then, "Hey, Allie. What're you doing here?" Inquisitive blue eyes noted Tyler's hand on the back of her chair.

"She's helping us," Casey said, and looked at Allie.

"Tyler said you wanted to know about the Finisterres! They come to all the recitals, so Casey wanted to know what I thought!" She blushed again. "They've picked me out! Isn't it great?"

"That's amazing. Well done," he said. He pouted slightly. "I was shooting around the theatre and I wanted to ask them about shooting in their other productions and Allan told me absolutely not. He told me they're a pair of sharks and refused to let me speak to them without him. He never trusts me with anything."

The four detectives laughed at him. "He got good reasons," O'Leary teased.

"Should I be worried?" Allie said.

"Oh, no. Likely you're fine, because they're into supporting new starters, but they drive a hard bargain with anyone established." He grinned. "If you're worried, you could have a chat with Allan – my manager," he explained, "and he'll make sure it's okay."

"That's so sweet!"

"No problem."

Casey shot him a glance. He smiled, and mouthed *later*. "Are you still modelling?" he asked.

"Yeah, sure! I have to cover my tuition somehow and it pays a lot better than waiting tables or any of the on-campus jobs." She smiled widely. "Stardance is happy to keep using me – I even got another Coronal shoot!"

"Great," Carval said.

"It wouldn't have happened without you!"

"The Finisterres are sharp cookies," Casey recalled the conversation to the case, "but they hide it. That's great. That ties up with what we know. Do you want to get a coffee before you get back to lectures?"

"Sure!" Allie smiled. "You have much better coffee than the school."

Tyler escorted Allie to the break room, though the rest of the team and Carval piled in behind him. Behind them, Estrolla scowled, and muttered something to Grendon, after which they both slouched out.

Casey made the coffee, unusually: O'Leary having nudged her. She was a little confused by that: normally he made coffee, claiming that she couldn't do it properly. When she noticed him tapping Tyler, however, she understood, especially as both men slid towards the door – out of Allie's hearing, but not hers.

"Estrolla's gone out," O'Leary murmured. "You might wanna walk Allie down."

"'Kay," Tyler replied. "Might shadow. Tell her first."

"Sneaky," O'Leary said. "You think you'll get rid of him?"

"Nah. Scare him shitless, though." Tyler bared his teeth, then converted it into a smile as the others took their coffee and he retrieved his sports drink from the fridge.

Nobody wasted time over their drinks: Casey was anxious to get on with the case, Carval received a text from Allan that sent him scurrying out, and Allie had to get right down to Washington Square. She favoured the team with a glorious smile, and started to sashay towards the stairs.

"Wait," Tyler said.

She gave him a questioning look. "What is it?"

"Estrolla's out there. Be right behind you if he's trying anything."

Allie blinked.

"Take Tyler up on it," Casey suggested. "Estrolla doesn't like any of us and we don't want you caught up in it."

"Okay! If you think I should, I'll do it. But I don't like it." She pouted, beautifully. The bullpen sighed from a safe distance, encouraged to stay there by Tyler's expression. "I'd better go!" Her sashaying sway riveted every straight male eye to her astonishing figure, as a result of which nobody paid any attention to Tyler's quiet exit ahead of her.

In the public area of the precinct, Tyler slipped through the crowd, doing nothing to draw notice. He couldn't see Estrolla, but he'd spotted

Grendon near the door. Time for some fun. He ghosted up behind Grendon, and as Allie exited the stairwell, grated into his ear, "She's got a boyfriend. Go near her, and you'll be in deep shit." Grendon spun around, furious, read Tyler's expression, turned sheet-white and ran. *Asshole*, Tyler thought, and searched the crowd for Estrolla, using all of his sniper's vision to keep Allie in view.

Finding Estrolla didn't take long, since he was moving in on Allie.

"Hello again," he oozed.

Allie looked around, favoured Estrolla with an uncertain smile, and then blanked. "Bye," she said.

"Don't be like that," he tried. "I wanna buy you a coffee. How about it?"

"No, thanks," she said. "I have a boyfriend." She took a step to the door, but Estrolla accompanied her. "Leave me alone," she said clearly. Tyler scythed through the crowd.

"It's just a coffee. C'mon, be nice," Estrolla said, and tried to catch her arm.

"I *said*, leave me *alone*," Allie yelled, loudly enough that the desk sergeant stood up. "Take your hand off me! I don't want you touching me and I don't want you anywhere near me! If you don't get *away* from me I'll report you!"

Tyler stopped in his tracks and watched, agape. Allie was making enough noise that the entire room, containing at least twenty witnesses, was watching– and supporting her. Estrolla's face turned black with anger – but unfortunately, from Tyler's point of view, he wasn't dumb enough to keep trying.

"Sorry, miss," he said.

Allie didn't answer. Tyler slid through the crowd to the door, and outside, where she arrived a second or two later.

"Handled him nicely."

"I've had plenty of practice," she said bitterly.

"Didn't need any help."

She managed a smile. "I knew you were there."

Tyler grinned. "Didn't need me, though." He paused. "Carval's show previews Thursday."

"It does? That's great!"

"Get to see it Wednesday. Want to come with us if Carval okays it? Team, so it's private." And, he thought, another person to hide Casey's dad from Kent wouldn't hurt at all.

Allie beamed at him. "Sure I do!"

"They'll tease me."

"That's okay," she smiled. "So will I!"

"Six Wednesday. Text you the address." His face changed. "If Estrolla comes near you again, tell me."

"Okay." She gave him a hug, plopped a kiss on his lips, and swung off.

Tyler returned inside, and up to the bullpen, grinning widely. As he examined Estrolla, malignantly hunched at his desk, his smile expanded.

"Wow," Andy said. "Tyler's smiling. Tell the newsies."

"Is Allie okay?" Casey asked.

"Fine," Tyler replied. "Estrolla's miserable. Hit on her. Handed him his balls."

"You did?"

"Allie."

The team's grins lit up the room. "Go, girl," O'Leary said.

"Coming to Carval's show. If Carval okays it – and if Casey's okay."

Andy whistled. "You're finally admitting you're dating? Guys, Tyler's showing an emotion! Stop the press."

"Shut up," Tyler said, looking at Casey.

Casey looked straight back. "Did you think of that first or after you invited Allie?"

Tyler squirmed. "After. Hides your dad. Allie gets attention."

She shrugged. "I guess. Whatever. Up to you and Carval."

"I think it's a good idea," O'Leary put in. "An' it's cute."

Casey made a dismissive gesture. "Can we get on with the case? You can rag Tyler as much as you like later, but we have a lot to do. Andy, you work out that book and those papers with Isabella's financials. Tyler, you're looking into the phone to go with the records. Anything immediate?"

"No."

"Why can't there be a helpful message up top – come meet me so I can murder you?" Casey complained.

"'Cause most killers ain't that dumb."

Casey muttered blackly, then refocused. "We need to talk about interviewing the actors, 'cause there's too many for us four and we need to decide how best to use our four officers. We wanna talk to Maisie again. O'Leary'll talk to Ron. I wanna finish reading the autopsy, so we know what she got hit with and what she got strangled with." Casey looked up and around. "Someone needs to talk to those two friends of hers, too."

"Phone might tell us what to ask friends and Maisie. Maybe actors," Tyler said.

"Same if I work out these financials."

"An' Ron."

"You all do those, I'll go with the autopsy, and we'll circle back before lunch."

They set to.

Nearly three hours later, they surfaced.

"What've we got?" Casey asked, sitting on her desk and contemplating the murder board.

"You start," O'Leary said. "Anythin' else in the autopsy?"

"Drugged with Flunitrazepam – Rohypnol. Enough that she'd be pretty much unconscious after less than an hour. After that, she was hit neatly above the ear – the left temporal. McDonald theorises a right-handed assailant – with a smooth, rounded, heavy object. Naturally, he can't tell us what it was, but he says it must have been close to or precisely spherical – not a baseball bat or a two-by-four."

"That's unusual." O'Leary frowned. "We better take a good look at the props. Might be somethin' that fits the spec in there."

"Good thought. Can you talk to Ron, and we'll go over and have that good look when there isn't a rehearsal?"

"I always like a trip out," O'Leary agreed.

"The strangulation was with fabric – not a rope or wire. Tiny fragments of artificial silk – rayon – CSU is still looking at it to try to give us colours and an exact fabric composition. I guess they need to turn up their microscopes."

"Likely a scarf," Andy said, "or something like that."

"Yeah," Casey agreed.

"Video," Tyler put in. "Scarves on half the cast."

"Those weren't scarves, they were wings," Andy contradicted.

"Whatever." Tyler wasn't the world expert in dress or costumes. "Silky stuff."

"It could easily be that," Casey said. "When we get more from CSU we can look. What about those papers and the financials?"

CHAPTER THIRTEEN

Andy grinned wryly. "Well…" he enticed.

"Spit it out."

"It's weird."

"We do weird every day of the week."

"There's nothing in her financials. Absolutely nothing. Unless she had another account, she wasn't blackmailing."

"Or wasn't dumb," Casey said cynically.

"Likely," Tyler said. "Two banking apps on her phone."

"Two!" Andy yelped. "Why didn't you say already?"

"Just found them. Messages first." It was his turn to smile. "Lots. Social media, too."

"Use a few more words and tell us properly," Casey instructed.

Tyler smiled some more. "Two banking apps. One for Chase – we knew about that, name of Betty Scarfield. One for Citizens Bank, name of Maisie Scarfield." Casey's mouth opened. "Already started on the warrant."

"Wow. Great find. Social media?"

"Lots of 'I'll call you' and 'I'll meet you' but no real names. When we're done, I'll set the uniforms on looking up real names."

"Why'd she use her sister's name?"

"How'd she set it up in her sister's name? Banks need verifiable photo ID to open accounts."

"Must've been in on it." Tyler's words stopped the conversation.

"Which means," Casey said bleakly, "that likely Maisie isn't our murderer, nor Gallagher – but someone connected with the play."

"*The play's the thing*," Andy quoted, to general derision.

"Maisie could be our murderer," O'Leary mused, crevasses cutting his brow, "iffen she got tired of not benefitin' from the money, or she didn't want to be second-best."

"Can't we cut *down* the motives?" Casey complained. "We have lots – every actor'll have a different one, Heyer hated her, Dacia wanted to star, maybe she was after the Finisterres – that's a quick way to get rich – there's Maisie, we can't write off the boyfriend yet, and we haven't even started on the two friends." She blew a sigh fit to shift O'Leary.

"We better get goin', then," the big man said. "Where'll we start?"

"Uniforms to find names," Tyler said.

"You set that up. First, though, we have a lot of interviewing ahead. O'Leary and I will take Maisie, but there are all the actors. O'Leary suggested we each pair with a uniform, to give them some experience?"

"I'll take Larson," Andy said quickly.

"I'll have Henegan," O'Leary said, with a slow, nasty smile. "I c'n keep him in order, an' I c'n deal with anyone makin' trouble. You take Fremont, Casey. He c'n keep up with you, an' you don't have no patience with anyone slow." Casey made a face at him.

"Adamo," Tyler said.

"I guess you all think it's a good plan, then?" she said, a touch sulkily.

"It can't hurt to teach them something," Andy said. "This way we know they're up to our standards."

"Or we send 'em back," O'Leary suggested.

"We'll try it. But if one of us has a doubt, we go back to normal, okay? I'm not sacrificing our closure rate for anything."

"Naw," O'Leary agreed.

"I think we should have another chat with Gallagher too – as a witness, not a suspect. He might know more than he thinks he does. You take that," she said to Tyler and Andy, "while we grill Maisie. We'll ask Fremont and Larson to go get her and sit her in Interrogation." She bared her teeth. "Scare her a little."

"Friends?" Tyler said.

Casey thought. "I think I want to finish with Gallagher first. If we can cross him off for good, it takes out a lot of complications. We'll take the friends after that – in case he says anything useful about them."

"We'll take Gallagher on home ground," Andy said. "We don't want him scared, so we won't bring him anywhere near you." Casey muttered darkly at him. Andy smiled sweetly back. "We can do that without having the Citizens Bank records."

Tyler strode off to talk to the four uniforms, and sent Fremont and Larson towards Casey.

"I want you to bring in Maisie Scarfield – Isabella's sister – and park her in Interrogation. Don't arrest her – unless she does something dumb, of course – but she doesn't get a choice."

"Yes'm," they said.

"O'Leary and I will question her. When we've found out what she knows, and Andy's done some financial wizardry, we'll start interviewing the actors." She smiled. Fremont and Larson didn't look reassured. "You four will get to play."

"Ma'am?"

"We'll pair you off with us. Larson, Andy's scooped you up. Fremont, you're with me."

"Yes, *ma'am*," they said, delighted.

"The other two will be with O'Leary and Tyler." She smiled. "Chance to learn."

"Yes'm. Thank you."

"Go get Maisie, please."

The two officers departed, cheer in every line of their uniformed backs. Casey wondered what on earth O'Leary had unleashed. Uniformed officers shouldn't be *cheerful* at her, they should be...something else. Not looking at her as if she'd given them a wonderful present. She humphed, and picked up her phone to harass CSU about the fabric threads.

Tyler, having despatched Fremont and Larson to see Casey, regarded Adamo and Henegan balefully. Henegan cringed. Adamo didn't.

"Going to learn about interrogating," Tyler said. Adamo's dark eyes sparkled. Henegan shivered like a reed in a gale. "Tomorrow, we're questioning the actors. Each of you is with one of us." Adamo grinned. Henegan paled to corpse-like. "Adamo, with me. Henegan, with O'Leary." Adamo quivered, but his eyes stayed bright. Henegan recovered enough colour not to look as if he would die on the spot.

"Yessir," Adamo said, faintly echoed by Henegan.

"Yes, *Detective*," Tyler corrected. "You don't *sir* us – but you *ma'am* Casey, or we'll know why."

"Detective O'Leary said that," Heneghan said.

"Remember it. Get started on those social media handles."

"Yes si-Detective." Adamo and Henegan replied, and got going.

Tyler collected Andy, and they went to see David Gallagher.

***

"Ma'am?" Fremont approached Casey. "Miss Scarfield's in Interrogation One. She's not happy."

"Good. I'm not happy with her." Casey stood up. "Ready, O'Leary?"

"Yep."

Casey marched into Interrogation One exuding menace, with O'Leary looming behind her.

"What do you think you're doing, dragging me out of work like that?" Maisie yelled.

113

"Quiet," Casey snapped. "You lied to me. I'll read you your rights, before we start."

Maisie gaped. Casey read the Miranda warning, Maisie paling with every coldly enunciated word.

"Do you understand your rights?"

"I haven't done anything!"

"Do you understand? Answer for the record."

"Yes, but I haven't *done* anything! You've no right" –

"You lied," Casey stated flatly. "You obstructed our investigation. You concealed material information." She stared at Maisie. "You're in deep trouble. You could go to jail for up to a year."

Silence fell. Casey didn't break it. Maisie's mouth opened, closed, opened, as if to say something, closed.

"I didn't!" she finally cried. "I didn't do anything."

"You told us David Gallagher had hit on you. When did he do that?" Casey waited, face hard.

Maisie's calculating gaze skittered around the room.

"We can check his movements," Casey said. "He's providing us with the swipe card data for his office. Every entry and exit is recorded." That rocked Maisie.

"What day was it?"

"I...I don't remember."

"You don't remember? You said" – Casey ostentatiously consulted her interview notes – "it was straight after he dumped Betty. When did they break up?"

"About a month ago," Maisie admitted sulkily, which agreed with Gallagher's information.

"You do know. You were mad at them breaking up, so don't tell me you don't know exactly when it was."

"It was Tuesday. They were supposed to go out on a date and that sonofabitch met her and told her they were done," Maisie spat.

"I see. When did he come on to you?"

"The next day."

"Time?"

"Just after six, when he got off work. He said he wanted to explain."

"Really? Where did you meet?"

"There's a coffee bar right by his office. I don't remember the name. We went there. They knew him."

Casey consulted her notes again. "That would be Peaky Barista." She frowned. "You went there after six?"

"Sure we did."

"That's interesting," Casey said coldly, "since it closes at six."

Maisie gulped. "It must have been another one."

"Really."

"Yes!"

"I see. What happened when you turned him down?"

"He stormed off to the subway."

"I see. He didn't return to work?"

"No."

"When I obtain his e-Tix account, I'll see his travel from 110th to 191st shortly after six p.m.?"

"Yes!"

"Liar."

Maisie jerked back at the flat, annoyed tone.

"I know you're lying because David Gallagher was working every hour there was for year end. I know that when I see his swipe card information, he won't have left before ten that evening, and he won't have gone out. I know that you didn't go to Peaky Barista because they were shut. That's three lies in less than ten minutes." Casey pinned Maisie with a full-force glare. "One more lie and you'll be in a cell."

"It's true!" But even Maisie didn't believe herself. She wasn't a tenth of the actress her sister had been, and guilt was written across her face.

"Detective O'Leary," Casey said with icy formality, "please have Miss Scarfield taken down to Holding and processed. The charge is obstruction."

"Of course." O'Leary stood.

Maisie burst into tears, which impressed Casey not one bit. "I didn't *mean* to," she wailed.

"But you did it."

"I didn't *mean* to," she blubbered. O'Leary sat down again. "I wanted to protect Betty."

"Betty is *dead*," Casey bit. "You didn't protect her from that, and you're not protecting her now. Stop lying!" she suddenly yelled. Maisie jumped a mile high and cringed when she came down. "Why did you lie about David?"

"He ditched her! He deserved to be in trouble. He had no right to look down on her and ditch her because he'd be some bigshot corporate suit and she was waiting tables in cheap diners."

"She wouldn't go to Chicago with him," Casey said. "He asked her. She refused. They broke up."

"What?"

"She wouldn't leave New York. She followed her dream. He followed his. They broke up over it."

"No! He ditched her. She was heartbroken. She really loved him."

"She loved her career more."

Maisie started to bawl again. Casey didn't move. O'Leary pushed a Kleenex at her, without noticeable sympathy.

"Stop cryin'," he said bluntly. "You c'n tell us the truth or you c'n visit a cell tonight an' be charged in the mornin'. You been wastin' our time outta spite, an' we don't like that."

Maisie snuffled damply, and made an unsuccessful attempt to stop her pointless tears.

"You lied about David Gallagher because you thought your sister had her pride hurt. Was there any truth in *anything* you said about him?"

"No," Maisie dripped. "He deserved it."

"He did not," Casey snapped. "Lose that attitude. It's not helping you." Maisie crumpled again, but Casey didn't regret her tone in the slightest. "Your next mistake."

"What?"

"Why didn't you tell us your sister used your name to open a bank account at Citizens?"

"That was *my* account."

"But your sister had full access. She had it on her phone. How did she have that if it was your account?"

Maisie rediscovered her trapped-rat demeanour.

"You can't get a bank account without ID. Either she stole your ID" –

"Betty would never!" –

"Or you provided it. Or opened it for her."

"Which is it?" O'Leary chimed in.

"You must have known she was using it, if you're so sure she wouldn't steal your identity. Or maybe she *borrowed*" – Casey's scepticism was patent – "your bank login credentials? How'd she manage that without you knowing?"

Maisie obviously wanted the floor to open and swallow her up. Sadly, the floor in Interrogation would not co-operate. "We shared it," she muttered guiltily.

"Why? You tell me absolutely *everything* about why that account was opened, what you were *both* doing with it, and everything else about it, or that cell downstairs is waiting for you." She held Maisie's gaze. "How will your parents feel about that? They've lost one daughter, and the other's actively obstructing the investigation into her death? I thought you were *best friends*, and so did they."

"We were!"

"Then tell us everythin'," O'Leary said. "Every detail."

"She said she needed an account that wasn't linked to her at all, and I said sure I'd help. She was my *sister*, of course I'd freaking help!"

"Why did she want that?"

"I don't *know!* I asked her, and she said she had things to do, but she didn't want anyone to know about them. That was years ago anyway. It's got nothing to do with her murder! Why're you talking about that when you should be out there finding who killed her!"

Casey ignored the tantrum. "Did you have access to the account?"

"No."

"Unusual."

"She would never do anything wrong. She wanted to act, that was all. She didn't have a cent to spare – you must have seen her apartment. She didn't do drugs or designer clothes or spending. It was all about acting and she worked and worked to be able to support herself and not need to take money from Mom and Dad. She'd never have done anything wrong."

"Who do you think killed her?"

"I don't know."

"No lies," Casey said ominously.

"I don't! If I did I would tell you. I don't know why she wanted that account – I don't even know her password. She changed it as soon as I set it up but she never told me."

"That doesn't matter. We'll get a warrant to give the bank permission to provide all the records to us." Casey looked at O'Leary. This mess would take all of Andy's financial acumen to clear up, so that they had the information they needed. The big man nodded. "Where were you from six p.m. on Thursday to noon on Friday?"

"But…"

Casey stared her down.

"I was home. I didn't go anywhere until I went to work Friday morning. I was in the office from eight Friday morning."

"Did you make any calls, watch TV, order takeout?"

"I made a couple of calls to friends from my cell."

"Write down its number, and the numbers you called." Maisie did. "We'll call you if we need your input for the bank records. Don't leave town. You can go. For now."

She staggered out, escorted by O'Leary.

***

"You again?" David Gallagher said to Tyler and Andy, in the same conference room. "What is it? Maisie telling more lies?"

"No. We know she's lying about you," Andy said. Gallagher sagged with relief. "We're trying to find out more about Betty – Isabella. Did you know she had a second bank account in her sister's name?"

"What?" Gallagher stared at them, mouth open. "She had what? No, I never knew that." His brow furrowed. "What'd she need that for? She sure didn't have any spare money – you must have seen her apartment. Basic wasn't the word. She needed every cent to support herself and her acting. She worked really hard. Didn't matter what it was. I respected that. She never asked me for anything and she said she couldn't ask her parents, because they'd done so much already. I would have…" He blinked, once. "I don't see what she would've had a second account for, because she didn't have money."

He looked from one to the other. "I guess you're thinking she was making money on the side. But I swear, she never had money. She had a temper, but she wouldn't have done anything like that." He stopped. "She really tried to be nice. She couldn't stand the girl she was up against, but she tried not to be bitchy. She knew the director was on her case, but she always made excuses for why he behaved badly. Like, she tried to forgive. She believed in being a good person – it didn't stop her being ambitious, she just didn't cheat to get there."

"Did she ever tell you anything about the rest of the cast?"

Gallagher thought. "I don't remember her saying that anyone was mean to her or that she'd had an argument – but that was before we broke up." He considered again. "There was one guy she said she was uncomfortable around, uh, Carson, Corman…Cordell! But she didn't say why. Nobody else. They'd only been auditioning at that stage, so she wouldn't have had much chance to know who was who or who would be in the play."

"Yeah. You didn't know she'd got the part."

"No." He blinked hard again. "If I had known…I would have tried to go see it, to see her succeed. Sure, we broke up, but I don't – didn't – want her to fail." His lips twisted. "I wouldn't have told her, though. I got some pride."

"Thank you, Mr Gallagher."

"Thanks."

Tyler and Andy left quietly to return to the precinct and catch up with the others.

***

"Okay," Casey said, "it sounds like there's nothing more to be done with Gallagher." She drew a big red X through his name. "We'll make sure we check his alibi, but an officer can do that."

"'Kay. Maisie?"

"Pathetic," Casey scorned. "She deliberately tried to get Gallagher into trouble, then cried like a baby when she was called on it. She didn't know anything useful."

"She admitted she helped Isabella set up the account, an' Casey scared her silly, so she'll co-operate iffen we need her to help us get into that account."

"She didn't know anything about it?"

"Naw."

118

"She doesn't have an alibi, either. Just a couple of cell calls which don't rule her out."

"Finish the warrant," Tyler said.

"Yeah," Casey agreed. "We can't go a lot further without knowing what's in that account."

"We could grill all the actors anyway."

"We *could*, but we don't have anything to grill them with. I don't want to wait," Casey complained, "but we need some information. Otherwise we're wasting our time and giving them a chance to mess us around."

"Better get on with findin' some info," O'Leary said happily, "but first I'm findin' some lunch, 'cause I'm starvin'. C'mon, Casey. That food truck is callin' my name."

"Give me a minute," she said, and whipped off, to return a moment or two later, grabbing her light jacket.

CHAPTER FOURTEEN

"Not there!" Carval snapped. "It's *wrong*. It needs to be *before* the shots of my cops sparring, otherwise there's no progression and no story."

"Okay," Allan said. "Move it to where it should be. Then go get lunch, because you're tired, hungry, and unreasonable. I don't want to see you back here till you've eaten enough to cool your temper and you can play nice again."

"It has to be *right*," Carval insisted.

"It won't be if you don't eat. Anyway, *I* want my lunch, and so do the technical staff." Allan made shooing gestures. "Go." Carval scowled at the photos and the wall. "If you don't, you'll be here on your own." He tip-tapped off. Carval barely noticed. It wasn't right. It had to be right.

"Go. For. Lunch." Allan's exasperation finally penetrated from his ears to his brain.

"You go for lunch. I'm thinking."

"I did. That was forty minutes ago. Do I have to walk you out of here?"

"Why didn't you bring me some?"

"Jamie! Wake up. You are not allowed to eat or drink in the gallery. For God's sake go get lunch before we murder you and your Casey comes to investigate us." Allan stretched up to Carval's shoulder, clamped on to it, and shoved until he moved. "Out!"

"But" –

"Out! Out, out, out!" Despite Carval's height and breadth advantage, Allan frogmarched him out of the gallery, and added a final shove before retreating.

Carval stomped off, to find, much to his surprise, that it was a beautiful day – and that he was ravenous. He visited the nearest sandwich bar, and shortly sat down in the sunshine to cram down a substantial lunch and drown his thirst in plain water. He was wired up enough without adding caffeine to the mix. Hunger and thirst satisfied, the sun warm on his back, he pulled out his camera, and took candid shots of the area around him: a small girl chasing a ball, her mother or nanny looking on protectively; a dog lying at its elderly master's feet, gazing up adoringly; an urban squirrel strutting along the sidewalk, chattering at unimpressed city pigeons. Longer than he'd had time for, and after an irritated text from Allan, he returned to the gallery, far more relaxed.

"I got it," he announced as he walked in, over Allan's remonstrations. "Like this." He started to arrange and move and order; directing the gallery staff and Allan as he went. Under Carval's assured, rapid direction, the show took shape.

"We're done for the day," he said, much later. The gallery staff disappeared, before he could change his mind. He looked around. "It'll be amazing," he murmured. "Everyone'll see how amazing they are."

"Time to go," Allan pointed out. "The staff need to lock up."

"I guess." Carval rotated on his spot, assessing. "Yeah."

Outside the doors, Carval remembered something. "Allan, I forgot to tell you" –

"Oh, God. What?"

"No, nothing bad, don't worry."

"That makes a change," Allan said sourly.

"You know Tyler's dating Allie?"

"Allie?"

"The model who I shot that the team used for the murdered models sting. She's a music major" –

"Oh, yes. I remember. She's still dating Tyler?"

"Yes. You knew that."

"I'm surprised they're still together, that's all."

"*Anyway*," Carval said, totally uninterested in Allan's thoughts about the pairing, "Allie's been noticed by the Finisterres and I said if she was worried you'd help" –

Allan choked. "You what?"

"I said you'd help her. You will, won't you?" he coaxed.

"Of course I will. But who are you and *what* have you done with the real Jamie Carval?"

"Huh?"

"Jamie, you have never in your whole entire life thought about helping anyone, let alone some girl who's being swallowed up by the machine. When have you ever offered that before to anyone you've photographed? Sure, you've done shots for free occasionally, when you're bored or fed up or you'd ditched whichever piece of arm candy you'd had last, but you've never actually offered practical help. Who are you, and where's Jamie?"

"That's not fair" –

"Really?"

"*You* said the Finisterres were sharks. *You* said *I* shouldn't talk to them. When will you talk to them so I can shoot in theatres with their productions, and can you find me some other productions too because I can't only rely on their experimental stuff" –

"Jamie! Stop getting distracted. Why did you tell Allie I'd help?"

Carval shuffled his feet, wriggled, and generally became an embarrassed five-year old who'd been caught out sharing his candy. "Dunno," he muttered. "Doesn't matter. You *will* help her, won't you?"

"I already said I would." Allan smiled. "I like it when you do something that proves you're not just a spoilt little boy. Growing up is good for you."

"Oh, shut up," Carval sulked. "It's 'cause she's with Tyler. It's like buying the team dinner."

Allan wriggled an eyebrow, and smiled knowingly. Carval scowled. "You work on getting me into theatres," he grumped.

"Not till this show is hung and opens. Friday morning, we'll know what the critics think."

"They'll think it's a triumph," Carval stated. "Because it is."

"There's my Jamie, back in all his egotistical glory."

"As long as they focus on the glory."

Allan sighed. "Shoo. I'll see you here first thing tomorrow." He bustled off to do whatever Allan did in his free time.

Carval checked his watch, found that it was close to shift end, and ambled off towards the precinct to see if anything interesting was happening.

He slipped in, surreptitiously taking photos in the entry hall, and wandered up to the Homicide floor. Nobody noticed him.

Carval, on the other hand, certainly noticed two officers. He recognised them as ones that Casey and the team had reduced to flinders on the sparring mats, and a third who'd been with Fremont, Larson and the rookie Adamo earlier. Though their voices were low, the tones were unpleasant, and the way they were standing implied that the two would-be sparrers weren't happy with the third man.

Carval casually palmed his camera, and strolled around the bullpen as usual, making sure to take as many shots as he could of the unpleasant scene. As he moved, he switched from camera to phone, and from photo to video, finally getting close enough to record the three officers and pick up most of the sound. The conversation was deeply disturbing. He'd talk to the team later, because he didn't want to mention it in the precinct.

***

The team had spent a frustrating early afternoon trying to extract blood from a variety of stones, also known as CSU and Isabella's second bank.

While Tyler had managed to prepare, submit, and have his warrant for the Citizens Bank account approved, the bank itself hadn't yet supplied any information. Casey had harassed CSU about the fabric traces until they'd told her, not politely, to get lost, or they'd ensure that she got lost. Since CSU probably had creative ways of disposing of her, she had, sulkily, left them alone. Before she started chewing the desk, or dismembering any uniform who couldn't run away fast enough, she had an idea.

"We can't do anything further with the actors or Finisterres till we get financials from Citizens, but we can go see Isabella's two friends. We've got time. One each?"

"Yep," Andy said quickly.

"You take Suzie Keller, and O'Leary and I'll take Anna Bulitt."

Five minutes later, they were gone.

***

"Suzie Keller?"

"Yes?" A tall, blonde twenty-something woman regarded them suspiciously.

"Detectives Chee and Tyler. We're here to talk to you about Betty Scarfield."

"Betty's *dead*," she said. Her eyes unfocused, and liquid puddled. "I still can't believe it," she said blankly. "She was starring in a play. She shouldn't be dead. She didn't return my messages since Thursday and then I saw it on Instagram. Her sister said she died and how can she be dead when she was *young?*"

"I'm sorry to tell you that Betty was murdered," Andy said.

"No! Why would anyone do that? Nobody hated her like that." Suzie's face crumpled.

"Can we sit down somewhere?" Andy asked gently. "We'd like to ask a few questions."

"Won't take long," Tyler added.

They went to a small room. Drinks were not offered, nor did they request them. Suzie was hanging on to her control by a hair: her mouth twisting and eyes blinking rapidly; any more stress, even as simple as asking for a drink, would send her over the edge. She dropped hard into a chair, slumping.

"Tell us about Betty."

"We met in a community theatre group, run by the community college I went to." Her voice shook. "She was a couple of years younger than me, but she was trying to get experience before applying to one of the stage schools, so she joined us. She was much better than everyone else, and a few people were bitchy about it, but mostly we were glad to have someone who could act well. It sparked the rest of us, you know? We all tried harder

123

and played up to her and it was much better." She gulped back choking tears. "Even when she made it to her theatre major and she was working so hard in dead-end jobs to pay tuition, she still came to us when she could."

"Did you meet her sister?"

"Maisie? Sure. She came to the group a few times, but when she realised she wasn't good enough to win big roles she stopped." Suzie paused. "She said all the right things about Betty's ability, but…sometimes I thought she was jealous."

"Mm?" Tyler encouraged.

"Um, little comments. They could've been constructive."

"Get it," Tyler said.

"She picked and pecked about Betty's boyfriend – David. Maisie didn't like him. I mean, David wasn't enthusiastic about acting as a career, but he was really into Betty and he tried hard to support her. I was surprised they broke up, but you never know, do you? David was ambitious too, and Betty couldn't expect him to put her first every time when there was a good opportunity for him."

"You knew about that?"

"Oh, sure. Betty told us – me and Anna – Anna Bulitt. Betty couldn't believe he'd choose the big promotion over her, but she hadn't gotten the role as Titania then and he'd asked her to go with him and she'd said no, so it wouldn't work. If he'd stayed, he'd have resented her, if she went, she'd have resented that. Anyway, Betty was really upset, but then she got the part and she, like, shrugged him off and went for it."

"We heard the Finisterres were supporting her," Andy said. "They're a big name in theatre."

Suzie snuffled. "It isn't *fair*. She'd just gotten her big break and they were totally on her side and helping her and *this* happens? It's *unfair*. She was going to be a star and she was, like, so *nice* to everyone. Always trying to help and never showing off. I mean, she couldn't have had much spare money and even her apartment was tiny, but she could always find a dime for a panhandler or if someone was upset she'd manage to get them a coffee or some candy." She paused. "She lived on a shoestring, so she could save any spare money for the things that really mattered to her."

"What do you mean?"

"Like, she'd say she had theatre tickets – not often, but enough – and even cheap tickets wind up to be expensive if you're going every six weeks. She supported an acting charity."

"Do you remember which?"

"Uh, it was for kids getting into theatre – Act Like A Child, that was it. She was always talking about how kids needed more support for creative stuff. She volunteered there."

"But you said she was living on a shoestring?"

"Apart from those, yeah. She didn't spend on clothes, or haircuts, or shoes, you know? She scoured the thrift stores for good stuff. She loved finding a good bargain – don't we all?"

"Sure do," said Andy, who hadn't entered a thrift store since the day he'd joined the NYPD – and never would again, if he had any say in it. Tyler nodded agreeably.

"She found this faux-silk scarf, a week ago, for, like, fifty cents, and she was so pleased. She wore it every day. It looked really stylish."

"What did it look like?" Andy asked.

"It was Paisley patterned, with a dark red background and navy/white pattern."

Tyler quietly took a note of the colours. He'd tell Casey as soon as they were done.

"Did Betty say anything about *A Midsummer Night's Dream?*"

"She was totally delighted to get Titania – who wouldn't be? – and she was really grateful that the Finisterres had made it happen, but the director was a real asshole, and the understudy was a total bitch."

"Anything else?"

"That was the worst, but she did say that all the old guys – it was all guys except her and her understudy. Weird, huh?"

Andy nodded.

"Anyway, she said all the old guys were bitching at each other." She wrinkled her forehead and scrunched her nose. "But it was weird. It was like she was, I don't know, like she knew something about why they were mean to each other, but she didn't say anything. She was kind of pals with the guy who played Egeus, but apart from that I don't think she got close with anyone. She said the guys playing the four fairies were pretty cool, but they were only interested in each other and skateboarding when they weren't acting."

"I see," Andy said easily. "Is there anything else you can tell us?"

Suzie considered. "No, I don't think so. It's unfair," she said again, and sniffed soggily. "She was just about to make it." Her control broke, and she sobbed in earnest. "It's not fair."

"Thank you for your time. I'm sorry," Andy said.

"Sorry," added Tyler.

Back down in their cruiser, they looked at each other.

"Interesting," Tyler said.

"Sure was. I wonder if Casey's getting the same story?"

"Go back, find out."

**

"Anna Bulitt? Detectives Clement and O'Leary." Casey proffered her badge to a small, dark woman, who inspected it carefully and then regarded Casey and O'Leary with worry.

"Yeah? What do you want?"

"You're a friend of Betty Scarfield?"

"She died," Anna said miserably. Casey saw the connection happen. "No! You're *investigating*? Was she *murdered*? Suzie told me she died and her sister put it on Instagram but we didn't know she was *murdered*." She grabbed her doorframe, so pale that Casey thought she might faint.

"I'm sorry," Casey said. "Could we come in so you can sit down?"

"Whatever," Anna faltered. "I don't get it. I saw her last weekend and she was fine. How could someone…" She couldn't force the word out.

"Tell us about Betty," O'Leary rumbled softly. She stared uncomprehendingly at him. "How did you meet?"

"We were working in the same diner on a Saturday, when we were in high school." Tears escaped.

"I get it. Hard work."

"Sure was," Anna snuffled, dabbed at her eyes and blew her nose. "She was a really hard worker. She put the effort in – she waited tables at Verdicchio and Carrie's Diner, 'cause she needed the tips to pay for her acting. She just got a big part and she's happy. It's her big break." She suddenly realised what she'd said. "It *was* her big break. It's not fair. She was happy…" She began to cry again. "I don't believe it. Who would do that?"

"We'll do everything we can to find out who and put them in jail," Casey said.

"That won't bring her back, will it?" she said bitterly.

"No," Casey admitted. "It won't. It's no consolation."

"I'll tell you what I can," Anna dripped.

"Thank you. You met when you were both working in a diner, when you were in high school. And you stayed friends when Betty went off to college?"

"Yes. I could never have acted – Suzie, her other close friend, she's an actress too, but she wasn't nearly as good – Suzie said that," Anna added at their questioning look. "She – Suzie – wasn't going to make a career of it. She wanted to act with a community theatre group and enjoy herself. Betty wanted to make it her life. I'd hate it." She shuddered, and blew her nose again. "Standing up in front of all those people… But Betty was great. She could make you believe in her. I went to see her in community productions whenever I could, then when she got into her theatre major I went to see that. She was totally brilliant."

"Did you meet her boyfriend?"

"David? Yeah. He was a stuffed shirt, but up till he ditched her he was pretty supportive. I mean, he wasn't into theatre or anything creative, but he came to watch her when he could and he was always nice about how she'd done. I didn't understand how they split up, but Betty said he wanted to move out of New York and there was no way she was leaving when some bigshot funders – Finneys, something like that" –

"Finisterres?" O'Leary suggested.

"Yeah, that was it. Weird name, anyway, they had put some muscle behind her and put her forward for a really big part, so she was sticking with it. He wasn't having it and was leaving the city, and if she wouldn't come, that was it. They broke up. She was devastated about it, but it sounded like they had incompatible goals, you know?"

"What about her sister?"

Anna's lips pinched. "I don't like her."

"Why not?"

"She was big on how she was Betty's best friend and biggest supporter, you know, and how they did everything together, and she said the right things but it never, like, sounded sincere. I think she was jealous. She dressed like Betty, but it never worked – Betty had style, and Maisie was pretty good looking and she dressed well, but it never looked as put together as Betty did with stuff from the thrift store."

"Betty bought her clothes from the thrift store?" Casey asked.

"Yes. She loved a bargain, but she was pretty short of money. She wanted quality, but she couldn't afford new. She made her own lunches most times."

"I see." Casey smiled sympathetically. "It must've been tough."

"It was. She had to watch every cent, but she worked really hard. She didn't want to take money from her mom and dad. She said they deserved nice things, 'cause they'd never had much when Betty and Maisie were kids."

"A good daughter," Casey said, ignoring her own guilt. She *was* a good daughter. She was.

"Yes." Anna's eyes flooded again. "She volunteered at a kids' charity, too. Act Like A Child. She really wanted the kids to get a chance."

"Paying it on," O'Leary rumbled.

"Did she talk to you about the Finisterres?" Casey asked. They'd follow up the charity later.

"She couldn't say enough nice about them. She, like, adored them. They'd given her a big break and she'd have done anything for them. She said they were the sweetest people, and she was so grateful for the chance."

"What about the people in the play – *A Midsummer Night's Dream?*" O'Leary asked.

Anna's mouth twisted. "The director was a real sonofabitch. Betty said he'd wanted the girl who was understudy, and when the funders insisted on her, he was really pissed. She couldn't do anything right, but he had to put up with her, or he wouldn't have the funding. He made her life miserable. She used to come to work and cry about it, but she wouldn't let him force her out. She said you only got one big chance and she wasn't giving it up."

"Brave," Casey admired.

"She was. That understudy was a total bitch. Always making sly comments and trying to get Betty into trouble – she told her the wrong time for rehearsal, but Betty always used to check with the doorman – she said he was a good guy, and he gave her the right times. He'd been an actor once, she said. She was awful. Wanted the part and didn't care how she got it – if she murdered Betty, you bet I'd believe that. I don't remember her saying anything much about the others – she said the guy playing Egeus was nice. She said that the four young guys were cute, but only interested in each other – I thought she meant they were gay, but that wouldn't bother her." Suddenly light dawned. "The older guys didn't like each other. There was a lot of sniping and nastiness. It sounded like they hated each other, but Betty said she was sure they'd pull it out for the show. It was weird the way she said it, though, like she knew they would. She never said more than that. I guessed she meant they were all professionals."

"Nothing else?"

"No." Anna stared at the table, and wiped her eyes again. "I can't believe she's gone. She was a really good friend."

"Thank you. If you think of anything else, no matter how small, call me. Here's my card."

"Okay."

CHAPTER FIFTEEN

"Waal," O'Leary said, as the four detectives shared their findings, back in the precinct, "seems like it wasn't all sweetness an' light between the sisters."

"Yeah," Casey agreed. "I bet these fabric traces are that scarf, but I don't remember a scarf on our victim when she was found. Do you?"

The others shook their heads.

"Gentlemen," she grinned, "We have the strangulation weapon." She scrawled it on the board with immense satisfaction. "I'll improve Evan's day, then we can carry on."

A quick call to CSU later, to advise Evan about the scarf and ask him to confirm that it was indeed used to strangle Isabella, they resumed.

"The stories pretty much match up," Casey summarised. "Both friends agree that Gallagher was genuinely supportive but in the end they had incompatible goals and broke up. They both confirmed that Heyer hated her, and that Dacia wasn't any better. They've confirmed that the older actors disliked each other, which we'd worked out from the videos and Carval's pictures, but they *also* both thought that Isabella knew something about why, though she didn't say anything. She volunteered at a kids' theatre charity. Finally, Maisie wasn't Isabella's biggest fan."

"Don't sound like it," O'Leary rumbled. "Sounds to me like Maisie was jealous of her li'l sis."

"Did one of the uniforms check Gallagher's alibi, so we can discount him?"

Tyler nodded. "Fremont. Gallagher's out."

"One down," Andy said sourly. "Only thirty or so to go."

"When will we get the second set of financials?" Casey asked.

"Probably not tonight," Andy replied. Everyone grimaced.

"What else can we do? I don't want to bring Maisie in again till we've seen these financials, ditto all the actors and Heyer – is there anyone left? We can tell the officers to dig into the charity so we know who to contact, but we can't go see them now because Kent won't authorise overtime if it's not urgent."

"Naw," O'Leary said. "An' that's good, 'cause it was shift end ten minutes ago, an' here comes your boyfriend."

"Hey," Carval said generally. "How's it going?"

"Stuck," Casey grumbled. "I want those financials."

"Good."

"What?"

"I need to show you something," Carval said, "but not here."

"Abbey?"

"No. My studio. I can put it up on the computer."

"Will there be beer?" O'Leary wheedled.

"Coffee."

"No beer?"

"You'll live," Casey said callously. "It's good for you not to have beer."

O'Leary mumped and mumbled. Nobody paid any attention as they cleared their desks.

Not long later, Carval led them to his studio and connected his phone to the computer and its large, high-definition screen.

"What's this?" Andy enquired.

"Watch and see," Carval said heavily.

"That don't mean nothin' good," O'Leary offered. "Waal, hell. What now? We already had Estrolla goin' after Allie, an' gettin' his balls handed to him…oh. Aw, *shit*." He was looking at the screen, which had brought up the start frame of the video. "That's Estrolla, Grendon and Henegan."

"Henegan's the one working with you?" Carval asked.

"Yeah," Casey said acidly. "Kent foisted him on to us so we could fix his weaknesses. Starting with finding him a spine and some guts."

"It don't look like he's good friends with them two any more," O'Leary pointed out.

"He doesn't have to be good friends with them to tell them stuff. He only has to be shit-scared," Andy noted. "That looks like shit-scared to me."

"Yeah," Tyler said. "Intimidation."

"That's all fine," Casey said, "but is there anything we can actually do something about? Can you play it?" she directed at Carval. He started the video.

Two minutes and thirty-six seconds later, the video finished. During it, none of the cops had said a word, but Carval had taken at least fifty shots of their changing expressions and their focused, investigative stares.

"Waal, that's" –

"Clusterfuck," Tyler swore.

"They didn't say a damn thing that couldn't have an innocent explanation, but Henegan looks like they beat him up in a back alley. He knows what they're really saying," Andy said.

"He's telling Henegan to keep him informed about things. People. *We* know he means me," Casey said, "'cause he's asking about people going out on their own."

"You an' Andy," O'Leary corrected.

"Chickenshit sonofabitch can't take me or Bigfoot," Tyler growled.

"Sounds to me like he's looking for information on our case," Andy added.

"An' there's Henegan, crumplin' like a wet Kleenex in a tornado. That man ain't got no spine at all, an' *now* what do we do?"

Casey winced. "You know what we have to do. We have to take this to Kent. I *know* it shows nothing," she yelled over the protests of the other three, "but he ordered it and we can't hide this. I wish we could. He has to have it." She looked up at Carval, standing silently by his computer. "You did the right thing," she said. "I just wish it wasn't…it hadn't been you. Now you're in it with the rest of us."

"He always was," O'Leary said gravely. "As soon as he started takin' snaps of us, an' this'll just bring it forward. Soon as that show opens, he'd've been in the cross-hairs too, 'cause Marcol knows who's goin' after him for copyright in that shot of you from way back. There ain't no way to keep him outta this."

"Yeah, but Marcol wouldn't go in for beating up. Estrolla and Grendon might."

"More than they bargained for," Tyler said.

Casey stared. "What?"

"Tyler took your boy on the mats. So'd I. He didn't do badly. Tyler took a couple of falls – I didn't," O'Leary smirked, "but even though Carval here got thrown all around the place by Tyler an' me, he put up a good show. He'd take them two. You an' Andy can, an' your boy's pretty much up to that level."

"You are?" Casey said. "Why didn't you say? You could've come sparred with us."

"I can't shoot straight with my hands or wrists in plaster, and anyway, sparring's your game."

"Why were you sparring with Tyler at all?"

"Workin' off his bad temper, just like you," O'Leary said to Casey. "An' he had a whole lotta temper to work off."

"Standing right here," Carval said.

O'Leary ignored him. "You know, next time you two have a fight, you c'n fix it on the mats. We'll come watch. It'll be a good show, an' I c'n always watch a good show."

Casey opened and shut her mouth a couple of times, without finding an acceptable answer. O'Leary smiled happily. Carval, having closed his dropped jaw, didn't try to say anything. Andy and Tyler grinned.

"That's not the point," she eventually said. "The *point* is that we need to take this to Kent first thing tomorrow when he's back. Can I have the recording, please? Then if we're done here, I have to go see my dad."

"I'll walk you down," Carval said, after he'd given her a flash drive with the video on it.

"Awwww," O'Leary teased, met by a scorching glare from Casey and a distinctly male smile (safely over Casey's head) from Carval. Her departure carried more stomp than style.

"Do you have to go?" Carval asked, at her car.

"Yeah," she sighed. "He needs me, and I have to explain about the show and timings." She peeped upwards. "I'd rather stay. You know that, don't you?"

Carval hugged her. "You can come back after, if you want. Lemme know." He kissed her firmly. "In case you needed encouragement."

"I'll text," Casey said, and suddenly hugged him back, leaning on him for a moment. Another moment later, she was pulling out, leaving Carval smiling at the tail lights. She'd never leaned in like that before. He lolloped back up the stairs, still smiling.

When he reached his studio, the other three were happily inspecting the photos on the corkboard – his construction sites.

"Not as pretty as us," O'Leary said.

"Bigger, though," Carval batted back. "Even bigger than you."

"Will that be the next one?" Andy asked.

"Probably. I need to wander around a whole lot of sites before I know. Maybe some demolitions, too, for contrast."

Tyler hummed thoughtfully, paying no attention to the conversation. "Casey coming back?" he queried.

"I don't know," Carval replied. "Up to her."

"Mm."

"It's up to her," Carval repeated. "I'm not asking her to choose."

"Good," Tyler stated. "Something else."

"Yeah?"

"Asked Allie if she wanted to come, Wednesday."

Carval choked. Tyler acquired a reddish tinge to his dark skin.

"See, he's fin'lly admittin' they're datin'," O'Leary said. "A'course, we all knew."

"You want Allie to come to the exhibition?" Carval squeaked.

"On Wednesday. With us."

"Why?"

"Estrolla tried to hit on her." Tyler bared teeth. "Was going to educate him. Didn't need to. Allie raised hell in public."

"Good for her," Carval said happily. "Couldn't happen to a nicer guy. Sure, she can come too, but you better bring her with you. I'll make sure Allan puts her on the list, then he'll know who she is so he can help out with the Finisterres if she needs it."

"Thanks," Tyler said.

"Where's your beer?" O'Leary asked. "All this romance makes me thirsty."

"Upstairs. C'mon. Let's have a drink."

***

Casey parked at her father's Brooklyn apartment, and went up, knocking but then simply letting herself in with her key. "Hey, Dad," she announced.

"Catkin! I didn't expect you," he said, "but it's nice to see you."

"I brought dinner," Casey reminded him, concealing how much it hurt that he hadn't expected her, when she'd told him on Saturday that she'd be there tonight. Sober, he was still forgetting things. She'd hoped his memory would be better, but it wasn't happening.

She made dinner while her dad set the table and put out drinks – there was only soda in the fridge, which was a relief – and then, as they ate, came to the point.

"You said you wanted to see the photo exhibition."

"Yes? Oh – yes. The one with you in it," her dad remembered, after an uncomfortable beat.

"There'll be a private viewing for us – the team – on Wednesday, and you're invited."

"I am? That's great."

"I'll need to go straight from work, but Carval – the photographer – said that you should come around eight and see it with me and the rest of the team."

"Sounds good to me. I'll write it in my diary," he said, and, ignoring his half-eaten dinner, hunted out an old-fashioned paper diary in which he scrawled the appointment. "There. That'll be interesting."

It sure will, Casey thought bitterly, *but not how you mean it*. "Are you going to finish your dinner?" she asked.

"Yes. I'm hungry, but I didn't want to forget the exhibition." He sat back down at the table and continued to put away a decent amount of dinner, which comforted Casey. He hadn't been eating properly before rehab. Eating sensible meals was a definite improvement. In a tiny corner of her mind, she thought *see, supporting him is working*, and was insensibly happier. Maybe this wouldn't be such a disaster after all. She could keep her dad and Kent apart, and they'd all get through the exhibition viewing.

Her cheerfulness increased as her dad carried on conversation without losing the thread or digressing randomly. He was more on the ball than for months, despite forgetting that she was coming. She stayed far longer than she'd intended, because she couldn't bear to stop him to leave.

Eventually, she left, two hours after she would normally have gone home, exhausted but content, agreeing to come around on Sunday. Supporting her father had been the right decision. She only needed to keep on doing it. Now that she *knew* it was working, it would be easier, and gradually she could back off as he recovered. He was getting better. Really trying.

Really succeeding.

She drove home smiling, and texted Carval. *Dad in good form. See you tomorrow?*

Shortly, she received back *Sure, at shift end?*

Yes, she sent, and fell asleep completely happy.

***

"Got financials," Tyler said, early on Tuesday.

"For the other account?" Casey exclaimed. "Great."

"Mine," Andy said. "Give them here so I can apply my genius."

Casey blew a raspberry at him.

"Genius? That what you call it?" O'Leary said. "Y'know, you should've been a beancounter, like Pete, you're so into numbers."

"But then I wouldn't have the adrenaline rush of catching criminals, would I?"

"Guess not."

"Shall we go through these financials so we all get the adrenaline rush of catching criminals?" Casey asked with delicate emphasis. "Where are we with the phone records? Andy, you take your beloved numbers. Tyler, you and O'Leary go through the phones and whatever our officers managed to match up to real names."

"What're you goin' to do?"

"See Kent," Casey stated. "Wish me luck. It might be goodbye."

"Naw. He won't dispose of you till after Thursday. Too many questions."

"Gee, thanks," she said sarcastically. "That makes me feel *so* much better." She reluctantly rose from her chair, and trudged across to Kent's office.

"Come," Kent said to her knock. "Clement. What is it?"

"I have to make a report, sir."

"Shut the door." She did. "What is it?"

134

"Uh, sir, you ordered that if there was anything at all we were to report to you…"

"Yes?" Kent snapped, instantly on alert.

"Uh, Carval took this video, sir" – she presented the flash drive, which Kent regarded with the same expression as if a spitting rattlesnake had appeared on his desk – "and though it doesn't show anything conclusive, it looks like Officers Estrolla and Grendon were, um, not pleased with Officer Henegan. They were asking him about people going out alone, and about our latest case, sir."

"You did right to bring it to me and not to take any steps yourself," Kent said judicially. "Do not take any actions. I will review it and if action is warranted, I'll take it. Dismissed."

"Sir." Casey scuttled off as fast as her feet would carry her.

Behind her, Kent regarded the flash drive with loathing, then shut his office door again, plugged it in, and watched the video. By its end, his square, choleric face was scarlet. There was *nothing* that he could officially censure or even take exception to. Reading between the lines, it was perfectly obvious that Estrolla and Grendon were looking for an opportunity to harass the misfits, whether that was in person or by messing with the case, but there wasn't a single word that Kent could haul them in on. "Dammit!" he said aloud. Couldn't he catch a staffing break?

He wished he'd never allowed that damn photographer anywhere *near* his precinct. Everything had started with that. Still, Darla was happy, which was something. He smiled fondly. She'd be delighted on Wednesday, which was more than he would be. Why he couldn't go for a couple of beers and watch a game, leaving her to it…

However. He couldn't manage his precinct and the misfit team without seeing both the full exhibition and the team's reactions, so he'd have to put up with it. He could always have a beer with Garrett of the Third the next evening. In fact, he'd set that up now.

"Garrett? Kent here."

"Hey. How's the prospect of fame?"

Kent growled. "Shut up. It'll be a mess no matter what I do."

Garrett laughed. "What d'you want?"

"I have to go see this exhibition, Wednesday. How about a beer Thursday? I think I'll need a sensible opinion to talk it through."

"Sure, but you're buying."

"For this, I'll buy."

"O'Lunney's at six. See you there."

"Bye."

Kent put the phone down, less aggravated than earlier, then carefully made a copy of the video, sealed the original flash drive in a handy evidence bag, and then, regretting the necessity every second, sent an e-mail to Dr

Renfrew, whose underling, Agent Bergen, was preserving all electronic evidence related to Clement's alcoholic father and his arrest history – and who was an expert in electronic manipulation. Kent didn't think that the flash drive or its video had been altered, but he would make damn sure he checked. If he got this wrong, the union would ensure he never had another chance to deal with the situation.

***

"Where are we with the phones and financials?" Casey asked, recovering herself with every step away from Kent's office.

"Financials are interesting," Andy said cheerfully. "The second account has everything I'd ever want to know."

"Yes? Something we can get a grip on?"

"Yep." He grinned. "It was a pretty active account. Come look."

Casey and the others gathered around Andy's desk.

"Here," he pointed, "we start getting money in. That's a few days after she got the role. The account was opened a long while previously, though, just like Maisie said, but it was used, went quiet, was used, went quiet..."

"Suspicious," Casey commented.

"The payments in are cash deposits."

"That ain't helpful," O'Leary said.

"No. But they're all smallish amounts – five to fifty dollars, mostly ten to twenty. There's a lot of them, and it added up to quite a bit flowing through. But there are these breaks, where nothing happens."

Casey's brow furrowed and her nose wrinkled. "This period of activity corresponds with Isabella's new role, yeah?"

"Yeah."

"Do the others correspond with other roles?"

"You think she was fleecin' the cast in every role?" O'Leary suggested.

"It's a possibility. Small amounts, in cash… you know, it almost feels like workplace collections to me, like for weddings or babies."

"Charity," Tyler said. "Anna and Suzie said she gave to that kids' charity."

"Is that blackmail, or was she just socially conscious?"

"To give, or not to give, that is the question," Andy pontificated.

"No culture," Casey said automatically. "Who'll search out her previous roles? Her parents would know, wouldn't they?"

"Likely they'll have scrapbooks," O'Leary smiled. "Keepin' a record of her success."

Casey consciously stopped her wince and blanked her face. Her mother had done that – not scrapbooks, but there had been all the silly little grade school Christmas programs with Casey as third angel at the back, or tenth sheep. They'd cleared them out. Neither she nor her father could bear to keep them. O'Leary flicked her a quick glance, but said nothing.

"Okay," she decided. "Either me or Tyler needs to ask Isabella's parents, before we talk about the phone records. Toss you for it?"

"Nah. You."

Casey picked up her phone. "Mrs Scarfield, it's Detective Clement."

"Yes, we do have leads, and we're following them all up as quickly as we can."

"It would help us if you could tell us about Betty's previous roles."

"You never know if someone from those productions might have gotten jealous."

"Thank you. I'll visit you right now."

She looked around the team. "I'll go on my own."

"An' I'll walk you down," O'Leary stated.

"Okay."

CHAPTER SIXTEEN

Mrs Scarfield looked as if she hadn't slept since Casey had met her: dark shadows ringing red eyes, her face drawn.

"I'm sorry," Casey said. "I know it's hard for you, and I'll do my best to make this quick and easy."

"Anything to help. You'll catch him, won't you?" she pleaded.

"We're doing everything we can, and this will help a lot." Mrs Scarfield needed all the reassurance and comfort that Casey could offer, and telling her that she could help would give her a purpose. In Casey's extensive experience, that was often more comfort than anything she could say.

"It will? What do you need? I'll – we'll do anything we can."

"We'd like to know what other productions Betty was in. We know how talented she was, and people get jealous of talent." Casey knew all about that from her Academy days, and was still dealing with the fallout. She'd be dealing with a damn sight more of it the following week, she thought bitterly, and pushed the thought away.

"She was," Mrs Scarfield half-wept. She swallowed, and forcibly calmed herself, meeting Casey's sympathetic brown eyes. "I have a scrapbook with all her roles. I'll get it for you."

"Thank you."

Mrs Scarfield dragged off, and drooped back with a large album. "Everything's in here. Do you have to take it away?"

Casey, who had been intending to remove it, looked at her miserable, worried expression, and changed her mind. "No, I don't. I can photograph each page, and that'll work fine. I don't want to take it away unless I absolutely have to."

Mrs Scarfield crumpled with relief. "Thank you," she gulped. "I don't want to lose it, but if you had to…"

"No, I don't," Casey said, snapping each page. It wouldn't be anything like Carval's shots, but that was fine. These pages were evidence, not art. "It's best if it stays with you."

"Thank you," she said again. "It's all we have left..." She started to cry.

Casey photographed as fast as she could, so that she could leave and Mrs Scarfield, trying vainly to hide her grief, could have privacy. It seemed hours until she finished, though objectively it was less than fifteen minutes.

"I'm done," Casey said. "Thank you. I really appreciate your help."

"Anything," Mrs Scarfield repeated. "Please find him."

"We'll do our very best."

Casey hurried back to the precinct with her information. "I got it," she announced to the team. "Every role since she was ten."

"Why?"

"It was quicker," Casey said, in a shutting-down fashion. "I took photos of it, instead of bringing the whole lot."

"Learnin' from your boy," O'Leary said happily.

Casey ignored him. "We can match up roles to the active periods on the second account."

"Send me all the photos," Andy said. "Or give me your phone so I can download them."

Casey passed it over, and went to get a drink. On her return, Andy was already head down in matching dates.

"What did the phone records show?" she asked Tyler.

"Contacts had initials. Match up to the book."

Casey grinned triumphantly. "The book matched to real names. We have a key to the phone calls."

"Yep. Officers working through it."

"Great. Progress. When'll they be done?"

Tyler smiled back at her in a way that indicated that the officers would be working their asses off to finish as fast as the team wanted. "Soon." Or he would know the reason why.

"Now?" she hoped, then grinned. "It's a little early for lunch, though." She thought for a moment. "If we can match phone calls to people, can we match phone calls to deposits?"

"Tried that," Andy said. "It doesn't work."

Casey scowled. "We have lots of little cash deposits. Are there *any* transfers, or checks, or anything that might have more information?"

"Nope."

Casey's scowl would have terrified tyrannosaurs.

"But the book does."

Scowl turned to astonishment. "Why didn't you say that first?"

"I was waiting for the optimum moment," Andy said mischievously. "It was worth it."

"What does the book give us?"

"Waaaaaaaaaalllllllllll," O'Leary drew out.

"My work. I'm telling her," Andy stopped him. "It doesn't say X person gave me X dollars. But it does say – eventually – X person contributed to X cause."

"Cause? Like, charity causes?"

"Exactly like. Her friend Suzie said that she gave to a kids in theatre charity, Act Like A Child. O'Leary set Adamo and Henegan on looking it up" –

"Why they haven't finished the names," Tyler interjected –

"And it fitted the abbreviations in the book."

Casey's brows drew together. "You're saying that she was demanding money from actors which she then gave to Act Like A Child?"

"Yep," Andy said, echoed by O'Leary and Tyler. "That's exactly what we're saying."

"That's new," Casey said blankly. "It'll be hell to prove, too, with those tiny amounts. Everyone'll claim that they were giving to a good cause. They were, too." She pondered further. "Why kill Isabella for that? I mean, sure you don't want to be tapped for cash every five minutes, even if it's only five dollars, but it's…"

"Disproportionate," Andy said. "Yeah. It is."

"It'd be like me killin' Feggetter for comin' round askin' for donations to someone's cute new baby," O'Leary joked.

Casey wouldn't know. The only member of the team who was ever approached for contributions to marriages or births was O'Leary, who then leaned on the others and gave the total to the unlucky requestor. Asking any other team member was invariably avoided, in the same way as the misfit team was generally avoided by the rest of the bullpen. It made everyone's life happier.

"I guess we'll be doing a lot of interviewing. I think we're back to old-fashioned detecting. We wanna find this scarf, and McDonald's smooth, round object that bopped her on the head. We wanna find where she might've had dinner – there weren't any dirty dishes in her apartment, and I don't remember CSU finding any prints there that weren't hers. Did she eat there, or did someone take her out? Or did she eat at Verdicchio when she was waiting tables? No, because she didn't wait tables on afternoons or evenings when she had rehearsal, so it couldn't have been there."

"Maisie said she thought there might be a new boyfriend," O'Leary reminded them. "We know she's a liar, an' we can't believe everythin' she's sayin', but mebbe there's somethin' in that. Or mebbe she's makin' more outta somethin' than there was."

"Bring her in?"

"Naw," the big man said. "We gotta search the props at the theatre first, an' interview all them actors."

"Oh, joy," Casey said dryly, but her eyes lit up.

"You go make nice with CSU" – the team laughed – "an' get them to meet us there. We'll all have some fun searchin', an' mebbe I'll have a nice chat with my pal Ron. I wanna talk about what he knew about Isabella, now that we know more."

"Call him and see when the next rehearsal is, so we don't miss the actors," Casey said. "Who'll give our officers the good news about interviewing?"

"Me," Tyler said.

"'Kay."

Casey suspected that Tyler was planning a motivational session with their four officers, and she didn't want to be anywhere near it. Tyler's motivational style owed more to a drill sergeant than to Dale Carnegie, and Casey preferred to induce terror less loudly. In the background, she could hear O'Leary's comforting folksiness talking to Ron-the-gnome, and evidently getting satisfactory results. Over to one side, Tyler was issuing terse orders, and receiving only instant agreement.

Casey herself called CSU, and the hapless Evan, who couldn't think of an excuse fast enough. She thought it would be good for him to get out more. It was positively her public duty to help him to have some more time outdoors and sunshine, or at least scenery of the outdoors and spotlights pretending to be sunshine. If he actually went out in real sunshine he might faint from the unexpected Vitamin D overload.

"Okay," O'Leary said. "Let's go search these here props. CSU meetin' us there?"

"Yep. Evan again."

"He'll turn into ash like a vampire iffen he goes out much more."

Casey smirked. "That'd be interesting, but I think you're confusing him with McDonald."

"Mebbe," O'Leary said, unperturbed, "or mebbe they're related."

Casey shuddered. "Don't give me nightmares. Come on. Searching time. Are the others coming?"

"Yep." O'Leary looked around. "An' there's Estrolla, givin' us the evil eye again. Don' he get tired of bein' an asshole?"

"No, but who cares? He's not bothering us, and Fremont and Larson'll keep him off Henegan for the moment. Kent can deal with him. He's not our problem – orders, remember?"

"Yeah."

The other two joined them. "C'n we get lunch on the way?" O'Leary whined, echoed by his stomach.

"Sure. There's that sandwich shop by the theatre, and while we're there we can ask if Isabella ate there or if they have cameras."

"Good plan."

After the server at the sandwich shop had surmounted his admiration of the sheer size of O'Leary's lunch requirement, he proved to be quite conversational.

"Yes'm, we sure do have cameras," he said as he put together the sandwiches. "The manager's scared we get robbed, so he had them put in."

"Do you keep the footage?"

"For a week, then it's recorded over."

"Good. We'll need the footage for Thursday and Friday. Can you show us what areas are covered?" Andy asked.

"Sure. I don't know if I can give you the recordings, though. I gotta ask the manager. Can I call him? He's not here – he'll come in at around two." It was barely a quarter after twelve.

"Yes, call him."

The server had a brief conversation. "He says he'll need a warrant, but I should make sure that the recording is taken out and locked away so it can't be lost. Will that be okay?"

"Sure," O'Leary rumbled reassuringly. "That'll be fine." He took a huge bite of sandwich, and smiled blissfully. "You do good stuff here," he mumbled.

"I'll come watch you secure the recording," Andy said helpfully, and trotted off behind the server to ensure that everything was done properly and the recording was locked away until it could be handed over. "Thanks," he said. "Did you see anything or anyone unusual, Thursday or Friday?"

"We close at four," the server said, "but I don't remember anything."

"Did you see this woman ever?" Andy carried on, passing over a photo of Isabella.

"No, I don't remember her."

"Okay, thanks."

They arrived at the theatre and knocked on the stage door.

Ron poked his wrinkled head around the door, rather like an elderly giant tortoise, and managed a half smile. "Hi. Four of you?"

"Yeah," O'Leary said, "an' the same guy from CSU as last time we visited. These three here an' CSU are goin' to have a li'l look at the props, an' you 'n' me c'n have another talk about Isabella. We got some more information, an' I wanna check it with you, seein' as you knew her best."

"I want them caught, whoever it was," Ron drooped. "She was a sweet girl."

"Sure you do," O'Leary reassured, "an' we wanna catch them. Let's you 'n' me have a nice cosy chat, an' that'll get us closer."

"I'll wait for Evan – our CSU guy. If you'll show Detectives Chee and Tyler where all the props are kept, Evan and I'll catch them up." Casey smiled. "Where am I going, or should I come find you when he gets here?"

"Find me," Ron said. "I'll steer you the right way. We got a lot of props, so you'll be busy."

"When you're finished with O'Leary, send him our way. He can cover a lot of ground when we're searching."

"I do the heavy liftin'," O'Leary said, and flexed a tree-sized bicep.

Ron managed a laugh. "Got a future in comedy, you have."

"They only ever let me be the strongman," O'Leary pouted. "Typecastin'. 'T ain't fair."

"That's because you're good at it," Casey said briskly. "Here's Evan, before you start to cry and drown us all." She grinned. "Hey, Evan."

"Hi, Casey, O'Leary, Mr O'Toole."

"Okay," Casey said to Ron. "Since Evan's here, could you show us where the props are, and we'll start while Detective O'Leary talks to you."

"Sure." Ron led them through a maze of backstage tunnels, until they reached a room marked, helpfully, *Props*. "Most of them are here," he explained. "When you're done here, I'll show you where the rest are – they're a bit scattered."

"Thanks," Casey said.

"Okay," O'Leary rumbled as Ron returned. "Let's you 'n' me have a nice chat about Isabella." He smiled hopefully. "C'n I get a coffee with you?"

"Yeah, sure. I could use a cup of tea."

O'Leary squashed into one of Ron's chairs, and tried to look unthreatening. "We've had a chance to look into all Isabella's family an' friends. I wanted to ask you about her again, 'cause we're confused. Seems like Isabella was a real nice, helpful sort. Her friends said she did community productions with them, an' though it sounds like she was head 'n' shoulders above them talent-wise – bit like I'm head 'n' shoulders above Casey height-wise" – Ron chortled happily, and noticeably relaxed – "she never made much of it, just played nice."

"She never put on airs with me," Ron agreed. "She was trying hard to learn everything she could, and she used to listen to my stories – paid attention."

"What sorta stories?"

"I been around here a longish time, and I've seen them come and go. She was interested in what makes a great actor, obviously, and what keeps you in work."

"She worked pretty hard to fund her tuition, we heard – dead end jobs an' all. Didn't want to leech off her parents."

"That's – that *was* – Isabella. Wanted to make it in her own right. Anyways, she was pretty interested. Always asking me about the other actors and directors that I'd seen."

O'Leary hummed encouragingly. "Is that diff'rent ones or some of the guys in this production?"

"Both, I guess. You see a lot of the same faces. Experimental stuff, 'specially Shakespeare, isn't to everyone's taste."

The big cop assumed a hopeful expression. "I like stories," he wheedled. "C'n you tell me a few about the guys in this production, same as you told Isabella?"

Ron regarded him cynically. "Looking for motives?"

"That's what we do," O'Leary said without a single tinge of embarrassment. "C'mon. Tell me the stories."

"Say a word and I'll have you fired," came from the door, where Carl Heyer stood foursquare, furious-faced. Ron cringed.

"You try stoppin' him assistin' the NYPD, an' *you'll* be arrested for obstruction," O'Leary said flatly. "Don't think I won't. An' now I'm *sure* there's some good intelligence in those stories, 'cause you wouldn't be tryin' to prevent them comin' out if there wasn't." He stood to his full, intimidating height, scowling down.

Try to hide it as he might, Heyer shivered and hunched defensively. "You can't" –

"Sure I can. You got no right to stop us investigatin', an' I don't give a crap iffen you're the director. You could be Steven Spielberg an' I'd arrest you iffen you obstructed me. An' it won't be me you'll deal with, it'll be Casey – Detective Clement. You don't want that."

"The hell I don't. Some two-bit girl cop?"

"The senior detective on our team," O'Leary said coldly. "Best solve rate in the NYPD. She don't pull any punches. You don't want to go there," he repeated with absolute sincerity.

"O'Leary," Casey herself called, turning up to Ron's room. "O'Leary – what's going on here?" Her tone hit absolute zero at the scene.

"Mr Heyer here doesn't want Ron tellin' me stories about the actors," O'Leary rumbled ominously. "Threatened to fire him iffen he did."

"He doesn't?" Casey regarded Heyer with less enthusiasm than she would have regarded a cockroach. "He's obstructing our investigation? Cuff him, and call Fremont to take him in and have him processed. He can wait for me in a cell." The dead flat voice said that Heyer had already been forgotten.

"You can't do that!" Heyer yelled.

"I can. Obstruction is a crime. Jail time might teach you better." She looked at O'Leary. "Get him out of here." A tiny wriggle of her eyebrows told the big man that something much more important had happened. He pulled out his phone and opened the contacts, to Heyer's horror.

"No! I didn't mean" –

"You thought you could coerce Mr O'Toole here into not co-operating by threatening his job," Casey said. "You thought wrong. How long will your job last if you're in a cell? I don't see the Finisterres getting you out, because as soon as I tell them you're obstructing the investigation into Isabella's death – *their* protégée – you'll be toast."

"I won't! It was just a" –

"Joke?" O'Leary snapped. "It didn't sound like a joke to me. I don't see anyone laughin'. I see Mr O'Toole lookin' downright frightened. That wasn't a *joke*."

"I can assure you I'm not joking," Casey bit. "Get Fremont here asap."

O'Leary looked at her face, and called. "Fremont. O'Leary here. Get to the Terpsichore theatre as fast as you c'n run. We got an arrest for you to take into Processing and Holding."

"Yessir," Fremont said, shocked into the *sir* by O'Leary's harshness. "On my way already."

"Turn around," Casey said, and put the cuffs on Heyer. He gobbled louder than a Thanksgiving turkey on the way to the chopping block, and didn't shut up until Fremont arrived and marched him off.

"You didn't cut him any slack," Ron wobbled.

"Iffen he tries anythin', let us know," O'Leary said. "We'll show him the error of his ways again."

Casey, half-hidden behind O'Leary, tapped out a text, and then put her phone away. "Mr O'Toole," she said with a reassuring smile, "can I borrow O'Leary for a few minutes? I'll give him back to you to listen to your information as soon as I can."

"Sure," Ron agreed, reacting to Casey's infectious smile. "I think I'll have another cup of tea. Steady my nerves."

"I didn't think you were British?" she teased gently. "All this tea – don't go to Boston or they'll float you in the harbour."

Ron chortled, restored. "I spent some time in London, and got a taste for it."

"Better you than me," Casey said. "I'll stick to coffee. I'll take O'Leary, but I'll send him back in a couple of minutes. Your information'll be really helpful to get a better view of Isabella and the other actors."

CHAPTER SEVENTEEN

"What's up?" O'Leary asked, as soon as they were out of earshot.

"We found something that might have been used to hit Isabella. A crystal ball type thing, buried right at the bottom of a props box. It's been wiped, but it's smeary. Evan's bagged and tagged it. We've found something that might be Isabella's scarf, but there are about fifty flimsy colourful scarves in there, so Evan'll have to bag and tag every single one." She grinned, face alight. "But it's progress."

"Sure is."

"CSU'll take ages, though," she grumped.

"Waal, that's as may be."

"I don't want to wait," Casey sulked. "I want to interview" –

"You mean interrogate" –

"Shut up – all those actors. And that asshole Heyer."

"Will you charge him?"

"No. I sent Fremont a text not to charge him – yet. I could. We have cause. But I want him to talk, and if I don't charge him yet we might force some information out of him, 'specially if he's spent some time in Holding with all the other dirtbags."

"Sneaky."

"We need something more than we've just found."

"Lemme go back an' chat with Ron. Sounds like there's plenty there."

"Yeah. We'll need all of it to interview the actors."

"Yup," O'Leary said happily. "I do like terrorisin'."

"You have to set a good example to the uniforms, remember?"

O'Leary pouted. "Why'd I agree to that?"

"You suggested it. I thought we could give the easy actors to our uniforms, but no, you wanted to pair them off with us."

"Why didn't you stop me?"

"'Cause it's like trying to stop an earthquake. It doesn't work." She smirked up at her giant partner. "All these years of it not working taught me something." The smirk altered to a smile. "You go back and keep Ron happy. I'll come find you if we finish this before you do, and if not, you and Ron come find us."

"Deal," O'Leary agreed, and tromped back to Ron's cosy den.

"You done with your spitfire?" Ron asked, eyes dancing. "She really stuck it to Mr Heyer."

"He shouldn't've tried to interfere," O'Leary said amiably. "She don't like that much, an' nor do I."

"I got that." Ron swallowed a gulp of tea. "Want another coffee?"

"Please. C'n we go back to the stories?"

Ron rapidly produced another large mug of coffee for O'Leary to wrap his paws around, and shifted into a comfortable story-telling position. "Let's start with Mr Heyer," he began. Malice flashed in his face. "Seeing as he can't bully me any more – I need to keep this job to make my rent – you can have the whole story. I was scared to tell it last time."

O'Leary leaned forward and almost waggled his ears with interest.

"Heyer thinks he's God," Ron opened. "Whatever he wants, that's what's gotta happen, right then and there. As soon as it doesn't, or someone doesn't get it first time, he loses it. Shouting, screaming – he even throws things around – squaring up to folks. He has a helluva temper, and he doesn't hold back."

"Mm? I knew he was gettin' angry with Isabella."

"Yeah. He couldn't stand that the Finisterres could force him to do something he didn't want to, so he took it out on her. She wasn't the first. He did that to most of the actors. If someone had killed him, you'd have most of the theatre world lining up to celebrate – and three-quarters of 'em would have a motive." Ron paused for breath. "Isabella didn't do anything to annoy him except exist. She never went near him for her charity collections – she had that much sense."

"Charity collections?"

"Oh, sure. Everyone knew that she was big into getting kids into theatre, and every so often she'd go around with a little book and try 'n' get a few dollars from everybody to pass on. I think – yeah. Act Like A Child, it was. You could get in touch with them."

"Yup," O'Leary said, and wrote it down.

"But she never went near Heyer that I saw."

"Don't blame her. You said he got mad with her. Did he ever come on to her?"

"Him? No. She wasn't his type. That Dacia, she's his type, and the boys. Those four youngsters, they'd be right up his alley, but they make damn sure they're always together when he's about."

O'Leary's caterpillar eyebrows almost met his buzz cut. "For real?"

"Yeah. Heyer's keen on pretty men as well as pretty women."

"Casting couch?" O'Leary asked.

Ron shrugged. "I don't know, but it wouldn't surprise me."

"Waal, I c'n see why he'd be in someone's cross-hairs, but that don't explain Isabella." O'Leary's forehead creased. "You said you never saw her go near Heyer?" Ron nodded. "Could she have tried an' you didn't know?"

"Guess so. I'm not here twenty-four/seven and I don't see or hear everything."

"'Kay. That's Heyer?"

"Yeah."

"What about the rest of them?"

"Julius is gay, but I didn't see Isabella having a problem with him 'cause of that."

"'Cause of other things?"

"Nup. She tapped him for contributions, but he always paid up with a smile. Never heard anything bad about Julius. He didn't come on to the other actors – he said once that he never fouled his own nest. Max, he's a sad story. He used to be a really good actor, Broadway and everything, but then his wife died and he started to rely on a drop or three of liquid help."

O'Leary nodded. He surely did know, and thanked the heavens and all the gods of interviewing that he was hearing this, not Casey. He could warn her before she interviewed Max – and she'd insist on doing that to prove to herself and everyone around her that her pa's issues wouldn't make any difference to her work.

"Heyer beat up on him a lot, which didn't help, and Max got put in a tank a couple of times, but I think Isabella got him out, 'cause he looked at her like she was the Second Coming and he suddenly seemed to be trying to keep it together. He paid up his contributions every time, no fuss."

Worse and worse, thought O'Leary, where Casey was concerned. "No stories about him? Awww."

"He's another one who'd happily have seen Heyer dead, centre stage, but I don't know any reason he would have killed Isabella." Abruptly Ron's face twisted. "Cordell's another matter."

"Mm?" O'Leary hummed enquiringly. "What's the problem with him?"

"He hit on Isabella," Ron said blackly. "She turned him down, and she was pretty mean about it."

"Isabella? Mean?" O'Leary exclaimed, thinking to himself that they'd known she couldn't be as much of a saint as she'd been made out to be.

"It's the only time I saw her furious. She was spitting fire – I'd never heard her use language like it. She was such a *nice* girl."

"What happened?"

Ron squirmed.

"How did you know, anyways?"

"She came running in here crying her eyes out." Ron admitted. O'Leary concealed his slight scepticism – Isabella was an actor, after all, and crying on demand was a pretty standard skill. "She couldn't stop. All her words poured out." He shuddered. "There were marks on her arms where he'd grabbed her."

Could be make-up, O'Leary thought cynically, without letting it show on his face. "Nasty stuff. 'T ain't no way to behave," he said aloud.

"Nope. Anyways, she told me all about it, and what she'd said to him, and then she went home with that sister of hers. I dunno what happened after that, but at the next rehearsal I guess he must've apologised, 'cause I didn't hear about any more hassle."

"Did Cordell pay any contributions to them charities?"

"I didn't hear that he didn't, but I dunno," Ron said.

"Did you?"

"She didn't ask me often." Ron wriggled uncomfortably. "I don't have a lot to give. Gave her a coupla dollars when I could, but she never pushed me."

O'Leary suddenly played back what Ron had said. "Her sis was here?" he queried.

"Oh, sure. She showed up a lot. Sneaked in, sat somewhere Heyer couldn't see her. Theatre-mad, she was."

"She knew about Cordell hitting on Isabella?"

"Could've. I don't remember if she was there – nope, she couldn't've been, 'cause if she was, Isabella would most likely have gone to her."

"You'd think," O'Leary agreed. "Nice as you are" – he grinned – "I'd'a wanted my sis if it was me."

"Me too," Ron said.

"Did her sis ever come talk to you?"

"Nah. She was star-struck, and I'm not a star. She hung around Julius if she could – and Cordell, until Isabella lost it with him."

"Julius?"

"He's a good-looking guy. I don't think anyone told her he's gay. She was pretty keen on the four that play the fairies, but they weren't interested in her." Ron wrinkled his face. "Fact is, no-one was interested in her, but they were all friends with Isabella, except Heyer, Dacia and Cordell."

"What did her sis think of that?"

Ron wrinkled himself into a hundred-year-old tortoise. "Dunno," he said slowly. "She said all the right things to Isabella, but…"

"Mm?"

"Sometimes I caught a look, like she was annoyed that Isabella got all the attention."

"Int'restin'," O'Leary mused, and changed the subject for the moment. "What about Vincent? He looked like he might be a boxer. I do some sparrin', y'know."

"Why am I not surprised?" Ron wondered, and grinned at him. "If Vincent was a boxer, he isn't now. He's a fine character actor. Got a lived-in face."

"Sure does. Ain't nothin' wrong with that. I got a lived-in face too."

"Vincent's a good guy. Don't hear anything bad about him."

"Did he contribute?"

"Yeah. Never missed."

"Thanks," O'Leary said. "That's been really helpful." He smiled. "Let's go help Casey find the next set of props."

"Okay," Ron said, drained his tea, and led O'Leary through the maze again. They found Casey, Andy, Tyler, and Evan of CSU, apparently disoriented by being out of his lab for more than three hours at a time, still searching through endless boxes, shelves and closets. A pile of evidence bags was stacked up on a small table.

"Finally joining us?" Andy asked cynically. "We're almost done here."

"There's one more room," Ron pointed out.

"Casey 'n' me'll start there," O'Leary said. "I'll do the top an' she c'n do the bottom, seein' as that's all she c'n reach. Show us where?"

Ron did, and then left, no doubt to find another cup of tea.

"What did you find out?" Casey asked.

"How'd you know there was anythin'?" O'Leary teased.

"You're looking smug. You got a lot from Ron, didn't you?"

"Sure did," O'Leary said, and downloaded everything as they started to search the room. Casey stiffened as he relayed the details about Maxwell, but said nothing.

"Maisie hung around the theatre?" Casey said quietly, focusing on a key point. "She didn't mention that."

"Maisie didn't mention a whole bunch of things. I'm beginnin' to think she's hidin' a lot of stuff."

"Her and Cordell. We'll have some fun with Cordell." She smiled viciously. "That tale from Ron – and yes, it could've been staged," she said to O'Leary's rumble – "goes right along with what the Finisterres said."

"So far, them and Gallagher are the only two tellin' us the truth. An' Ron, most likely."

"Likely, but not certain yet. I want to have a nice long chat with Heyer." she said, rifling through a box of masks. "We'll get Maisie, Julius and Cordell in first off. Second round, Max, Vincent, and two of the four fairies. We'll do Heyer when we get back to the precinct today."

"Sounds" – O'Leary's approval was interrupted by Casey's phone ringing.

"Clement," she rapped. "What? When? Get over to the ER and stay with her until I get there – you already are? Good." She swiped off. "That was Fremont. Maisie was attacked earlier this afternoon. When she regained consciousness, she asked for us to be contacted and the hospital called the precinct. Fremont got going right away and then called me."

"Good man, that Fremont."

"Yeah. Larson's doing well, too."

"Too scared of you not to," O'Leary teased. Casey made a rude gesture. "Guess we'd better be goin'?"

"Yeah. Let's tell the others – and Ron – and get gone."

"I'll find Ron. You tell the rest. Seeya outside."

Casey hurried back to the props room and briefed them. "I'll see you all back at the precinct," she wound up, and hustled out to find O'Leary already there.

"Fastest to walk back to the precinct an' pick up my SUV," he said. "I'll go, an' I'll pick you up on the way. I c'n go a lot faster than you."

"I'll be on Amsterdam."

O'Leary strode off, and Casey hurried towards Amsterdam. She really didn't like that just as they were getting somewhere, Maisie had been attacked. It didn't feel coincidental. She called Fremont. "You at the ER?"

"Yes'm," Fremont said briskly. "I spoke to the attending physician and I'm outside Maisie's room. She doesn't look great, but they say she'll be fine. Nothing life-threatening."

"What happened to her?"

"I'm not sure." Casey made an unhappy noise. "The doctor said, um, where I could hear, she's badly bruised with a big bump on her head" – Casey was sure that was a translation of medical-speak for brevity's benefit (and hers) – "but they can't tell how she got the bruises. She's also got a cracked rib, they say, but they don't know how."

Casey had a sudden, horrible memory of being beaten up by Sackson, and the boots to her ribs then. "Not nice," she said with huge understatement. "O'Leary and I are on our way. Stay put."

"Yes'm. She's asleep – doped, I think. Painkillers," he added hastily. "There's an IV in her arm."

O'Leary's SUV stopped beside Casey only a moment or two later, and she scrambled in. "Let's go. Fremont gave me what he had, but there's not much."

"Naw?"

"She's asleep. We'll need to wait till she wakes up – or the morphine wears off."

O'Leary parked, and they went into the hospital. The receptionist pointed them towards Maisie's room, outside which Fremont was leaning on the wall. He straightened up in a hurry when he heard the thumping of O'Leary's size fifteens, but came to attention when he saw Casey.

"She hasn't even blinked, ma'am," he said.

"Naw? She must be wakin' up soon. Where's a nurse or someone we c'n ask?"

"I'll go find one," Fremont said hurriedly, on catching their twin hard stares and taking the hint. He didn't run down the corridor, but he certainly walked fast. He returned shortly, with a smallish, chubby attending physician in a wrinkled white coat. "This is Dr Cairns," he said. "He admitted Maisie."

"Hey. I'm Detective Clement, and this is Detective O'Leary."

"Not Detective Grizzly Bear?" the doctor asked, with a sly smile.

"Only on Saturdays," O'Leary said happily.

"Visit the Zoo on your own time, O'Leary," Casey said. "Dr Cairns, Maisie Scarfield is a witness in a homicide we're investigating."

"Oh my God," the doctor said, turning serious in an instant. "I'm sorry."

"When's Maisie likely to wake up?" Casey asked.

"Soon, but that means any time from now to a couple of hours from now." He gazed apologetically at them. "It's not a precise science, and she's had a rough time."

"I see." Casey thought for a second. "Fremont, you stay here, and call me as soon as she wakes up."

"Yes'm."

Casey and O'Leary trudged out of the hospital and started back to the precinct. Two hundred yards down Broadway, Casey's phone rang. "Clement."

"Detective, it's me. Fremont. Maisie's waking up."

"Thanks." She swiped off. "Better turn around. She's waking up."

"Couldn't she have done that ten minutes ago? Now I gotta go around an' find parkin' again."

"Sympathy," Casey said, unsympathetically.

A few minutes later they were back in the corridor outside Maisie's room. Dr Cairns was in with her, explaining her injuries. The cops unashamedly listened in.

"You're badly bruised, and you have a cracked rib. There's a nasty lump on your head, but no fracture. You've been lucky. Try to rest, and I'll come back later."

Dr Cairns being finished, Casey tapped on the door and walked in. "Maisie, how're you feeling?"

"Hurts," Maisie whimpered. The IV was still in her arm, though there wasn't a tube in her nose or any other medical interventions. The monitors drew their regular green traces in perfect order.

"I bet. Can you tell me what happened?" She managed to summon up sympathy. O'Leary sidled in without drawing attention to himself.

"Someone shoved me in the back," she whined. "Really shoved, and I fell over, and then I think he stomped on me really hard."

"He? Did you see him?"

"No," Maisie sniffled. "It was so hard I thought it must be a man – oh. No heels." She looked at Casey for approval.

"That's good," Casey complimented. "What else can you remember? We wanna get whoever it was. Where did they push you?"

Maisie thought. "High up. Like, between my shoulders, not my waist."

"We'll ask the attending if there's a bruise there, if that's okay with you?"

"Sure. You'll catch him, won't you? If you'll catch him then I want the doctor to tell you everything that'll help."

"That'll be helpful."

"I'll go get him," O'Leary said, "an' then you c'n tell him yourself. That'll be good, 'cause then there's no delay." He smiled warmly at Maisie.

"They pushed you, and you fell. What made you fall?"

"Being pushed," Maisie said.

"Nothing else?"

"Uh…"

"Take your time. I know it's a nasty thing to remember, but try." Casey felt like she was talking to a small child, which wasn't helped by Maisie's coloured hair against the white, pained face over the flowered cotton hospital gown.

Maisie's hands gripped the cover as she thought. "Uh…there was this hard push, and then I thought I tripped on the sidewalk, like on a raised edge or something." She thought again. "Yeah. Like I tripped. I fell, and I was totally shocked 'cause it hurt – my knees are all cut up and they had to X-ray my wrists in case I'd broken something when I hit the floor."

"Ow," Casey sympathised. "I get what you mean. It takes a minute or two to pull yourself together when you fall."

"Yeah. But then it was like someone trampled right over me." Indignation rose. "I know it's busy in Manhattan, but hell, you don't step on people and kick them!"

"They kicked you?"

"Yes!"

"Someone shoved you, kicked you and stepped on you. Where did this happen?"

"Outside the office. I went out to get lunch – late 'cause we were busy – and it all happened and then Jim – he's from the office," she added, "went out for a cigarette" – she made a disgusted face – "and saw me. He called the ambulance."

"Lucky he did," Casey said. "You said late. What time?"

"Quarter of two, I guess. Usually I go out around quarter after one."

Casey considered. "Did you see anything or anyone unusual when you went out, before you were shoved?"

Maisie shook her head, winced, and said, "No. I didn't notice anything. I was in a hurry 'cause I was hungry."

"Thank you." Casey could hear O'Leary's tread approaching. "Is there anything else at all that you can remember?"

"No."

"Okay," Casey repeated. "Do you know why anyone would want to attack you?"

Maisie flinched, then looked defiantly at Casey. "No." Casey looked levelly back at her, and waited.

CHAPTER EIGHTEEN

"Now, Miss Scarfield." Dr Cairns bustled in at exactly the wrong moment, "Detective O'Leary says that you're happy for me to tell the detectives about your injuries?"

Casey rigorously controlled her face and feelings, though she would cheerfully have lacerated Dr Cairns for ruining the tension she'd deliberately established.

Maisie seized the moment. "Yes. I don't care if it was some random mugger, I want them caught."

"Detectives, Miss Scarfield has a cracked rib and some nasty bruising, with a large contusion on her head, though there's no concussion and the skull is intact. There's nothing too serious, but we're giving her some painkillers."

"Dr Cairns," Casey said, "I'm sure you have other patients to see. Could we come talk to you about the details when we're finished with Maisie?"

Dr Cairns appeared to realise, possibly from Casey's terse tone, that he'd interrupted something important. "Sure," he agreed. "Someone'll page me if you ask them."

"Thank you." Casey turned back to Maisie. "Do you know why anyone would attack you?"

"I already said *no*." The monitors showed her pulse rate kicking up.

"I don't believe you," Casey bit. "This wasn't a mugging. You haven't mentioned your purse, wallet or phone being stolen, and you'd have told me that right off the bat. Random psychos don't choose this area at lunchtime – they go for the subway and push people in front of trains, or stab them. They don't do shoving and kicking. Why don't you try again, with the truth?"

Maisie cowered. O'Leary regarded her with a flat, unfriendly gaze that matched Casey's irritated demeanour. "Tell the truth," he grated, at his most monstrously intimidating.

"I don't *know*," Maisie wailed.

"You have an idea," Casey said icily. "Unless you want the next place you go to be the morgue" – Maisie gasped – "or a cell, start telling the truth. *All* the truth, not some made-up nonsense to feed your sense of drama. You're not an actor and your sister's death isn't a play. She won't get up and take a bow and nor will you." She remembered something. "What were you doing hanging around the theatre all the time? Is that how you knew some of the actors weren't squeaky clean? It wasn't Isabella who told you, was it?" She stopped, projecting cold intimidation.

"She did!" Maisie cried. "She *did!*"

"Who did you tell?" O'Leary probed.

Maisie fell silent, the only sound the high-pitched, rapid beeping of the monitor. Her heart rate remained sky-high.

"You said something," Casey said. "How much did you say?" She flicked a glance at O'Leary. "Were you trying to make yourself more interesting to everyone? Trying to make sure the attention was on you, same as you did by making up stories about David Gallagher? Seems to be a theme with you – and this time you got your sister killed and almost yourself."

Maisie burst into hysterical tears. A middle-aged nurse came running in. "What's going on here?" she scolded. "You're upsetting Miss Scarfield."

"Miss Scarfield," said Casey with chilling formality, "is providing information in her *sister's* murder investigation. The attending physician advised she has no serious injuries and therefore no reason not to talk to us." She stared the nurse down. "We assumed that she would want her sister's murderer caught, especially as she herself has been assaulted." Casey let the nurse take the unstated implication, that the assailant had been the murderer.

"Uh," the nurse said. "Uh, I guess that would be pretty upsetting." She turned to Maisie, who was still snuffling. "Do you need some more pain meds to help you get through it?"

"No," Maisie whimpered.

"You call me if you do, you poor thing." The nurse departed, casting Casey a considerably friendlier and more respectful look.

"Let's try that again," Casey clipped. "What did you say, who did you say it to, where were you, and who might have overheard?" The tears trailing down Maisie's face didn't impress her at all.

"Betty said that there was a lot going on," Maisie whined. "Nobody liked anybody except the four young guys. She said there was stuff between the four main old guys. That director was such a sonofabitch and the understudy was a total bitch herself and it was *obvious* they were sleeping together though the director would've slept with a goat if it flattered him" – O'Leary muffled a chuckle – "anyway, Betty said that she'd done some digging so she didn't tread on any toes because if you make trouble you never get another role, and I said if it was that bad, people ought to know about it so *they* didn't get any more parts and she got angry and told me to keep my nose out and stop ruining her big break" – she finally stopped to breathe.

"An'?" O'Leary prompted, when she didn't continue, shamefaced and scarlet-cheeked.

"I...I...I got angry too so I yelled at her and everybody would've heard because the director yelled at us both for interrupting the rehearsal" –

"When was this?" Casey fired.

Maisie counted back on her fingers. "Thursday last week."

"An' there was a rehearsal that day?"

"Yes, but at the end of it the director said that they'd miss the next day because he needed a break from all of them and then he was horrible to Betty and then he told me if he saw me in the theatre ever again he'd have me thrown out and arrested for trespassing and everyone heard that too and nobody was even sorry for me!"

Casey was on Heyer's side for that one. She sure wasn't sorry for Maisie, who'd been acting like a spoiled toddler from moment one.

"On Thursday, you told the entire cast that Betty knew things about them which could ruin their careers?"

Maisie nodded.

"It didn't occur to you to tell us this, when your sister was *murdered* the same night?"

"It wasn't my *fault!*" Maisie wailed. The detectives said nothing, meaningfully. "It wasn't!"

"You've cost us almost a week, leading us down false trails and concealing relevant information, because you were jealous of your sister's talent and you didn't like her boyfriend." Casey turned away contemptuously. "I'll ask the doctor to document your bruises in case there's anything that will help us identify your attacker. I don't expect there will be, but right now *anything* would help."

"Iffen you think of *anythin'* that might help, however bad it makes you look, you tell us," O'Leary ordered. "Iffen you play any more of these games, we'll be askin' your mom an' pop to tell us."

"No!" Maisie begged.

"Betty'd had a meal an' a drink before she was killed. Who'd she go to dinner with? You said you thought she might have a new boyfriend, back before you started tellin' us all them lies an' dumb stories."

"I don't know! We were going to go home and then she said she didn't want to go with me 'cause she was still totally mad with me and she went back into the theatre and I never saw her again." This time, Maisie's tears were heartbroken. The cops weren't convinced.

"She went back into the theatre?" Casey said. "You'd come out?"

"That director was going to throw me out physically. He got right up in my face and I was scared and Betty came out with me but she was mad."

I'm not surprised, Casey thought cynically. As if Isabella-Betty hadn't had enough problems with Heyer, her over-dramatic, jealous sister had ensured that he'd had another reason to treat her badly.

"You don't know who she might have seen that evening?"

"No. If I did I would tell you!" Casey raised her eyebrows. "I *would!* I want him caught." O'Leary's eyebrows also rose. "I *do!*"

"One last question," Casey said. "Was Betty wearing a scarf that Thursday?"

"Uh, yes. She got it in the thrift shop. Red, navy, white, in those funny little comma shaped patterns."

"Thanks. If you think of anything else at all, you tell us right away."

"Okay," Maisie capitulated.

***

"Waal, we're lookin' at the cast again," O'Leary said as they drove down from the hospital back to the Thirty-Sixth. "Great. All them actors, all lyin' through them lovely white teeth."

"Yeah. But we'll start with Heyer."

"There's a man with a whole lotta 'splainin' to do." O'Leary's satisfied smile could have lit Broadway. "It's gonna be fun."

"I could use some. We have to go see Carval's exhibition with Kent tomorrow night." Casey sighed. "Do you think I can catch stomach flu before then?"

"Naw. You c'n get through it."

"At least Dad won't be there when Kent is."

"Yup. An' if he makes any trouble, I'll pick him up an' take him out."

"Kent or Dad?" she asked bitterly.

"Whoever won't fire me in the mornin'."

She didn't even raise a flicker of a smile. "Let's get back. It's way after five, and we need to talk about all we've learned today and work out next steps."

"Heyer," O'Leary said happily.

"Not tonight. I'll let him stew for the twenty-four hours I can hold him. We'll grill him tomorrow."

"I do like a good barbecue."

"Three oxen and a bear, isn't that it?" But there was a dragging at the back of her voice, which O'Leary heard.

"That's my share. You c'n have a hot dog. 'S all your teeny li'l stomach c'n take."

"Yeah."

"C'mon. What you need is some nice terrorisin', an' you've got plenty of that comin' up."

"I guess."

"Anyways, we're back. Let's go finish up the day an' then if you want we'll go get a beer, or you c'n snuggle up with your boy an' forget about it. That's what I'd do, iffen I was you."

"If you're snuggling up with Carval, Pete'll be upset."

O'Leary laughed. "You c'n keep your Carval. I'll keep my Pete."

***

Back in the bullpen, the team gathered around Casey's murder board and debriefed. Nothing more had come from the search of the props, but Evan had gone back to CSU with plenty to do.

"Did CSU say how long they'd take?" Casey asked.

"Nah. Do it as soon as they can."

"What about Maisie?" Andy asked.

"She got attacked outside her office. We need to get any street cam footage, to see if we can identify the attacker."

"I'll get it started before we quit for the day," Andy said.

"Thanks. In shocking news, Maisie didn't tell us everything – and neither did Heyer."

"I'm shocked," Andy droned. "Shocked, I say."

"Yeah," Tyler agreed.

"What did she lie about this time?"

"Turns out she yelled out in front of the whole cast and Heyer that Isabella knew bad things about them and she should make them public – on Thursday."

"Thursday night/Friday mornin', Isabella shows up dead. Don't seem like a coincidence to me."

"Heyer didn't mention that when we interviewed him," Casey pointed out. "I wonder why not?" She smiled nastily. "Heyer's in a cell for obstruction, and he's staying there tonight. Tomorrow, he'll be in Interrogation."

"Couldn't happen to a nicer guy."

"Anyway," Casey said, "Maisie and Isabella had a screaming fight in the theatre, so I guess they weren't the best pals Maisie made them out to be. It sounds like the friends who said Maisie was jealous weren't wrong."

Tyler nodded. "Never what it seems."

"Mm?" Casey inquired.

"Families. Siblings." Nobody asked him to expand. He'd talk if, or when, he wanted to.

"Tomorrow, we interview Heyer first – me and O'Leary. Andy'll get street cam footage – if any – from around Maisie's office. CSU can do their thing without us. Tyler, can you collect that camera footage from the sandwich shop and see if there's any at the gas station – or an attendant to interview?" She stopped. "Andy, could you keep Larson with you to learn about street camera footage? Tyler, choose one of the other three" –

"Adamo."

"Okay – and take him with you to learn something."

"What about the other two?"

Casey grinned. "I think – since Fremont's pretty useful these days – we should give the four of them these updates, whip out Larson and Adamo, and then let Fremont and Henegan have a go at working out who, and in what order, we interview. Let's see how they do."

O'Leary's grin matched Casey's. "You're thinkin' that Fremont might want to move into detectin', ain't'cha?"

"He might. If he does, let's give him a helping hand."

"Helping others? Where's that in the team rules?"

"I think we've adopted Fremont and Larson."

"Only 'cause nobody else'll talk to us."

"Whatever," Casey said. "They're doing fine, so let's encourage them. If Adamo starts looking good, we'll adopt him too. Like a litter of puppies. He's a rookie, though, so he's got a long way to go."

"We got a lot to do tomorrow through Friday," O'Leary pointed out. "You rememberin' we all got Saturday off?"

"Oh," Casey said. "I forgot."

"An' the exhibition tomorrow night."

"Stop reminding me," she snipped.

"But I'm goin' to be famous," O'Leary pouted.

"I said *stop* reminding me."

"'Kay. Are we all goin' home, or are we all goin' for a nice beer?"

"Home," Casey said firmly.

"Me too," Andy said.

Tyler nodded, words being unnecessary.

"No fun," O'Leary humphed. "Seeya tomorrow."

***

Casey reached the precinct on Wednesday morning with a twisting discomfort in her stomach, not linked to any physical cause. If it had been, she'd have popped two Advil and ignored it. Since it was entirely caused by the thought of the evening ahead, and nobody had yet invented painkillers for justifiable nervousness, she tried to ignore it. Fortunately, before an ulcer could arrive, the rest of the team appeared and her proper job, catching murderers, could take priority.

"We all know what we're doing. Who wants to brief our four officers?"

"Your turn," Tyler said.

Casey made a face at him, but went. The four officers spotted her approach and managed a reasonable facsimile of hiding their nervousness at seeing her.

"Listen up," she commanded, and ran them through the new findings from the previous day. "That means," she continued, "there's a lot to do today. Larson" – he straightened – "you'll work with Andy on street camera footage."

He beamed. "Yes'm," he said cheerfully.

"Adamo, you and Tyler are going out to collect camera footage from a sandwich bar and interview a gas station attendant. Watch and learn."

"Yes, *ma'am.*"

"O'Leary and I will interrogate Heyer," Casey said. Fremont and Henegan exuded severe disappointment. Casey grinned at them. "However, while we're doing that, someone has to work out who we should interview today and tomorrow, and in what order. Fremont and Henegan, that's you two. I want you to consider everything we already know, and be ready to defend your decision to the team" – they quivered – "when we're done with Heyer. Unless there's something major, this is where we'll each take one of you, like we said Monday, so you'll all get a chance to be in on a live interrogation."

"Yes'm!" Fremont celebrated.

"Yes'm," Henegan wavered.

"Fremont, you and Henegan get Heyer up to Interrogation, and then get started. Any disagreement, Fremont makes the call – but he'll have to defend that, so that'll keep you even. Larson, off you go to play with the tech. Adamo, Tyler's waiting." Adamo ran.

Casey went back to her own desk to wait for Heyer to be taken to Interrogation. Barely five minutes later, Fremont hurried up to her. "Ma'am, he's ready for you."

"Thanks." She turned to O'Leary. "Shall we?"

"Yep."

Heyer was considerably more dishevelled and less arrogant than he had been the previous day. A holding cell obviously hadn't agreed with him, though both detectives thought that anything that had punctured his unpleasant pomposity was a good lesson.

"Carl Heyer," Casey said. "Before we start, I will read your rights again." She did. Heyer, already pale and panicked, lost all colour.

"But...but...."

"Let's recap," Casey said coldly. "You tried to obstruct a murder investigation. That's punishable with up to a year in jail. Imagine that. It won't be nearly as pleasant as the night you've just spent in a cell." Heyer shook. "You directly lied to us. And you withheld relevant information." She exposed her teeth. It wasn't even close to a smile. "Trifecta. You lose."

Heyer couldn't force a single word past his chattering teeth. He stared at Casey, paralysed, for a full minute before he spoke.

"*Lady Macbeth!*" he exclaimed.

"What?" Beside Casey, O'Leary was struggling not to react, which had left him purple-faced and almost squeaking with suppressed laughter.

"That's exactly how Lady Macbeth should be. Small and feminine, with a steely glare and cold eye, imposing her will on everyone around her. Do you act?"

O'Leary spluttered. Casey took a breath.

"Mr Heyer. I do not care about your theatrical thoughts. You can be charged with obstruction. Shakespeare has no place in this room, although I'm sure you could attempt it in whichever jail you go to. Until I" – she stressed the pronoun – "decide whether to charge you, put you back in a cell, or release you, you will stop thinking about irrelevant matters and answer my questions wholly truthfully. No more lies, evasions, or references to anything outside my murder case. Death is more important than any production." She fixed him with a stony stare. "In this case, all the world is most certainly *not* a stage." She let silence hang heavy around them, until Heyer focused on her.

"What do you want to know?" he quavered.

"We'll start with why you didn't tell us about the argument in the theatre on Thursday night." Casey watched unlovely colour spread over his face. "Yes, we know about that. Tell me in your own words what happened." She paused. "We have a witness. Don't even *think* about lying or shading the truth."

CHAPTER NINETEEN

"That dumb woman kept showing up in the theatre. No reason to be there, and I don't want spectators." Casey and O'Leary shared a thought: *they might see how awful you are*. "They can buy a ticket when the play opens rather than scrounging cheap thrills. She couldn't even act."

"How d'you know that?" O'Leary challenged.

"Because I put her up on stage and made her try. She was a complete failure, like I knew she would be, but I thought if she was totally humiliated she'd keep out of my theatre." His pride in his idea radiated from him. Casey and O'Leary could barely conceal their disgust. "I told Isabella I wasn't having her there, getting in the way and distracting everyone, drooling over every actor. Why would any of them look at her? She was a dumb office drone trying to be interesting. Nobody cared. Isabella was totally wrong for my *Dream* but at least she had *some* talent – not much, but some. That woman had none."

"Rather than complainin', start tellin' us about the argument," O'Leary said sternly.

"Rehearsal had finished," Heyer admitted. "She was skulking up in the circle and Isabella went up to tell her to leave."

"How did you know that?"

"I told her – Isabella – to tell her to leave, that's how. She wasn't allowed in. She knew that. Isabella went up to tell her so, and the next thing she was screaming at Isabella that she should call out bad behaviour and not condone it by keeping quiet. Isabella told her to shut up 'cause she was jealous and she – Isabella – wouldn't make trouble because this was her career."

"You could hear all this? Who else could hear it?"

"The whole damn theatre could hear them. If Isabella could've managed half that fury on the stage she might have been useful" – he stopped at the cops' twin icy stares. "Everyone."

"I see. Why didn't you mention this earlier?"

Heyer shuffled his feet and squirmed in his chair.

"Because the bad behaviour was yours?" Casey jabbed. "You don't have a great reputation" –

"I'll fire Ron" –

"It wasn't Ron." Casey's words fell heavily. "You're known about. God complex, bad temper, throwing things, insults, threatening physical violence. Oh, and a dubious attitude to sexual consent." She stared him down. "What did you do that Isabella heard or saw?" Heyer failed to answer. "We'll be asking every member of the cast, whether you tell us or not. Every single one of you will be cross-questioned on their own behaviour and everyone else's. You can tell us your version or we can rely on theirs. Your choice."

"I didn't do anything wrong," Heyer insisted. "Nothing. That bitch heard *lies* and rumours. I haven't done anything wrong and you won't trick or intimidate me into saying I did when I didn't. Charge me if you want, but then I want my lawyer."

"I won't charge you – yet. You're free to go, but don't leave New York. We *will* be interviewing you again, and if anything arises that you haven't told us, then I'm sure it will come out."

Heyer ground his teeth. Casey and O'Leary exited, and sent in a stray uniform to have Heyer's effects returned to him.

They repaired to the break room, where they could relieve their feelings. After a soothing rant, Casey drained her coffee in one go.

"Why'd he want a lawyer anyway?"

"He's hidin' somethin'."

"Sure he is. Whatever it is, we'll find it and if we can, we'll charge him," Casey said vengefully. "It must've occurred to him that if it wasn't much, we wouldn't care."

"I dunno," O'Leary mused. "He's got enough ego to fill Yankee Stadium, so mebbe any li'l thin' that might make him look bad would set him goin'."

"Yeah. Let's go see how Fremont and Henegan are getting on."

"An' if Andy has that footage yet."

***

"Sandwich place preserved footage," Tyler said as he and Adamo walked up, "but…" He waited.

"Uh, they wanted to see a warrant?" Adamo tried.

"Yep."

164

"Does the gas station need to see a warrant too?"

"Haven't asked yet."

"What do you want me to do, si-Detective?" Adamo queried.

"Watch and learn in the sandwich place. Gas station, you tell me."

Adamo took a moment to think, having to walk faster than Tyler to keep up. "Uh, ask if they have cameras?"

"Yep."

"Ask if they keep the footage," he said a little more confidently. "If they do, ask for it, but expect them to ask for a warrant. If they don't, ask if the attendant is the same one as was on duty, um, Thursday night and/or Friday morning. If he was, find out what he knows, if not, find out who it was and how to contact them."

"Yep. You can do that. Good practice. Canvassing's a skill."

The server in the sandwich shop recognised Tyler, and nodded.

"Hey," Tyler said. "I have the warrant you need to see." He passed it over.

The server examined it, and nodded again. "Sure. I'll go get the recording."

"I'll come with you," Tyler said.

Adamo, without needing to be asked, produced an evidence bag, and followed. Tyler gestured to Adamo, who held it open for the server to deposit it, then tagged it in approved fashion.

"Thanks," Tyler said. "If we spot anything, we might come ask a few questions."

"Sure."

Tyler and Adamo departed for the gas station, where they found a bored, pimply youth, chewing gum and playing on his phone. Adamo's slightly frantic glance at Tyler indicated that he thought that the youth wouldn't be co-operative. Tyler declined to help, being a believer in the sink-or-swim method of learning.

"Hi," Adamo began. The youth popped his gum, but deigned to look at the cop. "I'm Officer Adamo, and this is Detective Tyler. We're investigating a murder."

"Murder!" the attendant said. "When? Where? How?"

"Near the Terpsichore," Adamo said confidentially. "We think you could help us."

"Me? Like, for real? Totally, man. What can I do? I love crime shows."

Adamo – and Tyler – suppressed their surprise at the change in attitude. "First up, what's your name?"

"Danny. Danny Werts."

"Nice to meet you, Danny. Do you guys have cameras or CCTV coverage around the station?"

"Sure we do. Do you wanna see it? When? We keep a month."

"Last Thursday and Friday would be great," Adamo replied. Tyler gently faded into the background.

"Sure. I'll go get it. D'you want a copy?"

"If you're offering."

"I'll bring one up. Holler if anyone comes wanting to get gas."

"Okay," Adamo said. "Can I come with you?"

"Sure."

Danny whipped off, Adamo following.

"Doing good," Tyler said to Adamo's back. "Carry on." Adamo had grown at least six inches under Tyler's benevolently authoritarian eye.

"Here you go," Danny said. Adamo dropped it into an evidence bag, and tagged it. The youth's eyes followed every move. "That how you do it?"

"Yes."

"I wanna be a cop," he said, "but I haven't finished college yet. As soon as I do, I'll apply."

"Go for it," Adamo encouraged. "It's great."

Safely out of sight, Tyler contemplated the enthusiasm of youth with the cynicism of age and experience. Still, they'd learn better as they got older, like raw recruits in the Army. Like he had. He didn't think he'd ever been as bouncy as Adamo, though. His brother'd beaten that out of him pretty fast.

"You got time for another couple of questions?" Adamo asked.

"Yeah."

"Last Thursday and Friday, did you see anyone or anything weird? Like, someone hanging around, or anything?"

Danny considered, which entailed popping his gum several times. "Nah," he said eventually. "I don't remember anything."

"That's okay. Is this a twenty-four-hour station?"

"Sure is. Last week I did the night shift: eight till eight. This week I'm on days."

"How's that work with college?"

"The semester finished three weeks ago, and I started the next day. I do this every vacation. Louis who runs it, he's a friend of my dad's."

"Good to have a job," Adamo said. "Who did days last week?"

"Louis's nephew. Darrell. Louis comes in at least once every shift to check everything's okay, though. Darrell'll be in at eight this evening, maybe ten minutes before that so we can hand over."

"Thanks. Look, we'll want to ask Darrell if he saw anything if the footage isn't great, but if you talk about this visit, he's gonna start thinking and remembering and if you've been doing your research about investigating you know that people can talk themselves into remembering things that weren't quite that way. I'd be really grateful if you didn't talk to him about it?"

Danny mimed zipping his lips. "I won't say a word," he promised. "Uh, look" – he coloured and looked at his feet – "uh, would you come by sometime and tell me about being a cop and all? The detective there, he's probably really senior and you don't look that much older'n me, uh...?"

"Sure I will," Adamo said. "Here's a card. They keep me pretty busy, but me and a pal could maybe come talk to you one evening."

"Thanks!" Danny said. "Anything you need, you come right back."

"Thank you," Adamo said, echoed by Tyler.

"Back to the bullpen," Tyler said, "look at the footage." He grinned. "Did good."

"I was gonna ask Fremont if he'd come with me," Adamo said uncertainly. "He's been around a lot longer, but he's pretty approachable."

"Ask him."

"Yes, si-Detective."

***

"What did you get?" Casey asked, as soon as Tyler returned to the bullpen.

"Footage," Tyler said. "Adamo'll bring it over." He grinned. "Make a useful cop."

"Oh?" the other three asked.

"Good interviewing. Easy subject. Still. Did good."

From the group of four officers, the team could hear Adamo. "He let me interview!" floated over to them, followed by a disgruntled mutter from Henegan. It might have been *some people get all the luck*. Shortly, the sounds of Adamo coaxing Fremont into meeting Danny arrived.

"If Henegan don't work out, we're keepin' li'l Adamo," O'Leary decided.

"We'll see," Casey said. "He hasn't met us when we're angry. See if he's still up to it then." She shrugged. "Let's have a look at this footage you brought back."

"I'll clean it up first," Andy said. "Show Larson how, and let him try on a copy of one of them."

"Your funeral," Casey said briskly. "I guess I'll go harass Fremont and Henegan."

"I'll come with you," O'Leary rumbled. "Make sure you don't harass them right out of the door."

Casey made a face at him. "No. If they need you to protect them, they're no good." She marched off to find her officers. "Fremont, Henegan," she announced, "let's talk about your conclusions." She directed them to a conference room, and sat down. The two officers hesitated, then sat too.

"What order do you think we should interrogate them in – and why? If you disagreed on anyone, then you both get to tell me your reasons and I'll tell you who's right. If I think you're wrong, I'll tell you why so you know for next time." She smiled. "This is a teaching session." She didn't soothe the two officers at all. She hadn't meant to.

"Ma'am...we agreed that Cordell should be first from the actors, and then Maxwell," Fremont said, Henegan nodding.

"Why? Henegan, you explain Cordell."

Henegan shivered and gulped. "Uh...ma'am" – the respectful term came awkwardly – "because there's a lot of bad stuff around him." He stopped.

"Continue."

"It's only rumours," he said with a little more confidence, "but if Isabella was murdered because she knew bad things and could have made trouble, then there's more bad around Cordell than we know about anyone else."

"Yes. Cordell first. Fremont, why Maxwell next?"

"Ma'am, we don't know what he might have done when he was drunk. Just because he's only been put in the tank doesn't mean that Isabella – or anyone else – didn't know about something worse, like bar fights or driving under the influence. Henegan thought that maybe he would be fragile and if you interrogated him he might spill a whole lot."

"Yes. You're right about those two." Both officers relaxed. "Next?"

They looked at each other. "We didn't agree here," Fremont admitted. "I thought that it should be Julius then Vincent."

"I thought we should take the four young guys," Henegan confessed, "but I didn't have an order for them."

Casey regarded Henegan with considerably more favour than previously. That was an interesting idea and certainly not what she'd expected to hear. She'd expected him to disagree with the order. "Why?"

"Uh..." Fremont nudged him to start him talking. "They were a *lot* younger than everyone else. They might have picked up stuff about the rest of the cast that no-one else did, or overheard, or had a different take on things. They might have talked to Isabella or Dacia or even that Maisie."

"That's a good reason. It might even be a good reason to take them before anyone else, but let's work that out when we've covered the rest."

Henegan looked as if he couldn't believe the praise, his cheeks flushing and the hunch of his shoulders easing. For the first time, Casey thought that Kent might have had the right idea by assigning him to the team, though she absolutely wasn't prepared to welcome him with open arms. Henegan was far too close to Estrolla for her to take that chance.

"Fremont, why did you think Julius and then Vincent?"

"They're older, and they've worked with Heyer before. They likely already know about his behaviour. Then, the four older men didn't like each other – that was in the notes but I don't know who said it – so if you took all four of them first they might spill about each other. I don't think Julius being gay should be a problem, but he might have been like that Chef Manoso and been predatory. Nobody's said anything much about Vincent except that he might've been a boxer, so he might have assaulted someone or been doing illegal steroids, but we don't have evidence for any of it."

Casey considered. "You both make good points and you've both defended your thoughts logically. Henegan, go grab the other three officers, Fremont, get the detectives, and then I'll tell everyone what we'll do."

It took less than two minutes for everyone to gather, though Andy, and, more quietly, Larson, were muttering about being called away from their technogeeking.

"What's up?" Andy grumbled. "We were finally getting somewhere with the footage and you've hauled us in here."

"You weren't doin' nothin' 'cept waitin' for the clean-up routine an' for your warrants for the building cameras at Inwood, seein' as there ain't many public cameras," O'Leary corrected. "An' it looks like Casey's got an idea. Don't make us wait," he directed at her.

"Fremont and Henegan were told to work out an order for interrogating our cast. Fremont said Cordell, Maxwell, Julius then Vincent."

"Sensible," O'Leary approved.

"Henegan said take the four fairies first." She paused. Amazingly, there were no cries of disagreement, though there were furrowed brows.

"Intel," Tyler clipped.

"Yep," Casey said.

"Nice," O'Leary said.

"Both are good plans. There are four pairs here. O'Leary, you and Henegan take two of the young men. Tyler, you and Adamo take the other two. Andy and Larson, you take Julius and Vincent. Fremont will be with me, for Cordell and Maxwell. I want O'Leary and Tyler to finish the first two before we start on the older men – if there's anything interesting from the young guys, I want to be able to use it, but we'll likely know that early on in the first two." She looked around the other detectives. "What do you think?"

The officers, sensibly, stayed quiet while the detectives thought.

"Take one kid each today," Tyler said. "Get any intel first. Then Fremont's order."

"Uh, ma'am?" Fremont said.

"Yes?" Casey rapped.

"I think Henegan was right," he blurted. Henegan jolted upright, staring at Fremont. They hadn't exactly hit it off – they'd almost had a stand-up fight in the bullpen – but Fremont had just made serious amends. The team's view that Fremont was a good guy increased.

Henegan squirmed uncomfortably. Casey made a sharp gesture to the others to stay absolutely quiet. His mouth opened, then closed, twisting on acid-bitter words.

"Ma'am?" he said, gaze fixed on Casey. "Ma'am…can I talk to you?"

Casey's next gesture dismissed everyone except Henegan. O'Leary met her eyes from behind Henegan, but when she gave a tiny *it's-okay* nod, left too.

"Talk," she said uninvitingly, as soon as the door had shut.

Henegan didn't appear to be able to find his words. His lips opened, then pinched as he didn't like the taste of the sentence in his throat. After a minute, Casey scowled. "Look, we've got work to do. Either start talking, or get to work."

"It's…Larson said you gave him a second chance…I…you…Captain put me with you but I…" he stopped. "He didn't…" Another pause. Casey womanfully resisted the urge to snap *Get on with it, idiot!* "Estrolla… You're keeping him away from me but…"

"Estrolla's pressuring you to tell him about any dirt on us, the investigation, and if Andy or I are going out alone," Casey said bluntly. "We knew that."

"You *knew?*" Henegan slumped. "How?"

"You were seen and heard. Captain Kent knows, too."

Henegan went green. "The *captain* knows? I'm fucked."

"He's known for a couple of days, and he hasn't fired you yet," Casey pointed out. "You've come clean to me, which took guts. You're not off my team yet. You have some choices to make, though. If I think you're squealing to Estrolla, Grendon, or any of that mob, you're dead meat. It's up to you." She stood up, leaning forward over the desk. "One chance, Henegan. We've all told you that. *Only* one chance."

She stalked out.

"What was that about?" O'Leary murmured.

"Henegan found some guts. Let's send Fremont and Larson out to get our four fairies in, and the four of us can go get some lunch and I'll tell you all together."

"Carval?" Tyler asked.

"Allan'll murder us if we take him out of the gallery today," Casey said, and shuddered. "I still don't wanna think about tonight."

"Get Fremont," Tyler said, and strode across the bullpen to do exactly that.

A few minutes later the misfit team left. O'Leary ambled. Casey and Andy half-jogged to keep up, until Casey slapped O'Leary's enormous bicep.

"Slow down," she complained. "We've got time."

"But you're goin' to tell me a story," O'Leary whined. "Good stories take time."

"Not this one," Casey flicked back. "Slow up or I won't tell you any story at all."

When they had all bought their lunches and found a handy space in Sakura Park, O'Leary attempted to bat his sandy lashes at Casey. "Story time," he rumbled.

"Big baby."

"That's me," he said happily.

"Henegan's found some guts. Told me about Estrolla pressuring him."

"What!" three men exclaimed.

"He did?" Andy said. "Wow."

"I told him we already knew, and Kent knew, and he nearly threw up on the spot. Then I told him he had choices, but he only got one chance with us. That's it."

"I wouldn't'a believed it," O'Leary said, then frowned. "You know what this means, don't'cha?" He grinned evilly. "We're goin' to get a reputation for fixin' people. You ain't done this team any favours, Casey."

"I don't want bad officers," she said defensively. "It's not like we'll add them to *us*." She grinned. "I'm sure not offering to reform Estrolla."

"Naw. We're good." Tyler and Andy nodded. "Anyway, we got Carval buzzin' round iffen we need extra."

"What we need is to start interviewing," Casey said firmly, and led them back.

Although the team had returned, Fremont and Larson hadn't, which didn't make Casey happy. She was still less happy when Kent summoned her.

"Clement," he said ominously. "I trust you have remembered your team's attendance at the gallery at six tonight?"

"Yes, sir."

"Good. Is there anything I should be aware of before then?"

"No, sir." Since her father wouldn't turn up till eight, there was no chance of Kent encountering him.

"Good."

She had a sudden thought. "Sir?"

"Yes?"

"Uh, we're allowing the four officers assigned to us to assist in our preliminary interviews of the actors. One of them with each of us."

Kent blinked. "Approved. It's about time you four helped officers to progress. Dismissed."

Casey fled, wondering how telling Kent about a good idea had turned into a reprimand that they hadn't been doing enough previously.

Kent watched his detective depart, thinking hard. He hadn't heard a single whisper of trouble. Just maybe his discussion with Travers of Narcotics had squelched any possibility that Marcol would cause issues. Kent didn't care why it was quiet, only that it stayed quiet. He didn't want to raise hell right up to the top of 1PP if it all went wrong, though he would if he had to. He couldn't expect loyalty from his precinct if he wasn't loyal to them.

If only he didn't have a constant feeling that the whole house of cards was about to come crashing down.

CHAPTER TWENTY

"Aren't Fremont and Larson back yet?" Casey grumbled. "I want to get started. We'll all have to be out of here by five-fifteen to make this viewing and Kent's *reminded* me about it. Anyone would think he didn't trust us to go."

"Anyone would be right," Andy said cynically. "Don't tell me you aren't trying to get CSU to infect you with some dreadful disease before then."

"I'm thinking about it. Do we still have cholera in Manhattan?"

"Don't be silly," O'Leary chided. "'S one evenin', an' it'll all be over. Anyways, here's Fremont."

"The four are all in separate rooms," Fremont said.

"Let's go."

Casey and Fremont took the first room. Before they went in, Casey turned to Fremont. "This is information gathering from a witness, not interrogation of a suspect – unless something comes out that *in my opinion*" – she stressed that hard – "changes that. That's not your call."

"Yes'm."

"If you have a question, tap me out of sight, then wait till he's finished answering mine – he might answer yours too – and then ask. If I tap you back, *don't* interrupt with your question, wait till I give you a signal. Take good notes." She smiled. "With some common sense, you'll do fine. Let me lead."

"Yes, *ma'am*." Fremont practically saluted. "Thank you, ma'am."

"And," Casey added, "you can do the introductions, since he's already met you."

"Yes'm," Fremont said, and opened the door for her. "Mr Jackson, this is Detective Clement, who's leading the investigation into the murder of Isabella Farquar. Detective, this is Deontay Jackson, who's playing Mustardseed."

Casey mentally gave Fremont extra points for courtesy and giving her all the relevant information. "Hello, Mr Jackson," she said. "Thanks for coming in." She saw a lean African-American, handsome, with brilliant mustard-yellow hair. He was wearing jeans and a t-shirt supporting the San Francisco 49ers.

"Hey," he drawled. "That was totally terrible about Isabella. I really liked her. We all did. She was sweet."

"It was terrible," Casey agreed. "We wanna catch who did it, and I'm hoping you can help."

"I don't know, but sure, I'll try."

"Start by telling me about her."

Deontay did, but he didn't say anything new.

"Thanks. Did you meet her sister, Maisie?"

He made a face. "She kept hanging around. I don't like Carl much – don't tell him!" he added quickly, "but the best thing he did was tell her to get out. She was always in our faces after rehearsal and trying to be part of it. We weren't interested and she wasn't half the actor Isabella was, though she – Maisie, I mean – thought she was shit-hot. She was really full of herself. You know, I don't think Maisie liked Isabella much. Far as Maisie was concerned, Isabella was simply a route to hanging around the maybe-famous, eavesdropping and pretending like she – Maisie, I mean – totally knew secrets. She saw Isabella trying to get contributions to that charity – Act Like A Child – and I think she thought it was because Isabella knew bad things about everyone."

"What sort of bad things?" Casey asked.

"This is totally confidential, yeah? Because I wanna keep acting and if this leaks I'll never get another role," Deontay fretted.

"We won't tell anyone what you've said unless it comes to a trial and it's vital evidence," Casey reassured. "But the Finisterres" – Deontay sat upright – "are keen to find Isabella's killer and see them put away." She watched Deontay take the implication, and relax. "Tell me about it," she encouraged.

For the first twenty minutes, to Casey's undisclosed disappointment, Deontay said nothing new. However, after that, he wriggled uncomfortably, and began several sentences which then veered off into known territory. "Um, we all hang together," he finally said. "But it's not 'cause we're, like, buddies from before. I never met any of them till this role."

"Mm?" Casey enticed.

"It was, like, totally because of Carl and Cordell, to start with. Julius never mixed with us – arrogant s.o.b," Deontay added, "and Max kept to himself and his bottle. But Carl and Cordell hit on every single one of us whenever we were alone. Vincent warned us to stick together, and then he told Cordell that the next time he heard about him getting pushy he'd take him out back and punch his lights out till his pretty face couldn't be used for Caliban without plastic surgery."

"Wow!" Fremont emitted. Casey nudged him hard to shut him up.

"Cordell even hit on me – said I was really hot for a black guy, so he'd make an exception for me. I wasn't flattered. Racist pig."

"Did either of them threaten you?"

"It was totally clear that if I didn't put out then they'd badmouth me as not a good team player, if that's what you mean?"

"That's exactly what I mean."

"Then yeah, I guess so."

"Did Isabella know about this?"

"I don't see how she could've missed it. Vincent was pretty loud about it."

"What about Maisie?"

"Nah, she wasn't there. Too early – she never showed up till early evening."

Fremont tapped Casey under the table. She gave him a tiny nod. "Do you think Maisie might have found out about it later?" he asked.

"She could've, I guess," Deontay said after thinking about it, "but I didn't hear them talking in the theatre." He thought further. "But yeah. After Vincent waded in, maybe a couple of days later, Maisie was dropping hints. She wasn't explicit, but I think she knew by then."

"What sort of hints?" Fremont asked, which was the right question.

"Like, had Cordell ever done any boxing, one time. What did he think of actors getting plastic surgery? That sort of stuff."

"Not terribly subtle," Casey said. "Did you think Cordell caught on?"

"Oh, sure he did. He was totally pissed, but he wouldn't say anything in front of the whole cast because Vincent would have called him out."

"Did she do the same hinting about Carl?"

"I don't think anyone had called out Carl – we all need the next role, and even if nobody likes him he can screw you over by putting the word out." He wriggled. "But when Carl told Maisie to get out, Maisie said something about *bet the Finisterres wouldn't approve*, and Carl went white. It sure didn't stop him throwing her out, though."

"Who else did she hint about?"

Deontay's eyes dropped.

"C'mon," Casey said. "I'm only interested in murder. If you or one of the others jumped a subway turnstile, I'm not interested. All I care about is catching this killer."

"She hinted about everyone," Deontay admitted. "But I didn't get a lot of it."

"What did she say about you?"

"I'd told Isabella about this girl. She's totally cute and really hot. I asked her on a date, and she drank too much, and it turned out she was under twenty-one so she shouldn't have been drinking at all. Maisie made a few comments."

"Wasn't she carded?"

"Fake ID," Deontay said, "but it was damn good because it fooled me too."

"I don't care about that. What was Maisie saying?"

"Just, like, stuff about cradle robbing – I mean, *I'm* only twenty-three, for fuck's sake. She was twenty!"

"How'd you know?"

"She admitted it when I called her the next day."

"You called her?" Fremont said. "Boy, she must be cute." Casey elbowed him.

"She is," Deontay said, with a broad and sappy smile.

"Anything else that rang a bell with you?" Casey asked.

"She tried getting at Julius, but he's such a good actor I couldn't tell if she scored a hit."

"That's helpful, thank you. Anything else you remember?" She realised something. "Was there anything about Dacia?"

"Dacia was such a bitch to Isabella that nothing would have made a difference. She never said a word to Maisie – completely ignored her."

"Last thing, we think Isabella went for a drink or dinner with someone after rehearsal on Thursday. Do you know anything at all about who or where?" Casey asked.

Deontay wrinkled his nose, thinking. "Uh, I don't know. She never said anything about a date, but she liked Babbalucci, though I thought she was as broke as the rest of us. If she did go for dinner, someone else most likely paid."

"Thank you, Mr Jackson. Here's my card. If there's anything else you remember, even if you don't think it matters, let me know." She smiled at him. "Officer Fremont will take you out."

***

O'Leary and, behind him, Henegan, entered Interrogation Two to find Ji-Hoon Park, who was playing Cobweb. He wore a plain t-shirt and chinos, though his hair was dyed in silver streaks to simulate ethereal cobwebs. O'Leary privately thought that it was too obvious, but it wouldn't have been Mr Park's choice.

"Mr Park," O'Leary rumbled. Ji-Hoon looked up, and gaped. "Hey. I'm Detective O'Leary, an' this here is Officer Henegan."

"Hello," Ji-Hoon said in a cultured accent. "Uh, nice to meet you?"

"We're investigating Isabella's murder, an' we'd like to chat through what you know."

"Sure. I remember you from the theatre. Your colleague didn't make Carl happy."

"Naw. She don't make lots of people happy. Still, she ain't here, an' I wanna talk about Isabella. C'n you tell me about her?"

"She was, like, totally into helping kids get into theatre. Always trying to raise money to give to one particular charity – Act Like A Child. But if you didn't have any cash that day, or you were broke, she never pushed. Not like that sister of hers. She – Maisie, the sister – was totally pushy and she wasn't even part of the cast."

"Like how?" O'Leary asked.

"She was always hanging around at the end of rehearsal and it was a total pain. I'm sure she eavesdropped, because she kept bringing up things, in a totally *I-know-what-you-did-last-summer* kind of way. Anyway, she tried pushing for cash when I'd said no – I'm living on freaking ramen, I haven't got fifty cents let alone five bucks to give to charity and I'm working half the night every night to make my rent – and I told her to, um, fuck off out of my face. I wasn't the only one she did it to. The older guys, they paid up, but they've likely got some money. I don't, and her hassling me wouldn't make money show up out of nowhere."

"What'd she know about you? I know it ain't bad, 'cause iffen you had a record we'd'a known already."

"Grew up in foster care," Ji-Hoon said. "She was trying to make out like it was a bad thing."

"Iffen it was, which likely ain't the case, it's not on you," O'Leary pointed out. "Babies don't choose their lives." He redirected the discussion. "You told her to quit it. Who'd'a heard you an' her gettin' into it?"

"Isabella, but I think she told Maisie to stop 'cause it didn't happen to me again."

"What about others?"

"I don't know. She sure did a lot of hinting at bad things, so pretty much everyone hated Maisie. If it was Maisie who was dead I wouldn't have been surprised, but everyone liked Isabella, except Carl and Dacia. Oh, and Cordell, but he's a total asshat." His profanity didn't match his cultured demeanour and voice.

"What was up with Cordell?"

"I don't know, but most likely he tried to hit on Isabella and she shut him down. He tried it on all of us four, but Vincent threatened to beat the hell out of him and he stopped."

"Can't say I disagree with Vincent," O'Leary drawled, "though iffen he actually did start hittin', we wouldn't be too happy." He smiled, his homely face open and friendly. "What sorta thin's was Maisie hintin' at about the others?"

"It was a weird reference, but I thought she was getting at Julius. Something about him being a good fit for William Gladstone, with all his evening walks."

"Don't get that," O'Leary rumbled.

"Me neither," Ji-Hoon said, "and I sure wasn't going to go looking it up." He thought. "She went on about different types of booze, and Max didn't much like it but everyone knows he's on the sauce. We all already knew that Cordell was bad news, but she made some reference to casting couches in Hollywood and Cordell and Carl both got antsy. I wasn't surprised."

"What about Vincent or Dacia?"

"Maisie tried to make a crack about starring in the next Rocky, but Vincent laughed and said everyone who mattered knew he'd boxed and yeah, maybe sometimes it wasn't the American Boxing Federation in charge but who cared, it'd paid his rent."

"An' Dacia?"

Ji-Hoon squirmed. "Small but totally mean. Maisie tried to wind her up once, and Dacia got right in her face and slapped her. Told her to fuck off and never come near her again. But then Dacia went after Isabella too. She was screaming at her that she had to keep her sister under control. After that, Carl told Maisie she couldn't come to the theatre."

"I get it," O'Leary said. "D'you think Dacia pushed Carl into it?"

"Could've. I don't know. Dacia hated Isabella anyway, 'cause Isabella got the part and she was only the understudy."

"Would Isabella have gone out for a drink with her iffen Dacia said she wanted to make up, or somethin' like it?"

Ji-Hoon's face wrinkled in consideration. "Isabella was big on being nice, but I don't think so."

"Did she mention meetin' anyone Thursday night?"

"Not that I heard." Ji-Hoon's fine features twisted. "Someone took her on a date and then killed her? That's awful. I mean, I wouldn't have dated her: she wasn't my type, but...she was *nice*."

"I'm sorry," O'Leary said. "Is there anything else you c'n tell me?"

"No, I'm sorry, I can't think of anything."

"If you do, don't matter how li'l or trivial you think it is, give me a call. Here's my card." O'Leary handed it over. Ji-Hoon took it in two hands, read it, and then carefully put it away. "Thank you for comin' in, Mr Park. Officer Henegan will show you out."

***

In Interrogation Three, Andy entered to find Craig Devine, also known as Peaseblossom, languidly admiring his lilac-and-white hair in the one-way mirror. *Lucky Carval isn't here*, Andy thought, and a quick look at Larson showed that the officer wasn't impressed either.

"Mr Devine?" Andy said, "I'm Detective Chee, and this is Officer Larson. We'd like to ask some questions about Isabella and the play generally." Andy smiled. "I was impressed with the way it came across in rehearsal."

Devine's self-admiration fell away immediately. "You saw rehearsal? You're interested? It's not just another case to you? Then anything I can do to help. I knew Isabella from before because we went to the same theatre school, but I was a senior when she was a freshman. She had real talent and I was pleased we'd be in the same play, but then Carl hated her and Dacia was a total bitch and Cordell was hitting on me, her, and the other fairies, and it wasn't what I'd thought it would be, you know?" His long lashes were actually damp, and he sniffed. "It wasn't fair. She was *nice* and she wasn't all conceited about the Finisterres pushing her – I would've been," he said with devastating honesty. "I would've wanted to shout it to the gods in every theatre."

"I bet," Andy agreed.

"I guess she was a better person than me."

"I wouldn't say that," Andy contradicted, "because you're helping us. She'd have approved of that." He smiled. "Tell me about Isabella."

Craig did, but he didn't add anything to Andy's knowledge.

"Thanks," Andy said. "We know that Isabella had a meal and a drink on Thursday evening, Do you know if she was meeting anyone?"

"You know," Craig said slowly, "I think she was."

"Mm?" Andy hummed.

"She'd taken off her stage make-up. Usually she left it on – I guess she took it off at home. Her hair was different. Carl wanted Titania to have loose hair, wild. Like, not groomed. He said it was *evoking the Wild Magic of an elder age*." Craig made a face. "Yeah, right."

"A touch pretentious?" Andy said with a gamin, theatre-goers-together grin.

"Yes," Craig admitted. "But I'm not saying that near Carl. Anyway, she'd tidied her hair" – he closed his eyes – "yeah, and it wasn't up but she'd done one of those braids that starts here" – he tapped the front of his head – "on each side, loose-ish, you know? I thought it looked really cute."

"French braids," Andy said. "That's helpful. She didn't say anything about who?"

"No. She said she was single, but mostly I thought she was spending time with this charity she supported." He talked about her charity collections for a while, all of which Andy already knew.

"What about the rest of the cast? I saw how it all came together when Dacia stepped in, but I didn't get the impression everyone outside you four were totally comfortable together?"

"Vincent, Julius, Cordell and Max hated each other," Craig spat. "They created a really bad atmosphere. I don't know what their history was, but there was obviously plenty. None of them liked Carl much, either, but you can't turn down work and you *really* don't turn down anything the Finisterres are funding. They sucked it up."

"Would Isabella have gone out with any of them?"

"I don't think so." Craig frowned. "I don't think she would have bothered doing her hair like that for any of them and apart from Max she didn't talk to any of them. It was her sister that kept hanging around. She was a nasty piece of work. Sneaking around the theatre poking her nose in, trying to be fake pally with us all, and when she'd found out things she tried to blackmail us."

"Blackmail?"

"She was always dropping hints about what she knew, and I think she was trying to get money out of some of them, but I don't have any spare. She dressed it up as wanting contributions to the charity, but if she was going to hand it over, I'll eat my Peaseblossom tunic. Maisie liked nice things, and she made a few cracks about not needing to buy out of thrift shops, but it wasn't like she had a top paid job. She was another office drone, and didn't we all hear how great she would be as an actor if it wasn't for that?"

"How'd she know any of this stuff?"

Craig made a rueful gesture. "Isabella was always happy with how close she and her sister were, and I think she told her pretty much everything."

"Did you think they were close?"

He shook his head. "Isabella might've, but I don't. Little things: looks and comments. Then they had a fight in the theatre because she yelled that if Isabella knew bad things she should report it, and Isabella said she wasn't going to make trouble. Then Carl threw her out. Isabella was crying."

"What day was that?"

"Thursday, maybe? Yeah. We have a rehearsal every second or third day, though next week they'll be daily. Thursday. Then…" – it dawned on him. "Oh my God. She got Isabella killed because she told everyone Isabella knew bad things and someone – oh, *fuck*, it's one of us. One of the cast." He went whiter than his bleached hair.

"Breathe slow and deep," Larson said: the first time he'd opened his mouth. "That's it. Keep going." Craig recovered a little colour. "That's better. A few more breaths, nice and deep."

"Thanks," Craig said. "But…"

180

"We don't know that yet," Andy said. "Leave it to us. *Please* don't go investigating yourself. Either you'll get hurt, or you'll mess up something and we won't be able to bring Isabella's killer to justice."

Craig briefly looked mutinous, but then relaxed. "I get it," he conceded. "I wanna, but I won't do anything."

"You can do something," Andy said. "You can keep your eyes open and if you hear anything, or think of anything, tell me." He handed over a card. A thought entered his head. "Did anyone leave Thursday's rehearsal at a weird moment?"

"Don't think so."

"Thank you for your time, Mr Devine, and if you think of anything at all, call me."

"Find them. She didn't deserve this."

CHAPTER TWENTY ONE

Tyler, followed by Adamo, strode into Interrogation Four in no great mood. Actors, acting, and theatre were not his thing, and interviewing an actor wasn't the way to continue a day which would end badly anyway. Why Kent wanted to *observe* the team at the exhibition, he didn't know. Kent should go back to being a stern but remote captain, far away from Tyler and the others. Consequently, he was scowling blackly as he entered.

The young man sitting there took one look at Tyler and quaked in his seat. "Am I in trouble?" he quavered. "I haven't done anything."

Adamo gave him a bright smile. "Hey," he said. "Mr Thakkar?"

"Uh, yes?"

"This is Detective Tyler, and I'm Officer Adamo."

Tyler managed to correct his expression. "Thanks for coming," he said, assessing the man before him. Brown skin, mid-height, dark eyes, hair that should have been pure black dyed a dusty brown. "Mr Sunil Thakkar, you're playing Moth in Carl Heyer's production of *A Midsummer Night's Dream*."

"Yes?"

"You know we're investigating Isabella Farquar's death. Tell me about her."

Sunil did, briskly, no doubt hoping to leave Tyler's intimidating presence faster. He didn't say anything new.

"What about her sister, Maisie?"

"Total pain," Sunil said with some venom. "Came straight to the theatre after work every time we were rehearsing. Isabella said she was being supportive. My ass she was."

"Mm?" Tyler hummed.

"Nasty little comments, though Isabella didn't notice, then hanging around the rest of us and making nasty little comments to everyone. Carl's a total prick, but he fixed her. Put her up on the stage and humiliated her. Horrible, but it worked for a while. Then she came again and started yelling at Isabella that if she knew bad things about people she should report them. Everyone heard. Carl threw her out."

"Think Maisie knew what Isabella knew?"

"Sure she did."

"Whole cast heard?"

"Half of Upper Manhattan probably heard."

"When was it?"

"Thursday last week." Sunil clearly hadn't made the connection.

"We think Isabella might have been meeting someone Thursday night."

Sunil considered. "That makes sense," he said. "She'd done her hair differently – oh, I know!"

"What?" Tyler said.

"She'd said, like, a week before then, that the Finisterres would want an update. I bet that's where she'd be going."

Tyler blinked. The Finisterres hadn't mentioned that. "If it wasn't them, anyone else it might be?"

"I don't know," Sunil said. "She was cute, so lots of people might've wanted to date her, but she didn't mention anyone."

"Any of you?"

"Maybe Craig. I'm…committed. Ji-Hoon isn't interested in girls. Deontay's seeing someone." He frowned. "But she wasn't seeing Craig, certainly not Thursday night. He left with me and the other two – we stuck together to avoid Cordell. Predatory prick." Frown turned to outright scowl. "Carl was nearly as bad, though Dacia managed to hold on to him. She was a total bitch too, but she'll be totally amazing as Titania. She's what'll make it work."

"Affair?"

"I guess. She'll make Carl's name with this, and we'll all get kudos too."

Tyler clocked the motive, but it wasn't news.

"Thanks," he said. "If you think of anything else, call." He gave Sunil a card.

"I will. I want her killer found. She was *sweet*," Sunil said miserably.

***

"Waal," O'Leary said, "I dunno iffen I'm happy that we got motive or unhappy that *everybody* got a motive."

"Not the four fairies," Casey said. "All of us agree that they're genuinely unhappy about Isabella. They're all pretty consistent, too. Carl and Cordell were predators, Maisie was a bitch but Dacia was a bigger one, the four old guys hate each other, Max was a drunk and Vincent was protecting the younger ones from Cordell."

"Finisterres," Tyler said.

"Yeah. That needs to be followed up stat."

"That, Clement, means first thing tomorrow. It doesn't mean tonight. You are not excused from the viewing." Kent hove heavily into view. "It's quarter after five. Shift is over. Be gone. I'll see you all in forty-five minutes."

"Sir," they said, packed up, and repaired to the Abbey for a fortifying drink.

Kent also cleared his desk. Darla had been thoroughly enthusiastic, though his popularity at home didn't make up for the waste of time that looking at *snaps* would be. Still, making Darla happy was good. He smiled fondly and left, making his way to the gallery, where he'd arranged to meet his wife.

***

Kent scowled at Allan, who was at the door to meet him, taking the place of one of the gallery's staff. "Captain Kent," Allan said, "and this must be Mrs Kent."

"Hi," Mrs Kent said. "Call me Darla." Kent scowled harder.

"Hello, Darla," Allan said politely.

"Thank you for setting this up. Gareth and I are delighted." Kent didn't look delighted at all. "We visited *New York's Ugly Underbelly* and I was truly impressed. I'm looking forward to finding out how Mr Carval does it."

Allan managed not to say that Jamie did it through sheer instinct and monumental self-confidence – and never letting common sense, the word 'no' or good manners stop him. "Come into the gallery," he invited.

"Are Clement and her team here?" Kent enquired, still black-browed.

"Not yet," Allan said. "I'll take you to meet Jamie till they get here." Darla followed him, radiating enthusiasm. Kent stumped after her, radiating irritation. "Jamie," Allan announced, "here are Captain and Mrs Kent."

Carval spun around. "Hi," he said, switching on his public personality under Allan's meaningful stare. "Nice to meet you." He extended a hand to Darla, who shook it. "Allan said that you'd seen *Underbelly*?"

"Yes. I loved it. How did you manage to take those shots?"

Carval explained. Kent fell into an at-ease posture as Allan returned to the door, to find his four detectives and a stunning Latina woman arriving.

"Hey," Casey said. "We're here. You know Allie, don't you?"

"I don't think so," Allan said, "but I recognise her from Jamie's shots. Nice to meet you. Tyler's brought you along, hasn't he?" he added a touch mischievously.

"He sure did!" Allie bounced. "I can't wait to see the shots!"

"Kent's here," Allan said. Four detectives' faces fell. "And his wife. They're talking to Jamie."

184

"Guess we'd better go in," O'Leary said dispiritedly. They trudged through behind Allan. Kent, looking thoroughly dyspeptic, was watching his wife talking and gesticulating with Carval, who was regarding her with some surprise and a lot of interest.

"Clement," Kent said, and then noticed Allie. "Miss, er…"

"Despero," Allie reminded him. "I, um" –

"You helped out on the modelling case," Kent said. "Good work." Allie blushed, and tried to hide behind Tyler.

Mrs Kent turned around, and frankly stared at the assorted collection. "Hello," she said, then, "Gareth, would you introduce me?"

"Darla, these are my detectives – the ones the exhibition is based around. Detective Clement" – Casey nodded – "and her partner Detective O'Leary" – O'Leary extended a paw. Darla's eyes widened at his size – "Detective Chee" – Andy nodded and smiled – "and Detective Tyler, with" – Tyler blinked at Kent's sly smile – "his friend, Miss Despero. Miss Despero assisted on a case."

"Pleased to meet you all," Mrs Kent said. Unlike her scowling husband, she appeared genuinely happy to see them.

"Now that you're all here," Carval said, "you can go see the exhibition. You have to start here," he explained, gesturing them forward. The detectives hung back to let their captain go first, and to avoid his beady stare.

Kent stopped dead in the doorway, half a step behind his wife, and stared, goggle-eyed. It was only when she tugged him forward that he moved, and even then it was only two steps. "What the *hell?* Detectives, get in here!"

Carval followed everyone else in, and, in obedience to Kent's previous orders, ensured that he was next to Mrs Kent, who was also staring at the centrepiece. "That's amazing," she breathed. Carval preened. "How did you do it?"

"I went to the store for milk and they were there at a crime scene," Carval said. "I've always got a camera, and the shot was right there."

"Instinct?" said Mrs Kent acutely.

"Uh…yeah." Carval was completely disarmed. He'd expected a shrill wannabe culture-vulture, and instead, here was a well-groomed but otherwise unassuming small woman who'd seen straight to the core of his talent in one word.

"I thought so," she said, and smiled. "Taking your chances when you see them."

"Yeah."

Mrs Kent stared at the central shot of Casey again, and then at Casey herself, and then back at the shot, but didn't say anything.

"Do you want to move on?" Carval asked.

"Yes."

Behind them, Captain Kent was also staring at the central shot of Casey, seemingly transfixed by it, his thick brows drawn together.

Allan came up beside him. "That's what Jamie does," he said. "That's why he insisted on shooting your team and your precinct."

"I'd still rather be at the ball game," Kent muttered, "but that's astonishing."

"Shall we move on?" Allan said, after another moment in which Kent neither shifted his gaze nor spoke.

"Yes." Kent stepped to one side, scanning the next sequence: recruits at the Academy, in physical training, keeping one eye on his team as they entered.

Casey and the team, with Allie, gave Mrs Kent plenty of space to move on, and only then began.

"Wow!" Allie exclaimed. "That's stunning! You're totally focused and *wow*!"

Casey couldn't answer. It had been bad enough seeing that shot on Carval's corkboard. Seeing it at full size, as the opening shot of the exhibition, centred and unmissable – she wanted to run right out of the gallery and straight to the airport.

O'Leary's hand landed on her shoulder. "Breathe," he murmured. "Iffen you don't, you'll faint."

"I don't faint!" Casey snapped.

"Then you better get some colour back, before you turn into a ghost."

Casey grimaced at him. "Look at it," she said. "Everyone'll see that. I don't *want* to be seen. I'll be notorious."

"Naw, you'll be famous."

"Notorious," Casey repeated. "The media will give us hell."

"Won't," Tyler said firmly.

"Huh?"

"Look around," Andy expanded. "Stop staring at that picture and look at the rest. Even a quick glance around tells me that Carval's single-handedly shown the NYPD in its best light. C'mon. Let's go see."

"Yeah," O'Leary chimed in. "Just 'cause you like lookin' at your own face, don't mean we have to. I'm goin' to find all them snaps of me, an' stare at them."

Casey spluttered furiously, but moved, surrounded by the team and pushed on by O'Leary's huge paw.

"Hey, look!" O'Leary enthused. "There's the recruits trainin', an' there's us showin' how it's done" –

"There's us turning Estrolla and his cronies into ground beef," said Andy. "That'll improve bullpen harmony."

"This one," Tyler said, smirking as he pointed to a sequence showing Casey tearing Andy to pieces, and then beating out pain against O'Leary. Casey winced. "Got you perfectly."

"Awww, there's me an' the baby. Don't I look cute?" O'Leary said happily.

The team moved on, teasing each other as they went.

Captain Kent dropped back behind Darla and Carval, leaving them to discuss culture. "Now what?" he said to Allan.

"Critics' previews tomorrow, then we open Friday at ten. It's already booked out for the next two months," Allan replied smugly. "It'll be great, not that I'll tell Jamie that."

"I didn't mean that," Kent said irritably. "What about my team and the press?"

"That'll come from the reviews – the critics will get the ball rolling, and we'll get requests from their colleagues. Your press liaison and I will set up a conference."

"When?"

Allan was about to answer, when one of the gallery staff requested his attention. "Excuse me," he said, and tapped off to the gallery's entrance to see a small man, a little shaky, his gaze a little off-centre.

"Hello?" Allan said.

"Er, hello. I'm David Clement. Um, my daughter said I should be here."

"Of course," Allan said smoothly, inwardly aghast. This was Casey's father? He shouldn't have arrived for nearly two hours, but here he was. "Come on in. Let me take your coat." Nobody else had had a coat, in the almost-hot weather of early June in New York City.

"Thank you."

"Wait here for a moment while I get someone to show you around. I would," Allan lied, "but I have to make sure everything keeps running smoothly." He hurried into the gallery, and frantically looked around. He couldn't bring Casey out. His eye fell on O'Leary. Though Allan had far more in common with Andy, O'Leary was the right choice here. He tapped the big man's arm, and when he turned, Allan put a finger to his lips.

"I gotta use the restroom," O'Leary announced, to derision, and wandered out, conveniently disguising Allan's rapid exit. As soon as they were out of the gallery, he stopped. "What's this about?" No trace of hayseed softened the irritation.

"Casey's dad's here," Allan said.

O'Leary's face crashed. "He's what? He ain't s'posed to be here for another hour at least. Casey told him eight, an' it ain't even quarter of seven yet." It was barely after six-thirty. "What're we goin' to do now? We can't send him home. Waal, *shit*." Quick thoughts raced over his wide face. "You did right not distractin' Casey. Go get her, an' tell her what's happened. I'll go deal with her pa, an' steer him so's he stays behind Kent. Tyler'll help, an' his Allie-girl's a big distraction to most people."

"Okay," Allan said, and hurried off.

O'Leary ambled to the vestibule of the gallery, and smiled down at Casey's father. "Hey," he greeted him. "You're Casey's pa?"

"Yes. David Clement." He looked all the way up. "You're one of her team." He hesitated. "You're…." Silence.

"I'm O'Leary," the man himself said, "but Casey calls me plenty of other thin's, 'specially when she's mad at me."

Mr Clement managed an uncertain smile. "She does?"

"Oh, sure. Big bully's her fav'rite."

"You're certainly big."

"Come see the show with me."

"With you? But…but I thought Catkin would show it to me."

"She's inside, an' I was nearest. Anyways, I'll take you in."

O'Leary was already worried. No stranger to small signs, he could see that Casey's dad was shaking slightly, though, thank the Lord, he didn't seem to have been boozing. He was looking nervously around for Casey, who, if she had any sense, would be in a well-timed restroom break to straighten herself up before this all went to hell in a hurry.

"That's *Catkin!*" Casey's dad exclaimed, disastrously clearly. Every person turned towards him, except O'Leary, who hadn't taken his eyes from Casey (who hadn't had sense) since he walked back in with her father. She went dead white, right down to her bloodless lips. Carval, in a moment of true stupidity, precipitately abandoned Mrs Kent to sling an arm around Casey and prove to absolutely everyone that he wasn't merely the photographer shooting her.

"Dad? I told you *eight.*"

"Did you? I…don't remember. Did I get it wrong?"

Casey's face blanked. "It doesn't matter," she said. "Come and see Carval's show."

"Who are all these others?" he asked.

"I'll introduce you. You already met O'Leary, and that was Allan Penrith, Carval's manager, who brought you in." She led her father to the rest of her team. "Tyler, with Allie Despero, who helped us on a case recently." Her gaze dropped to Tyler's hand, suspiciously moving back from Allie's, and she managed a brief smile and lift of eyebrows. "This is Andy." She turned. "Captain Kent, and Mrs Kent."

"Pleased to meet you," Mrs Kent said, echoed by her husband, who added a piercingly assessing gaze which was lost on Casey's father, but not on Casey.

"Who's this?"

"Jamie Carval," Carval said. "I took the shots in this exhibition."

Casey's father looked at him. "You did?"

"Yep." Carval smiled, and cut off any commentary that might have covered *why were you hugging my daughter*. "Come see."

Mrs Kent joined them. "Mr Carval's been telling me all about how he took his shots," she said. "It's compelling. Let's start at the beginning again, and I can look at them through fresh eyes now that I know what he did."

"Are you sure?" Casey's dad faltered.

"Oh, yes." She gave Carval a look that didn't allow arguments. Carval, looking at Casey, didn't argue. Casey needed to be separated from her father, fast.

"Will Catkin come too?"

Oh, shit, thought three detectives, one captain, and one photographer in perfect unison.

"Of course I will," Casey said with total calm. "I just need a couple of minutes." She disappeared in the direction of the restroom. Carval, trapped with Mrs Kent and Casey's father, twitching with the desire to go after her, couldn't move. O'Leary, not in the slightest daunted by Kent's approach to the team, followed Casey.

"Casey," he said gently. She stopped. O'Leary took the two strides to reach her, and stood between her and anyone in the gallery. "You okay?"

"Do I have a choice? I have to be." She turned half away. "This'll be awful. Didn't you see Kent watching?"

"Yeah. We gotta get through it. That Mrs Kent knows that somethin's up. Didn't you see her makin' herself a barrier between your pa an' Carval?"

"Yeah."

"C'mon. We'll keep him on track. You stay with your pa, an' the rest of us'll run interference anywhere we need to."

"I wish I'd never come," Casey said bitterly. "I wish I'd never listened to you and never told Dad."

"An' you might be right, at that, but it's too late now."

"Too fucking right," Casey spat.

O'Leary, entirely undeterred, hugged her. "Go clean up, an' then we'll all get us through this."

Captain Kent was none too happy to see Clement and O'Leary disappear, but he also didn't want to be official at an off-duty event. "What's going on?" he asked Andy.

"Casey's dad wasn't supposed to be here this early," Andy admitted.

"Oh? Explain."

"She didn't want him to interfere with your order that we attend with you so you could see our reactions."

Kent processed that against what he knew of Clement's father, and reached an unpleasant conclusion without any difficulty. "I see. Tell

Clement and O'Leary to see me before they start going around with her father."

"Yes, sir," Andy said formally.

Kent strode off, thinking furiously. Thanks to Clement's father's untimely interruption, now he wouldn't get a proper sense of the team's reactions to the show, though Clement's shock at the centrepiece wasn't reassuring. He'd barely had a chance to see more than the first few groupings himself, though he had to admit that Carval, infuriating as he was, had gotten under the skin of the subjects, and that opening shot of Clement was show-stopping. That wouldn't be helpful, especially if any of the precinct – or Detective Marcol – saw it. Kent was glumly sure that they would, if only to try to make trouble. He cast a bleak glance at Carval, whose actions on Clement seeing her father had spoken louder than a shout. There was a man who might not know it, but was six feet under and drowning in his feelings. Kent shrugged. Carval wasn't a cop and wasn't involved in cases apart from taking photos, therefore his feelings for Clement were not Kent's problem.

Clement's reactions to the show, however, were. Kent growled to himself, and decided that he would have to join her, her father, Carval – and his wife, who was the one bright spot in this complete disaster.

CHAPTER TWENTY TWO

Casey blotted her eyes, blew her nose, dragged up composure like a shroud, and exited the restroom to find O'Leary's comforting mass waiting for her.

"Let's go do it," he rumbled soothingly, "an' then we'll pack them all off home and we c'n go get beer."

"Yeah," Casey drooped, and then straightened. "Better know the worst."

The worst started immediately with the approach of Captain Kent. "What is your father doing here?"

"He was supposed to come at eight," Casey almost-snapped, holding Kent's scowl with a scowl of her own. "So that he didn't get in the way. You ordered us to be here at the same time as you so that you could watch our reactions, and Dad being here will affect that."

Kent noticed with considerable interest that shock had removed Clement's normal perfect respect in favour of belligerence. He'd let it pass, this one time.

"He's gotten confused?"

"He must have. I was crystal clear. He even wrote it in his diary."

Kent noticed a tremor in her voice, and fear in her eyes. There was far more to this than a forgetful parent. He added up what he knew about Clement's father's records, and decided that her father was much closer to serious illness than he'd understood. His decision not to call her on her tone would stand: she was focused on her father and adding to that strain was poor management.

"I see. We'd better join them," he said.

"Yes, sir."

Casey and Captain Kent joined the small group, to which Carval was explaining technical details of lenses, focal length, light and shade, and anything else he could think of to cover the complete awkwardness of the situation. Casey's father looked completely bewildered. Mrs Kent seemed to be following quite readily.

"Let's start," Carval said. "We'll go around, and you can ask me anything you want. I won't lecture you about the shots, because you'll all have your own reactions. I won't tell you what to think." He smiled, and moved the group from its position directly in front of the centrepiece to the first set of shots.

With every sequence, Casey's tension wound higher. Carval hadn't only pinned their souls to the gallery walls, he'd exposed every tiny flicker of emotion in every event he'd shot.

"Catkin," her father said querulously, "why are you wrestling with men much bigger than you?"

"That was sparring training," she dissembled. "There aren't many cops who are as small as me, so I have to practice with bigger guys." She forced a laugh. "Even with O'Leary."

He fell quiet as they moved on to the series of shots from the very first case for which Carval had been present. Kent stared at the shot of his misfit team, Casey in the lead, walking towards the camera, ready for war. He shook his head. Chalk that team bond up to his hunches, he thought smugly.

Smugness incinerated in an instant as he heard Clement's father's angry distress.

"Catkin, *what happened?*"

Kent looked at the shot of Clement unconscious on the floor of a dark corridor, none of her team obvious, and thought back to some extremely careful wording about who had been present on that occasion. His face darkened.

"Dad, we talked about this back when it happened," she tried. "It wasn't too bad."

"You didn't tell me you were *unconscious!*"

"She's very brave," Mrs Kent tried.

"She's my *daughter.* She shouldn't be doing this!"

Casey paled. "Dad, it's my job" – she began, but it was too late.

"That big guy should've done that. And you" – he turned to Kent and jabbed a finger at him – "if you're her boss, you should be making sure she's properly protected." He turned back to Casey. "If you'd been a lawyer" –

O'Leary swept in and frogmarched Casey's father out of the room before the situation could deteriorate any further.

"Sir, I apologise for my father," Casey said, bloodless and frozen-faced. "He doesn't understand."

Kent certainly did understand, but it wasn't the time for that discussion. "It's not on you, Clement," he said.

Carval moved around to stand slightly behind Casey, a tactfully hidden arm supporting her.

Allan hurried up. "Mrs Kent – Darla," he altered, at her look, "how about I take you around for a moment or two while your husband talks to Casey and Jamie?"

"That won't be necessary," Kent said. "I'll take my wife around. Carval will join us in a few moments."

Carval opened his mouth to protest. Casey jabbed him. "Go with them," she said. "I'll be fine." She gave him another little push. "I need to go see if O'Leary's accidentally broken Dad." Her voice stayed light. Her eyes...told a different story.

"If you're sure," he said. "If that's what you need," he murmured, inaudible two feet away. He couldn't resist the quick hug, but he didn't linger, obedient to her request.

Casey vacated the gallery fast enough to scorch her feet, aiming for the restroom. Almost there, she stopped at the sound of O'Leary's ominous bass.

"You gotta choice. You c'n go back in there an' see the rest of the show, an' you keep your thoughts to yourself, or you c'n go home. Either way, stop upsettin' your daughter." An indistinct mutter, flavoured with shame. "No. You don't go back in without agreein'. Casey might be your daughter, but she's my pal an' our team boss. You don't upset her any more. Iffen it's all too much, you tell me or one of the others an' we'll take you for a break." More muttering. "We'll go back in, an' you stay with me."

Casey fled before she could be noticed. Facing her father was beyond her overstressed composure. If O'Leary would take charge of him, she wouldn't argue about it. She slumped down in a stall, drained, determinedly dry-eyed. She could get through, if everyone pretended the last half-hour had never happened; if no-one offered sympathy; if no-one talked to her about it.

If the team did what it did best, closed around her and allowed her *not* to mention it.

She washed her hands, and walked out: armour in place, ignoring O'Leary and her father, joining Andy. Tyler and Allie were strolling round, engrossed in the shots and each other, though Tyler flicked her an assessing glance.

"Come on, Casey," Andy said. "I want a better look at the sparring shots." Andy could see Casey's father and O'Leary moving towards the shots of Casey interrogating Caveman Bill and his wife, and he wanted to keep them as far apart as possible.

Carval rejoined Kent and his wife and met Kent's gaze squarely. "Yes?" he said combatively.

"What you and Clement do isn't my problem. You don't work for me."

"No."

"But the can of worms you've opened up here *is*."

Carval raised cynical eyebrows. "Oh?"

"Apart from Clement's father, what exactly do you think will happen when certain elements of the precinct see those?" Kent gestured to the shots of sparring.

"I think you'll deal with it," Carval snapped. "Just like you already do. It doesn't matter what you say, because this exhibition isn't changing 'cause you don't like something. Anyway, Casey and the team can take care of themselves in the precinct. The *problem* here is her father, and she won't let that get in the way of her job." He glared.

"Gareth," Mrs Kent said gently, "I think I'd like to see the rest of the exhibition." To Carval's utter amazement, Kent fell silent. "Shall we?" she added, and moved on, to look at the same pictures of interrogation that O'Leary had just left.

Three hours after they'd arrived, Allan had managed to collect the ill-assorted assembly into one place, ready to shoo them out. O'Leary had kept Casey's father away from Casey for the whole time, and by judicious muttering had also kept him from voicing his thoughts above a whisper. The team was collectively quiet, though Casey's colour hadn't returned since her father's explosion. Allie's eyes sparkled with delight, and Mrs Kent freely expressed her awe.

Captain Kent's face was ominously stern. "This is what the public and media will see?" he enquired coldly.

"Yes." Carval didn't try to soften his answer.

"Congratulations," Kent said, and smiled. "You've portrayed the NYPD in a great light. We can work with this." He turned to Allan. "The press office will call you, if you haven't called them first." The team tried to shuffle away. "You four will report to me tomorrow morning to discuss your part in the media circus." They drooped.

Kent and his wife departed, much to everyone's relief. Casey looked at her father, who was shuffling uncomfortably. "Do you need a ride home?" she asked. O'Leary's mouth opened, and then closed.

"No. I'll take the subway."

She shrugged. "Okay." Trying to persuade him otherwise was too much for her, tonight. "I'll see you for dinner on Sunday."

"Bye." He plodded off. Casey didn't try to hug him, or do anything more than watch him go.

"Give me a minute," she said, "then let's go get a drink."

"I better get home!" Allie said. "That was great!"

"Take you," Tyler said. They departed, to knowing, sly smiles from the others.

"I better go too," Allan said. "There are a few things to fix up before the critics tomorrow. Jamie, don't be late. They'll expect you there, bright eyed."

"Yes, Mom."

Allan sighed, and disappeared into the subway.

Ten minutes later, the remains of the group had found its way to a wine bar near the gallery. Despite O'Leary's mutterings, it proved to have beer as well as wine.

"That could have gone worse," Andy said.

Casey stared. "How? Dad showed up far too early, laid into Kent, and had to be escorted around by O'Leary to stop him doing it again every time he didn't like a shot – which was a lot. I could see him frowning at every other photo."

"Everyone else thinks the shots are brilliant, though. Even Kent was pleased."

"He's not the one who'll have to face the media."

"He will," Andy pointed out. "It's his precinct. It all comes back on him."

"Waal, we can't fix that, an' I don't want to try," O'Leary said. "An' we can't stop your dad from dislikin' the shots, an' I don't want to try that either. Let's try drinkin' our drinks an' relax." He set an immediate example by draining his beer, and then grinned. "It ain't such a bad show."

"It's great!" Carval whipped back. "Everyone'll love it."

"Dunno," O'Leary threw in.

"Yeah," Andy added. "It's unbalanced." He snorted as Carval's colour rose.

"Unbalanced?" Carval squawked. "Unbalanced? You don't have a clue" – O'Leary's gusts of laughter clued him in. "You got me. But that was *mean*."

"Keepin' you grounded. You'll get so many kudos from the critics that you need your pals to keep your head outta the clouds."

"That's what Allan's for," Casey said cynically.

"Waal, we'll help."

"But seriously," Andy said, "it's amazing." He smirked. "It's even worth you following us around and annoying us."

Carval grinned back at him. "It's worth me putting up with all of you," he riposted.

"Like you needed any encouragement," O'Leary said with a grin. "The problem would've been stoppin' you."

Where Casey would normally have added a snarky quip, there was only silence. "Casey?" O'Leary said.

She looked up from her glass of wine. "Huh?"

"Were you listening?"

"No. Did I miss something important?"

"No," Andy said. "Carval preening."

"Oh." She drank her single small glass of wine, and sank back into her own thoughts.

"You okay?" Carval asked.

She shrugged. "What does it matter? He hates it and he hates what I do." Carval put an arm around her, which didn't seem to help. "Why couldn't he be happy that I'm happy with my life?" She tossed the rest of the wine down her throat. "I'm out," she said. "I'll see you all tomorrow."

"I'll come with you," Carval suggested.

"No. I don't want anyone else tonight." She fixed O'Leary with a cold-eyed gaze. "That means you too."

"'Kay. Night." His words were echoed by the other two.

"What did you do to her dad?" Carval asked O'Leary as soon as Casey had gone.

"Told him to stop upsettin' Casey, then walked him around so's he couldn't talk to anyone."

"Did he hate the show?" Andy asked.

"He sure didn't like seein' Casey all cold an' hard or injured. Iffen I were Casey, I'd be upset with him too. Didn't you notice that she didn't try to talk him into a ride home?"

"Maybe this time she'll leave him to it."

"Mebbe this time he'll die," O'Leary said bluntly. "'Cause I think he's gone home to drown his fuck-up in a bottle, an' I'm tired of watchin' Casey kill herself to try an' keep him dry."

"Hard words," Andy said, but didn't contradict them.

"Hard place for Casey to be," O'Leary pointed out. "She won't leave him till he leaves her." His cheerful moon-face turned stern. "An' the sooner that happens, the better, for my money." He finished his beer. "Anyways, I'm goin' home. Night, all."

The others took the hint.

***

Casey, having barely slept for fear of Kent's likely commentary on her father's behaviour, made worse by the acute perception and outright brilliance of the exhibition, gave up and went to the precinct hours before she should have. If Kent caught her, she'd be in deep shit, but she was likely so far up shit creek already that a little further wouldn't make a difference.

She settled down at her desk and considered the state of the case. They likely had the weapons – both of them, but they didn't have a source for the roofies that had been used, nor did they have a place where those roofies had been administered. They had a suspect list, which was far too long, but no easy way of shortening it.

In fact, they had a long and tedious path ahead of them. Great. Why couldn't they have a sudden (and completely unbelievable) coincidence that pointed them to the murderer? Then they could all go home, or in her case take a long holiday to somewhere without cell service or a forwarding address. She gloomed at her murder board, searching vainly for a hint, or something they'd missed. A few officers and detectives hit the bullpen, but Casey didn't notice.

"I hear you're gonna be a star."

Casey jumped. "Officer Grendon," she said coldly. "Do you have some information on a case of mine?"

"Naw," he drawled. "I'm gonna go see this show, along with some pals."

"Are you, Officer Grendon? How interesting." Captain Kent had ghosted up behind them. "My office. We'll discuss your visit, with particular reference to 1PP's orders." Grendon paled. "I said, *my office*. Now!" Grendon went. The implications as Kent's office door closed with a sharp crack weren't lost on a single cop in the precinct.

Casey breathed a sigh of relief, and went back to poring over her murder board. She entirely failed to notice Grendon slouching back, with a pitch-black expression which boded ill for his blood pressure, nor did she detect his discussion with Estrolla.

"Mornin', Casey," O'Leary boomed, half an hour later.

"Hey. Why don't I have any new leads?"

"'Cause we're still workin' through all them actors."

"Oh joy," Andy added. Tyler grunted.

"Clement. Your team, my office."

"Great," Casey muttered.

They followed Kent to his office, and stood at strict attention.

"After last night's viewing, I am content that you will be able to handle the media. You will be informed when you're required to speak to them. Regardless of the status of your case, undertaking that interview has priority over everything except life-threatening emergencies."

Casey shivered. Kent was gazing directly at her. She clamped her mouth shut.

"Do you understand?"

"Yes, sir," they said in perfect unison.

"Clement, remain. The rest of you, dismissed."

"Sir," the three men said, and left.

Casey continued standing at parade attention.

"At ease, Clement." She shifted to parade rest. "You aren't responsible for your father."

"No, sir."

"Is there anything that will affect your work or your ability to undertake any media conferences?"

"No, sir."

Kent fixed her with a firm gaze. "Are you sure?"

"Yes, sir."

"If your father becomes ill, or if he is picked up or arrested, report to me immediately."

"Yes, sir."

"Dismissed."

"Sir." Casey scarpered, before Kent could change his mind about her father's idiocy.

***

"Okay?" O'Leary asked.

"I'm alive. I'll take it. Let's think about the case. First up, we – you and me, Bigfoot – need to go see the Finisterres. If they were supposed to meet Isabella on Thursday night, why didn't they tell us?"

"I thought they were bein' pretty straight."

"So did I, but they're still actors at heart." She looked at her board. "Second, we need to follow up with that charity. Andy, Tyler?"

"On it."

"Third, is there *any* clue at all from her phone where she was going on Thursday? Set Larson on that. He's good at methodical. If we can't get it from the phone, we'll need to get it from the cell towers, and that's not exactly accurate or quick."

"Not Larson. I want him to finish with the footage. He's got an eye," Andy contradicted.

"Henegan and Adamo, then. Henegan ought to have experience, and Adamo'll keep him on the straight and narrow." Casey still didn't trust Henegan as far as she could see him. Right now, her back was to him and so she couldn't see him at all. "Fremont can follow up on camera footage from Inwood. If we get that, we might get a proper idea of who attacked Maisie."

"Waal, we know why," O'Leary said. "Someone thought Maisie knew about them, same as someone knew – thanks to Maisie – that Isabella knew about them. I guess that someone was tryin' to get rid of Maisie."

"Guard," Tyler said.

"Good point. Let's get an officer sitting on her hospital room, stat. Anyone that we know isn't part of Estrolla's gang."

"On it," Tyler said, whisking off for a brief discussion with Sergeant Tully and returning. "Done."

"Thanks," Casey said. "After the four of us get back, we start on the actors. Oh, joy."

CHAPTER TWENTY THREE

Casey and O'Leary made their way to the Finisterres' plush apartment, informed the doorman that if he gave any warning, it would be taken very badly indeed, and went up to rap on the door.

"Who is it?" fluted from behind the entrance.

"Detectives Clement and O'Leary," Casey announced.

"Oh! Just a moment." They heard the rattle of the safety chain, and then the tumblers of locks turning over. The door opened. "Have you come with news?" Claudia asked. "Do come in. Some tea?"

That wasn't what Casey had been expecting, if the Finisterres had been hiding a meeting with Isabella. No matter how Oscar-worthy their acting, there should have been some hint of worry or fear.

"Yes, please," she said.

"Madeleine, two cups of Earl Grey for our guests, and I shall have camomile. Henry?"

"I think I shall have Rose Oolong," Henry said. "And perhaps some pastries?"

"I think so. Thank you, Madeleine."

"What can we do for you, Detectives?" Henry asked.

"We have received information that Isabella was meeting you on Thursday evening."

The Finisterres stared at her. "I'm sorry? Meeting *us*? There must be some mistake. She was to meet us on *Saturday*, but obviously that was prevented. There didn't seem any point in mentioning it."

"When did you arrange that?" No matter how well they could act, that was genuine astonishment, Casey thought.

The Finisterres thought. "My dear, I think it was last Thursday."

"Yes," Claudia agreed slowly. "I thought it was simply a progress report – she was grateful for our support, and we had agreed with her that she would let us know how she was doing. We had had two meetings" –

"Three, I think," Henry said.

"Perhaps it was."

"You didn't think that there was anything significant in this meeting?"

"No, but she had called from the theatre. I could clearly hear lines from the *Dream* in the background." Claudia stopped. "Why should there be anything significant? I didn't – she didn't say anything. She was upset, but she'd been upset with Carl every time we spoke. I didn't think anything of it. I simply forgot about it until now." She blinked hard. "My dear, what if she had wanted to tell us something important?"

"My God," Henry exclaimed. "She never had the chance." They stared, wide-eyed and horrified, at Casey. "Could that be why she was" – he hitched at the word – "killed?"

"We don't know yet. We're looking at everything."

"Could I see your phone call log, please?" O'Leary asked.

"Of course," Claudia said, and handed over her phone, opening it for him. Henry pulled his out, and did the same for Casey's inspection.

"See, here is her call."

"Six oh-five on Thursday," O'Leary said. "An' you say they were still rehearsin' in the background?"

"I think so," Claudia said. "I thought I heard *So shall all the couples three/Ever true in loving be*. Almost the end of the play. They should have been finishing the rehearsal, though I'm certain that Carl would have had many, many points and corrections."

Casey and O'Leary exchanged looks. Anyone who hadn't been on the stage could have overheard Isabella. In fact, even people performing on stage might have heard. The acoustics in the Terpsichore were pretty good.

"Did Isabella mention going out to dinner or for a drink with anyone?"

Claudia thought hard. "She said that she would be busy that evening, and probably Friday, but she was free on Saturday," she said slowly. "She sounded…upset." She thought some more. "I asked her if there was anything wrong, but she said no. I didn't press her. If I had…I wish I had. Maybe she would have told me and she'd still be alive." She sniffed damply, and blotted her eyes. Henry put an arm around her, and she turned into him, seeking comfort, or absolution.

"It's not on you," Casey said. "If Isabella had said more, you would have helped her."

"Of course we would," Henry said sadly. "I only wish that we could do so now."

"She said," Claudia spoke with miserable realisation, "that she had always wanted to do more for Act Like A Child, and that maybe she would be able to because of Carl's *Dream*. I thought she meant that she'd be better known, and earn more."

"You knew about her charity work?"

"Oh, yes. It was part of why we supported her, though she didn't know that we support them. She gave back. She had told us that she wished she had had access to that when she was young. She helped there, too. She gave them such money as she could, and she sought contributions from the other cast members, but her biggest gift was her time. She gave that generously."

"Did her sister help out?" O'Leary asked.

"If she did, I don't remember it ever being mentioned."

"I see," Casey said. "Thank you for your time. We're doing everything we can to solve this."

"If there is *anything* more we can do, please tell us. Anything."

"We will."

"Let me see you out," Henry said.

Casey and O'Leary didn't say anything until they were safely in O'Leary's giant SUV.

"Waal," O'Leary said heavily. "Looks like we're settlin' on the cast, don't it?"

"Yeah. I want another go at Maisie, though. She's one big barrel of lies and omissions. She got her sister killed, and nearly herself."

"Let's see what Tyler an' Andy got from the charity."

"'Kay."

"An' while we're on the way, you okay?"

"I guess. I don't want to think about Dad. I don't want to see him. He could've gotten me fired and how would I get past that if he had? If it hadn't been for you…" She swallowed. "I heard you telling him to behave. Picking up the pieces again."

"We're pals. We've always been pals, an' we always will be. You did plenty for me – that chef case, last up. We don't count up or keep score."

Casey blinked hard as O'Leary patted her shoulder. "Pals," she agreed soggily.

"An' Kent wouldn't fire you."

"No?"

"Waal, not 'cause of your dad, an' not 'cause of Carval neither. Iffen you try'n shoot him, then that'll do it."

"Carval?" Casey said blankly.

"The man's head over heels about you, though he don't quite know it, but Kent an' his wife sure saw it. Look how he was there holdin' you up." O'Leary pouted. "Thought that was my job, an' there you are, goin' off with some other guy."

202

"You went off with Pete first," Casey replied automatically. *Head over heels?* Nope. That had to be wrong. Far too soon. They needed time – what? "I can't deal with that. It's too soon and Dad's too much and I don't need to have any more complications. Not now."

"'T ain't complicated 'less you make it so. Don't shut him out. You need someone to hug you when it's all gettin' too much, an' he's there." The big man smirked. "I wanna be a bridesmaid in one of them pretty frilly dresses with flowers an' a sparkly tiara."

Casey choked. "Is that before or after the circus parade when you carry in the elephants, one on each arm?"

"There. Now you're back to normal, an' here we are at the precinct. Let's go get our lunch, 'cause I reckon we won't have time to get it as soon as the others get back."

***

Tyler and Andy pulled up at the community centre where Act Like A Child was based. As soon as they stepped out of the cruiser, they could hear enthusiastic noise. They simply followed the sounds to a large hall towards the back of the building, where they found a group of around fifteen pre-teens being shepherded into different groups by four adults.

"Darnell!" one adult yelled over the hubbub. "Pay attention! You're a firefighter, big and brave. Help Jodie with the hose."

"But Miss Savannah, there's two men coming in."

Savannah whirled around. "This is a private session," she snapped.

"Detectives Chee and Tyler," Andy interrupted, showing his shield. "Can we talk?"

"Can you wait ten minutes till the session ends?"

"Sure," Andy said. The cops wandered over to a row of seats against the wall, and watched. The work appeared to be a short play about firefighters rescuing puppies from a blazing animal shelter. Since it was for pre-teens, all of the animals were saved.

"More freaking toys," Tyler muttered.

"I don't think you're allowed to use real puppies," Andy said dryly.

Tyler grinned. "Total chaos," he said.

"This isn't?" Andy said, watching the children leave.

"No," said Savannah sharply, "this isn't. What do you want?"

"We're here about Isabella Farquar – Betty Scarfield."

"Isabella? But…but she died. She didn't show up on Friday and then it was on Instagram." Her eyes dampened. "Why are you here?" Her fingers twisted together, tightening, as she tried to deny her suspicion. "Why are you here?" Savannah asked again, desperately.

"I'm sorry to tell you that Isabella was murdered" –

203

"No!" Savannah cried. "No!" She half-fell into a chair, knees giving, blood draining from her shocked face.

"Put your head between your knees," Andy ordered, worried that she would faint. "Take a moment."

"Isabella," Savannah sobbed. "Oh, Isabella."

"What's happened. Savannah, what's wrong?" An older woman, hair in beaded braids, hurried up and took Savannah in her arms.

"Mom, Isabella was murdered. It wasn't just a horrible accident. Someone *killed* her." Savannah sobbed harder, joined by her mother. The two other adults rushed across to join them.

"Harvey, Keiron, Isabella was murdered," the older woman wept, slumped by Savannah.

"Murdered?" Both men paled, lips tight, shoulders bent to endure a blow. All four stared at the cops, as if staring would change the awful news.

"She meant a lot to you?" Andy tried.

"Yeah," one of the men said, tight-lipped to hold emotions inside. "She came to help out twice a week, regular. The kids loved her. We all did." His voice cracked, and he sat down hard.

"She was a big supporter," the other said. "Donated what she could, but her time was much more important. She was an inspiration. Those kids *believe* they can do it. She did that." He gulped, loud in the grief-ridden silence of the hall.

"She donated time and money?"

"Yes," Savannah's mother managed. "She gave…"

"Take your time," Tyler murmured.

It took several minutes for Savannah, her mother (Atalanta, they discovered) and the two men to recover anything close to composure. Shock still stained their faces when they'd calmed a little.

"You said Isabella helped out twice a week."

"Yes," Atalanta sniffled. "Wednesday and Friday. She didn't have rehearsals then – she said that if rehearsals were daily then she'd have to take a break and she'd done that before so I didn't worry when she didn't show up on Friday… I should have reported it then."

"If you saw her last Wednesday," Andy reassured, "then nothing you could have done would have made any difference. We might have talked to you sooner, because we'd have known about you earlier, but you couldn't have stopped it." Atalanta began to cry again. Savannah hugged her, looking about to sob herself.

"When she was here on Wednesday last week, how did she seem?"

"I thought she was worried," Kieron said.

"Worried?" Tyler queried.

"Yeah. She was a little distracted, but she pulled it together for the kids. When we were done, though, we went to make a coffee and she wasn't with us at all. But she said nothing was wrong, and told us she'd raised another seventy dollars – that's another fourteen sessions for a kid who can't afford it" –

"How are you funded?" Andy interrupted.

"Savannah?" Kieron suggested.

"The Finisterres fund us up to a point – hall rental, small salaries for the four of us, a fund for costumes and three-quarters of the fee for every child, but every little bit helps us add another child, or take one who can't pay anything."

"I see. Sorry, you were saying?"

"Yes, she'd raised another seventy dollars. She said she'd transfer it that afternoon, and she did." He blinked rapidly, and then sniffed. "She did all she could."

"Were there a lot of transfers?"

"Oh, sure. At least one a month. Never big, but…constant, you know?"

"Could we have your bank details, then we can check it off?"

"Sure, sure. Kieron, go get a copy statement for them." Kieron trotted off, and brought one back.

"Did her sister ever help out?" Tyler asked.

"Sister?" Kieron said blankly. "I never saw her sister."

"Me either," Savannah agreed. Atalanta and Harvey shook their heads. "I don't remember her ever mentioning that her sister might want to help out in person here. We'd have been happy for her to, but I guess she wouldn't have had time."

"Her sister wasn't involved here?"

"Not in person, no."

"Thank you. Did you know if she was seeing anyone?"

"She broke up with her boyfriend, David," Atalanta said.

"She was going to meet someone, Thursday," Savannah said. "She said that she was going after rehearsal, but I didn't think it was a date. More of a business meeting, you know? I think she was hoping they'd contribute to us."

"Do you know who?"

"No, but it was one of the actors." Savannah's brow creased heavily. "You know, I said her sister wasn't involved here, but I'm sure Isabella mentioned that her sister was supposed to go with her."

"She was? Why would that be?"

"Isabella said her sister was her best friend, and she trusted her. Likely she wanted a second opinion, I guess."

"Most likely," Tyler said neutrally. He and Andy exchanged a glance. Maisie, not for the first time, had outright lied.

"If you remember anything more, or think of anything else, give one of us a call," Andy said, handing over a card to each of them. "That's been helpful."

"Catch him," Savannah said brokenly. "Make him pay."

"We'll do our very best," Andy promised.

***

"Are you ready?" Allan fretted.

"Yes. Stop fussing. Are *they*?" Carval smiled arrogantly. "They've never seen anything like this before."

"They're all packed into the ante-room. Let's go."

Suddenly, it all hit him. His feet failed to move, and the air held no oxygen.

"Come on" – Allan began, and then looked at him properly. "What's wrong?"

"What if they don't like it?"

"*What?*"

"What if they don't like it? What if…what if I've done all this and put the team out there and it's *wrong*?"

"Jamie" –

Carval's heart pounded. He'd never had stage-fright in his life, never doubted his talent or skill. He wanted to vomit. "What if it's *wrong* and I've ruined Casey's life for *nothing*?"

"Stop that," Allan snapped. "It's wonderful that you're worried about someone other than yourself, which I have to say is a welcome sign of maturity which you've never displayed before – but now is *not the time*. Get your head out of your ass and *move*." He shoved Carval's shoulder.

"I wanna throw up." Carval twined his fingers, and took two deep, slow breaths.

"There's a fire bucket behind you. I don't care how you feel, get out there and make the critics happy."

"You're supposed to support me."

"Nope," Allan said unsympathetically. "This show is *my* biggest triumph yet and you won't ruin it because you've suddenly managed to grow up."

"Yours?" Carval squawked. "This isn't *your* show, it's *mine*!"

"Go open it, then. Or I will. This'll be *amazing* and if you don't want the credit, I do."

Carval gawped at Allan, then took five more slow, deep breaths, pushed away his terror – he didn't need to be scared: Allan had said this exhibition was *stellar* – remembered who and what he was, and switched on. By the time he'd hit the front of the room, he blazed. Allan briefly introduced him.

"Thank you for coming, everyone," Carval said, and smiled brilliantly, drawing answering smiles from the throng. "This exhibition was only possible with the co-operation of the Thirty-Sixth precinct of the NYPD: some of New York's Finest, who've let me follow them around for most of a year." He grinned infectiously. "I think I got the best end of that deal, but they haven't pushed me into the Hudson yet." The critics laughed. "Seriously, though, the cops I've been trailing have been outstandingly professional and dedicated. I hope that you'll see them through my shots in the same way that I did." He caught up the critics' gazes. "Go see!"

The media walked decorously to the door – and the first two to reach the gallery entrance stopped dead, gasping.

"What's the hold up? Lemme *see*!" those behind called. "Move up!"

"It's *stunning*," said the first few, standing still.

In an instant, ordinarily civilised, cultured men and women of the media shoved and elbowed, and then, as they halted in amazement, were shoved or elbowed in their turn.

"I told you so," Allan said smugly to Carval. "Let's see how they do with the rest."

"Yeah," he replied, grinning like a fool. He hadn't realised how much it would mean to him that the critics were rocked out of their socks by the centrepiece; he'd been completely confident until ten minutes ago. His relief overwhelmed him.

"You okay?" Allan worried, as Carval stopped again.

"Yeah." He smiled widely. "Yes. Everything's going to be *great*."

"You'd better go join them. Let's ride the wave."

"I can't see you surfing, somehow," Carval teased.

"I leave the stunts to you. I keep the show on the road."

"You sure do," Carval said, suddenly serious. "You really do. Thank you."

Allan gaped. Carval, embarrassed, skittered off to join the critics. Allan, still dumbfounded, trotted after him.

The first gallery was full of noise and buzz. References to great photographers of the past were being thrown around like confetti at a wedding; sounds of astonishment formed an undercurrent.

"You said you followed cops around?" one man asked. "How did you get permission?"

"I asked," Carval said simply, failing to mention the, um, less simple aspects.

"Did the NYPD demand approval?" another, more cynical, questioned.

"No, and if they had, there wouldn't be an exhibition. I don't let *anyone* censor my work. The only person who gets to edit my shots is me." He smiled self-deprecatingly. "Any mistakes are mine."

"Complete free rein?"

"Yes. I had to blur the faces of witnesses and suspects – as you'll see, but that's to prevent any possibility of prejudicing trials or putting witnesses at risk." A gentle hum of approval rose. "But nobody stopped me taking any shots I liked."

"Is that a real cop in the picture?" That was one of the tabloid rags.

"Yes. That's Detective Clement."

"Didn't know they grew *those* in the NYPD," he said lecherously. Someone else elbowed that critic, not gently.

"They grow giants, too," Carval distracted.

"Giants?"

"Sure. Here's the resident giant in this sequence here. How about moving around the exhibition? There's plenty of time and you'll all get to talk to me and Allan while you look." He moved the first bunch along, and heard another round of amazement behind them.

CHAPTER TWENTY FOUR

"What did you find?" Casey asked as soon as Tyler and Andy walked in.

"'Cause we found *clues*," O'Leary added smugly.

"Too damn many clues," Casey muttered, "and Maisie will have another truly unpleasant go-around with me very, very soon."

"We found clues too," Andy said. "Let's match them all up. Hope you got your lunch."

"We did. You go first."

An hour later, the four detectives grinned at each other.

"Isabella passed on every cent to the charity, whatever the rest of the cast thought she was doing," Andy said. "But get this, the reference on the *charity's* bank statement is the right number but the wrong account name. It's Isabella's name."

"What the hell? Maisie said Isabella had asked her to set it up in her name."

"Yeah. *After* she'd claimed it was her account, that they shared it, that she didn't know about it, that she never had any log-in details... I don't think Maisie ever set it up."

"You c'n change the name on an account pretty easy, iffen you wanna. 'Specially if your li'l sis thinks you're her best pal and is happy to tell you the log-in. Wasn't it on-line access?"

"Yeah," Andy confirmed. "I'll find out when the name changed."

"O-*kay*. Maisie knows a *lot*, and my guess is she's going in for blackmail."

"Don't she *read*?" O'Leary asked. "In ev'ry story I ever read, witnesses goin' in for blackmail get dead. Ev'ry time. They prob'ly used that storyline in Ancient Egypt, never mind now."

"Dumbass," Tyler said, clearly directed at Maisie.

"The Finisterres are likely out of it, or at least low down the list, and so is the charity. But we *do* know that Isabella was meeting one of the cast, and that Maisie was supposed to go with her." Casey smiled. "We're narrowing down the list."

"CSU report on the props?" Tyler wondered.

"Came in a minute before you did," Casey said.

"A minute before you yanked Evan's guts out through the phone, you mean," Andy snipped.

"Naw," O'Leary drawled. "She was givin' him at least two minutes."

"Thinking about our murder here," Casey said, "I'll read it when we're done. Andy, will you see what Larson and Fremont've come up with? Tyler, you talk to Henegan and Adamo. We'll regroup in twenty minutes with the results."

Twenty minutes later, the four detectives gathered once more in front of Casey's murder board.

"The gas station and sandwich shop footage doesn't give us anything," Andy said disgustedly, and then grinned. "But the Inwood footage is better. We can definitely rule out Dacia from the attack on Maisie, and I think we can rule out the four fairies too. Fremont's running it through enhancement to see if we can go further."

"CSU confirms that the crystal ball and the red-navy-white scarf are the murder weapons – traces of Isabella's blood on the ball and DNA on both. They have partial fingerprints but they don't match anything in the databases. There's DNA that doesn't match Isabella on the scarf, but it's not in the databases either."

"That matches up to none of our actors havin' any record," O'Leary rumbled, "but it still ain't exactly helpful."

"On the other hand," Casey said, "all we have to do is put a glass of water in front of them in interview and see if they drink from it."

"You think that'll work?"

"No, because thanks to the endless round of cop shows on TV, pretty much everything we might do is on air seven days a week. But I'm still going to try it because *some* criminals really are that dumb. We'll ask them if they'll give fingerprints."

"They won't," Andy said cynically.

"Phone records don't help," Tyler said. "Need to know the cast's numbers."

"We could ask the four we've ruled out," Casey said suddenly. "They all said they wanted to help, so let's push them on it."

"Good thought. Let's each call one, and see if it all matches up."

"Sneaky," O'Leary said admiringly to Andy.

"I give good sneak," Andy smirked.

"Interview the four older actors," Tyler said. "Heyer too?"

"I think so. Didn't the Finisterres say he had money?"

"Yeah. Someone thought Julius did too."

"We don't have nearly enough for warrants for anyone's financials except maybe Carl. If any of those prints had pinged, we would, but we don't. Let's think about what we *can* do."

"We c'n look up what Maisie meant with that comment about some guy called Gladstone, for one," O'Leary said. "'Cause none of us know what it means, an' I think we should."

"That's what Google is for," Casey said, and tapped in *William Gladstone evening walks.*

"Walks?"

"Yeah, because Ji-Hoon said Maisie mentioned evening walks by this guy – wow! First up, references to prostitutes. British Prime Minister back in the day, who spent his evenings walking around red-light districts. Well, well, well. What was Julius doing – and with who?"

"How'd Maisie know?"

"Unpack, Tyler! How'd she know *what?*"

"Don't know that reference. British. Maisie wasn't scholar of the year; found that out when we ran her. Never done an elective in British history. How'd she know? Even Andy didn't, and he's cultured."

The cops looked at each other. That was a good point. If none of them knew – pub quiz champions by a crushing margin – then where had Maisie gotten it from?

"Another thing to push her on," Casey said, and made a note.

"Maisie's the key to this whole thing," Andy said.

"Yeah," Casey said. "Let's speak to the four and then start fresh in the morning. I can see Kent glaring at us even though my back's to him."

"Leastways he hasn't mentioned press conferences again," O'Leary said.

"Did you have to remind us of that?" Casey muttered.

"Sword of Damocles," Tyler said.

"You what?"

"A sword hanging by a thread over the head of a courtier," Andy said, "to teach him about the fragility of a luxurious existence."

"Song from Rocky Horror," Tyler said. Andy wailed, fruitlessly, as Tyler laughed.

"Calls, guys," Casey said firmly, and set the example by dialling Deontay. "Mr Jackson?" she said. "There's something you can do for us, to help us find Isabella's killer." She explained.

"Sure," Deontay said. "I could come over and you could take all the contacts off my phone."

"Can you come now?"

"In half an hour? We're finishing up rehearsal. Uh, do you want all four of us? 'Cause it looks like the other three got the same calls."

"Yes, that would be good. See you in half an hour."

The four young men appeared half an hour later, and were taken to four separate rooms, which didn't reassure them enormously.

"Thanks for coming in again," Casey said. "Would you write down the phone numbers that you have for any other cast members – with names, and including your own number – and for Carl Heyer. Could you say if it's not a cell number?"

"All of my contacts are cell phone numbers," Deontay said.

"That makes it easier." Casey gave him paper and a pen. "Please don't take the pen away. We don't have many," she smiled. Deontay relaxed, and started to write.

In three other rooms, three other detectives had the same conversations. Ten minutes later, four lists were handed over, the actors were effusively thanked and sent on their way, and the detectives started cross-checking the four lists against each other by the simplest method of Casey reading out a name and number and the other three checking it off. It took them almost half an hour, and at the end of it there hadn't been a single discrepancy.

"Waal, that was a waste of time," O'Leary said.

"Nope, it means that they gave us the right info – or they all had the same wrong info," Casey said. "Can we match up these numbers to Isabella's unnamed contacts?"

"We" – Andy started.

"You can, tomorrow," Kent said. "It's shift end. I have not approved overtime, nor will I. Clement, do I have to remind you about my rules on doing overtime?"

"No, sir," Casey said. He didn't have to. She merely wished he wouldn't enforce them.

"Out, then. You have five minutes to clear your desks and go."

"I'll use the five minutes to ask Adamo to put the actors' contact list into a spreadsheet that I can match against Isabella's phone records. That'll be much faster tomorrow."

"We'll tidy you up while you do that."

"Abbey?" O'Leary said hopefully.

"Nope. I'm going home to a good book."

O'Leary glanced at Casey, wriggled his bushy eyebrows, and grinned. Fortunately for his good health, he didn't say anything.

"Nah," Tyler said, and didn't say why.

"Nope," Andy followed. "I'll find some culture at La Mama. You can join me."

"Naw. I'll go be lonely. Pete's outta town tonight."

"See you all tomorrow," Casey said.

***

Captain Kent watched his misfits leave, and breathed a sigh of relief. He knew Clement had been in far too early, but he'd let that pass – this time. She needed a break, but his precinct wasn't a rest cure. He glanced at his watch, and found that he should be on the way to meet Garrett already. He could use a beer or three after the previous evening, and some company that didn't want to talk about culture.

He reached the bar ahead of Garrett, and ordered a beer. When Garrett hadn't turned up after the first was done, he had another.

"Starting fast there," Garrett said, looking at the two empty bottles of beer already in front of Kent as he sat down. "I guess it didn't go so great?"

"Try absolute fucking disaster," Kent said bitterly.

"Your misfits were that bad?"

"Not the misfits, though I'm pretty antsy about how Clement's taking it all. But her father showed up, way earlier than he was supposed to, and he didn't take any of it nicely."

"Mm?" Garrett encouraged. "Start at the beginning. What's this exhibition like?"

Kent scowled, growled, and harrumphed. "Don't say I said so, but it's amazing. It's the best PR we'll have this century. That smart-ass photographer's managed to shoot the absolute best of the Academy, catching suspects, interrogation – how he's done it and made those four look as if they're saving the world when they can't get along with a single other person in the precinct for more than ten minutes, I don't know. It's stunning." He harrumphed again.

"If it's that good – hey, maybe I'll go see it. Didn't you say there were pictures of you?"

Kent's harrumph at that idea nearly knocked over his beer bottle. Garrett sniggered. "Anyway," Kent grumbled, "the shots are great. Darla loved it."

"But?"

"*But*, Clement's father took exception to most of it. Starting with the shots of her being beaten up by a suspect – now in jail – and unconscious."

"Not exactly surprising," Garrett noted. "I'd be pretty upset if I saw photos of my kid unconscious on the floor."

"Yeah. Then he laid into her team for not protecting her, and then started on me" –

"Brave. Dumb, but brave."

"Then told her she should've been a lawyer. I got the feeling it wasn't the first time. Then O'Leary swooped in and carried him out, and he must have read him the riot act 'cause he simmered right down, though he was muttering all the way through."

"Oh."

"Yeah, *oh*. Now I don't know what reactions were down to those shots and what was down to Clement's dad, and *that* means that I have no more idea than you how she'll handle the media."

"The others?"

"They'll be fine. They look like heroes, and for all their bitching they're pretty pleased with how they're shown. But Clement's front and centre, and that photographer's head over heels for her and it shows. Every damn shot of her. He should've written *I'm in love* on every single one. That's a whole new can of worms."

Garrett pulled at his own beer, thinking. "So you say," he eventually said, "but you've seen a lot more of them than the public or critics have. Anyway, aren't photographers supposed to love their subjects – while they're shooting? Don't go looking for trouble. You've got enough of it with this business with her dad and not knowing how she'll react."

"Yeah. I don't like this. If she gets it wrong in front of them, the media'll crucify her simply because they can. If I don't put her in front of them, they'll go digging and find everything we don't want them to find." He sighed. "Helped by the officers they took apart on the mats – all of which Carval shot, and then put in this exhibition."

"Haven't you managed to deal with them yet?"

"No. They haven't done anything out of line. When they do, I'll come down hard. Until they do, I don't have cause. I can't expect my cops to do things right if I don't."

"No."

Kent downed the rest of the beer, and went to get another. "I don't have a choice. I have to put her in front of them. Hell."

"When?"

"Critics' preview today. Grand public opening, ten tomorrow morning. Press conference – don't know yet. That prissy-faced manager is fixing it up with the NYPD press liaison officer. I have to give the whole team the time to show up. My detectives should be out detecting, not fielding the media. None of it'll do any good for precinct harmony, not that those four care about that."

"The price of fame," Garrett said, smirking.

"Thanks," Kent said sardonically. "I'll send them all to you for a while, and you can have the fun."

"No, thanks. I'll have another beer, though, and toast your success."

Kent laughed, and bought him one.

***

At the end of a long day of the critics' previews, Carval's feet, hands, head, and possibly eyelashes all hurt, and he wanted nothing more than a stiff drink and some food. Allan looked even more tired than Carval felt, which was saying something. They ushered the last critic, still casting glances over his shoulder at the centrepiece shot, out of the door, shut it firmly (to the amusement of the gallery staff), and sat down hard on the benches.

"I think you did it," Allan said.

"Who are you and where's Allan?" Carval asked, without malice. "You never predict success before you read the critics' columns. Are you feeling okay?"

"I don't have to read them this time. I only had to listen. You did it, Jamie. You blew them away." He slumped, which Allan never did. "I'd toast you, but I'm too tired. Everything rested on this, and you did it. Public opening in the morning, but it'll be packed. Every ticket sold."

"You said," Carval yawned. "Can we go home now?"

"Home? You don't want to go out partying on the high of success like usual?"

"I'm too tired."

"That's new. Maybe you really have grown up." Allan smiled. "Yes, go home. I'll see you tomorrow, at the studio. I need to arrange the cops' press conference, because the critics'll be on to their colleagues by now."

"It can wait till tomorrow," Carval said. "We won't need to hurry. They'll all wait for us."

"There's my Jamie back in all his wonderful arrogance." Allan heaved himself up, sighing. "Home. Get some rest. You'll need it."

Carval monumentally failed to mention that when he'd said *home* he'd actually meant Casey's apartment. As far as he was concerned, *home* was a generic term covering any place he put his head down for the night. Allan might fuss at him if he admitted that he wasn't going to the studio, and now that it was all over, he was careering down the adrenaline crash-slide at full Cresta Run pace. He wanted, he decided, food, his nice snuggly Casey and about ten hours of sleep. The stiff drink could wait.

***

"Who – Carval? What are you doing here? Shouldn't you be at the gallery?"

"We're done. They *loved* it. Can I come in?"

"Sure."

Carval ambled in and instantly swept Casey up into a bear-hug. "They *loved* it," he repeated.

"Great." Enthusiasm didn't dominate her tones.

Carval, restored to complete happiness, didn't notice, and planted a smacking kiss on her lips. "If it wasn't for you four, I'd still be looking for a theme, and I have this, and construction, and theatres, and more of you."

215

He kissed her again. "Have you had dinner?" he asked. "I haven't and I'm starving. I don't think I had lunch either, but I don't remember."

"No. It's only seven o'clock."

"Oh. I feel like it's much later. I'll get us takeout."

"I have food," Casey pointed out.

"Whatever you want," Carval said expansively, "but if we get takeout you don't have to do anything."

"Whatever. Takeout."

A few moments later, dinner organised, Carval had planted himself on Casey's couch and planted Casey next to him. He gradually realised that she was, even for Casey, unusually quiet, and, contrary to his earlier hopes, decidedly not snuggly.

"What's up?"

"Nothing."

Carval didn't believe her, but asking again wouldn't get any more answers. "Okay."

"How do you know it's a success?" she asked, sounding far away.

"Allan said so," he answered, realising, before both feet entered his mouth, that *because they were astonished by the centrepiece* wouldn't be an acceptable answer.

"Allan?" Casey squeaked, immediately engaged, "Allan *never* tells you that."

"He did!"

"He did? Wow."

"Isn't it amazing? He *never* tells me that."

"I just said that," she pointed out dryly. "Why are you here?"

"Huh?"

"You've been showing off your exhibition, it's been successful" –

"Stratospherically!" Carval interjected.

"– so you should be out partying or something. But you're here."

He developed an interesting line of colour along his cheeks. "Uh," he said, which wasn't informative. Casey acquired her interrogation stare and silence, against which Carval wasn't proof. All his usual savoir-faire and suavity was dissolving under Casey's patented technique, which was simply *not fair*. "I wanted to." More silence. "I just did, okay?" The silence acquired a steely quality, with sharp edges. "It had to be a success," he blurted. "Otherwise I'd put you out there for *nothing*."

The tension snapped. Casey's jaw plummeted.

"I was *scared* they'd hate it," he babbled. "I'm *never* scared but it had to be a success or it was all going to backfire on you" –

"Stop."

"I couldn't" –

"I said *stop*."

Carval stopped.

"You were scared? You? Mr Arrogant? Mr I'm-the-greatest-photographer-since-cameras-were-invented? *You* were scared because of *us*? Not because a bad exhibition would hurt your pride?" She finally breathed.

"Uh…yes?"

Casey firmly told her skittering, shaken mind to sit down and calm itself. She couldn't have heard what he'd just said, surely? That would mean – nope. Not going there. Not. Going. There. Evasive manoeuvres definitely required.

"Who *are* you?" She prodded him. "You can't be Jamie Carval."

Carval scowled. "None of you appreciate me. Allan was rude too. Just because I" –

"Grew up a bit?" Casey suggested.

"You're all mean to me."

"Not growing up a bit, then."

"If I grew up I'd have to be an adult."

"You haven't managed that yet," Casey teased.

"You love me anyway," Carval flipped back.

Casey's brain fractured. Her face went scarlet, and she failed to find any words that weren't *uh*, or worse, *eep*. She should have found a laugh and a comment approximating to *sure I do, just like I love small cute animals or O'Leary*. She didn't. Instead she was blushing like a fourteen-year-old and completely devoid of a snappy retort. She took the line of least resistance and most cowardice and fled for her bathroom, leaving a flabbergasted Carval behind her to deal with the takeout delivery.

Casey emerged some five minutes later, pale but composed. "Is that dinner?" she asked before Carval could say anything. "I'm hungry."

"Lychee chicken," Carval said. "Special treat."

"You mean it's the only thing you remember."

"No, it's the only one that's practically rubbed out because you tap it so often."

Casey grumbled, but then applied her chopsticks to excellent effect, both on her dinner and on Carval's libido. By the time they'd finished eating, he'd dropped any idea of returning to her peculiar reaction in favour of some more direct action. He shifted the plates to the kitchen counter, returned, and promptly slung an arm around her. She smiled slowly, and turned her face up in invitation.

Carval liked being given invitations. He liked accepting invitations even more. When those invitations came from Casey, he never declined. In fact, he accepted with alacrity. Alacrity, however, didn't mean that he had to hurry, and he didn't. Casey's mouth, capable of delivering hard, lacerating interrogation, was soft on his, offering more invitations which it was his pleasure – and hers – to accept. Kisses turned hotter, hands roamed, and shortly they mutually decided that the bed was far more comfortable than the couch.

Carval, who'd thought earlier that all he wanted was food and sleep, found, to his complete lack of surprise, that what he wanted first was Casey. *All* of Casey. Starting with uncovering all of Casey, which action was only marginally hampered by Casey uncovering all of him, after which both of them didn't bother with any sort of coverings for some time, until the bedcovers were needed to keep them warm.

CHAPTER TWENTY FIVE

Carval cuddled up to Casey, comfortably happy and sleepy. Casey, however, didn't feel sleepy. She fidgeted and turned over, then back, then fidgeted some more.

"Whassup?" Carval muzzed.

"Nothing."

Even Carval's half-unconscious brain recognised that as meaning *plenty is wrong but I don't want to talk about it*. In lieu of words, he pulled her closer and petted soothingly. "Is it the shots? The critics?"

"No. Maybe." She curled away from him. "Dad."

"Mm?"

"He hated them. What if…" She trailed off. "He's stayed dry. But…"

"But?" Carval was rapidly waking up, though he didn't move. Casey had talked about important matters maybe once or twice. She almost never talked about her father; in fact, she'd only told him about her family history in the last couple of weeks. Talking should be encouraged, especially to him. It made him feel closer, less of a boyfriend and more of a partner.

"But he even said it in front of Kent," she muttered miserably. "Didn't you hear him? I should've been a lawyer." She fell silent. Carval waited, sure that there was more. Sure enough, there was. "He yelled at Kent. Is he trying to trash my career? After" – she stopped dead, and buried her face in the pillow.

"After?"

"He asked me to make his second hearing go away. Said I could *fix it*. Cops could fix it, he said. I told you that."

"Yes," Carval recalled.

"I thought it was only a hope, not asking me to do something that would finish me. That he was drunk, and flailing around for anything to save him from his own bad choices. But…he's yelled at my boss. Told everyone I should've been a lawyer. He doesn't believe in my job." She stopped again. "He doesn't believe in me, and now he's trying to force me out of my career."

"Do you think he's doing this deliberately?"

"It doesn't matter," she said desolately, into the pillow. "Accidental or deliberate, if he keeps doing it, sometime it'll all come crashing down on me."

"No."

"Huh?" emerged from the pillow.

"He's an adult. What he says isn't on you. What he does isn't on you either, even if you pick up the pieces afterwards. As long as you don't cross your own lines, it's not on you. And you haven't." He plucked her out of the pillow and replaced her on his own broad chest.

"That won't stop anyone," she said acidly.

"No, but you can't stop them either."

"Is that supposed to help?"

"Nothing I say will help. There isn't anything that will help here. You're the only one who can decide what to do." Carval clasped his hands at the small of Casey's back, and shut his mouth before he could ruin the moment with more words. Casey could, and had to, make her own decisions. None of this was up to him. Scandal sold exhibition tickets, a cynical voice pronounced, but scandal would set Casey running like a rabbit, which was worse than a poorly attended exhibition.

She lay, quietly miserable, against him. Gradually her breathing evened out, slipping into the soft cadences of sleep, into which Carval rapidly followed her.

Deep in the night, Carval woke. The reason for waking was simple: Casey wasn't there. Surely, *surely*, she hadn't gone out running, or to the precinct? She'd stopped running from him – hadn't she?

He listened, and then sat up, but he couldn't see a line of light anywhere, nor could he hear anything – until he did: the quiet *floomf* of a cushion squishing beneath someone's body, followed by the click of a glass or mug on the table. When he reached out, the place where Casey had been was no longer warm. The glass clicked again. Carval swithered: to join her, to stay there… After an indecisively long while, he stumbled out of bed, thinking that he could always plead that he had been going to the bathroom if she objected.

No lights were on, but as the curtains weren't shut, the dim glow of the city at night provided enough illumination for Carval not to fall over his own feet or the furniture. Faintly, he could see a hunched form on the couch, enveloped, he noticed as he approached, in that same oversized robe that she'd worn when he, with O'Leary, had heard the truth of her mother's death. Though he wasn't trying to be silent, if she had realised he was there, she gave no sign of it.

He peered through the gloom, and found that her eyes were closed. "Casey?" he murmured, and without thinking, "Sweetheart, it's cold out here. Come back to bed." She gave an unintelligible mutter, and sank deeper into the unlovely robe. Carval, who thought that, even for someone as small as Casey, sleeping on a couch would be uncomfortable, took the easy option, simply lifting up the whole Casey-bundle and taking it back to bed. He didn't try to disinter her from the robe, or tuck her under the covers. Shortly, he was asleep again.

Casey opened her eyes and gazed into the dark of the bedroom. She'd risen to think, without disturbing Carval, her brain spinning fruitlessly around the problem of her father. She knew, deep in her heart, that she should cut him loose so that if he chose, he could drown without dragging her down too; but she still couldn't find the strength to do it, no matter what he did or how his actions hurt her. She'd dozed off again, still hoping for a better answer. Next thing she knew, there'd been a whisper around her. *Sweetheart*. It wasn't a Carval word: old-fashioned and affectionate, nothing like him at all. Except that tonight he'd lost all of his usual over-abundance of egotism and self-confidence, terrified for *them*: her team. And, of course, her. Which was not like the Carval she knew and –

Oh. Oh, *shit*. No.

Don't think about that, Casey. Just because it's not totally casual any more doesn't mean that. Instead, she thought about Carval's astonishing admissions. Scared that the exhibition wouldn't be a success because it would damage the team? Carval was *never* unsure about anything. Oh. But *she* was. Unsure about the exhibition, that was.

Jamie Carval, obsessive photographer who never let anything get in the way of his shots and his purposes, completely confident to the point of overwhelming arrogance about his own talent and ability, utterly unbothered by any qualms anyone else might have about his work – had been *worried about the effect on the team*? Which really meant *worried about the effect on her*, because the others didn't run the same risks as she did, if her history were known.

Casey finally turned her deductive ability on to Carval's changing behaviour, examined it as if it were a murder case, and barely stopped herself gasping. The last thing she wanted was to wake Carval. She didn't want to wake *herself*, because this had to be a dream. There was absolutely no reason why Carval should be changing because of her. She hadn't asked him to change. She would never have done that. She'd even said to Kent that she wouldn't stand in the way of his photos. It wasn't like he'd tried to change her.

But she had changed, she realised. Carval hadn't tried, but it had happened all the same. She still wasn't into sharing, but she had turned to him when she needed someone; had talked to him. He knew…everything that O'Leary, her best and oldest friend, knew. Oh. How had that sneaked up on her? However it had, there it was. No point in thinking about it now.

She yawned, turned over and into Carval, and fell asleep in seconds.

***

"Okay," Andy said, five minutes after eight on Friday morning. "I've run the cross-match against Isabella's phone records and we can match up most of the calls. The rest are her family, the charity, and the Finisterres, same as you found yesterday."

"Do we have anything that might tell us where she went Thursday?"

"Not from the phone records."

"Isn't there *anything*? I mean, can we track her phone off the towers and see where she was?"

"I guess," Andy said. "It's not exactly accurate. There aren't many towers up this end of Manhattan. I'll give it a go, but we might do better with her GPS data. If there is any."

"Do it. Let's get Maisie back in, too. Or do it in her hospital room."

"Call," Tyler said, and called the officer he'd put there. "She's been discharged to her parents."

"Bring her in?" Casey asked.

"Yes," Tyler said. "Me and Bigfoot." They strode out.

"Coffee, and then let's take a look at the cleaned-up Inwood footage to see who attacked Maisie, and see if we know where her phone went."

"We can't do anything about location till we've got her phone," Andy pointed out. "Like I just said, GPS data's our best bet."

"Can we pull up that Inwood footage?" she said impatiently, as soon as they'd made their drinks.

"Sure. Stop fussing at me." Andy tapped a few keys, and the footage came up. "Ah," he said, "Larson's helped Fremont run the clean-up program." They ran it forward.

"There's the attack," Casey said. "Frame by frame?"

"Not my first rodeo," Andy rebuked mildly.

"I know." It was an apology. "It's been a week, and we're nowhere. I want this case done."

"You need a vacation."

"We all do. We haven't had time off since Thanksgiving, really. Only the usual shift pattern."

"You could go somewhere with Carval," Andy said mischievously.

Casey said nothing, remembering a call from San Francisco, remembering Carval's suggestion that they should be tourists there. She

222

hadn't been on vacation with another adult since…since her mother passed. She wasn't sure she was ready for that.

"Footage," she said. Andy glanced at her, saw her expression, and moved the footage forward frame by frame. They watched it right through, twice.

"That's not Dacia, and not the four fairies."

"We *knew* that. But I can't tell who that might be. They're all bundled up in a hoodie."

"I can tell you who it's not," Andy said smugly. "It's not Vincent. He's short and square. That person isn't wide enough."

"Any other people it isn't?"

"No. The rest of them are all pretty much the same build: taller and leaner; even Carl. I can try running it against their PR photos but I don't think it'll tell us anything definite."

"Let's try. Another one down, though. In that case, we'll talk to Vincent first, see if he can narrow anything down for us."

"Tyler and I'll do that, as soon as they've brought Maisie back in."

"Okay."

Not long after, Tyler came up. "Left O'Leary with Maisie. Two," he said.

"I'll go down. You and Andy get to talk to Vincent," Casey replied. "See you later."

She reached Interrogation Two in time to hear Maisie let loose a string of insults and profanity, which, from O'Leary's bored expression, he'd heard before.

"Maisie Scarfield," she said. "Here we are again." Maisie indulged in another round of vituperation. "Did you already read her rights?"

"Yeah, but we should do it again. I don't think she was listenin'."

"I agree. Maisie, we will read your rights for the record." Casey raised her voice above the cursing. "You can yell all you like, but we know you've told us a whole bunch more lies, so all bets are off. O'Leary, make sure you can be heard above that toddler tantrum."

He obliged. Faced with the twin stern, cold faces of the cops, offering no sympathy, Maisie shut up.

"Do you understand?" he growled. "Answer aloud for the record."

"Yes," Maisie mumbled.

"Last time we interviewed you," Casey snapped, "we warned you about obstructing our investigation. You clearly didn't understand that, because you've lied and withheld more information. The only place you're going after this interview is a cell, so you'd better co-operate in full because I won't be recommending a deal to the district attorney, I'll be recommending that he charge you to the maximum level possible. You're out of options, Maisie."

"I didn't lie! I didn't leave out information."

"Don't make it worse by lying again," Casey said boredly. "You lie as often as you open your mouth. Let's start with the easy bits. You didn't tell us Carl had barred you from rehearsals. You didn't tell us that you were sitting in on rehearsals. You didn't tell us that you were dropping hints about events that could make any of the cast or Carl look bad *before* you had the argument with your sister that the whole cast heard. You didn't tell us that Dacia Kraven slapped you in front of the whole cast and then told you to fuck off when you tried to needle her. You *certainly* didn't tell us that you knew that Isabella was going to dinner, or for a drink, or to a meeting with one of the actors immediately after that same screaming fight and that you were supposed to go with her because *she trusted you*. What a mistake she made with that," Casey added contemptuously. Maisie cowered. "You knew who she was supposed to see before she was killed and you haven't told us that. You haven't even mentioned it. That's concealing material evidence. You're toast, Maisie. I can't say I'm even a tiny bit sorry."

Maisie stared, appalled. "How" – she began, and stopped. Her hands knotted.

"How do I know? Because we're detectives, and we *detect*. We interview. We look at evidence. And most of all, Maisie, we find the truth. No matter how many lies people tell us." She bared her teeth in a savage smile. Maisie looked as if she wanted to run, but she had nowhere to run to. "You confirmed everything we've discovered. You knew everyone's secrets – and you haven't told us any of them. One of those secrets is the reason your sister was killed and you were attacked. You knew who your sister was meeting. Whoever that was might be her killer and is certainly a suspect. You didn't tell us that."

"You don't want the killer found," O'Leary pronounced. "You were so jealous of her talent that you didn't care. You'd rather have seen her dead than successful." His face and voice carried equal disgust. "You hated her, didn't you?"

"No! I didn't!" Maisie cried.

"You didn't kill her, but you're grateful to whoever did. Now she's not taunting you with her success. Your parents are only proud of you. You don't have to share their attention or look at the scrapbooks or listen to them praising her." Casey's mouth pursed.

"She thought you were her best friend. Everyone says she loved you, thought the best of you, an' tried to take you along with her. You threw all that back in her face an' got her killed."

"You're a murderer, Maisie."

Maisie gasped. "I'm *not*!" All the blood had left her face.

"You might not have done the deed but you set it up. You made sure everyone knew Isabella knew things – and someone killed her for it."

"Now they're comin' after you. You've already been attacked once. Who's to say it won't happen again?"

"You should protect me!" Maisie cried.

"No. We don't have the resources to protect everyone, and we protect people who deserve it," Casey said casually. "We don't protect murderers. That's up to the prison guards."

"I'm not a murderer!"

"Just a nasty, jealous sister who got her killed. Sounds like a murderer to me. Does it sound like one to you, O'Leary?"

"Sure does."

Maisie, astoundingly, wasn't crying. Instead, her face had twisted with vicious anger. "I should have been a success," she spat out. "I was the oldest. They should have given *me* the chances. Betty should have let me do it, not taken it for herself. It wasn't fair that she got offered the auditions and I didn't. Mom and Dad should have made them try me."

Was Maisie *four*? That wasn't how the world worked. "Carl did try you," Casey pointed out. "You weren't good enough."

"I could have been!"

"That's not what the director thought. You hung around to make trouble, weren't you? Isabella" –

"Betty! Isabella was a dumb name" –

"*Isabella* thought you were being supportive, same as she thought at the community theatre group, but her friends knew differently. They spotted all the nasty little comments. Were you hoping that the *Dream* cast would turn on her and throw her out? That wouldn't help you, because Dacia would take over. Or were you planning to take Dacia out? How? She wouldn't put up with your scheming – she already told you to get lost. Carl wouldn't have had you – he already made you try out and you were a flop."

"Carl was a *rapist*!" Maisie screamed. "He and Cordell *boasted* about it. He'd have made me a star or I'd have told the Finisterres and he'd never have gotten another production."

Casey and O'Leary stayed silent, though Casey was restraining a shriek of *you should have gone to the cops*, not that that would necessarily have achieved anything.

"That pompous *prick* Julius, he was out looking for rent boys every other night and pretending like he was cultured and civilised and above all of that. Max and Vincent hated it as much as they hated Carl and Cordell but Max never did anything about it and Vincent got mad with him too about that."

"How did you know to call him Gladstone?" Casey whipped out. "Do you know who Gladstone was?"

Maisie looked unconvincingly blank.

"You do know, don't you? Didn't you Google what you were calling him?"

"Of course I did! I knew. Some old guy in Britain who went out walking the red-light districts for working girls."

"How'd you know that? You take a history class? British history? That didn't come up when we looked at you."

Maisie reacquired her trapped-rat demeanour. "Max."

"Max told you about Gladstone? I don't believe you. I don't believe any of them *told* you anything. What did you overhear?" Casey's stab in the not-quite dark hit home. Maisie jerked.

"I overheard. So what?"

"*What* did you overhear?"

"Max told Julius that all his wandering around pretending he was helping homeless youths to safety like William freaking Gladstone" – that sounded like a direct quote to Casey – "wasn't fooling anyone and if he wanted to help he'd give to a charity."

"You turned that into *lookin' for rent boys*? Not sure how you got there, but then, all you cared about was blackmailin' them, wasn't it? You thought that's what Isabella was doin' with all her subs."

"Course she was. She was making up for having no money, dressing it up like she didn't need anything from Mom and Dad. That's 'cause she was topping up from all of them."

"She wasn't." Casey's statement dropped like a calving ice-shelf. "She gave it all to charity. We matched every last cent." She paused. "Why *was* that account in your name?"

Ghastly silence fell.

"Why?"

No answer.

"You lied to us about how it was set up, didn't you? You made us think you'd opened it so Isabella could use it in secret, but that wasn't true, was it? She opened it normally. You changed the name. When we go back to the bank, they'll show us the audit trail of when it was changed. You changed it on Friday, after we told you about Isabella's murder, didn't you? I bet you were upset when you found there wasn't any money there."

"She was always demanding contributions! There should've been cash there."

"Why did you want that account? Goin' in for blackmail like you thought Isabella was?"

"Why not? They all had money. It wasn't fair."

"But all you got was attacked," Casey said wearily, "which is pretty much what you deserve." She paused. "Who was Isabella seeing last Thursday night?"

"Max. She said she was seeing Max."

226

"That better be the truth," O'Leary rumbled.

"Maisie Scarfield," Casey said, "I am arresting you for obstructing governmental administration. Stand up." She handcuffed Maisie, as O'Leary stood ready to stop any stupidity. "You'll be taken to a cell."

"What a mess," O'Leary said, Maisie gone.

"Yeah. Max, though?"

"Don't seem likely. I was bettin' on Carl or Cordell."

"Guess we'd better get him in."

CHAPTER TWENTY SIX

Carval dashed into Allan's office as soon as he'd returned from Casey's on Friday morning. "What did they say?" he demanded. "Did they love it?"

Allan drooped. "No," he said sadly.

"What? They didn't?" Carval's face collapsed. "But they – they were stunned. How didn't they love it?" He looked straight at Allan. "What about the cops? Didn't they love them? Tell me they didn't trash them! What went wrong?"

"Nothing."

"But" –

"They didn't love it, they *adored* it." Allan smirked. "They liked it even better than *Hands*. I told you so."

"You…you *toad!*" Carval yelled, utterly furious. "You made me think – you *rat!*" No matter the provocation, he never swore at Allan. He'd been trained out of that very quickly. Carval liked the bills being paid and the lights staying on.

"You're the toast of New York," Allan said serenely. "Stop shouting and allow me a little revenge for all the times I've picked up after you."

Carval muttered for a moment more, and then grinned ruefully. "You were mean," he sulked. "But I'll forgive you."

"I always forgive you," Allan pointed out. "Far more often."

"Stop gloating, and tell me how big of a success we are."

"It couldn't be better. Top billing in every critic's column, and several of the papers have brought it forward into the main news. The NYPD is a draw."

"Are they nice about the team?"

"Yep. Really complimentary. It's all about how good the NYPD looks. You can check the scrapbook when I've put it all together, or do a search through the online media if you want to feed your ego further. But we've done it, Jamie. You've done it. You're more golden than Midas."

"Show me," Carval said, enthusing like a small child at the zoo. "C'mon. I know you've cut them all out already."

"Okay." Allan spread the clippings out on his desk, and Carval bounced over to read them. His grin grew and grew until he could barely contain his delight.

"I'm the *best!*" he crowed. "No-one's ever going to top this!" He read on. "They *loved* them."

"Them?" Surely this wasn't Jamie actually thinking about *others* for a change?

"The team! They can't say enough good things about them. We did it! I told Casey it would be okay and it is! Better than okay. They're *loved*," he repeated. "They're untouchable."

"Let's hope so," Allan said. "We'll organise a media conference – that is, I will, with Leanne from the NYPD press office."

"I'll go see the team. They'll be" – Carval stopped. "I guess they'll mostly be relieved. But they'll be stars. The public opening is at ten, isn't it?"

"Yeah. Which is only half an hour away, so if you want to see them before the doors open, you have to hurry."

"I don't need to be at the public opening, do I?"

"No, but you might want to sneak around and listen to what they think."

Carval made a face. "If there's nothing interesting at the precinct. But you said you'd find me construction sites and talk to the Finisterres about shooting in their theatres, and you haven't done that."

"We were hanging this exhibition," Allan reminded him. "There's only one of me, even if I could use a couple of clones to keep you in line."

"Mean."

"But fair. Once I've fixed up the media, I'll talk to the Finisterres. Then I'll see if there are any obvious construction sites, but you could as easily wander around central Manhattan with your camera for a couple of days and talk yourself on to them – you're not exactly short of confidence. If you keep a note of the addresses, then I can talk to the architects or project managers if there are any problems." He smiled. "You should buy yourself a hard hat and a high-vis jacket. You'll need them if you want to go into live sites."

"I guess." He looked at Allan. "Where?"

"Work it out," Allan said callously. "You can Google as easily as I can, and I have much more to do today than you. I'm flying to Pittsburgh on June 20th to deal with *Hands. Murder on Manhattan* will be fine without me."

"But" –

229

"No, Jamie. You don't need me here and you do need me to set up in Pittsburgh. The Manhattan galleries' staff know their stuff inside out, but I don't know about Pittsburgh because we've never shown there before."

Carval pouted. "I think there *should* be two of you," he grumbled. "You need to be in both places."

"You'll live," Allan said. "Pittsburgh isn't that far. I can get back if there's a problem."

"I guess," Carval groused. "If you won't help, I'll go see the team."

***

Tyler and Andy looked at Vincent across the table, preliminaries dealt with.

"Isabella and her sister had a fight in the theatre last Thursday, where Maisie accused Isabella of knowing damaging information about unspecified cast members, which should have been reported to the proper authorities."

Vincent shrugged. "Yeah. She – Maisie – was trying to paint all of us as criminals. It was ridiculous." He took a sip of water.

"But you knew that Carl, Cordell and Julius weren't squeaky clean."

"No. I knew that they were likely to hit on the boys, because Carl and Cordell would hit on anything that wasn't actually dead, but I didn't know whether they'd ever done anything they could be charged with. The boys were nervy, and I told them all to stick together. Julius wouldn't have gone after the cast. He never fouled his own nest. If he was picking up rent boys…he was discreet about it. Max knew, and told me, and I said if Max knew anything actually illegal he should report it, but Max said it was all rumours." He sighed. "Nobody would believe Max as a witness anyway. He was half-drunk half the time." Another deep sigh. "I don't like Carl, or Cordell, or Julius. Max would be fine if he was sober, but most of the time he isn't."

"Thought he'd been getting better?"

"Isabella had words, and he did. But then…after… He went straight back to his bottle."

"Get it," Tyler said.

"Isabella collected a lot of cash, didn't she?"

"Yeah. It all went to that charity – Act Like A Child. We all knew she collected for them and even Carl, who's Scroogier than Scrooge, coughed up. She didn't ask for much. Max gave more, after a bit." He coloured slightly. "After… I set up a regular payment. Not a lot – actors don't make much, but some. In her memory." He squirmed, falling into silence.

"Who was Isabella meeting last Thursday?"

"Oh, that was Max. She wanted him to volunteer at the charity – said he had a lot to pass on."

230

The two detectives stared. "Nobody told us this?"

"No, because it didn't happen."

"Huh?" Tyler exclaimed.

"Isabella was so upset by Maisie she cancelled on Max. He wasn't happy – I think he'd psyched himself up to take some positive steps to getting dry – but he could see that Isabella was wiped out. He was going to walk her to the subway, but she wouldn't have it."

"Do you remember anyone else offering to go with her, or going out about the same time?"

"No, but we were all packing up and leaving."

"One more thing," Andy said. "Was there a rehearsal on Tuesday?"

"No."

Dammit, Andy thought. If there had been, then whoever beat up Maisie would have been late.

The cops covered everything that Maisie had tried to turn into blackmail material, but Vincent couldn't hand them a smoking gun. He also couldn't hand them an alibi for himself or anyone else. Mid-morning, they thanked him and let him go. The glass he'd handled went into an evidence bag for fingerprinting.

***

"Something's got to give sometime," Casey growled. "There must be some way to find where Isabella went. Andy, did we manage to get any location data from her phone or the towers?"

"There wasn't when I came in" – he opened his e-mail – "but there is now," he cheered. "We've tracked her phone from the towers. She switched off her GPS, like you should" –

"None of your technogeek hobbyhorses, please. How quickly can you narrow it down?"

"I'll start now. Larson can help." He trotted off to excise Larson from the group of officers, and the two of them started analysing, oblivious to the others' discussion.

"Max next, I guess," Casey said. Her nose wrinkled, pondering. "Do we have enough for warrants for the GPS data from Carl, Cordell and Julius's phones if they won't give it to us? I don't think we can justify Dacia or Vincent on what we have, or even Max."

"Call Vincent, ask him."

"Do it," Casey said to Tyler, who promptly did.

"Be back. Andy can extract it."

Vincent hadn't gone far, and returned in short order. Andy, with permission, took his phone, tapped his GPS history, and then downloaded it. "Thanks," he said. "That'll be helpful." Vincent's lack of any protest further cemented his view that whoever had murdered Isabella, it wasn't Vincent.

After a few moments, Andy summoned the rest of the team. "I sent Larson to get Maisie's phone to strip its GPS history. He'll have to ask her to agree to it: if not, we'll need a warrant. That won't be a problem, but it will slow us up."

"I'll start on the warrants," O'Leary drawled. "We're goin' to need a few of 'em." He turned to his computer, and tapped.

"Yeah. I'll plot everyone's GPS and see if they intersect with Isabella – and when."

"Pretty pictures," said O'Leary. "I do love me a pretty picture."

"Go get a Degas print, then."

"I'm disappointed. I thought you wanted that shot of you and Tyler clasping forearms," Carval said from behind them.

"That's not a *pretty* picture," O'Leary said. "That's brotherhood. Totally diff'rent." He grinned. "I already got it, seein' as you didn't give it to me."

"How?"

"Allan gave me a copy of it, right after the *Hands* exhibition." He smiled sweetly. "He thought I deserved it. Reward for puttin' up with Casey there."

Casey spluttered crossly.

"Me too," Tyler said. "Same reason."

"Why're you here?" O'Leary asked.

"The exhibition's a success," Carval said, his grin wrapping around his head, "and the press thinks you're all wonderful. We did it!"

Larson marched up, interrupting him. "Detectives, ma'am," he said. "Maisie agreed. Here's her phone. I got her to sign the agreement."

"Good man," Casey said. "Go add it to Andy's pretty coloured lines."

Carval, leaving the cops to their work now he'd told them the good news, ambled happily around, shooting anything he felt like, totally relaxed.

"Come look," Andy said. "We can definitely rule Vincent out of the attack on Maisie, and he didn't go anywhere near Isabella after the theatre. Nor did Maisie."

"Shame," Casey said. "It would have been nice to catch her in another lie."

"She went home." Andy grinned. "But I know where Isabella went."

"Where?" the other three said.

"Here." He pointed at a spot on the Manhattan map.

"Where's *here*?" Casey snipped. "No games. We've a murderer to find."

"Cove Lounge. Caribbean food and cocktails. Way above Isabella's price range."

"Someone with money," O'Leary said, smirking. "Your boy should take you, Casey." Carval, hearing, grinned, and filed the thought for later.

"Fremont and Larson can take each other – oh. It doesn't open till four. Let's get Max in. They can go get him instead."

Tyler sent the two officers off.

"When it opens," O'Leary said, "we c'n send two of our good officers – I'm thinkin' Larson an' Henegan." Casey raised her eyebrows. "Larson got through to Henegan. A li'l bit of reinforcement won't hurt – to see what there is in the way of cameras, an' mebbe do some canvassin' of the staff."

"Good plan," Casey said. Her phone interrupted. "Clement." Her blood chilled. "What? When? I'll be there asap." She swiped her phone off. "Dad," she said. "Arrested in Queens. Again. Same station." Her face contorted. "Birkett's precinct."

"Go see Kent first," O'Leary suggested. "He c'n head off Birkett."

Casey's expression curdled further.

"C'mon. He said we had to report *anythin'* that went wrong. This is definitely an anythin'. If you don't, he'll find out anyways an' you'll be so far up shit creek we won't find you with a GPS."

"I guess," Casey said unhappily, and trudged off to Kent's lair.

"Come in." Kent looked up. "Clement. What is it?"

She swallowed. "My father has been arrested again, sir," she forced out. "In Queens. The same precinct – 112th – as last time."

"Captain Wetherly," Kent said.

"Sir." She gulped again. "Officer Birkett, at that precinct, is a close associate of Detective Marcol."

"I'm aware. You don't need to say anything more. I'll speak to Captain Wetherly. I assume you need to leave to collect him?"

"Yes, sir."

"Not yet. Wait while I speak to Captain Wetherly."

"Sir." Casey didn't want to wait. Every moment's delay was another when her father would be languishing in a cell, easy prey for Birkett's lurking malice.

"I have reasons. Sit down, and say nothing."

Kent tapped in a number. "Wetherly? Kent here, from the Thirty-Sixth. Yes, me again. I understand you have David Clement in your cells?"

"Yes," the speakerphone said.

"Your sergeant called Detective Clement a few moments ago to collect him, and she came straight to me to request permission to do so. I expect you'll be issuing another desk appearance ticket?"

"That's procedure, yeah."

"Good. Do it."

Casey gaped, caught Kent's eye, and remained as silent as he had ordered.

"My officers would do that without your input. Why are you getting involved?"

"That's why I'm calling. Have you seen the papers, or read the culture-vulture sections? I sure don't, but if you do, you'll have noticed there's a huge photo exhibition, starring the NYPD, that opened to the public this morning. The critics love it, and it's the best PR the NYPD'll have this year. 1PP are absolutely determined to make sure that nothing spoils it."

"Yes?" Wetherly said suspiciously.

"The show's based on the team that Detective Clement leads."

A peculiar, strangulated noise came from the phone. "You're kidding."

"No. Detective Clement, David Clement's daughter, is the centre of this show."

Casey muffled a wail of protest. Kent scowled at her. The unmistakable sound of rapid deductions came through the speakerphone.

"But you want him charged?" Wetherly said slowly.

"Yes. I don't want *any* suggestion that the NYPD does favours for friends or relatives."

"You didn't have to get involved," Wetherly pointed out. "Last time, Detective Clement was clear that he had to be treated like any other drunk." Casey winced. "I'm sure she'll do the same when she arrives. What else is going on?"

"You have an Officer Birkett in your precinct." Casey's eyes widened. Oh, *shit*.

"Yes?"

"I have been informed" – Kent didn't specify how, or by whom – "that Officer Birkett, who attended the Academy with Detectives Clement and Marcol" – Wetherly sucked in a breath – "may not understand 1PP's strong desire to keep the NYPD's reputation pristine."

"I see." Wetherly's tone indicated that he saw more than Kent had said. "Don't worry, Kent. I'll do what I can."

"Thanks."

Kent cut the call, and looked at a flabbergasted Casey. "Do you understand?"

"You're ensuring nobody can question my integrity, sir. If they do, you can correct them."

"That was one point. I'm also making the point, which you appear to have missed yesterday, that you are not responsible for your father. I don't hold you responsible for his words or actions." He scowled. "I don't expect to have to repeat that a third time."

"Sir."

"Dismissed. Go get your father. Do not come back to finish your shift. You can make the time up in future or take leave. You're not on shift tomorrow, and if I hear that you've been into the precinct I'll bench you without pay. Report his condition to me on Monday morning."

"Yes, sir. Thank you, sir."

As soon as Clement had left, Kent picked up the phone to Dr Renfrew, FBI profiler. "Dr Renfrew?"

"It is I."

"Captain Kent here. Clement's father was arrested earlier. Can your agent urgently acquire a copy of his arrest record including today's arrest – and then details of everyone who accesses that record between the moment of his arrest and, say, the end of the weekend."

"You believe someone will make trouble," Renfrew stated.

"I believe someone may already be making trouble," Kent said, observing his precinct through his office window. "That someone will regret it. Deeply."

"How unfortunate," Renfrew said, without a trace of sympathy. "I shall make arrangements immediately. Agent Bergen will download the access records daily, unless you consider that he should do so more often?"

"No. It won't help us stop anything."

"No. I take it that we should confer as I receive the results?"

"Yes. Thank you, Dr Renfrew."

"My great pleasure."

Kent put the phone down, and reflected that Renfrew might be a pompous, patronising ass, but when the chips were down, he was a man to be relied on. He contemplated his bullpen. Clement was talking urgently to her team; and then hurried off, O'Leary walking her out. Not, he noted, Carval. Kent nodded. The order that she wasn't to leave alone wouldn't be rescinded until he, Kent, was certain that any possibility of trouble had departed.

The remains of Kent's morning passed without incident. Shortly before lunchtime, however, his phone rang.

"Captain Kent?"

"Yes."

"It's Leanne Marloe, from the press office."

"Yes?" Kent queried, fingers suddenly tapping.

"I want to arrange a press conference for you and your detectives, Monday morning. We've had several requests already, and we expect more. The publicity is great, and the top brass want to ride it."

Kent breathed out very, very slowly. "Of course," he said, concealing his relief that it hadn't been a completely different call. "Let me know when and where."

"Oh, where's easy," Leanne chirped. "At the gallery. We've agreed with Mr Penrith that that'll give the best impression. I'll tell you the time as soon as it's arranged. Thank you, Captain."

"Thank you," Kent managed, not thankful at all.

He marched out of his office to the three detectives currently present. "Detectives," he said ominously.

"Sir?"

"There will be a press conference on Monday morning, at the gallery," Kent pronounced. "You will all be present. Tell Clement. I'll inform you of the time as soon as the press office have told me."

"Yes, sir."

Kent stalked off, and only long after he'd gone home and had a comfortable dinner with his wife did he realise that announcing the press conference in the middle of the bullpen might not have been the best strategy.

CHAPTER TWENTY SEVEN

Casey had a hurried confabulation with the rest of the team and Carval, then, escorted by O'Leary, almost ran for her car, knowing what she'd find at the 112th.

She did.

The desk sergeant brought up her father, shambling drunk, eyes unfocused and wandering, stumbling over his own feet. The odour of stale alcohol hung around him, though, thankfully, it appeared that he had neither vomited nor soiled himself. Given his state, that was a win. She signed the papers to take him, and collected the desk appearance ticket.

Forty-five silent minutes later, Casey pulled up outside her father's block. She'd had to keep the windows open to be able to breathe through the fug of sweat and drunkenness, and her throat wouldn't have formed words even if she'd had any to articulate. She escorted him out of the car, upstairs, and opened his door.

She stopped dead.

"Ca'kin."

The word moved her into the mess of her father's apartment. Usually, it was moderately tidy. Now, used glasses sat on the side table and by the sink. Papers and photographs bestrewed the couch, the table and most of the floor; an empty whiskey bottle lay in their midst. Face up, stained with liquor, was a photo of Casey and both parents, taken on the day she graduated from Stanford.

Her father stumbled in. "I was trying to fin' a photo," he slurred. "Coul'n't."

She began to collect up the papers.

"You an' Anne, t'gether. Wan' t' remember." He scrabbled around in a pile of photos, and lifted one. "No' the one I want." He stared fuzzily at it. "You're nothing like your mom."

237

The comment stabbed. "No. I'm not. You've made that clear for months."

But his whisky-sodden mind had flitted on. "You'll be famous." His mouth turned down. "Famous cop." He shuffled through the room, picked up an empty glass, and stared into it. "All gone."

Casey continued to pick up photos and papers, squaring them off in her hands, not looking up from the chaos that she was reducing to order.

"All gone," he said again, and slumped on to the cleared couch. "She's gone." He heaved himself up again.

"Sit down, Dad."

"Wan' a drink." He opened a cabinet, and found a bottle; poured and knocked it back, poured again. "Wan' Anne. My Anne."

"You think I don't want Mom?" Casey said quietly. "You think I don't miss her?"

"I miss her more. Loved her so much."

"So did I," Casey said tightly. "So did I."

"No' like I did. Nothin' like I did. You don' show anything. You go' over it."

"No. Not like you did." Her voice remained quiet and cold. "*I* didn't start drowning myself in liquor. *I* didn't get fired or picked up drunk or arrested or try to ruin my daughter's career. *I* didn't change my job to be a lawyer like you thought I ought to be or like you said Mom wanted me to be. *I* didn't do any of that, so I guess you think I don't care. I *do* care. I loved her as much as you. I'm going home. Drink yourself back to the hospital or drink yourself unconscious or do whatever the hell you want. I can't fix you and I can't save you and I can't deal with you any more. Whether or not I love you because you're my *dad*, you don't love me."

She slammed out of the door, leaving her father slack-faced behind her, ran downstairs and took off, screeching the tyres as she went. Anger stopped the tears flowing, she had always found.

At home, she couldn't settle, couldn't force herself to eat a long-delayed lunch, moving restlessly from one thing to another. She would have gone to the precinct, but Kent would be told, or be there, and if he weren't, then, with her present luck, Estrolla would take the chance to make trouble. Suddenly, she felt the need to move. She threw off her work clothes and tugged on running gear, slipped her phone into its pocket, fastened on her shield and gun for safety, and left, to run herself to exhaustion. She didn't like herself much right now: she'd lost her temper with her father, but it wasn't his fault, it was the alcohol. He wouldn't have drunk if he hadn't gone to the exhibition, she immediately added bitterly. She should never have listened to the others: she should have hidden it from him. He'd never have seen the papers, he'd never have found out.

He'd never have gotten drunk again.

She kept running, but she couldn't outrun her guilt and pain; her anger with herself that she'd pushed him right back into the bottle; the suppurating wound of his disappointment with her, his only child. Running, for the first time, wasn't calming her.

***

"We'll carry on," O'Leary said, after Kent had delivered the unwelcome news of the press conference. "Casey needs to know we're doin' it. Max is on his way in, so…leastways she's spared that. Her interrogatin' a lush ain't goin' to help anyone. Tyler, you 'n' me'll take him. Andy, you find out when Maisie changed the bank name, an' we'll ask Max to let us into his GPS first, so you c'n play with that. C'n you finish up with those warrants I started, an' get them through?"

"Sure."

Carval watched O'Leary seamlessly take hold of the team exactly as Casey would have, and knew that however much O'Leary would've wanted to go support his best and oldest friend, doing this for her was more important. He couldn't go, either. He wanted to, but until Casey asked him, he couldn't intrude. Instead, he flitted around the bullpen, invisible to most of the cops, but with his ears as open as his camera lens. He didn't hear anything interesting, though he noted that Officers Estrolla and Grendon bore unpleasantly satisfied expressions.

***

"Detectives, ma'am – uh." Fremont stopped as he realised that Casey wasn't present.

"Max in Interrogation?" Tyler said.

"Yes, Detective," Fremont said, and sensibly didn't ask about Casey's absence. Larson followed his lead.

"'Kay," O'Leary picked up. "Was he drunk?"

"Not so's I'd notice," Fremont replied, Larson nodding. "He seemed fine, and he's walking straight, but he's chewing on a breath mint."

O'Leary caught the gazes of the other detectives and Carval in a moment of shared thought. *Thank Christ Casey's not doing this one* hung deafeningly between them.

"Tyler, let's go. GPS first, an' then Andy c'n work magic or write warrants, dependin'."

In Interrogation, Max sat slumped and unfocused, not looking up as the detectives walked in. A glass of water, so far untouched, sat in front of him. O'Leary mentally gave the two officers points for learning and applying their knowledge.

239

"Maxwell Stephens," O'Leary said. "Mr Stephens, thank you for comin' in. Before we start, Detective Tyler here will read you your rights, so's we're all correct an' tidy."

Tyler recited the Miranda warning, letter perfect. Max didn't react in any way. "Do you understand?" Tyler asked.

"Yes."

"First up," O'Leary said, "c'n we take your phone an' search the GPS history?"

Max limply waved a hand in assent. "Sure," he droned. He fumbled in his pocket and pulled out the phone, automatically swiping it open for them.

O'Leary exchanged a quick glance with Tyler. Max's state was concerning both detectives. "Detective Tyler'll take it up to our tech expert, an' we'll have it back to you before you leave." Max simply nodded, as if his head were too heavy for his neck.

Tyler strode out, returning in only a moment.

"We're all back. Let's talk about Isabella. Tell me about her, Max," O'Leary enticed.

"She was..." his bloodshot eyes glistened. "She..." He put his head in his hands. "I need to have a drink," he pleaded. "I didn't when she was there because I couldn't disappoint her but I need to have a drink."

"You c'n get a drink iffen you want one, after we're done. Help us, an' Isabella wouldn't be disappointed with that."

Max looked up. Without his stage make-up, his cheeks were cracked with broken veins, his nose a little bulbous, his eyes dull. "She shouldn't have died. She didn't do anything wrong. She wasn't the one threatening to report stuff."

"What stuff?" Tyler asked, more gently than his usual brusqueness.

Max cringed. "I don't...I need to keep this role. I'm" – *halfway to washed up*, the detectives thought – "It's the best I've had in two years. I have to impress the Finisterres. I have to keep it." His voice had risen, with a disturbing note of panic.

"We ain't goin' to tell anyone what you say," O'Leary reassured. "We won't be quotin' you. It'll only matter iffen we arrest someone, an' then they won't be able to mess you up."

Max sat back, taking the water glass and emptying it.

"Want another?" Tyler asked.

"Please."

Unobtrusively, Tyler took the glass through a Kleenex, took it out, gave Adamo rapid orders, and returned with a clean glass of water. "Stuff?" he repeated.

Max's breathing turned shallow.

"Take your time. There's no hurry."

"I didn't even think she knew." *Knew what?* "I mean, Cordell hit on her and she was really upset by it, but I didn't think she knew he had a history. She could blow him off because she had the Finisterres behind her so he didn't dare but everyone knows he...he..."

"He coerces people into sex?" O'Leary said, in lieu of the bald word *rape*.

"Yes," Max admitted, defeated. "He and Carl both. But Carl hated Isabella so much that he wouldn't go near her, and anyway Dacia was pretty happy to sleep with him because he'd give her good parts. She'd have slept with a real donkey to be the star."

"Did she sleep with Vincent? He was playin' Bottom, wasn't he?"

"No – oh, no, I didn't mean that. She wasn't. Just that she'd have done pretty much anything. But she didn't need to be asked. She was all over Carl from moment one."

"Carl and Cordell got a history of bad behaviour?"

"Yes. Maybe Isabella did know? I don't know. Her sister knew. She made a whole lot of references and some of it was to past productions. I don't know how she knew that stuff." He downed half of the glass of water, and stared into the remaining fluid.

O'Leary had a sudden thought, and scrawled a small note, nudging Tyler under the table. *Ron?* Tyler nodded once.

"What about Julius?"

"He's gay. I don't know. Maybe he was doing stuff but I don't know about it." He glanced up, pathetic and miserable. "Isabella shouldn't have died. She wouldn't tell anyone anything if she didn't have really hard evidence that would get them convicted."

"Do you know whether Isabella was meetin' anyone after rehearsal Thursday?"

Max shook his head. "Not me. She'd asked me to meet her, but after her sister...she couldn't. She'd said she wanted me to come along with her to that charity she supported – we all contributed, but she asked *me* to come and teach the kids something. She had faith in me. I would've done it, too, but..." He gulped. "I couldn't go without her. I didn't dare." He stared at his fingers. "I would have needed a drink without her. Just like I do for rehearsal."

"I see," O'Leary murmured. "C'n you tell us where you were Tuesday lunchtime?"

"Tuesday? I don't remember."

"An' Thursday evenin' last week?"

"I guess I went home. I don't remember anything." He dropped his eyes again, ashamed. "I likely went home and had a drink."

"Thank you. We'll get you your phone back, an' you c'n go. We might want to talk to you again, so mebbe don't go too far from Manhattan."

241

Tyler retrieved Max's phone, and let him leave.

"There goes a man I'm glad Casey didn't see today," O'Leary said heavily. Tyler grunted in agreement. "Let's go see what Andy and Adamo've found."

Andy was muttering blackly at his computer. "Dumb machine," floated back to them. O'Leary and Tyler looked at the back of Andy's head, noted Larson's nervousness next to him, and decided that seeing Adamo was a far better idea. Andy rarely lost his cool with tech, but when he did it was better to let him fry circuits in peace. Nobody wanted their screen saver adjusted or small electronic sheep wandering across their warrants as they typed them.

"What've you got?" Tyler said to Adamo, who leapt to attention, as did Henegan.

"I sent the prints to CSU – Evan – but he hasn't gotten back to me yet. We don't have the results from Vincent either. Henegan said to ask."

"That's right," O'Leary rumbled. Henegan looked relieved, and even managed an almost-confident smile. "You two were goin' through Isabella's phone to see about Thursday. We know where she went, but c'n you point to anythin' that might tell us who with?"

"There aren't any texts or calls to or from anyone except Maisie – two unanswered calls from Maisie to Isabella. Whoever it was," Henegan essayed, "it was set up beforehand and nothing changed."

"Waal, that ain't no help at all," O'Leary said. "I guess Fremont an' Larson'll be gettin' their outin' to the Cove Lounge this afternoon."

"All off tomorrow," Tyler said.

"We c'n leave these fine officers chasin' down anythin' we need to have chased."

"Uh," Henegan said, "me and Adamo are off tomorrow too."

Tyler grinned. "Hope you're watching the Yankees."

"Sure am, si-Detective," they said in unison.

"Good. Can't work with us if not." He laughed, and the two officers managed a slightly unnerved laugh with him.

When Tyler and O'Leary returned to their own desks, Andy was still grumbling at his computer.

"What's up?"

"Dumb program's having a hissy fit." Andy scowled. "Waiting for it to reload."

"Switched it off an' on again? That always works."

"Of course I did. Who's the tech whizz here?"

"Not me," O'Leary said peaceably. "I guess that means we don't know where Max went yet?"

"No." Andy turned a Casey-rivalling glare on his tech, which, amazingly, still failed to co-operate. "Lunch, while I wait for this machine to behave itself." He glared at it again. It produced a pathetic little beep, and didn't improve its output.

Fortunately for the continued survival of Andy's computer, when they returned from a late, hurried lunch, it had recovered itself. Andy re-uploaded the GPS history from Max's phone – and whistled.

"What'cha got?"

"Well…" Andy drew out, "Max didn't go anywhere near Isabella on Thursday."

"But?" O'Leary asked. Tyler marched up to find out too.

"But, he was up in Inwood on Tuesday lunchtime and look at this intersection with Maisie." Andy pointed to the coloured lines crossing. "This looks like Max was right there when she was attacked."

"Max?" O'Leary said blankly. "That…ain't what I expected."

"Nah," Tyler added. "Said he couldn't remember Tuesday."

"I reckon he was sodden drunk," O'Leary supplied. "But iffen he don't remember nothin', then we gotta prove it, 'cause we won't get anythin' from him." His wide brow wrinkled into fissures. "I think we got enough for a warrant to search his place. We won't get it back today, an' we're all off tomorrow an' I don't see Kent approvin' the overtime – 'sides which, I think Casey might be needin' the team then."

"Why?" Tyler queried sharply.

"Got a feelin'. Hopin' I'm wrong." He sat down, frowning. "Or mebbe hopin' I'm right. She can't keep runnin' after him." He changed tack. "Anyways, we don't got enough to arrest an' charge Max without findin' more, an' twenty-four hours ain't no good when we ain't here."

"No," Andy agreed.

"Fremont and Larson to Cove Lounge, soon as it opens. Brief them." Tyler swung off to instruct the officers.

"Not much more we c'n do today, 'cept tidy up an' make sure we're all good for Sunday." O'Leary pouted, sending a small ice-shelf out in place of his lower lip. "I don't like workin' on the weekend. I don't get no proper time with Pete."

"If we tidy up, you'll get home to Pete sooner," Andy pointed out acerbically, "and you won't face the wrath of Casey on Sunday."

"Aw, Casey won't get angry at me. An' if she does, what's she goin' to do?"

"Set Animal Control on you."

The three men laughed, and set to.

***

Some way down the western edge of Central Park, as Casey turned back up towards home, her phone rang. She stopped, not totally displeased to take a break, saw it was her father's number, and almost swiped ignore.

Almost. A stab of guilt made her answer. "Yes, Dad?" She couldn't hide her irritation.

"Need you," he gasped. She heard vomiting, a cry of pain, then the call cut.

She dialled 9-1-1, gave the address, told them she'd meet them there, and grabbed a cab to get her car. What else could she do? If it were a false alarm...

But all her training told her that it wasn't. All her experience said that this call was real. Her gut clenched. She was suddenly sure that this was more of that horrifying blood-soaked vomit. She threw bills at the taxi driver, and dashed up to her apartment for her purse and car keys. In the car, she flipped on lights and sirens, prayed that nobody would ever ask why, and, by breaking every traffic rule, made it to her father's apartment as the ambulance pulled up.

"I'm Katrina Clement – his daughter," she said to the EMTs. "I have a key. I called you." She was already halfway up the stairs to her father's apartment, the EMTs following, her heart racing and terror whipping her on; hand shaking as she unlocked, then flung the door open.

Automatically, she moved clear to allow the EMTs through. She couldn't panic. Mustn't panic. Let them work.

But there was so much blood, and in the middle of it her father lay, small and crumpled, white. *He's dead.* She sat down hard, ducked her head between her knees. She'd seen messy murder plenty of times – even a few short weeks ago – but this was her *dad.* All her training wasn't directed at her own – her only – family.

"He's still alive," the EMT announced, and the medical machine moved to stabilise, lift, take him away to the same hospital as before, Casey following: shell shocked, *he's not dead not dead not dead* looping in her head. He'd looked dead. So much blood. *Who'd have thought the old man had so much blood in him*, the play had said: Lady Macbeth, sleepwalking through endless nightmares caused by her own actions. But she'd been a good daughter, she told herself, over and over as she parked, waited, and waited some more. She had. She'd tried and tried to save him. She paced the waiting room, sat, stood, paced, sat, stood, paced; unable to stay still, unable to stop the guilt or the terror. If she hadn't told him about the exhibition...if there had never been an exhibition in the first place...

If she'd never met Jamie Carval again.

If she'd never met Jamie Carval again...her father would still have drunk himself to death, in much the same timescale. He'd been far, far down the track before he ever knew about the exhibition. She'd been told nearly three months ago that he was too far gone to recover.

She'd thought – hoped, desperately, vainly – that he wouldn't make it worse. She paced some more, waiting. Surely the longer she waited, the more there was hope? They would have told her if.... She scrubbed at her eyes. They would have told her.

If only she'd never told him about the exhibition.

She slumped down on a hard plastic chair, and tried to restrain her tears. Time slid by, every minute seeming an hour, every entry of a nurse or doctor sending her heart rate spiking. She worried her fingernails down to the quick; and that tic exhausted, twisted her hands together; then stood, paced, sat once more. A further time passed: her watch showed thirty minutes more, her emotions told her three hours. With every moment, her stress rose and her confidence fell. More time dragged by, from six, to seven, to eight.

CHAPTER TWENTY EIGHT

"Miss Clement?"

She jerked into life. "Yes?"

"Come with me." The doctor smiled gently, sadly. "We've managed to stabilise your father for the moment. It's taken a while, but he's asleep, and when" – Casey heard *if* – "he wakes, he won't be in pain. I'll take you to see him, and then we can talk."

"Thank you." Casey scrubbed at her eyes, and blew her nose. It didn't make the slightest difference, no matter how many times she repeated the actions in the short walk to her father's room.

She stopped in the doorway, appalled. So much worse than last time; so small and yellow and crumpled in the smooth white of the sheets; so frail between the tubes and wires, the machines and monitors attached to him; the IV line into the cannula taped to the back of his hand, between the age spots. She'd never noticed the age spots before.

He could have been a corpse already, for all the life he showed. Tears ran unheeded down her face as she stared at the wreckage of her father.

She couldn't bear it; stumbling out of the room to a blurry seat, collapsing into it and weeping hopelessly into her hands. The doctor pushed a Kleenex into her fingers, and simply waited, silent, until she'd gulped her way back to a semblance of calm.

"That's *stabilised?*" she challenged, her voice breaking again. "He looks like he's already dead! How is that *stabilised?*"

"Miss Clement…" the doctor began.

"I know," she said helplessly. "It's all necessary. But it looks…" She swallowed hard. "He looks…" Another gulp. "Eleven weeks ago, your colleague said…told me…there wasn't much chance for him."

Another Kleenex arrived in her hand, and shortly, the sodden mass dropped into the trash can.

"Now he's here again and his apartment was covered in blood and vomit." She gazed at the doctor through agonised eyes. "He won't make it, will he?" The doctor hesitated. "Tell me the truth," she pleaded. "I have to know the truth."

"I'm sorry," he said, and passed her the box of Kleenex. "He may recover this time, but if there is another episode…" He trailed off at her expression, which didn't need the sentence to be completed. "Would you like some time alone?" She didn't answer, unable to speak, and he stood up. "I'll come back in a little while."

"I want to sit with him," she whispered. "I can't leave him. He…I don't want him to be alone."

"I'll take you back."

"Thank you."

The pity in the doctor's eyes nearly broke her again.

Sitting in an uncomfortable chair, she held her father's limp hand, hoping that somehow, some way, despite his unconsciousness, he'd know she was there and be comforted. *In his last hours* crept into her mind, and refused to leave. More time passed. Her father's eyelashes fluttered, and for an instant she thought that he was waking, but then they stilled again. An hour later, Casey had moved no more than had her father, still clinging to his lax hand.

He blinked. "Catkin?" he breathed.

"I'm here, Dad. You're in the hospital."

"Hurts."

"I'll call the nurse." She hit the call button.

"Really hurts." His face twisted, and the little colour remaining left his lips as the electronic beeping of the monitors speeded up. Casey hit the call button again, and kept pressing. "Catkin…" His hand tightened till his grip hurt.

"I love you, Dad," she whispered, and then, "We'll fix it," as a nurse rushed in and raked one assessing glance over her father.

"Move back," the nurse rapped, and pressed a different button. Suddenly the room filled with light and noise; medical staff frantically working on her father. The nurse ushered her out, but she'd already seen the electronic trace begin to falter.

A few moments later, it was all over. The room was quiet, empty except for Casey, sitting at her father's side, weeping silently.

***

"Miss Clement?" someone murmured after a long while, in which she hadn't stopped crying for more than a moment. "Is there anything you need?"

"No, thank you." *I need to have my dad back.* "What happens now?"

"We will certify the death, and take care of him until you can make arrangements."

"Thank you." She forced the words out.

"You can stay with him as long as you want to."

"No. He's not here any more." But she didn't move at once, and when she did, she rose as if she were a centenarian, slowly unbending, stiff and sore from the long vigil.

The staff member pressed a card into her hand. "For making arrangements," she said softly. "So you have it when you're ready."

"Thank you," she said again, and stumbled out to her car, half-blind with swollen, reddened eyes, her nose raw from blowing it, an empty, gaping hole in her chest. She had to drive back to Manhattan, but, thank God, she was off-shift tomorrow. She blinked frantically to clear her vision, but she couldn't start the engine for more stretched-out, numb moments.

***

She didn't go home. Without ever having to think about it, she knew that she needed not to be alone. She parked at Carval's block, calling his entry phone; first the studio, then his apartment. A sleepy, angry voice answered.

"What the fuck? Who is this? It's one in the goddamn morning!"

"It's me," she blurted. "Dad…"

The door unlocked instantly to let her in, but she stood in the hall, completely drained, any remaining energy ebbing away and tears running once more down her face. Carval came crashing down the stairs, saw her misery, and caught her before she could crumple.

"What happened?" he murmured, steering her towards the stairs. She didn't answer until they'd reached his austere apartment, when he'd drawn her down to sit with his arm around her, tucked into him.

"He haemorrhaged," she sobbed. "He's gone."

"I'm so sorry, sweetheart," he breathed into her hair, and pulled her on to his lap as if she were a child, letting her cry out her grief into his broad chest. She couldn't stop her scraped-out, raw-edged sobbing, no matter how she tried. Carval simply held her, and tried to soothe her pain, whispering attempts at comfort into her dark curls and stroking her shuddering back.

"Come to bed," he said, when she was still crying almost an hour later; his t-shirt sodden at the shoulder, the trashcan full of Kleenex. "It'll be warmer, and you're cold." When his suggestion produced no response, he simply picked her up and took her through to sit her on the bed, as malleable as a rag doll; removed her shoes and light jacket and hugged her again. "C'mon. I'll lend you a t-shirt so you'll be more comfortable, and then you can stay here. I'll be here. I got you."

248

Slowly, painfully, Casey took off her pants, socks and shirt, dropping them on the floor without thought. Carval produced an old, soft t-shirt from which her head emerged, the rest of her swathed in the oversize garment. Her bra joined the rest on the floor, and she slipped into Carval's bed, where he joined her, curling her back into him. She was disturbingly empty and lax.

But she'd come to him, he realised. Come to him: though after the exhibition she had gone home alone, raw and bleeding from her father's behaviour. Now, in her worst moment, she was here, seeking him out to comfort her. She was still crying, but the tears were slowing, the sobs quietening. He continued to hold her close, and didn't try to stop her tears or talk. Finally, she was still, exhausted, though he didn't think she was asleep. He still didn't say anything. It was long past two, and sleep would be the best thing for both of them. He took his own advice, and without letting go of Casey for one second, fell back into slumber.

Casey wasn't asleep, but, pillowed against Carval's chest, the steady beat of his heart was drawing her down into calmer rest. She couldn't have moved if she'd wanted to, drained. It was all over. She'd never flinch at an unknown number again; never have to face the pity of Carla Jankel or the contempt of other cops or judges.

She'd have faced them all a thousand times over to have her father back.

Eventually, she drifted miserably into sleep.

***

Carval woke briefly around eight, at which time, unusually, he had a thought which wasn't *urgh*. This thought said *warn Allan*. A short text message later, he slid back into bed. Casey hadn't twitched as he'd arisen, but tear trails had marked her face, and there had been ugly black rings below her eyes. In the few moments he'd been absent, she'd curled into a tight ball, buried beneath the covers where he could only see a few strands of her hair. He didn't try to wake her: if her alarm hadn't gone off, she didn't need to be awake. On off-shift days, which this must be, she slept longer – at least, she did when he was there. He yawned hugely, and wriggled down further. Shortly, only a soft whiffle broke the silence.

Slightly over an hour later, Carval woke again, washed, dressed, and went to talk to Allan.

"Casey's dad died late last night," he said bluntly. "She's upstairs, asleep."

"Sorry to hear that," Allan said, then, catching up, "She came here?"

"Yes," Carval said impatiently, "but the important thing is that her dad is gone."

"I get that." Allan frowned. "I'd better cancel the press conference. That's Monday morning – and Casey doesn't know about it yet, I guess."

"Don't do it without talking to her. I don't know what she'll want to do, but I bet she'll go to work tomorrow." Bitter realisation tinged his tone. "That's how she'll cope."

Allan looked sharply at him. "You're forgetting something, which even for you is pretty good after less than ten hours."

"What?" Carval snapped.

"She came here. Far be it from me to indulge your excessive ego" –

"Hey!"

"– but the first thing she did to cope was came here. If she goes to work tomorrow, that's the *second*. Try thinking with your brain instead of your hurt feelings for a change. You might even like the answers."

"My feelings aren't *hurt!*" Carval complained. "She needs to *de*-stress, not deal with all the crap in the precinct and then a press conference which she'll hate."

"What press conference?" Casey demanded from the doorway.

"You're awake," Carval said in a statement of the completely obvious.

"I'm sorry for your loss," Allan said.

"What press conference?" Casey rapped again.

"The one your team will tell you about if you call them," Allan said calmly. "They'd have left you alone last night, wouldn't they?"

"Yeah," Casey agreed, her momentary flash of ire dying away. "I'll go call – oh. You can tell me, can't you?"

"Before we knew...uh..." Allan was unusually tongue-tied, "anyway, we agreed with Captain Kent that the press conference would go ahead at ten on Monday morning. He ordered you all to be there, but, er, he might change that."

"I'm doing it," Casey stated. "It won't get any better so I'm going to get it out of the way." She stared Allan down when he thought about arguing with her, then glanced at Carval. "Do you mind if I go call O'Leary from your apartment?"

"No. Or the studio?"

"No. You'll want to work there." She didn't say *I want privacy*, but Carval heard it anyway.

"Okay."

Safely out of view, Casey called O'Leary.

"Casey? You okay?"

"Dad...Dad died," she faltered, and began to cry again.

"Aww, Casey. You at home?"

"Carval's," she snuffled.

"I'll be there in half an hour." He cut the call.

Casey stared at the phone blankly, then, when she'd stopped crying, trudged back down the stairs to the studio. She'd better wait for O'Leary, because trying to stop him arriving would be like trying to stop a tsunami.

She sat in an uncomfortable chair, and gazed into space, trying not to think. If only she could block out the memory of the blood; of the small, wrecked body in a hospital bed.

A hand landed gently on her shoulder. "Are you okay?" Carval asked. She shook her head blindly. "C'mere," he murmured, and knelt in front of her, bringing her head in to his shoulder and patting soothingly.

"There was so much blood and it's still there," she dripped. "All over the floor and I've seen messy murders but this was *Dad.*" She dissolved again. "I'd shouted at him and that's the last thing he knew. I said I loved him in the hospital but I don't think he heard and then he died." The floodgates opened. "It was awful. I thought he was dead already. So much blood on the floor."

Carval cossetted, and managed not to offer solutions, though *get a cleaning service to deal with it* trembled on his tongue. He couldn't imagine walking in on a scene that sounded more like an abattoir than an apartment: his father had had a massive heart attack; his mother, only a year later, had effectively died of a broken heart. He'd been devastated, but not suffered the horror that Casey had, and certainly hadn't felt the guilt that she was displaying.

"He heard you," Carval said eventually. "He'd have heard you say you loved him." He paused. "The important thing is that you said it to him. He knew. You didn't end on a bad note." She wept harder at that. "You didn't. You did everything you could for him."

Carval was still trying to calm her half an hour later, with many repetitions of *you did everything you could,* when the thunderous noise of the O'Leary juggernaut shook the stairs and then the floor of the studio.

"Casey," he rumbled, and simply picked her up as if she were a doll. "The others are on their way too. Team. We got this." He managed a wry smile. "Carval got this, but we're all goin' to be here."

"All of you?" she sniffled.

"Team. All of us. We're not leavin' you to bear this alone, an' if you're thinkin' we should, you're thinkin' wrong."

"No…" she whispered. "Team."

"While we're waitin', you c'n tell me whether you did the sensible thin' an' came here straight from the hospital?" She nodded. O'Leary looked at Carval for confirmation. He nodded. "Good. Doin' somethin' right."

"There was blood everywhere," she said again. "All over the apartment." Carval thought that she couldn't get that picture out of her head.

O'Leary patted her, finally setting her on her feet, though he kept a huge hand on her back so she stayed close. "They're here," he noted, as feet sounded once more on the stairs.

"Sorry for your loss," Andy's light tenor arrived almost before he did, echoed by Tyler's deeper voice. They tucked around Casey, surrounding her: protective in a way that Carval hadn't seen before, every man with a hand on her shoulder or back, unspoken comfort. He watched, and felt shut out.

Until Tyler caught his eye and beckoned him into the group. "Belong," the burly man said, and made a space. "Casey here last night?"

"Yeah."

"Good."

Casey's bedraggled, woebegone form straightened as the team simply stood there around her: saying nothing, doing nothing beyond their touch on her back and shoulders, asking nothing of her.

"What'cha wanna do?" O'Leary finally asked.

"Work," Casey said. "Take my mind off it all. I have to block it out, but" – her voice cracked – "I have to make the arrangements. We're back on shift tomorrow, so I need to go home and do it now."

"We c'n come with you?" the big man offered uncertainly.

"No. You can't do it for me." She sniffed soggily. "I wish you could. I need to start by calling a cleaning service to deal with his apartment, and a funeral home. I need to find his will, but I can't go back in there. I can't look at the blood and mess…" She blinked back tears.

"You c'n cry if you want to," O'Leary said. "We won't judge."

"Big girls don't cry," she said, but she couldn't make it humorous. She swallowed, and pulled on composure like a shroud. "Time for me to go home."

O'Leary hugged her again. "'Kay. Call iffen you need anythin'. We're all here."

"Yeah."

"I'll walk you down to your car," Carval said.

"Okay."

She didn't speak until they reached her unit. "Thanks," she said, looking up.

"Call me if you need anything," Carval said, echoing O'Leary.

"Yeah," she said again, but it didn't sound as if she were agreeing, just like it hadn't been agreement with O'Leary's offer. He leaned down and hugged her, but she didn't relax into it. "See you," she said absently, mind already elsewhere.

Carval went back upstairs, and with no surprise found the other men still lounging around his studio, drinking his coffee.

"She gone?"

"Yeah."

"Fuckit," Tyler exploded. "Should've stayed."

"Doin' it all herself, like she always does. She never let us help with her dad an' she's not startin' now. Most she's ever let us do is listen," O'Leary

252

disapproved. "First sensible thin' she's ever done was to come here afterwards. She shouldn't go in tomorrow, but I ain't goin' to stop her."

"Kent?" Tyler queried.

"Iffen she don't tell him before this conference, I will." O'Leary became stern. "You sure this is goin' to go off okay?"

"We've done everything we can," Carval said. "Kent'll be there too, to squash anything."

"Good enough. I got stuff to do. Seeya."

O'Leary, trailed by the other two cops, departed, leaving Carval uncomfortably wondering what he should do. *Not* go to Casey's, no matter how much he thought she could use company, no matter how much he wanted to cosset and comfort her. He hoped desperately that the press conference would be uneventful.

CHAPTER TWENTY NINE

Casey arrived in the precinct far too early, having barely slept. She'd spent Saturday dealing with the awful administration for a death, had had to go to her father's apartment to allow the cleaning service access. She had forced herself to return much, much later, when they were finally done, almost gagging on the smell of lemon cleaner and bleach, to collect her father's will and then lock up securely. She had barely managed to force herself to do that, but sometime soon she would have to enter again. Just…not yet. She blew her nose, and determinedly focused only on the case.

She swiftly realised the team had left it completely tidy for her. She read through – what? *Max* had been there when Maisie was attacked? *Max?* Here, received late on Friday night, an approved warrant to search Max's apartment. She read on. O'Leary's report of the interview with Max, to her miserably experienced eyes, screamed that Max had been drinking before he'd been brought in, and had been drunk on Thursday night after rehearsal and again on Tuesday. She strongly suspected that Max had drunk himself to oblivion as soon as he'd learned that Isabella had been killed, only barely surfacing for any rehearsals between Saturday and today.

Fremont and Larson had been to the Cove Lounge, but though they'd ensured the bar's CCTV would be preserved, the manager had demanded a warrant before it was released. They had left her a completed warrant, for her to check and file. That she *could* do. Action.

She sniffed, blew her nose, and checked the warrant, which was all in order. She filed it with the court, and then made yet another espresso. Maybe the hot liquid would warm her chilled hands and insides. She hadn't been warm since she left Carval's apartment, and it was cooler than the previous day. She wished she'd worn a thin sweater over her silky t-shirt, and shrugged her blazer back on to keep her warm, wrapping her hands around her coffee cup.

She knew what she had to do. Bring Max into interrogation, using everything she'd learned from dealing with her father to analyse Max's actions and reactions; statements and omissions. That way, her father's death could be turned to good use, not simply be the horrible memory of blood and vomit, pain and misery.

She fled to the restroom, locked herself in a stall and sobbed. It wasn't *good*. It was a needless death. He could have stopped drinking and lived. He could have.

He never would have. Not once her mom had gone. Now she didn't have any family, because she hadn't been enough family for him. She wiped her eyes, and pushed back more tears. She had her team and Carval. They'd been there for her. One short call to O'Leary – and without asking, all of them had been there, holding her up, the family she didn't have.

She squashed down her misery, and ignored the intrusive thoughts: if she'd never told her father about the exhibition; if she'd been a lawyer like he'd wanted – he'd have stayed dry. He wouldn't have. But deep down, she couldn't believe that. Swallowing hard, she returned to her desk to bury her misery and guilt in the haven of her work.

As her team arrived, each of them passed by her desk and touched her shoulder, not speaking until she greeted them, following her lead. Once all of them were there, silent sympathy in every eye, she gathered them at her murder board.

"We have to interview Max again," she said. "I'll take point."

"You sure?" O'Leary said.

"Yes. I" – she stopped for an instant, recovered herself – "know what to look for. How to find the truth behind the blackouts and the lies."

Carval, in time to hear her, winced. *I don't need a hero*, he thought, hearing her voice from months ago. She didn't need to be protected. He knew that she'd bury everything in the job…but when the case was over, he'd still be there to comfort her. He hoped she would allow it – but she'd come straight to him, which had to mean something.

"You're with me, Bigfoot. Tyler, Andy, while we're doing that, you execute the search warrant. Take Fremont and Larson if you can, but first, they – no. Larson and Henegan to go get Max, and you go with them with the warrant. Take the other two if you think you'll need them." She met their eyes. "I want Larson to knock a spine into Henegan, like the other day."

"Will do."

"Do we have our warrants in for the GPS on Carl, Cordell and Julius's phones?"

255

"Yup. We did that Friday, an' they should all be back." O'Leary tapped at his e-mail. "Yeah. Here they are – duty judge must've had a slow afternoon yesterday to do that."

"I'll take it. We need to bring them in and get that done." She looked around, meeting each of the others' eyes. "We've got a lot to do today."

The team nodded, and, except for O'Leary, dispersed.

"You c'n keep it back for a while," he murmured, "but when this case is done, take the time, huh?"

"We'll see," Casey said. She didn't want to have to face her feelings any time soon. If working would keep her guilt submerged, she'd keep working till Kingdom Come.

O'Leary dropped his voice further, to a sub-woofed whisper. "Let him look after you," the world's largest Cupid said. "He wants to, an' it'll help."

"I guess." She shook off emotions. "Let's get on with this case. Surely with only three real suspects we can solve it soon?"

"Iffen we get Max outta the way, we c'n concentrate on the others. Likely he'll crumble like a stale cookie, an' then we'll get on."

"I'll chase down the duty judge for the Cove Lounge warrant," she said. "We need that. I wish we'd had it back yesterday with the others."

"It still won't open till one," O'Leary said, "but that's a whole lot better'n four like on the other days – an' it's closed on Monday so I guess some chasin's a good plan. You go chase, an' I'll make sure everythin' else is in order."

Casey chased, and shortly had her warrant. Before she could get frustrated with any delay, Larson and Henegan reappeared to inform her that Max was in Interrogation. She gave Larson the warrant, and instructed him to collect the footage the moment the Cove Lounge opened – and if he could do it earlier, that would be good. The accent on *good* implied that he should push hard.

"Yes'm," Larson said. "If you're busy, shall I run it through the clean-up program too?"

"Yes. Good idea."

Larson swelled at the praise. "Thank you, ma'am." He strutted off to his desk, and could immediately be heard trying the Cove Lounge. Since it was barely nine a.m., he wasn't successful, but Casey appreciated his enthusiasm. He'd massively improved in the last three months, she thought, as she and O'Leary approached Interrogation.

The sour smell and slumped figure almost sent her straight back out to the restroom to vomit. She stopped in the doorway, desperately trying not to breathe. O'Leary stopped behind her. "You okay?"

"Yeah." She took another shallow breath, and stalked in. "Maxwell Stephens. I'm Detective Clement."

"'Member you," he slurred.

Casey held cold composure. "Before we begin, Detective O'Leary will read you your rights again." O'Leary did. "Your phone data showed that on Tuesday lunchtime you were in Inwood, at the same time and place as Maisie Scarfield was attacked." She paused. Max stared vacantly at the table. "You said you didn't remember where you were." Another pause. "I don't believe you," she snapped.

"I..." Max dropped his head into his hands.

"Look at me." He did. "What do you remember?"

"I don't," he slurred.

"I don't believe you," Casey repeated. "You remember enough. You're a drunk, but if you were sober enough to take the subway to Inwood, you were sober enough to remember why."

"I washn't...I didn't...She...It was her fault Ishabella died!"

"Explain." Casey's tone would have made God Himself explain.

"If she hadn't told everyone Ishabella knew thingsh...Ishabella believed in me and that little bitch spoiled it. She got Ishabella killed. She desherved it."

"What did she deserve?" Silence. "What did you do?"

"I had a drink. I don' r'member what I did," he said sullenly.

"Liar!" Casey's anger spilled over. "You remember. We have film of someone beating up Maisie, and we're searching your apartment. You were drunk and angry and you went to take it out on Maisie."

"She desherved it! She got Ishabella killed and she washn't even shorry!" he sloshed angrily. "She ruined it. Ishabella b'lieved in me and she was goin' t' help me and that jealous bitch shpoiled ev'rything." He slumped back down, a waft of stale whisky rising from him. Casey swallowed down vomit and bad memories of her father's drunken anger. "I only meant t' tell her so...but she din' even look sad an' I shoved her an' then...I don' r'member."

O'Leary's phone rang.

"Interview suspended," Casey said for the record. They left, and O'Leary flicked on the speaker so that they could both hear Tyler.

"Found a hoodie and boots. Looks like blood on them. Sending them to CSU."

They went back in. "We've found bloodstained clothes that match those on camera. Maxwell Stephens, you are under arrest for assaulting Maisie Scarfield." She stood up. "Take him away." She took three measured steps out of the interrogation room — and then ran for the restroom, where she threw up until only bile remained.

She staggered to the sink, rinsed her mouth until the vile taste had gone, and tried not to cry again: furious, frustrated tears. She had wanted to shout and scream at Max, spit out all her anger at her father; all her pain.

She hadn't. She clung to that knowledge: she'd stayed professional, she hadn't crossed any line, hadn't even come close. She'd held it together.

She trudged out, to be met by O'Leary and Carval, both wearing worried expressions. Screened by O'Leary's bulk, Carval didn't hesitate to hug her, though not for long.

"You're green," O'Leary said. "Iffen you don't want to be mistaken for the grass in the park, come 'n' get some coffee an' sit down."

"That was rough," Casey admitted. She shivered. "He was like Dad…" Carval stepped in again, patting her shoulder as would any of the team.

"Coffee," O'Leary repeated, and led the way to the break room: huge hands delicately preparing Casey's espresso, then drinks for Carval and himself. He met Carval's eyes as Casey stared into her coffee rather than throwing it back in her usual fashion, and deliberately moved his gaze to the ratty couch in the corner, helpfully out of view of the door and window. "You need a few minutes," he said, and removed Casey's espresso so that she had to follow: gently pushing her down on to the couch. Carval, at O'Leary's meaningful stare, sat next to her and then put an arm around her. O'Leary looked on benevolently. "There," he said. "That'll help. Drink that teeny li'l coffee an' sit a spell. Let your boy give you a hug an' relax. We can't do anythin' till we c'n get that footage from the Cove Lounge, anyways, an' Larson ain't back yet."

"Back? He's gone?"

"Yup, he went just as we'd finished up with Max."

Casey checked her watch. "He must have gotten hold of the staff before they open – it's barely eleven-thirty."

"You got time for another coffee an' to stay quiet."

"'Cause Casey talks so much normally," Carval teased.

"I talk when there's something worth saying," Casey retorted.

"Naw, you talk when you're givin' orders or insultin' me."

"Overgrown Bigfoot," Casey said, proving his point. "Is there more coffee?" she asked.

"Iffen you want. How long've you been here? You c'n put Mount Rushmore in the bags under your eyes, but that ain't surprisin'. I get you wanna forget thin's, but you gotta sleep tonight. We got that press conference tomorrow an' you don't want Allan doin' your make-up so's you don't let us good-lookin' men down."

Casey snorted.

"An' thinkin' of that, I know Kent ain't here today" –

"Good," Casey stated –

"But you better tell him about your dad."

Casey went white. "Tomorrow."

"Naw. Not tomorrow. Today. Now."

258

"No." O'Leary gave her a direct look. "No. He'll order me home and I *have* to work. I can't be on my own. I have to have something else to think about. Even if it's hard, it's better than being home alone."

"I'd stay," Carval said softly, and tightened his arm around her.

"Yeah," she said, "but that's not what I need. It wouldn't…it wouldn't take my mind off it. If I'm here, there's work to be done. I…later, yeah." O'Leary moved away to the coffee machine, obviously concentrating on that and equally obviously *not* listening. "Later, I'll need you there. Now, I need to work."

Carval nearly swallowed his tongue stopping the words queuing up in his throat. She *needed* him. No limitations or qualifications. "Okay," he said.

O'Leary gave her another espresso. "I get it," he said. "But I ain't goin' to be protectin' you at shift end when Kent turns you into ashes for not tellin' him this mornin'."

"You wouldn't anyway," Casey said with a damp smile, downed her espresso in one mouthful, and stood. "I can hear Larson and Henegan. Let's see what they have."

The two officers grinned at her. "Ma'am," Larson said, "we got the footage."

"Put it up, and we'll see what we have." Casey, O'Leary, and Henegan crowded around Larson, who put his newly acquired technogeeking skills to good use and rapidly pulled up the correct evening, starting at about the point rehearsal had finished without needing to be told. Casey noted his further improvement, and also that Henegan wasn't cringing as badly. She concluded that Larson had been applying some attitude adjustments.

"What's this?" Andy said, pushing in, followed by Tyler.

"Footage," Casey said. "Larson's showing us. You're in time for curtain up." The footage began. For a few moments, nothing happened.

"Okay," Larson said. "We went via the theatre, timed our walk, and we took ten minutes from the scene to the bar. We think Isabella wouldn't have been much different – maybe a little slower."

"Good thought," O'Leary rumbled.

"She should've been coming into the bar about here."

"There she is," Andy said. "This is nice footage. Sitting down – there's a scarf around her neck. She doesn't get a drink" –

"Pause the film," O'Leary said, "while we think. That goes with bein' broke."

"Yeah. It says to me," Casey said, "that she wasn't sure the other person would show up, and she didn't want to be stuck with the check. We said it was too expensive for her. Move on."

They watched Isabella check her slim watch, shifting fretfully. Then, "There. She's seen whoever it is she's meeting."

"She don't look happy about it."

"No. Come on," Casey said to the footage, "show us who it is." A figure arrived at the table, but all they had was a fine view of the back of his head. "Male. Great. We knew that."

"Couldn't Isabella have sat on the other side of the table?" Andy complained.

Another couple of minutes elapsed. Drinks were brought – it looked like two cocktails – and a plate of wings. The man paid.

"Wish I could hear them," Casey muttered.

"Uh, ma'am," Henegan quivered.

"What?"

"I can sorta lip-read, ma'am."

"*What?* Larson, pause that footage. Henegan, explain."

"Uh, a pal at college was deaf and he showed me. It was a way to pick up what the faculty was talking about, and it came in pretty handy at the Academy" – he squirmed – "uh, anyway, I'm not, like, professional but I can try?"

"Damn right you'll try," Casey said, but she smiled approvingly. "Andy and Larson'll clean this up if they have to, but as soon as we've watched it through, you can have a go. I'll be surprised if you get much, but anything will be good. Start it again, please."

The unidentified man appeared to be talking, with considerable gesticulation. He waved towards the bar, and Isabella looked away from her glass.

"Roofie," Tyler said. "Helluva risk."

"Sleight of hand. We didn't see any stage magic in the background checks?"

"Naw."

"Hmph. Keep running it."

Nothing more happened as Isabella and the man finished their drinks and the food, though Isabella, under the influence of the drug, had obviously relaxed. When they stood to leave, it was evident that she wasn't entirely sober.

"There!" Andy said. "Go back a few frames. It's a flicker, but I think we have a face there." Larson obeyed. "Frame by frame. Don't move on till I tell you."

One frame, two, three – "Got you!" four detectives said in unison. Carval shot their elation, as he'd been shooting the intent faces of all six cops. Fremont and Adamo came hurrying up to see what they'd got.

"That's Cordell," Casey said viciously. "Fremont, Larson. You're biggest. Bring him in. Any trouble, frogmarch him. He isn't a witness, he's a suspect."

"Yes'm."

"When you get him here, get the GPS out of his phone – we've got that warrant. I want him processed asap. Fingerprints, DNA if he consents, if not, start a warrant for that. I'll put a glass in front of him, but I don't think it'll work."

"Not likely," Tyler said.

"When we have fingerprints, Tyler, you get them to CSU and light a fire under Evan to match them to that glass ball. I don't want another delay like we had with Manoso's murder. I want those prints back stat so I can hit him with them. Andy, make the GPS dance."

"Yep."

"You goin' to let him stew a spell?" O'Leary suggested.

"Yeah. If he's the arrogant sonofabitch everyone says, he'll think he can act his way out. He can't. I want him wrapped up like a package by the end of the day." She glanced around. "Go get him."

The officers ran.

"Food," O'Leary said. "It's lunchtime an' you hafta eat somethin' so's you c'n interrogate."

"Yeah," Casey said, not notably enthusiastic. "Something easy."

"C'mon, then. The four" –

"Five!" Carval exclaimed.

O'Leary laughed. "Thought that'd get you. The five of us'll go eat. The boys'll take at least an hour."

CHAPTER THIRTY

Lunch sat uneasily in Casey's stomach as she waited for Evan to respond with the fingerprint data. Cordell was in Interrogation, but time was ticking. She tapped fretfully, and sipped water to try to settle her stomach. Being unable to *act* was leaving far too much space in her head for her father's death. She'd made the arrangements call yesterday, ensured that the funeral director had received the death certificate, asked for a dozen copies. She'd agreed the funeral would be held Wednesday: there was no reason to delay. She sniffed, and tried to put it out of her mind. In his corner of the bullpen, Henegan was still poring over the film, trying to read lips.

She grabbed her phone as soon as it rang. "What've you got, Evan?"

"Match. It's only a partial on the glass ball, but it's enough for you to use it. Can you get me DNA?"

"The warrant to take it went in an hour ago, but if the partial is that close, I can charge him and then we'll have more time. The DNA will be confirmatory."

"Does that mean you won't call every hour asking for it?"

"Maybe," Casey said, to Evan's sigh. "Thanks." She picked up her folder. "O'Leary, we're good. The partial print is a match."

"Time to interrogate."

Cordell was not a happy man, and, as soon as Casey and O'Leary entered, he made his immense unhappiness manifest with oration, declamation, and theatrically overdone anger. Neither detective was impressed. They waited until he stopped, and regarded him icily.

"Have you finished?" Casey enquired. "I will read you your rights. If you shout over them, I will read them again, and again, until you've had a chance to hear every word."

Cordell's gaze should have incinerated her where she sat. Casey remained entirely unaffected. She read the Miranda warning, clearly enunciating each separate word. Cordell confirmed his understanding.

"Cordell Andrews. You are an actor, presently rehearsing as Philostrate in Carl Heyer's production of *A Midsummer Night's Dream*."

He nodded.

"Answer for the record, please."

"Yes."

"The actor playing Titania, Isabella Farquar, was murdered. We have evidence that you were the last person to see Isabella prior to her death. We also have evidence that you administered an unknown substance to her. The autopsy identified that she had been drugged with flunitrazepam, also known as Rohypnol or roofies. Do you have any comment?"

"You have no evidence," Cordell pronounced.

"Here is a still shot taken from the bar's CCTV camera, showing the substance being administered. Here is a second still, showing your face. You will notice that the stills are time-stamped."

"That's hardly convincing," Cordell said, but Casey could see that he was shaken.

"In the light of these stills, did you meet Isabella in the Cove Lounge bar at approximately six forty-five p.m. on Thursday June 1st?"

"No comment."

"The GPS from your phone shows that you were in the Cove Lounge at the same time as Isabella, and that you and she left together to return to the Terpsichore Theatre."

"No comment."

"Your partially wiped fingerprint was found on a glass ball, hidden in a props box in the Terpsichore, together with the scarf Isabella had been wearing when she met you. We have recovered DNA from that scarf. The DNA is not Isabella's. You have refused to give a DNA sample" –

"That's my right. If I don't want to give DNA, you can't take it."

"That's only partially correct. If you don't consent to giving DNA, we can't take it without a court-approved warrant."

Cordell stared.

"We have already applied for that warrant. We expect to receive it shortly."

His face froze. Before Casey could continue, a knock sounded on the door of the interrogation room, followed by Henegan's nervous head entering. "Detective Clement, ma'am, may I have a word?" he said.

"Interview paused," Casey said, and left O'Leary to ensure that Cordell stayed scared. "What is it, Henegan?"

"The film, ma'am. I think I got some words."

"You did? Show me."

Henegan pulled up the film. "See, here. When Isabella sees him walking in. That looks like her saying *Cordell*, but I'm not an expert."

"We'll find an expert. Right now I'll take speed. Carry on."

"This bit here, where they're both pretty animated. I *think* she's saying *tried to rape me*."

"Enough. Get with Andy to get an expert in here stat. He'll clean up the tape so they have the best chance." Henegan blinked. "Good work. *Move!*" He moved.

Casey waited the instant that would ensure Henegan went straight to Andy, and returned to Interrogation, where Cordell was regarding O'Leary's stony face with worry. He looked up when Casey entered, registered her expression, and paled.

"Isabella greeted you by name," Casey stated. "She accused you of trying to rape her. That fits with everything we know about you. You assaulted her in the theatre. You were warned off the four actors playing the fairies by Vincent, who threatened to assault you if you didn't leave them alone." Her mouth twisted. "You don't discriminate, it seems, despite the rumours that you're blatantly homophobic and racist."

"I didn't assault her."

"We have evidence that you did." Casey paused. "We have evidence of everything."

"I didn't kill her."

"Your fingerprint is on the murder weapon."

"That ball's not the murder" – he stopped. "I used it as a prop in *Macbeth*."

"How do you know it wasn't the murder weapon?" Casey inquired casually.

"She was strangled," Cordell said, with a nastily arrogant air of *you should know that, idiots*.

"How do you know that?" Casey pounced. "We haven't told anyone how she died. How do *you* know?"

Cordell shut his mouth, too late.

"Cordell Andrews, you are under arrest for the murder of Isabella Farquar, aka Bettina Scarfield."

***

"Now that's done, you hafta call Kent," O'Leary reminded Casey, who was sitting miserably at her desk, having wound up the appalling day by informing Isabella's devastated parents of the arrest and charge. "C'mon. You c'n tell him about your success."

"Doesn't feel like a win," Casey muttered. "He was a nasty piece of work. I didn't even have to goad him."

"Don't matter iffen it's anti-climactic. Solved is solved, an' this one was good old-fashioned detectin' by elimination. Even Henegan did good. You can't have drama every time."

"I guess."

"You're mis'rable 'cause of your pa, an' that's natural, but you still gotta call Kent, or I will."

Carval ambled up and sat on the edge of her clear desk. "Case closed?" he said. "Good." He didn't remark on Casey's pale, tired face, nor the way her fingers locked together.

"Call," O'Leary said firmly.

"Bully." Casey picked up her phone and departed to a conference room. "Sir, it's Clement."

"Clement? Why are you calling?" In the instant's silence, Kent realised. "What has happened to your father?"

She choked, and swallowed. "He..." She forced the words out. "He died on Friday night."

"I'm sorry." He paused. "Are you in the precinct?"

"We solved the case, sir."

"That wasn't what I asked."

"Yes, sir. Sir, please don't bench me. I have to do something. I can't sit at home." She gulped. "Please, sir?"

Kent sighed. "I should. You should take time off. But I'll allow you – do you seriously expect to attend the press conference tomorrow?"

"Yes, sir. I've already told Allan – Penrith – that I will. I want to get it over with, sir."

Kent thought furiously. "I see. I will permit it. Reluctantly, Clement." He paused. "Have you arranged the funeral?"

"Wednesday, sir."

"You will take the full day. Your team will also take the full day. I have no doubt that they will wish to attend."

"Thank you, sir." Casey bit back a sob.

"Go home. Take your photographer with you."

"Sir."

The implication of Kent's comment didn't hit her until she was back at her desk. Carval, O'Leary, Andy and Tyler ranged themselves around her, hiding her from the bullpen.

"I've to go home," Casey said. "Kent ordered it. Told me to take Carval with me."

Carval gleeped. "He what? Why?"

"'Cause he ain't dumb. He saw all them photos same as we did, an' it wasn't exactly subtle, cuddlin' Casey in front of him." O'Leary caught Carval's eye, gesturing at Casey. "You do what Kent told you, an' take yourselves home. You c'n work out which home between you. We'll finish off the paperwork an' see you tomorrow. Get some dinner an' some sleep." He flapped huge hands at them. "Shoo."

"I'll take you home," Carval said to Casey's unresisting form.

"Yes."

"We'll deal with Carl," Andy said.

"Everything," Tyler added.

O'Leary simply bear-hugged her, then pushed her towards the exit. When she'd gone, he looked at the other two. "Who's goin' to tell Carl, an' who's goin' to tell the Finisterres?" he asked. "I reckon I oughta do the Finisterres, 'cause I've met them an' you haven't."

"You don't want to talk to Carl," Andy said sourly.

"Naw." O'Leary turned serious. "An' I wanna be able to go iffen Casey calls. I don't think she will, 'cause I think Carval'll take care of her, but...anyways." His phone rang. "O'Leary – sir? Yes, sir, she left a few minutes ago, after she spoke to you. Yessir." Pause. O'Leary's eyebrows joined his buzz cut. "Yes, sir. She will? Yes, sir." Pause. "We'd'a asked you, sir, but she ain't told me yet. Yessir. Thank you, sir." He swiped off. "That was Kent. Funeral's Wednesday – I guess Casey'll tell us later – an' we all have the day."

"Dress uniform," Tyler said. "Perfect order." The other two nodded.

"Let's get Heyer an' the Finisterres dealt with, an' then we'll all be tidy for this press conference tomorrow mornin'."

"Casey's *doing* it?"

"Yup."

"She's crazy."

"Naw, she wants it over 'n' done. Closed off." O'Leary heaved his immensity into standing. "Let's go. Back here when we're done."

An hour later, the team reconvened.

"Done," Tyler said.

"Lots of hysterical overacting from Carl."

"The Finisterres were shocked an' badly upset. Anyways, we're done."

O'Leary looked around the bullpen, noted that Henegan was still within the protective mantle of Fremont and Larson, ignored the scowling, lurking unpleasantness of Grendon and Estrolla, and smiled bleakly at his colleagues. "Let's finish up the paperwork an' take the pain off Casey."

***

"Do you want me to drive?" Carval asked. Casey nodded, which was entirely unreassuring. The last time he'd asked that, he'd been firmly told *no*. He drove them to her apartment, walked her up, and gently put her on the couch, without a single protest. "Dinner," he said, and investigated the fridge. Unusually, there was nothing there, only a few cans of soda and a nasty-looking brown mass that might have been salad four days previously.

He threw it in the trash. There wasn't anything, except some ice-cream, in the freezer compartment either. "You don't have any food," he said blankly.

"Oh."

"What do you want?"

She shrugged. "Whatever."

Carval realised that Casey wasn't able to make decisions, and simply ordered without further consultation. He sat down, and snuggled her in.

"I need to tell everyone about the funeral," she dripped.

"Tell me. I'll tell them."

"Wednesday. Two. Cypress Hills. Kent's given them all that day. He didn't have to…" she dissolved again. Carval tapped it into his phone. He'd send it on when Casey was sleeping, which from the look of her wasn't far away.

She tried to eat, but only managed a few bites; drank nothing but some water, and sat, beaten down and exhausted, tucked into Carval's chest. He petted undemandingly. "Go have a hot shower," he suggested, "and then try and sleep."

"Yeah." She stumbled to her bedroom.

Carval tidied up: the majority of Casey's dinner going into the fridge. That done, he could hear the shower running. He texted the funeral details to the team, and sat quietly messing with his phone until the shower finished. Casey didn't reappear, and when, after another few moments, he went to investigate, she was invisible below the quilt, balled up in soundless unhappiness. He patted the lump, but she didn't uncurl or react.

"I'll be in the other room," he murmured, "unless you want me here."

"Minute," she gulped.

Carval took that to mean that she'd come through in a moment, and tactfully withdrew, though he wanted to scoop her up, quilt and all, and take her to sit with him and be comforted, to fall asleep there in his arms.

Casey dragged herself through a short time later, muffled in her oversized robe, and came straight to him. He caught her as she sat down, and firmly repositioned her so that he could cosset her in. His shirt grew damp, but for a long while she said nothing.

"What if it was my fault?" she whispered. "What if I hadn't told him about the show? If he hadn't gone, maybe…"

"Maybe. But there would've been something else."

"Yeah," she said acidly. "I could've been injured again. That's what began it. Sackson."

"Did it?" Carval asked softly. "Did it really?"

She didn't answer that, simply curled further into herself. "I'm glad you're here," she breathed. "I needed you." On the breath, she finally fell into the sleep she needed, leaving Carval to think over her words as he

267

carried her to her bed, tucked her in, and ambled back to make himself a coffee and, eventually, join her.

***

The team sat uncomfortably on a low dais, flanked by Leanne, the NYPD press officer, and Kent at one end and Carval and Allan at the other. As far as they were concerned, ten on a Monday morning should be for analysing their cases and drinking whatever they could make in the break room. It was not for facing the metaphorical execution squad in best dress uniform, examined by Kent to ensure their belts and buttons were mirror-shined, their shoes reflecting the lights, and not a crease in sight. Even Casey's curls had been gelled into perfect submission, twisted away into a smooth bun.

"We can still call this off," Allan said. "I'd have to say that it was due to bereavement, but if you want me to call it off I can."

"No," Casey said. "I want it over and done. Move on." She winced. "If it's delayed, I'll never get through it. The PR and hype is bad enough already. I don't want them" – she gestured at the hall in which the press were collecting – "having any time to pry."

"We're good," O'Leary rumbled. "Let's do it."

Everyone looked at Captain Kent. "Start the show," he said brusquely.

"Thank you all for coming," Allan opened.

The cops collectively thought that he should be thanking *them* for not running off to Alaska, which had seemed like a great plan ten minutes earlier.

"I hope you've all had a chance to visit the exhibition, but if not, you can go in after this." Scattered smiles from the assembled media. "Let me introduce the team." He did, subtly stressing all the points that had been agreed with the press office and the cops. By the time he'd finished, all four of them were blushing beautifully. "With them," Allan finished, "is Captain Kent, in charge of the Thirty-Sixth precinct." Kent's stern face remained impassive as he nodded, once. "Without further ado, we invite questions."

Questions came thick and fast: how had each of them decided to be cops, why become detectives, how did they cope with the messiness of murder? What was it like having Carval around? Was it difficult being a woman in a predominantly male environment?

"No," Casey said. "We all have our own strengths."

"But you were injured?"

"It happens to all of us." She grinned, and only her team could tell it was forced. "Except Detective O'Leary here, of course." The room laughed with them.

"What about being gay?"

268

"Waal, nobody minds about that." There was a sceptical noise from the newsies. "Naw. Not now. I'm not sayin' as it mightn't've been different a while back, but it's good. I even got to take vacation when I got married."

"What's it like being in the Academy?"

Unseen, Kent's knuckles tensed.

"Tough," Casey said.

"Yeah," Tyler agreed. "Even if you're ex-military, it's a tough course. You really have to work at it."

The other two nodded. "You don't get through if you're not up to it. There aren't any shortcuts," Andy said.

"But doesn't it impact your families? I understand you don't get time off from the Academy."

"Naw," O'Leary said. "You don't get time off, but it's worth the time in." The rest of the team nodded firmly.

"How did you four become a team?"

The four looked at Captain Kent. "Detectives Clement and O'Leary had been paired up for some time. I thought that their talents would benefit from someone with a completely different background and experience – Detective Tyler, who is ex-Army – and from the addition of a computer specialist – Detective Chee. Together, the four of them form a formidable unit." Kent smiled. "There's always a little luck involved in personnel matters, and that was it."

The room shifted a little, but before Allan could draw the conference to a close, a slight, blond man stood up.

"Jared Margoly, of the *Manhattan Daily Diary*. This exhibition, you told us, shows the best face of the NYPD." Kent nodded. "Why, then, is it featuring a woman who's been misusing her position to get her father off charges of drunkenness for months, the third time this weekend?"

The room erupted. Kent stood up. "Silence!" he ordered. Utter silence fell.

"Sit down, sir," Casey said. It wasn't a request. She stood in turn, white as marble, eyes as hard as diamond. Command presence surrounded her, and every eye was on her. "Mr Margoly. Whatever you have been told is a lie. My father has been arrested three times, all in the last nine months. He has attended court twice and been found guilty twice." Acid laced her tones. "Hardly 'getting off'. Had you checked your facts, you would have known that. He would be facing a third hearing following his third arrest, except that he died at eleven o'clock on Friday night."

Margoly looked frantically around him at the other media representatives, and found no assistance, only scathing contempt. Kent controlled his face rigidly.

"I do not think that my late father's failings are relevant to my career. Nor are they a suitable subject for innuendo and lies, especially while I'm arranging his funeral." Her voice was glacial. The team, Kent and Carval recognised the iron control that she was exerting not to break down. "Since you clearly didn't have correct information, perhaps you would like to amend your question?"

A frisson of hostility rippled around the room, directed firmly at Margoly.

"No."

"Stand down, Clement," Kent murmured. "That's an order. I'll take it from here."

"Sir," she whispered back, and sat.

"As you have heard," Kent said, "the accusation that Detective Clement had corruptly favoured her father was an outright lie, intended to derail this press conference from the professionalism of the NYPD, as shown in the outstanding exhibition next door. Are there any further questions?"

There were none.

"Thank you all for coming," Allan said. "The exhibition is on the left, if you want to see it."

CHAPTER THIRTY ONE

The team left as a body through the back of the room, followed by Carval, Allan, Kent and NYPD Press Officer Leanne. As soon as she was out of sight of the media, Casey fled for the restroom.

"What the *fuck* was that?" Carval demanded, turning on Allan, Kent and Leanne. "You said you had this under control! How did that asshole get that information?"

"I will find out," Kent said heavily. "Detectives, take the rest of the day. I'll deal with this."

"Can't you haul the reporter in?" Carval snapped.

"No. Reporters don't need to give up their sources. Protected."

"So you can't do anything? What fucking good is that?" Carval spat. "Casey'll be trashed and you all let it happen." He stormed off after Casey.

The rest of the team regarded Kent, Allan and Leanne.

"Dismissed," Kent ordered, as if they were in the precinct. O'Leary started to say something, then stopped before a single syllable emerged.

"Sir," Andy said. They turned as one, and left in the same direction as Carval.

"This is a fine mess," Kent said.

"No," Allan contradicted. "You watched Casey. I watched the rest of the press. Amazingly, they didn't like what Margoly – tabloid rat – did," he directed at Kent. "They don't like Margoly, period. He's got a bad reputation and he made it worse. Casey did exactly the right thing: she didn't try for sympathy, and she pointed out that he was using bad information without checking his facts. They'll go with the program."

"He's right, Captain," Leanne said. "Margoly is a thorn in everyone's side. For once, we've found someone who isn't with the NYPD that the press will happily trash."

271

"Some well-judged calls and conversations should ensure it," Allan added. "I'll be making them today." He regarded Kent closely. "I guess you'll be taking some action of your own."

Kent everted his lips, which didn't qualify as a smile, and declined to answer, marching briskly out.

As soon as he reached his office, he shut the door with a decided crack, and called Renfrew. "It's Kent," he rapped. "I need your agent's data on who accessed the arrest file on David Clement."

"I take it there was an incident?"

"Yes. Some tabloid rag knew that Clement's father had been arrested three times."

"That was a little over-clever."

"Yes. We'll find out who. I'll clear it all with Wetherly at the 112th."

"I will speak to Agent Bergen immediately, and we will call you back as soon as possible – oh."

"What?"

"Agent Bergen is presently away. He will not return until Wednesday. We will speak to you that afternoon."

"Thank you."

***

Carval didn't let manners, etiquette or the fact that he hadn't entered a women's restroom since he was old enough to close his own zipper stop him going after Casey. He barrelled in without hesitation.

"Casey!" He couldn't hear a thing. "Casey! Are you in here?" Still nothing. "Casey! Talk to me. Please."

"This is a *women's* restroom. Leave."

"Not till I know you're okay."

"I'm fine. Go outside."

"Nope," Carval said. "You're not fine and I'm staying here till you come out and I can see for myself."

"You'll be waiting a long time. Go outside. There aren't any other exits."

"Casey…"

"I need to be on my own."

He left. That tone had gone straight to his spinal cord and moved his feet without his brain intervening.

Outside, he found the other three cops, bleak-faced.

"She wants to be alone," he said.

"She won't cry in public," O'Leary said. "Not till she gets home. Give her time. We were all there Saturday, an' she's still blockin' everythin' till she c'n deal with it better. Iffen she's still like this after the funeral, we'll worry about her then."

"Wait for her," Tyler said. "All of us."

"No question," Andy added, almost as terse as Tyler.

It took another fifteen minutes before Casey, pale, cold and red-eyed, emerged. "Let's go," she said. They fell in around her.

"Kent gave us the rest of the day," Andy said.

Casey stopped. "I don't want it," she replied.

"We have it. If you go in, you'll be sent home."

"Oh." For a moment, her shell broke, and liquid puddled in her eyes. "I guess I'll go home, then."

"All going." Tyler put a hand on her shoulder. "Not alone. All of us together."

"Okay." Which, from Casey, told the rest how shaken she was. Carval, without a word, put an arm around her shoulders and drew her in, falling into step with her and not letting go for a moment.

The four men squeezed into Casey's apartment, disposing themselves around her living area. Carval and O'Leary bookended Casey, who had collapsed on to the couch. Carval had an arm around her. Tyler annexed a chair; Andy sat cross-legged on the floor beside the coffee table, apparently perfectly comfortable.

"Now what?" she said desolately, a break in her voice.

"Waal, I guess Kent's got work to do," O'Leary said, "'cause he shoved us outta the way pretty fast."

"Allan's got work to do too," Carval bit. "He was supposed to *stop* anything like that."

"Kent and Renfrew said they could manage it," Casey snuffled. "They didn't. Where does that leave me?" She abruptly turned into Carval, and all four men pretended that they couldn't see or hear her.

"Exactly where we were," Tyler said. "Team. *Top* team. Can't spoil that."

"No," Andy agreed. "No-one liked us before, so what's new? The brass know it's not true, so it doesn't matter. *We* don't care."

"At least Dad won't see it," Casey tried, and buried her face in Carval's shirt again.

"Call Allan," O'Leary directed at Carval. "Find out what he's doin'."

"That sonofabitch and his rag are never getting into one of my shows again," Carval said viciously. He pulled out his phone and jabbed Allan's number, putting the phone on speaker. "What's happening?" he snapped. "Tell me you've dealt with that shithead."

"Calm down. Have some faith in me. The critic from that rag couldn't say enough good about the show, and I spoke to them immediately after the press conference closed. Margoly is *toast*. He'll be out of a job by five. Such a shame that the critic is the son-in-law of the owner – and, like most of the others, is a friend of mine." Allan didn't mention the other piece of information that he'd received. The last thing he, or anyone else, needed was for Carval to go off on another Casey-related crusade. The last one had led them right here to this disaster.

"What about the rest of them?" Carval said, less angrily.

"I've been making calls for the last hour, pointing out that anyone repeating lies will be sued for libel or slander, depending on the medium. Since everyone in the hall was told it was a lie, and can easily check the facts, they won't have a leg to stand on. As far as the media is concerned, it's already dead."

Carval breathed a long sigh of relief. "Hear that?" he said to Casey. "It's gone."

"Thanks," she gulped.

"Will you tell Kent and the press office?" Carval asked Allan.

"Yes. I'm waiting for Leanne to call me back. She can deal with Kent. He was out for blood, and I don't want to get in his way."

"Thought so," O'Leary said heavily. "Don't guess the bullpen's goin' to be a happy place pretty soon."

"No," Tyler and Andy said together.

"It'll all be our fault again," Casey said bitterly, punctuated by another gulp. She sat up. "Great. Tomorrow'll be hell." She sniffed, and blinked hard. "I still have to finish arranging the funeral. It's on Wednesday, Cypress Hills. Two. The main things are done, but…I have to deal with some stuff still."

"Carval told us. We'll be there."

"All of us," Tyler said. "Not alone."

"Naw," O'Leary said. "All together, like we always are."

"Yeah," Andy confirmed.

"And me," Carval said.

Suddenly, O'Leary grinned hugely. "Group hug?" he said, and met derision and cat-calls with equanimity. Even Casey managed a soggy smile. "Guess not. Phew. I thought we were all gettin' soft an' fluffy for a moment."

"Nope," Carval said. "Still as hard and cynical as the day I met you."

"Good. C'n we get some pizza or somethin', 'cause I'm so hungry I'm goin' to start eatin' this couch iffen we don't get some food."

"You call," Casey said. "I have soda, but if you want beer you'll have to order it."

"'Kay," the big man said, and put in a pizza and beer order which would have fed half of New York state. "Now, c'n we do anythin' to fix thin's up? I know you didn't want anythin' from us Saturday, but iffen you know different, we c'n help."

"Not now," Casey replied. "Thanks. Maybe later, when it's clearer." She blinked rapidly. "I don't wanna think about it. I want to keep working." All three cops raised eyebrows. "It'll…I have to, okay?"

274

"Iffen you want. But iffen you need us to pick anythin' up, you gotta say." The other two nodded. "You've been there for us when we needed it. We'll be here iffen you do." O'Leary patted Casey's slim shoulder. "Team."

"Team," Casey said, and put her hand over O'Leary's paw. "All of us."

"Yeah. *All* of us," O'Leary said.

In true Musketeer style, Tyler and Andy added their hands. Carval, completely unable to resist, flicked out his camera and took a few shots of the clasp, and then a few more.

O'Leary looked at Carval, looked at Casey, who was on the verge of tears again – and chortled. "One potato, two potato," he said, and brought his ham hand from bottom to the top of the pile.

"What?" Andy said.

"You never played that?"

"*I* don't have nieces," he said. "I guess this is some kids' game?"

"It's an Irish game," O'Leary said smugly. "You know I got Irish ancestry."

"You've never been to Ireland. Your *grandmother* never went to Ireland. You're about as Irish as my shoes. Wearing head to toe green on St Patrick's Day doesn't make you Irish."

"Does," O'Leary pouted at him.

Casey simply sat, not distracted, as O'Leary had hoped, from her imminent sobs, but before they spilled over, the pizza arrived.

Tyler answered, paid, and brought the boxes in; Andy made free of Casey's cupboards to find plates and glasses; O'Leary opened beers and sodas. Casey didn't move, once again completely disconnected from the activity around her, lost in her own thoughts. She mechanically took a plate and glass when they were handed to her, but didn't take any pizza to put on it; didn't pour or drink any soda.

Carval nudged her. "Eat," he suggested.

"I'm not hungry."

"Have a soda." He put one in front of her. Casey picked the can up, but didn't drink, staring emptily at it, eyes glistening with unshed tears. Somehow, though none of them seemed to move, the team closed around her. She leaned forward, face hidden, shoulders shaking.

O'Leary met Carval's gaze, and put his enormous arm around Casey. Carval shifted slightly back, just far enough to allow O'Leary to take over.

"Dad's gone," she half-sobbed. "He was my only family." She gulped. "If I'd been…if I hadn't been a cop. If I'd called you when I went after Merowin…he couldn't take me getting beaten up. He couldn't deal with me being a cop any more. He was disappointed in me and then he saw the show and that finished him." She sobbed, once. "I should never have told him. If he'd never seen it he wouldn't have…"

"He would," O'Leary said. "You listen to me. Grievin's one thin', but blamin' yourself, that's dumb. I've been right there beside you all the way, an' I knew you before your mom passed. I've seen all this play out, an' your pa had been gettin' worse an' worse long before you got beat up, long before this show. This ain't your fault, an' before you mess up that too, it ain't Carval's neither."

"'S not his fault," dribbled out from under Casey's hair.

"Waal, I'm glad you c'n see that. You need to see that it ain't your fault either. You did ev'rythin' you could to save him, an' a lot more than you should've. Any of us would'a cut him loose to drown a long time back. You didn't. He's gone, but that's not on you or anythin' you did."

"They were *disappointed*," she cried. "Mom died disappointed in me and so did Dad."

"That ain't true," O'Leary said sternly, and made a gesture towards the only photo in Casey's living room. Andy retrieved it and gave it to O'Leary, who shoved it under Casey's nose. "See that there? Your boy'll tell you that photographers can't counterfeit pride like that. Right then an' there, they were *proud* of you graduatin' the Academy – top by miles – an' becomin' a cop."

"But Dad said" –

O'Leary cut that off instantly. "Your pa was drunk, an' hurtin', an' takin' it out on you. Iffen you'd looked more like your mom, he'd'a been worse, earlier, but even though you don't look anythin' much like her, ev'ry time he saw you he'd be reminded of her. Babies," the big man pontificated, "tie you together, an' I bet you got some of the same expressions an' turns of phrase that she did. Daughters get like their moms, most often."

Casey made a heartbroken noise, and Tyler, Andy and Carval all moved in still closer.

"You grieve as much as you need to. Ain't no shame at all in grievin' your dad, an' iffen it's all too much – 'cause I know that however much you oughta stay home tomorrow, you won't – we'll be makin' sure that nobody makes anything outta it. Won't we?"

"Yeah," three men said, coming to attention at O'Leary's tone.

"Try'n eat somethin', 'cause not eatin' won't help, an' have your soda, 'cause otherwise you'll be gettin' a nasty headache iffen you haven't got one already, an' stop tryin' to blame yourself for somethin' that wasn't ever down to you."

Casey finally raised her head, tears tracking down her cheeks, eyes and nose red. Carval passed her a Kleenex, and swapped his arm for O'Leary's. She moved slightly into him, but her gaze was fixed on her huge partner. "Really?" she said desolately.

"Promise," O'Leary answered. His tone took Carval right back to their beginning: the team, the bond, the first two. O'Leary, rock solid in support, as he had been then, as Casey had been for him; and then, a little later, Tyler, then Andy, joining him. Foursquare, four corners, one unit. He'd shown it to the world, but it still hit him hard.

"Have some pizza." O'Leary handed her the plate again, and proffered a box. "Pepperoni, an' I know you like that best so don't try tellin' me you don't. An' since your teeny li'l fingers don't seem able to pop the tab on your soda, I'll do that for you."

"Thanks, but I think I can manage to open a soda," Casey said, achieving barely a tenth of her normal snark. She did so, and took a sip, followed by a much longer drink. "Have I told you I hate you when you're right?"

"Yeah, but it don't stop me an' it don't make me wrong. Eat the pizza, before monster-mouth Andy here eats the lot." Andy squawked indignantly, but Casey's grey face lightened a fraction, and she took a bite. The heaviness in the room eased as she did. Discovering she was hungry, she finished the slice and picked up another.

"That's better," O'Leary said. "Iffen you don't eat you'll waste away."

"Yes, Mommy," Casey snipped.

"That's better. More like usual." O'Leary patted her head, which gained him a fearsome glare and an accompanying growl. "Yup. That's our sunshiny, friendly, outgoing Casey."

Tyler and Andy didn't muffle their snorts. Casey glared around, at perhaps a third of normal wattage, but, Carval saw with considerable relief, the gentle joshing had helped her to recover a little colour and normality. He wasn't about to take his arm away: he could still feel small shudders, diminishing as she ate and drank.

When Casey put her plate down, it was clear that O'Leary thought she should eat more.

"It's enough," Casey said, answering the unspoken question. "If I have more, it won't be pretty."

"Okay," he said easily. "I won't make you." He took another slice of his own, and for a few minutes there was silence while everyone except Casey ate. Casey sipped her soda, comforted by the team around her, and as much comforted, she dimly realised, by Carval.

O'Leary finished the pizza, and stood. "I think it's time to go. I guess you'll hit the bullpen in the mornin'?"

"Yeah. I need to," Casey said, mouth twisting.

"Waal, iffen Kent sends you home, don't go shootin' him. You don't look good in orange."

Casey flipped him the bird.

"Seeya tomorrow," O'Leary said, and led Tyler and Andy out as soon as they'd added their goodbyes.

"I could tidy up," Carval offered.

"No," Casey replied, and turned into him. "Just…just stay here?"

"Sure," he said, and followed up by bringing her into his lap. Suddenly, she buried her face in his shirt. He stroked her back, and wished he had any words to make it better. She was crying, again. He didn't try to stop her. Grief was grief, and better to grieve than bottle it up.

"Thank you," emerged from his shirt.

"You don't need to thank me. I *want* to be here," he said without any thought at all. "Even if you're devastated, I'd rather you came to me than be alone."

"I didn't want to be alone. You were where I wanted…" she trailed off, and didn't look up. "I…you were the right place. Even O'Leary wasn't."

"I'm here. You don't need to be alone if you don't want to be."

She sniffled again. "No family," she breathed, still into his abused shirt.

"The team's your family. You four are closer than most families ever manage."

"Five."

"Five?"

"You're part of us too."

Fin.

ABOUT THE AUTHOR

SR Garrae grew up in Scotland and then worked in international finance in London until her retirement. She lives in the UK with her family, who are somewhat bemused by but supportive of her complete change of career.

She always loved books, but didn't start to write original fiction until after she retired. She now balances writing with travel, reluctant but very necessary gym visits, and designing her own book covers.

Modern, romantic cop stories are the stories she had always turned to as a go-to read, and always loved.